A Court of Bones and Sorrow

Lunaria Realms
Book 2

Alex Frost

GREYMALKIN

Published by Greymalkin Press
www.greymalkinpress.com

Copyright © 2024 by Maddox Grey
All rights reserved.

No part of this book may be reproduced in any form or by any electronic or mechanical means, including information storage and retrieval systems, without written permission from the author, except for the use of brief quotations in a book review.

This is a work of fiction. Names, places, characters, and events, and incidents are the product or depiction of the author's imagination and are completely fictitious. Any resemblance to actual persons, living or dead, events or establishments is purely coincidental.

Dev & Line Editing by Proofs by Polly
Copy-editing and Proofreading by Rachels Top Edits
Cover Design by Cover by Jules

Ebook ISBN - 978-1-963368-02-4
Paperback ISBN - 978-1-963368-03-1

The Lunaria Realms Series

A House of Fangs & Deceit

A Court of Bones & Sorrow

A Throne of Blood & Vengeance

Note From Author

A gentle reminder that this is a why choose romantasy, which means there are going to be multiple love interests. And our dear, sweet Samara will not be choosing between any of them.

You can still pick a favorite though. I won't tell.

Let's chat real quick about what to expect in this book. This is a fantasy novel that contains adult content and situations. If it was a movie, it would probably be rated "R" for violence, language, and sexual content. If you want to go into this book completely blind and prefer not to read content warnings, you can skip on ahead, my friend.

If there are certain topics that you need to avoid for the sake of your own mental health, or that you simply don't like, please take a look at the list below for some things you will find in this book.

- Explicit consensual sex scenes (there is no dub-con or non-con)
- Blood drinking
- References to parental death
- Cheating but **not** between love interests

Note From Author

Also... quick little note on language. I am a strange, strange person, and I've lived a bit of an odd life. I was born and raised in California, but was mostly raised by my Canadian grandmother and was then unofficially adopted by an Irish family in my late teens. You might be wondering why I'm mentioning this, and the reason is that I have a bit of a magpie approach when it comes to the English language.

Sometimes I like the American English spelling... sometimes I'm really attached to that extra "u" and go for the non-American version. Variety is the spice of life y'all.

Bless the soul of my copy-editor because she just sighs heavily at the start of each manuscript and deals with my eccentricities. So if you're an American and looking at a word and thinking it's not spelt right... it is most likely the non-American version of the word.

To PollyAné, Rachel, and Lisa. For leaving the absolute best—and occasionally unhinged—comments during the editing process.

And Fiona for never failing to catch the things we miss.

Y'all are amazing.

CHAPTER ONE

Samara

THE GORGEOUS PRINCE with enchanting blue eyes wanted to marry me, but I wanted to stab him in the heart and set his corpse on fire.

He was the reason our people were dying.

The wards that had protected our outposts for over a century were failing and the wraiths were getting in, and he was the fucking reason. My memory helpfully served up the image of a discarded doll from the last outpost that had been slaughtered by the shadowy monsters. That child had died, and Prince Draven was the Moroi who had let the monsters in.

Fury burned through my veins as I desperately struggled to keep it off my face. It'd been three days since we'd learned the truth at an abandoned temple in the badlands. The wraiths were actually the Unseelie Fae. Somehow, they'd pushed their shadow magic too far and turned themselves into monsters. We'd killed three of them when the prince had left with their leader, Erendriel.

Now Prince Draven was here, standing on the wide stone stairs that led to the inside of House Harker. *My home.* I kept my gaze on him, but from my peripheral vision, I didn't see any guards with him, and the only people I'd seen since we'd walked through the gates had been ours. We'd covered our tracks well at the temple. Was his being here a coincidence?

"This wasn't exactly the response I was looking for," the prince drawled, the smile never slipping from his face even as something else flitted through his eyes. His hair fell in a straight, black curtain to his waist, the silver streaks glittering in the bright sunlight.

"Apologies, my prince." I forced the words out as I bent my knees, giving a slight bow, hoping he mistook my rapidly beating heart for excitement about him being here. Though it was possible he knew exactly what we'd been up to and was just toying with us. "I'm beyond delighted by this news; it simply caught me off guard is all. Given how things went with my first marriage"—I lowered my eyes and clutched my hands together in front of me in what I hoped was a convincing show of uncertainty—"I just never expected another offer to come my way, and certainly not one like this."

Warm fingers titled my chin up, and I barely restrained myself from slapping the proprietary touch away. Something in my expression must have given that away because Prince Draven smoothly pulled his hand back.

"I've always thought Demetri was an over-entitled fool, and the fact that he did something to drive you away only confirms that." Prince Draven's expression was charming, but there was an edge to his voice. "Would you think poorly of me if I told you I was secretly delighted when I heard the two of you were ending things? And that I might have a chance with you?"

His smile morphed into a sheepish but unrepentant grin.

Die.

Instead of voicing how I really felt, I forced the corners of my lips to curl into a sultry smirk. One that always made men think of wicked things. Out of the corner of my eye, I saw Kieran's jaw harden, but he remained a few steps behind Prince Draven. He hadn't been with us at the temple in the badlands and had no idea the prince was the traitor we'd been looking for. I hoped he knew everything I was doing right now was an act and that I wasn't actually falling for the prince's charming bullshit.

Alaric hadn't said a word but remained a steady, calming presence as he stepped from my side to be one step above me, as if to put himself between me and Prince Draven. I couldn't see Vail without turning around, but I assumed he was still somewhere behind me. Probably glowering and very obviously plotting murder.

They would all die if I failed to play this right. We didn't know what Prince Draven knew. We'd killed all the wraiths who had seen our faces . . . hopefully. But it was clear the wraiths had been using that temple regularly, which meant Erendriel had surely returned there at some point. It wasn't like he wouldn't have noticed that the three wraiths he'd left behind were no longer there.

Prince Draven's showing up here now couldn't have been a coincidence. Maybe he didn't know who had been in that temple, only suspected someone from House Harker. Maybe he did know it was us but wanted to find out what we knew and who else we had told, but two could play this game. We had questions, so many moonsdamned questions, and he had the answers.

I might not be much of a fighter, but when it came to politics and deceptive words, there was no one better than me. This was a game I knew how to play.

"My prince," I purred, "you're too kind."

"There's no need for titles, Samara." He gave me a smile that was pure sin and took another step, forcing Alaric to back up until he stood by my side. "We've known each other our entire lives—Draven is fine."

It didn't escape my attention that he could have gone to my other side instead of stepping into Alaric's space. I wasn't the only one who knew how this game worked. Draven not only survived, he flourished in the Moroi courts. I needed to be careful. He held an arm out for me, but I shook my head and waved a hand at my clothes. "I don't want to get dirt and grime all over you."

There was a very real chance that if I had to hold his arm like he wanted, I'd lose my temper and sink my claws into his flesh. That would kind of ruin the whole flirting thing.

"They're only clothes." He shrugged and kept his arm extended. "I'm more than willing to pay the price of a little dirt on me if it means you'll be by my side."

I forced myself to let out a breathy laugh and slipped my arm around his, fighting against the revulsion at the contact, and allowed him to lead us up the stairs towards the main entrance. A dull ache was already settling into my cheeks from how hard I'd been smiling. As we walked past Kieran, I brushed my free hand against his, our fingers curling together for the briefest second. Then I glanced over my shoulder at Alaric as Draven led me inside, and I found him staring at the back of the prince's head with a look of absolute hatred.

The staff and courtiers of House Harker scattered as we strolled down the hallway, Kieran's and Alaric's footsteps trailing behind us, but I couldn't tell if Vail had followed or not. I was a little surprised none of the higher-ranking nobility were here, trying to capture a moment with Prince Draven.

"I've already spoken to many of the advisors and officials," he said with a thick note of satisfaction.

"Oh?" I tilted my head towards him and arched an eyebrow.

A wry, mischievous smile played across his lips. "You were

wondering why a hundred Moroi aren't lining these walls, trying to beg a favor of me so they might have a better chance of getting my mother to agree to whatever they are scheming."

"Was I?"

"You were," he said confidently.

A laugh slipped from my lips, and this time, it wasn't forced. I'd forgotten this, how easily Draven could make me laugh. Growing up, we'd spent a lot of time together because I'd visited the Sovereign House regularly. Not as much as I'd spent with Alaric, Kieran, or even Vail, but in the moments when Draven had let go of the charming prince act . . . he'd become someone real. Someone I'd liked.

And that was dangerous. I shored up my mental defenses, my smile becoming sharp like a blade.

"Kieran and I got here early this morning, so I passed the hours by pacifying them to ensure I could have your full attention. I might have implied that I would be willing to speak with them further if they left us alone this afternoon." He leaned closer to me as he spoke, and I just barely heard a growl slip from Kieran . . . and Alaric. If Draven heard them, he ignored it as he tugged me down a hallway that led to a balcony overlooking the beach.

It was one of the best views from the main house, and I was a little surprised he remembered it. He'd only been to House Harker a handful of times to my knowledge. Although I hadn't seen him much over the past couple of years—maybe he'd visited more often while I'd been living in House Laurent.

When Alaric and Kieran moved to follow us out onto the balcony, Draven turned and took a step towards them while raising his hand. "Would you mind giving us a moment alone?"

They both looked at me, and I could see the word "no" in their eyes, but further in the hallway, I saw Vail slip into one of the side rooms we used for storage. I didn't exactly love the idea of relying on Vail to come and save me if the prince tried anything, but it wasn't like we could deny the request without an explanation.

"It's fine," I told Kieran before nodding at Alaric. "Go and get cleaned up, and then we can catch up over dinner. Maybe find that book I need in the library. Kieran can probably help."

Alaric's bright eyes held mine, a completely unreadable expression on his face. "Of course." Then he spun around and stalked back down the hallway. I hoped he understood my unspoken request to fill Roth and Kieran in on what we'd learned. Kieran's jaw flexed as he looked between me and Draven before following Alaric out. Something was going on with him. He didn't know what we knew about Draven, so I didn't understand why he was so apprehensive about leaving me alone with him.

I'd make him tell me later after I thoroughly made it clear I had no interest in a marriage to the prince. Kieran was mine and I was his. Nobody would be getting between the two of us. Well . . . I wouldn't mind Roth between the two of us, but I was pretty sure they were more likely to pin *us* down with those rather useful blood ribbons of theirs. A shiver ran down my spine as I remembered what it had felt like to have the hard wood of the library table pressed against my back while Roth kneeled between my legs and lashed me with their tongue.

"Samara? You alright?" Humor sparked in the prince's blue eyes, as if he knew what I'd just been thinking about. "You look a bit . . . flushed . . ."

"I'm just glad to be home is all." I walked over to the corner of the balcony wall and leaned against it, letting my elbows rest on the sun-warmed stones. Draven hopped up onto the wall and took a seat with his back to the beach so he could fully face me. Then he lazily planted a hand on the stones and leaned on it, radiating an easygoing confidence.

If he knew we'd been the ones at the temple, he was truly

skilled at hiding it. Granted, he wasn't acting like someone who was responsible for the deaths of hundreds of Moroi either.

"So," he started, "I'm guessing you have questions?"

Why are you doing this? Why betray your own people? I thought bitterly. "You've never wanted to marry," I said lightly instead. "I believe your exact words when I told you I was marrying Demetri were, *'That's unfortunate. Hopefully I have better luck at avoiding such a fate.'*"

He winced. "To be fair, I do really dislike Demetri. Always thought he was a pompous ass."

"That literally describes over half of the Moroi court." I frowned. "Probably closer to three-quarters at House Laurent. As the Heir of that House, I suppose he never really had a chance."

"I suppose that's accurate," he replied with a chuckle. "It's rather amazing when you think about it. A century ago, we were barely managing to survive, hiding behind the thick walls of the Houses. Now, we've outgrown the Fae fortresses, have dozens of thriving outposts, and we've reached the point where some of us have nothing better to do than float about the courts of the Houses and gossip while making deals with each other behind closed doors."

"It's the same in the Velesian realm," I admitted. "Although they're less about the secretive deals and more about the violently overthrowing each other."

"They're shifters." He shrugged. "Their animal nature is an intrinsic part of them."

"If you're about to go into a spiel about how much better we are than the Velesians because of their *animal nature*, I will shove you off this balcony." Despite my words, I smiled brightly at him. "Fair warning."

"Ah." He let out a raspy chuckle. "I see you've heard Marvina Laurent rant about those *filthy mongrels up north*."

"Unfortunately."

"Alas, you will have to find another reason to push me off this balcony, because I didn't mean any disrespect by that." He leaned further back, resting on both hands this time before tilting his head back. For a few seconds, I let myself admire the early afternoon sunlight reflecting off the silver strands set against his inky black hair. I'd never met anyone who had hair like his, and more than once over the years, I'd had to fight the urge to run my fingers through it.

When I drew my attention away from his hair, I found Draven smirking at me. If his hair was different, his eyes were truly unique. All Moroi had two-toned eyes, a dominant color and a secondary color that expanded whenever our emotions were heightened. Usually, those two colors were similar shades. Bright blue and green. Brown and gold. Odd colors popped up here and there, particularly with the bloodlines that ruled the Houses.

The Nacht bloodline, Draven's bloodline, all bore the same eyes, which were a deep blue, like the color of the sky just after the sun dipped below the horizon, and dark red threads ran through the blue. I'd only seen Draven truly pissed off once, and his eyes had turned almost solid bloodred, only the thinnest lines of blue had still been visible. It had been years, but the memory had stuck with me.

"Just think of how often you can stare at my hair if you marry me." He winked.

"Please." I snorted. "We both know you love being the center of attention."

I turned so I was fully facing the beach. If I hadn't seen Draven at the temple speaking with the wraiths with my own eyes, I wouldn't have believed it. Right now, he was acting so . . . normal, but he'd definitely been there. I frowned. Was it possible to control someone with blood magic?

No. I was just trying to come up with excuses because I didn't want him to be the bad guy. It was terrible enough to know a Moroi was betraying us. I didn't want it to be someone I had a history with. Someone I liked.

Brick by brick, I erected a wall around my feelings. I needed to look at this rationally and be open to any possible explanations. Including that Draven had fooled me all these years and wasn't the charming and often kind male I thought he was.

Draven slid off the wall and turned so he was leaning on the railing next to me before bumping my shoulder with his. "Something troubling you, Sam?"

I frowned up at him. "I don't think you've ever called me that."

"It's how Kieran always referred to you." He shrugged, but there was a forced casualness to it. "Given that we're considering marriage, I thought I'd try out nicknames."

My stomach tightened. I let my gaze fall back to the white, sandy beach stretching out beneath us and the impossibly blue waves rolling in and out.

"Nothing is troubling me," I lied smoothly. "I was just thinking about how much I missed this view during my marriage to Demetri. House Laurent is on the coast, but their fortress is set back further from the water. More than once, I longed to be able to hear the tides while falling asleep."

"The Sovereign House is far inland," Draven pointed out.

"Then you'll have to work quite hard to convince me to marry you and move there," I said in a breezy tone, not taking my eyes off the water even as I was acutely aware of just how close he was standing.

"Kieran can tell you just how persuasive I can be." I went still at his words before slowly turning to face him. Draven cocked his head and studied my expression. "You didn't know about us? Given how close the two of you were growing up"—he gave me a knowing smile—"and how close the two of you are *now*, I assumed he told you."

I smiled wide enough to show my fangs. "First you remind me that the Sovereign House is nowhere near my beloved ocean, and now you try to drive a wedge between me and the man I love with my entire soul. You used to be far more *charming*, prince."

Draven stared at me for a long moment, and the deep red threads that ran through his lapis blue eyes widened slightly like dark rivers of blood. I cocked my head to match his movement from earlier, and for a moment, his eyes flashed almost entirely red before he let out a deep, rumbling laugh.

"There you are." He chuckled. "With all the false politeness and flirting you greeted me with, I was worried the Samara I knew had been lost to the bullshit of Moroi House politics. I knew when I got you alone out here, the real you would bleed through."

"You're the prince," I said flatly. "You are the walking embodiment of *Moroi House politics*."

"I am what I have to be." He nodded in acknowledgement. My brows furrowed before I caught the movement and smoothed it out. What had he meant by that?

"You didn't answer my question from earlier. About marriage," I clarified.

"Technically, you never asked a question." He shrugged a broad shoulder.

"Don't play coy with me, Drav."

He smiled at hearing the nickname I'd given him long ago. "I never wanted to marry because I'm surrounded by people all day who are only married for political gains. The Houses are all cutthroat with each other, fighting over resources and always trying to get one over on someone else. Even knowing everyone enters into these marriages willingly"—his lips twisted down—"it wasn't a future I ever wanted. So I made sure to make myself useful to the queen in other ways."

This wasn't the first time I'd heard Draven refer to his

A Court of Bones and Sorrow

mother as "the queen." When we were having private conversations, he'd almost always refer to her as "Velika" or just "the queen." Only when he was addressing her in front of others did he call her Mother.

I'd always wondered why but had never asked because it'd felt too intrusive, and because I hadn't wanted to ruin the times when Draven had shed the charming prince persona around me.

But everything was different now, and I couldn't afford to let Draven keep any secrets.

"You mean your mother."

"Sometimes she's my mother." His frown tipped up into a smile, but I knew it was false. "Sometimes she's the Queen of Monsters."

"And was it the mother or the queen who suggested the marriage between us?" I asked carefully.

"You could do worse." He glanced at me with an amused expression. "I *am* a prince. Most people are impressed by that."

"I'm not most people."

"No," he said slowly, "you most certainly are not."

We both turned back towards the ocean and watched the tide roll in and out in companionable silence for a few minutes. I didn't know what to say or think. All I knew was I needed to find the others so we could strategize.

"If you don't mind, I'm going to go get cleaned up now and then rest for a bit." I pushed off the balcony wall and took a step back as Draven turned around to face me, leaning his back against the stones.

"Will Kieran be *resting* with you?"

"Careful." My gaze turned flinty as I told him my next lie. "I'll consider this marriage, but I will not tolerate you coming between me and Kieran or harming him in any way."

For a second, Draven's expression faltered, and something

akin to sadness flashed across his face before he slipped on his charming and carefree mask once more.

"Understood."

"Good." I nodded. "I'll see you for supper then."

"Wonderful." He smiled, but it didn't reach his eyes. And I couldn't help but wonder how often he lied with his easy grins. "Enjoy your *rest*."

CHAPTER TWO

Samara

I'D BARELY MADE it to the hallway when Vail appeared at my side like a wraith. He didn't touch me or speak a word, just walked by my side as I made my way to the library, where I had no doubt the others were gathered. Since we'd made it out of the temple, Vail had been careful to keep some distance between us. This was the closest we'd been in the last three days.

A phantom pain flared along my shoulders where he'd clawed through my skin while I'd been lost in my bloodlust. Without meaning to, my gaze drifted to his neck and the throbbing pulse it contained. He'd saved my life by allowing me to feed from him, and I still remembered how his blood tasted.

Wild. Dark. Intoxicating.

My fangs slid a little further out of my gums. Normally, I kept them tucked away, hidden from sight unless I was feeding. It was considered a sign of weakness if you allowed your fangs to be out at all times. The Moroi were monsters but tried very hard to pretend we weren't.

I was getting tired of pretending.

A few people slowed and tried to catch my eye as I walked

at a brisk pace down hallways and up multiple sets of winding stairwells, but whatever they saw in my face caused them to snap their mouths shut and quickly walk away. Vail's menacing presence by my side likely had something to do with it as well. Whatever they wanted, I'd need to deal with later, since discussing the Prince Draven situation with the others was my top priority.

The dark wood doors of the library were closed as we approached, and no sound came from inside, which meant they had the silencing spell activated. I opened one of the doors and slipped in, Vail following and closing the door behind us before leaning against it with his arms crossed.

Roth and Alaric were seated at a table, books and scrolls stretched out in front of them. Roth's hazel eyes lifted from the page for a moment as they looked me over, then they returned to reading. "Don't come near my books until you've bathed."

"I would never, Roth," I said aghast while holding a hand to my chest.

Their gaze lifted once more, the burnt orange lines that wound their way through the hazel darkening into a smolder. "Good girl." Once again, their eyes lowered to the page, but based on the way their lips curled slightly, I knew they'd heard my heart skip a beat.

My eyes slid to Alaric, who was staring at me with an indecipherable look and a clenched jaw that usually meant he was pissed. The list of things he could be upset about was long, and I had no doubt he held me responsible for most of them, but he'd just have to stew in his shitty mood for a little longer. I only had one priority right now.

Kieran was paused mid-step from where he had likely been pacing back and forth—and probably driving Roth insane—in front of the table. His blond hair was tousled as he stood there, like he'd been roughly running his hands through it. I hated the uncertainty in his eyes, waiting for me to say something.

So I closed the distance between us and cupped his face in my hands. "I don't care. About any of it. You are mine, Kier." Then I kissed him. He just stood there for a second, frozen in place before gripping me to him. His tongue slipped between my lips and grazed over a fang, causing sweet, coppery blood to light up my taste buds.

Just as he swallowed my groan, someone cleared their throat, and we reluctantly pulled apart but didn't completely release each other. Instead, I let Kieran spin me around so my back rested against his chest as he wrapped his arms around me. Then I inhaled his scent and enjoyed the last lingering drops of his blood.

Vail's eyes glittered at me from across the room, his gaze locked onto my mouth and the fangs hidden behind my lips. His throat bobbed once before he looked away.

"What did the prince say to you?" Alaric asked, drawing my attention away from Vail. "Do you think he knows it was us in the temple?"

"Unclear. I don't think so, but I acknowledge the timing of his arrival is suspicious. He could be in the same boat as us. Maybe he only knows that something happened to the wraiths and a Moroi is responsible. Or maybe he knows it was us but doesn't know that we know he is the traitor." I blew out a heavy breath, a headache already forming at all the possibilities. "This whole marriage proposal could be a cover for him to spend time here, figuring out what we know and who we might have told." Kieran's arms tightened around my waist, and I pressed further against him.

"You already married one fool," Roth drawled, not taking their eyes off the page, "I'd prefer you didn't repeat that mistake."

From Roth, that was practically a declaration of love with chocolates.

Alaric glanced at them for a long moment before shaking

his head and returning his attention to me. "Did you tell him no?"

"Not exactly," I hedged. "We need to figure out what he knows and why he's really here. If I flat-out reject the proposal, he's not going to just go away. We'd be forcing his hand to take more drastic measures, assuming he knows it was us at the temple. I'll play along for now to buy us time to figure out our next move."

The muscle below Alaric's left eye ticked as he looked over my shoulder to Kieran. "And you're fine with that? Letting her *play* with the prince?"

Kieran stiffened, and the chains I'd been keeping around my temper broke. "First, nobody *lets* me do anything." I pointed a finger at him in warning. "Stay the fuck out of my relationship with Kieran. Second, you're more than welcome to walk your pretty ass down the hallway and bat your eyelashes at the prince. You'd make a beautiful consort," I crooned mockingly.

The turquoise coloring of Alaric's eyes bled into a seafoam green until they were practically glowing like blue fire. It made his already gorgeous eyes absolutely breathtaking. I smirked at him, and his fingers clenched around the book he'd been reading.

"You break my books, I break you," Roth snapped. Alaric dropped the book and leaned back in the chair, crossing his arms over his chest.

"Have your lover's spat later," Vail growled.

I gave him a cool look before slipping out of Kieran's embrace and slumping into a chair at the head of the table next to Alaric, Kieran sitting on my other side.

"Draven was a little cagey about it, but he implied it was his mother's idea for him to marry me."

Kieran nodded. "Carmilla was the one who told me about the proposed union between you and Draven. She said it was the queen's suggestion but that she thought it was a good idea and that you might be open to it."

I mulled that over. My aunt and I had discussed my future quite a bit since I'd returned to House Harker. In all our conversations, I'd made it clear I wanted to stay here and fully step into my role as Heir. I hadn't exactly said I didn't want to marry again, but I'd thought she'd understood I wasn't looking for that. Especially since the ink had barely dried on my divorce papers to Demetri. "And Draven?"

It was odd she would have agreed to such a thing without checking with me first. I needed to find a way to talk to her without the queen knowing.

Kieran's eyes darkened. "He does whatever his mother tells him to." The muscles along my jaw ached as I clenched my teeth. Whatever had happened between him and Draven had hurt him deeply. I didn't feel any jealousy towards what they'd had, only rage at someone hurting Kier. He deserved better, and I'd make Draven pay for putting that wounded look on his face.

"That was the impression I got in my conversation with him." I pursed my lips. "What if Queen Velika not only knows what her son is up to, but she's ordering him to do it?"

Vail scoffed. "You believe the Sovereign House has betrayed all of the Moroi and allied with the wraiths? After everything they've done to protect our people?"

I narrowed my eyes at Vail. His blind loyalty was almost as annoying as his dismissive attitude towards me. "That's exactly what I'm saying."

Vail started, "There has to be some other explanation—" but Kieran cut him off.

"I promise you there is nothing Draven does without the queen's knowledge." He swallowed and stared at the table. "Trust me. I know him better than any of you. If she told him to walk in here and slit all of our throats, he'd do it without hesitation."

"Why though?" Alaric frowned. "Velika is ruthless—she has to be to keep all of the Moroi Houses in line, but why would she agree to help the wraiths? What could they have offered her?"

"We need to find out," I said darkly. "Carmilla is at the Sovereign House, and Draven said she'd be there for a while."

Aggression poured off Vail, I could feel it even from where he stood across the room. "You think they're holding her against her will?"

Of course the idea that the Sovereign House was harming Carmilla would get him to immediately cast aside his devotion to them. There was no one Vail was more loyal to than my aunt.

"I don't know." My frustration with Vail left me, and dread replaced it. "Carmilla and Velika have always been close."

"Carmilla is *not* involved in this," Vail growled.

"Calm yourself. I trust my aunt more than I trust you," I snapped, and Vail's lip curled. "Carmilla would never sacrifice our people for a promise of power, certainly not from the monsters who have been hunting us for centuries, but Velika is her closest friend and she trusts her. If the queen asked her to stay in the Sovereign House as a personal favor, my aunt wouldn't closely examine the reason."

"Which means we have to be very careful," Alaric said. "Carmilla could pay the price if we make the wrong move."

Vail glanced at Kieran. "When did you and the prince leave the Sovereign House?"

"We both left five days ago but split up. He said he had something to take care of . . ." Kieran looked away, his jaw hardening. "He met me last night at the Faybell outpost, and we left first thing this morning. Only arrived here a few hours before all of you."

"So he went to the temple after splitting up with Kieran. We saw him there and left while he was busy serving up our people on a silver platter to that wraith prick." I frowned as I did the math in my head and then looked at Vail. "How did he make it there so fast? Granted, we stopped to rest a couple of times, but we still made good time, and we didn't pass Faybell until this morning."

We'd taken the quickest route to get home, but that still meant we'd had to travel north from the temple, then ride east all the way to the coast before traveling south down to House Harker. There were no roads that ran through the forests in the center of the Moroi realm. It was too dangerous.

Vail grimaced. "He must have cut through the forest. The roads are safer, but they take you out of the way. Through the wilds from the temple to Faybell is almost a direct shot, but he couldn't have ridden a horse through that. It would have been too loud and likely would have broken a leg at anything faster than a trot."

I thought back to Draven perching on the ledge, soaking in the sunshine. It was hard to picture him racing through the woods at night on foot. Then again, I never would have imagined him cutting deals with the wraiths either. Apparently, the prince was just full of surprises.

"All of you will keep working on what the wraiths—the Unseelie Fae," I corrected myself, "are up to. It seems like they want to return to their original forms and need those black stones to do it." I thought about the shiny, obsidian stone stashed safely in Roth's quarters. Our human ancestors had used the stones in the ritual to turn themselves into monsters. Into us. What made the stones so special, we had no idea—but the wraiths had been ransacking our outposts looking for them, so clearly, they were important. "We need to know more about whatever ritual they're doing and what they might have offered the Sovereign House to make them betray us all."

"And what will you be doing?" Alaric asked, even though the prick already knew what my answer would be. He just wanted me to say it out loud.

"I will be flirting with and distracting Draven." I waved a hand dismissively. "Keeping his attention off all of you and also trying to figure out more of his role in all of this."

Alaric looked at Kieran, and some unspoken conversation passed between them. Then Kieran's mouth flattened into a hard line as he glared at his best friend, who only returned the expression with a hard stare.

Yeah, I wasn't touching whatever was going on there. I had enough of my own drama to deal with.

"If our suspicions are right and the Sovereign House is really working with the wraiths, then we can't trust any of the other Houses." I rubbed my face tiredly. "Some of them will almost certainly be in on it too."

"I think we can pretty much count on it with House Corvinus," Kieran said bitterly. "They'd do anything to stay on Velika's good side."

"Tepes and Salvatore are wild cards," Alaric noted. "They could go either way, which means, for now, we definitely can't trust them."

"True. Although I doubt Salvatore would agree to ally with wraiths," I said. "Last I spoke with Dominique, she was still feeling overwhelmed at the loss of her parents and sister and also the pressures of stepping in to rule the House." The stoically beautiful, young Moroi was only twenty-five years old, one year older than me. Her elder sister had been the Heir, so Dominique had never planned on leading. Based on all the interactions I'd had with her, she hadn't been upset by that. She had loved her sister and had been happy to play a supporting role, even planned her life around it.

Then her parents and sister had been killed on a trip to visit House Tepes along with ten rangers and almost twenty other members of House Salvatore. Outside of the recent outpost attacks, it had been the deadliest wraith ambush in almost a century.

"For all we know"—a dark look passed over Kieran's face as he spoke—"Dominique arranged that attack to seize power. Maybe she's been playing everyone all this time."

I wanted to disagree, but if someone had told me two weeks ago that the Moroi Queen was plotting with our enemies, I would have laughed in their face. Nothing and no one could be trusted anymore.

"As much as it pains me to say," I said with great annoyance. "I don't think House Laurent would ally with the Sovereign House. Marvina has always hated Velika and would try to undermine the Sovereign House at any opportunity. She always did it on the sly so it wasn't super obvious, but I don't think she was faking the hostility."

To say my ex-mother-in-law and I didn't get along was an understatement. During my three-year marriage to her son, she'd bounced back and forth between indifference and hostility towards me. My leaving House Laurent and dissolving my marriage with Demetri had almost as much to do with that as it did finding Demetri in bed with someone else.

It still felt odd that merely months ago, I'd been living at House Laurent in a loveless marriage and growing more and more frustrated with my daily life. Given our current problems, my life wasn't exactly perfect now, but I was happy.

And I'd kill anyone who tried to take that away from me, even the Moroi Queen.

"What about House Devereux?" Alaric asked.

Roth let out a humorless laugh. "Trust me, they're not allied with the Sovereign House, but they won't help us either."

As a member of the Devereux line and someone who grew up in the House, Roth likely knew better than all of us. But of course Alaric wasn't willing to let it go.

"But you must know somethi—" he started.

Roth slammed their book shut and rose from the table. "I think I'm onto something with the black stones, but I need quiet to focus on it. I'll be in my quarters."

They gathered a stack of books before stalking towards the door, and I practically jumped up from my chair to dart across the room, cutting them off. Roth paused when I rested my fingers on their forearm.

"Please be careful. We all need to watch ourselves while Draven is here. Your room is far from all of ours, and there are no other living quarters around it." Roth had taken over a small room just down the hall from the library. Most of the rooms in this wing were used for storage or as guest quarters for lower-ranking members of other Houses while they were visiting. Roth liked it because it was close to the library and quiet, but it also meant they were isolated from the rest of us.

A dark red ribbon unwound from their forearm and gently brushed some of my hair back over my shoulder. "I'll be fine, Samara," Roth said in a low, even tone. "He probably has no idea who I am or what I'm doing here. I'll keep to my room and the library as much as possible and hopefully just avoid the prince altogether."

Then the ribbon wrapped around a thick section of my hair before giving it a sharp tug. "You can come check on me later though, if you're worried."

"I'll think about it," I murmured as Roth stepped around me and headed for the door. The ribbon trailed down my backside before wrapping back around their forearm as they stepped out of the library. Once the door closed, I glanced at Vail, who had stepped aside to let Roth leave. "Could you possibly get one of your rangers to keep an eye on Roth in an unobtrusive manner? They'll get cranky if they know the guard is there."

Vail's lips quirked up into the faintest hint of a smile.

A Court of Bones and Sorrow

"They'll get *crankier* if they know the guard is there," I amended.

"I'll take care of it."

"What now?" Kieran asked.

I plucked at the dark green fabric of my tunic and scrunched my nose. "Now we get cleaned up and pretend to go about our day as we normally would, which to be fair, with Carmilla gone, there are some House responsibilities Alaric and I need to deal with. Then we'll attend dinner tonight with the prince, where we'll find out just how good of a liar he is."

"Want me to grab you some food and meet you in your study?" Kieran offered as he rose before walking over to join me.

"Yes, please." I smiled at him, and Alaric grumbled something under his breath that I chose to ignore. Kieran shot his best friend a sharp look before planting a quick kiss on my lips and slipping out the door.

"I told him starting things with you was a bad idea." Alaric reached for a book across the table and began flipping through its pages. "Neither of you are lovestruck teenagers anymore. You're the Harker Heir, and he's just a courtier."

"Kier isn't *just* anything," I hissed.

Alaric continued like I hadn't spoken. "Sooner or later, you'll have to marry again." He raised his eyes from the book and speared me with a cruel glare. "Although I suppose for your next marriage, you'll clarify beforehand if your spouse is expected to be loyal to you or if fucking courtiers is on the table. Wouldn't want a repeat of Demetri, now would we?"

Something in me snapped. Between the tension of conversing with Draven earlier, the stress of the last few days, and the revelation that the queen we'd all sworn loyalty to had betrayed us, I was fucking done. The slim throwing dagger I kept strapped to my thigh was in my fingers within a second, and the next, I was hurtling it through the air at Alaric's face.

He slid out of the way, but not quite fast enough as a thin line of blood opened up on his cheek. Slowly, he raised his hand and touched his face, his fingers bloody as he pulled it away.

Then I spun on my heel and stalked towards the door, glancing up at Vail as I jerked it open. "Do you have something to add?"

A feral light glinted in his eyes. "Nice throw."

CHAPTER THREE

Alaric

I STARED at the bright red streak across my fingers. Samara threw a *knife* at me. At my fucking face. Sure, it wouldn't have killed me, only decapitation or massive trauma could take down a Moroi, but it would have fucking hurt. And if she'd taken out an eye, it would have taken me days to regrow it.

She'd never endanger your eyes, a voice in my head whispered. *She enjoys them too much.*

My cock stirred as I remembered the number of times I'd caught Samara admiring my eyes. Usually, I hated being stared at. I was well aware that many people found me attractive, but while Kieran thrived on that sort of attention, I loathed it. Yet when Samara looked at me like that . . . it definitely wasn't loathing I was feeling.

"Fuck it all," I muttered under my breath before wiping the remaining blood off my cheek, the cut already healed, since it had been little more more than a scratch. A glint of silver drew my eye, and I grabbed the dagger from where it had embedded itself in a bookcase, just barely missing a book. I smiled. If Roth ever found out about this, they'd make sure to punish Samara in a way the brat *didn't* enjoy.

I couldn't wait to let this little detail slip in the future and watch that play out.

Vail tracked me with that stony gaze of his as I stalked towards the door, dagger in hand, aching to hunt Samara down and finish our conversation because I was far from fucking done. I'd warned Kieran that this would happen. Now his heart was going to get broken because of Samara's fucking games.

It wasn't like I expected her to actually marry the prince, but Kieran would have to watch her flirt and lead him on for the next few days. Maybe even weeks or months. Who the fuck knew how long it would take us to untangle this nightmare?

And while, this time, the end result wouldn't be marriage, I knew it eventually would be, because the Heirs of Houses didn't marry lowly courtiers.

Just before I reached the doors, Vail slid into my path, blocking my exit. I was in excellent shape, but I was built on the leaner side, and the amount of running I did only emphasized that. Vail was nearly six and a half feet tall and covered in slabs of muscle. The cloak he wore over his brown leathers only made him appear larger.

I halted, eying him warily. The Marshal of House Harker had always been an enigma to me. On one hand, he was one of the most disciplined people I knew. All of the rangers who answered to him did so with respect and something close to veneration, but there was a wildness to Vail, as if his bloodlust was always simmering beneath the surface, just waiting to be let out.

I still remembered what it felt like to be hunted by a Strigoi, a Moroi who had lost all traces of their humanity. When a Strigoi looked at you, it was from cold, predatory eyes. Vail's gaze always felt the same to me.

"Is there a problem?" I asked cooly, forcing myself not to

take a step back and add more distance between us, even as my fingers tightened around the dagger.

Vail's stare never dropped from my face, but his lips curled as if he was acknowledging I had the blade and found it amusing that I thought it would make any difference in a fight between us.

"I don't understand you." He cocked his head, and the pieces of bone braided into his hair and beard slid against each other like little reminders of death. "Usually, I kill things I don't understand."

"That's because you're firmly in the brawn category and less in the brain one." My fingers tightened around the dagger's handle, even as I kept a bored look on my face.

"Hmm," he hummed. "You have feelings for Samara. I'm pretty sure you're in love with her, and that scares the shit out of you, so you strike out to hurt her. You did it before when you hinted that Kieran would cheat on her, and you did it a few minutes ago by bringing up Demetri and throwing that in her face." He leaned forward, crowding my space, and I stiffened but held my ground. "I might not be as well-educated as you, but my instincts are never wrong."

"I don't have the time to tell you how wrong you are, nor would I be interested in wasting the time if I did have it." I held his unflinching gaze. "What I don't understand is why you would even bring this up now."

"Because the prince has information we need. As much as it pains me to say this, Samara's plan has merit." Vail shifted back with a grimace. "You need to be the coldhearted bastard I know you're perfectly capable of being and keep your mouth shut around Draven. Samara has enough to handle without dealing with your emotional bullshit."

"I'm sorry"—I narrowed my eyes at him—"haven't you tried to kill her *twice* in the past month?"

"My bloodlust got a little out of hand in the temple," he said flatly. "But I'm the reason she got out."

"So you don't deny *deliberately* leaving her behind when the kùsu attacked us on the road?" He didn't say anything, and I snorted. "That's what I thought. Maybe you should worry more about your own *emotional bullshit* when it comes to Samara and less about mine."

Vail eyed me for several long seconds before standing aside, and I left without another word.

FIFTEEN MINUTES LATER, I barged into Samara's suite. My temper had only increased on my walk over as several advisors had stopped me to fill me in on various issues that had arisen while I'd been gone. With Carmilla at the Sovereign House, Samara and I were responsible for running things. While most of the more senior advisors were capable and smart, hand-picked by Carmilla over the years for their hard work and dedication, some serious problems had occurred while we'd been gone and needed to be dealt with soon. As if we didn't have enough fucking problems.

The large seating area that made up most of her living space was empty. Well . . . empty might be the wrong word. My lip curled as I took in the chaos of the room. There were stacks of books everywhere. On the low table in front of the settee. On the floor. I picked up one that had been haphazardly placed on the back of the lounge chair and flipped through it.

It was written in the Fae language, so I couldn't read it, but I was pretty sure it was the Unseelie dialect and poetry, based on how the lines were arranged. Was this what Samara did in her free time? Read poetry in a dead language?

"Careful, Alaric." Samara breezed into the room with nothing but a towel wrapped around her. "If you keep frowning like that, your face might get stuck, and think of how sad all the lovely, young courtiers would feel if they were robbed of your beauty."

I gritted my teeth. I knew exactly who she was talking about. There was a group of courtiers who regularly visited from Kieran's old House—Corvinus—mostly comprised of young, female Moroi who were on the hunt for a good marriage. There was nothing impressive about my bloodline, but my parents had served Carmilla as her top advisors, as I now did. Between this and my appearance, several courtiers from that group had set their eyes on me.

"Sounds like that would be to my benefit, so I think I'll keep the sneer, if it's all the same to you." I tossed the book back down and crossed my arms.

"Suit yourself." She shrugged and started pawing through the piles of clothes that, like the books, were scattered everywhere. Samara frowned as she tossed aside dress after dress before finally holding up a rich mulberry-purple one triumphantly.

"If you just put your clothes away like a normal person, you wouldn't have to go on a scavenger hunt for the ones you want," I said dryly.

Samara just rolled her eyes and walked back towards the wide-open double doors that led to her bedroom and bathing chamber. My eyes instantly fell to her ass and the way it shifted beneath the thin fabric. Why did that towel have to be so short?

"I'm sorry, why are you here? Generally, when someone throws a knife at your face, that's a sign that maybe they don't want to be in your company."

"I'm here because I wasn't finished with our conversation when you pulled that stunt," I ground out and looked away from that treacherous towel. "Thanks for that, by the way."

"Don't be an asshole and you won't get knives to the face,"

she said in a breezy tone as I followed her into the bedroom. A large bed with a midnight black headboard and deep red covers took up most of the space. My mind instantly went to Samara in those sheets. I suspected she slept naked or in some type of extremely indecent nightgown. "Alaric?"

I blinked slowly, dragging my gaze away from the bed to where Samara was standing next to it, holding the dress in one hand and dangling undergarments from the other. Suddenly, the only thing I could hear was the rapid pounding of my heart, then twin flashes of pain erupted from my gums as my fangs extended. Throughout it all, my expression remained stoic and slightly annoyed. I wasn't as good at rotating through different masks as Kieran, but I was excellent at this one.

Samara arched one perfect, dark eyebrow. Okay, maybe I was less than perfect at maintaining this mask. Why did she have to continue to be the absolute worst?

"What?" I bit out.

She let out a husky laugh, and the way my dick reacted, one would have thought she'd reached her hand into my pants and stroked it. Fuck. That thought was not helping.

"You just gonna stand there and scowl while I get dressed?" She twirled the black undergarments around her finger. "Because that's not normally the reaction people have when I'm about to get naked in front of them."

"Who exactly are you getting naked in front of?" The sharp words came out before I could stop them.

"Currently?" She tilted her head back and looked up at the ceiling, like she had to think hard about the answer.

"Samara," I growled.

"Alaric," she mockingly growled back as her gaze fell to me again. Maybe Vail would kill her and solve all my problems? When I continued to glower at her, she sighed. "Only Kier and Roth. Despite what you think of me, I do actually care quite a great deal about the two of them, and the three of us have discussed the dynamics of our relationships. Not that our business is any of your concern."

"Kieran is my best friend, and your involvement with him will not end well," I argued, even as I ignored the relief I felt that she wasn't seeing anyone else.

Her lips curled into that flirty grin that I couldn't decide if I adored or hated. "I promise you that I've given Kier more than one *happy* ending."

Argh.

"I'm being serious, Samara." My fingers tightened into fists at my sides. "If you would just think rationally about this—"

"Stop." Black streaks darkened her purple eyes until they were depthless voids. I shifted uneasily. It hadn't escaped my notice that she hadn't put her fangs away since we'd left the temple, and her eyes had been shifting between the colors more than usual. These were all signs that pointed to a Moroi's bloodlust being dangerously close to the surface.

As a Harker, Samara had better control over hers than most of us. It was unlikely she'd ever fully lose control and become a Strigoi. Growing up, she would regularly slip in and out of her bloodlust as if it had been nothing. Even though she hadn't put her fangs away the last few days, she hadn't been acting any differently. Just the same old, frustrating Samara who had always slipped under my skin like no other.

But despite that fact, seeing her like this made me tense. My cousin had turned Strigoi, and I still had nightmares about it.

She squeezed her eyes shut and inhaled several deep breaths. When they opened a few seconds later, they were back to their startling purple that always reminded me of the night sky. They were perfectly stunning, just like the rest of her. Not that I'd ever tell her that. Samara's ego was big enough on its own. Plus, that would be admitting to the attraction I felt towards her every day.

And that would absolutely not be happening.

"I'm done with this conversation," she announced. "And I'll be getting dressed now. Leave."

"We're not done with this conversation, and you can get dressed in there." I pointed to the bathing chambers.

"It's my room, and I'll get dressed wherever the fuck I want." She raised her chin in challenge.

"Not leaving." I crossed my arms. Knowing Samara, she would deliberately take an hour to get dressed just to avoid having this conversation. She'd already stormed away from me once, I wasn't letting her get away again.

Something wicked danced in her eyes, then she tossed the clothes onto the bed and whipped the towel off before I could object.

Fuck. I kept my eyes locked on hers. For three seconds. Three *excruciatingly* long seconds.

My gaze dropped, and I was pretty sure my heart stopped with it. I'd seen Samara naked before, but it'd been steamy and she'd been lying down at the edge of the pool . . . with Kieran's head between her legs. There had been a lot to process, and I'd stormed out before either of them had noticed just how hard my cock had grown at the sight of them.

Well, Kieran had spotted that fun fact. Samara might be oblivious to my frustrating interest in her, but he wasn't, and he absolutely loved to push me about it, because I was apparently surrounded by assholes.

I should have looked away, or better yet, I should have fucking left the room. Instead, I stood there and drank in every delicious inch of her. Samara was nothing but enticing curves. She had the most glorious chest to ever exist resting above the soft curve of her stomach and thick thighs that would feel amazing wrapped around my head. I couldn't see her ass from this angle, but I knew it would be plump, round, and something that would beg me to grip it. Hard.

"Have you looked your fill?" she drawled. "Because I really need to get dressed so I can get some work done."

I snapped my eyes back up, my jaw tightening at the amusement I saw written all over her face. She was the one who'd been naked in front of me, and yet I was the one blushing like crazy.

"I hate you," I said flatly before turning around and stalking towards the door, Samara's deep laugh following me out.

"Good talk, Alaric!"

CHAPTER FOUR

Kieran

I surveyed the plate resting on the worn, wooden, raised table at the center of the main kitchen. Leora—the Moroi in charge of the kitchen staff at House Harker and the best baker in existence—was shooting amused glances at me from across the room, where she was baking some honey biscuits. They were a common snack, since they required few ingredients to make and honey was one thing we had in abundance. Almost all of our sweets were honey-something. Luckily for me, I loved honey and never got tired of it. Samara was the same, which was why half the plate was made up of freshly baked biscuits.

"Are you waiting for them to speak some words of wisdom to you?" Leora mused. "I admit, I am rather talented, but even my skills have limits."

"Perhaps I'm debating if I want to bring them to Samara or if I simply want to hoard these all to myself?" I grinned at the older Moroi woman who had been a staple at House Harker for as long as I could remember.

She rolled her eyes and plucked two more biscuits off the tray before placing them on the plate. "There." She made a shooing motion. "Now out with you so I can get back to work. You're distracting me."

"Leora, my wondrous beauty." I gave her my best smile that usually resulted in panties being thrown in my direction. "You know I would marry you in a heartbeat if you would only ask."

"You're just as ridiculous now as you were when you first arrived." She picked up the plate and thrust it into my hands, her light brown eyes glittering with mirth. "And if Calus hears you talking like that, he'll wallop you good."

I laughed and kissed her cheek. "We can't have that. Tell him I'll stop by later this week. It's been a while since we chatted."

Grabbing the food, I beat a hasty retreat. I knew from experience that Leora would go from teasing and laughing to prying into my personal life if I stayed any longer. Her husband, Calus, was the same way. The two of them were fourth-generation Moroi, like Carmilla, and were considerably older than the mid-fifties they appeared to be. We'd celebrated Calus' 130th birthday over the winter, and Leora was only a few years behind him.

When I'd first come to House Harker as a jaded fourteen-year-old, they had instantly taken me under their wings. Everything was so different here than House Corvinus. My parents were high-ranking advisors there, and they'd viewed me and my siblings as nothing more than pawns in their scheming. Growing up, I'd learned quickly to control every single facial expression and measure every word carefully.

It was common for Houses to trade courtiers amongst themselves. Usually the children of people like my parents or the lower-ranking family members of whatever bloodline ruled the House. Everyone knew these courtiers were loyal to their birth Houses, and yet the practice continued, because there was always the chance you could sway their allegiance and then get information about the inner workings of the House they'd come from.

Our survival depended on the Moroi Houses working together, both for a solid defense against the wraiths and other monsters, and for resources like the gems that powered our wards. Every House controlled at least one unique resource, and the negotiations between them were ongoing and tedious. Samara loved dealing with all that bullshit. Alaric liked it too.

But that wasn't where my skills lay. I was excellent at getting people to like me, and when people liked you . . . they talked to you. Carmilla had never asked me to spy on other Houses or collect information for her benefit. The first few years here, I'd been practically holding my breath, waiting for her to make the request, the demand.

It had never come.

And that was why my loyalty would always be to this House. Carmilla wanted her people to be happy, and so did Samara. Both of them could be cunning and underhanded at times when it came to dealing with the other Houses—there was simply no surviving in this world without a little bit of that—but Carmilla knew the names of every single person who worked in this House, down to the lowliest maid. Samara worshiped her aunt and was the same.

House Harker was home to me.

I smiled at some of the servants as they walked by, heads bent as they whispered to each other and giggled, but then my pleasant mood vanished as I heard Draven's name. I'd been trying very hard not to think about him for the last twenty minutes. Not exactly a long-term plan, given his reason for being here and what Samara and the others had discovered about him, but not thinking about Prince Draven had been my go-to strategy for almost a year now.

As if summoned by the brief slip of my thoughts, the dark-haired prince appeared at my side and snatched a biscuit off the plate.

"There you are." He broke a piece off the sweet pastry and popped it into his mouth, then his eyes closed as he savored the flavor, and I couldn't stop my gaze from lingering on his strong jawline, remembering the number of times I had run my tongue across it before grazing his neck with my fangs. I'd never drank from him, nor him from me—that'd been one of the few lines we hadn't crossed in our time together.

I snapped my gaze up and clenched my jaw when his eyes opened and he caught me looking at him. "These aren't for you." Then I quickened my pace down the hallway, smiling tightly at others who passed us as they tried to subtly check out the prince before looking at me curiously. I knew what they were thinking. Why was the Moroi Prince talking to a simple courtier who held no sway in this House, especially when he'd been dismissive of the higher-ranking advisors all morning?

I gritted my teeth. As much as I loved collecting gossip, I didn't like to be the source of it.

"So touchy." He chuckled darkly. "At least you're speaking to me now. It was quite impressive how you managed to avoid me while you were at the Sovereign House and then not speak to me on the entire ride here . . . I recall you being a bit more vocal in our interactions, especially that one time—"

A growl ripped from my throat as I grabbed Draven by the arm and dragged him into an empty meeting room. Then I shoved him away from me and slammed the door behind us, dropping the plate onto the table, resisting the urge to throw it at him. He smirked at me like he knew exactly what I was thinking.

"It's been fun, but I'm bored now," I said coldly, repeating the words he'd said to me. "Also, watch how you speak to me in the future, courtier."

The smirk slid off his face as he tossed the half-eaten

biscuit onto the table before letting out a bone-weary sigh. "I had to say that, Kier. The wrong people were noticing how much time I was spending with you, and it was getting dangerous for the both of us."

I flinched inwardly at hearing him call me that. Until Draven, only Sam had ever called me Kier. Hearing the nickname from his lips again caused all the confusing emotions to swirl up inside until I ruthlessly shoved them back down.

"I'm assuming by 'the wrong people,' you mean the queen?" I asked flatly. The muscles along his jawline flexed, but he said nothing. I snorted and shook my head. Queen Velika was a puzzle to me. On the surface, she appeared to be a fair and just ruler who loved her son, although she was occasionally frustrated by his disinterest in helping her rule. But during my time with Draven, I knew there was more to her, something darker.

There was nothing specific I could point to, nothing I'd witnessed with my own eyes, but Draven was a different person around her. It was subtle, but no one was better than me at reading body language. He obeyed her no matter what, but it wasn't out of love. If I didn't know better, I'd say he was frightened of her. And every once in a while, I'd catch her looking at him in a way that reminded me of a predator circling wounded prey.

It was why I had probably been the least surprised when Samara had theorized it was actually Queen Velika who was allied with the wraiths and Draven was doing her bidding. What I'd never understood, though, was why she had such a hold over her son.

Draven's dark eyes met mine. "What have you told Samara?"

"Nothing yet." I waved a hand at the plate I'd set aside. "But I'll be telling her *everything* soon enough."

"She was always the one you wanted." He shrugged a

shoulder casually, as if our time together had meant nothing to him. "So I can't say I'm surprised."

"Fuck you, Draven," I snarled. "You weren't a fucking backup plan to me. I fucking—" The words died in my throat, and I took a deep breath. "My feelings towards you were genuine and unique to what we shared. I never hid what I felt about Samara from you. I'm perfectly capable of loving two people at once."

He sucked in a breath, and for a moment, I swore his heart stopped beating.

"You shouldn't have ever loved me." The bloodred threads in his eyes expanded as he pondered me like I was a creature he couldn't understand. "I told you *not* to love me."

"That's not how fucking feelings work, Drav!" I shoved my hands against his chest, and he staggered back a step. "If you hurt Sam, I swear to the gods, I'll kill you."

"I don't *want* to hurt her," he bit out.

"But you will if you're ordered to," I scoffed bitterly.

"Please, Kier," he pleaded. Usually, Draven soaked up attention with his tall frame and broad build, but now, he hunched his shoulders, and there was a desperation to his expression I'd never seen before. I barely managed to stop myself from wrapping my arms around him and telling him that we'd figure it out. That he just had to tell us what the fuck was going on. But I held it all back because, despite the churning feelings burning inside my chest, Draven couldn't be trusted.

"You don't understand what's at stake," he rasped. "Samara is trapped in this, but you don't have to be. Go visit your friends in the Velesian realm. Just leave the Moroi realm."

The urge to hug him instantly turned into a desire to strangle him. Did he seriously think I would leave Samara behind to face all of this on her own?

I picked the plate up off the table. "I don't abandon those I love. Maybe that's something you should consider in the future."

His expression shuttered, but he didn't say anything as I opened the door and left, something inside my soul cracking when he didn't stop me.

Samara was already seated behind her desk in the cozy little study she'd reclaimed as her own upon returning to House Harker. There were larger rooms available in the wing where Carmilla's spacious study was located—as the Heir, Samara could have kicked out any of the advisors and set up in one of those—but she'd always loved this space the most.

Before she'd left for Drudonia, she'd study here for hours. I'd always keep her company while she buried herself in books, scrolls, maps, whatever she could get her hands on. Even Alaric had joined us sometimes, although that had always devolved into the two of them taking verbal—and sometimes physical— swipes at each other. I let out an amused breath. Nothing had changed there.

Dark purple eyes lifted from the page they'd been reading and latched onto the plate. "Freshly baked honey biscuits?" she asked hopefully.

"Leora just made them." I smirked and walked over to the small seating area I'd crammed into the space. The outer wall was mostly windows, and the other three were lined with shelves. Samara hadn't been keen on adding more furniture to the already small space, but I'd insisted. Her desk and two chairs were on one half of the room, and I'd brought in two more chairs—with far comfier cushions—and tucked them away in the corner next to a window.

I placed the plate onto the table in between them and sank into one of the chairs. "If you want one, you're going to have to come over here though." Her brows furrowed as she frowned at all the papers scattered across her desk. "I promise whatever you're working on will still be there after you've taken a break and eaten something."

She let out an exaggerated sigh but rose to join me. I smiled to myself. Samara was always worried about Roth getting caught up in whatever they were working on and forgetting to eat or otherwise care for themself, but she was the same way. My lovely Samara had a bad habit of putting everyone's needs before her own.

Luckily, she had me, and I had no problem putting her needs before everyone else's.

"This is heaven," she groaned around a mouthful of biscuit, her hair still damp and clinging to the deep purple dress she wore. The color almost perfectly matched her eyes and made her golden brown skin practically glow. I was imagining peeling it off her later when she asked the question I'd been dreading. "So what's the deal with you and Draven?"

A cool dread solidified in the pit of my stomach as I rose to close the door and activate the silencing spell. Samara drew her legs up beneath her and settled further back into her chair as I took a seat again, her expression patient and supportive.

"It was hard when you left for House Laurent," I started. "It's not like I didn't know you'd be marrying Demetri, but when we were growing up, that was always something distant in the future. Even when you went to study at Drudonia, you'd still come back often, but when you left . . ." I swallowed. "It felt like someone had ripped out a piece of my soul, and I didn't know how to fix that."

Her eyes darkened, and her voice was rough as she spoke. "I'm so sorry, Kier."

I shrugged and forced my lips to curve into a small smile. "It's not your fault. Like I said, it's not like I didn't know what was coming."

"Still, I shouldn't have gone through with that marriage." She twisted her hands in her lap as she stared at them with an unseeing gaze. "I was so obsessed with doing what I thought was the right thing for House Harker. After my parents—" Her voice caught on the last word, and my heart clenched.

She never spoke about her parents, and I never pushed her about it. Everyone knew how the previous rulers of House Harker had died. They'd been gone for years before I'd come to live here, and whenever their names were mentioned around Samara, I could practically watch the emotion drain from her face. Everyone seemed to think she had handled the loss of her parents well and had rallied to support House Harker. They praised her as if she were the perfect example of everything a House Heir should be.

I didn't understand how no one could see how, over a decade later, Samara was still devastated by the death of her parents. Her grief was a never-ending well that she did her best to keep covered. I didn't know how to help with that because I'd never lost anyone I'd cared about as deeply as Samara did her parents. The only person I'd ever loved was her.

And Draven.

"I probably should have brought us a bottle of wine in addition to the biscuits." I blew out a deep breath, and Samara chuckled wryly.

"Yeah . . . or maybe some shots of whatever liquor Leora has hidden away in the bottom cupboard of the storage room." Her lips trembled for a second before she caught it and pursed them together. "After my parents died, I felt like I had to do everything perfectly. Everyone was counting on me to uphold their legacy. The alliance with House Laurent was my way of furthering House Harker's power." She shook her head ruefully. "And it was a complete failure."

"Not your fault," I said sharply. "Demetri is a piece of shit, and that House never deserved you. I should have told you back then how much I loved you and begged you to stay."

I'd been too scared that she would acknowledge that she felt the same . . . and then go on to marry Demetri anyway. Because that was what had been expected of her, and she never would have let her House—or more importantly, her aunt—down.

Samara raised her gaze from her hands to look at me and gave me a soft, genuine smile. "I'm sad we wasted so many years." Then her eyes became hard and possessive. "You're mine, Kier, and I'll never leave you again."

"You have no idea how much I want to fuck you right now," I growled as my cock thickened at her words and the truth I felt behind them.

"You can." She winked. "*After* you tell me about Draven."

I sighed and slouched in the chair. "Being at House Harker was hard after you left. So I started traveling even more than normal. Checking in with the outposts, visiting some of the other Houses and also the Sovereign House. During one of those visits, the queen was throwing one of those ridiculous masquerades she loves."

"They're such a waste of resources." Samara's mouth twisted in distaste. "I've brought it up to Carmilla before, hoping that maybe because she's Velika's friend, she could get the queen to tone them down or at least do them less often, but apparently, Velika feels very strongly that it's important we build up and maintain a Moroi culture."

"A culture that only the elite can take part in," I pointed out, and Samara scrunched her nose as she made a noise of agreement. "I was leaning against the wall, watching all those gathered engage in all kinds of wild debauchery, when Draven suddenly appeared next to me. Even with the mask on, I knew it was him."

"He does have a certain . . . presence about him," Samara admitted.

I nodded. "That he does. I didn't know what to do or say to him. We'd been in the same room before, but he'd never directly spoken to me. He just turned to me with a wicked grin and said, 'So, are you having fun collecting all sorts of gossip and potential blackmail material, Kieran?'" I let out a soft chuckle. "I was so fucking surprised not only that he was speaking to me but that he knew my name, that I almost dropped my wineglass."

"He didn't leave my side for the entire party. Other guests would come up and ask him to dance or join them in conversation, and he just politely declined. We spent the entire time pointing out who was fucking who, which House was trying to screw over another one on a trade deal, and any other saucy tidbit we could think of." I chewed on my bottom lip for a moment. "It was the first time I forgot about my longing for you and just . . . enjoyed life."

Samara leaned forward and stretched her arms out so she could clasp my hands in hers. "I'm glad, Kier. Whatever else Draven has done and whatever the future holds, I'm glad he at least gave you that happiness, if only for a night."

"Oh, there were *many* nights he gave me *happiness*." I arched an eyebrow as my lips curved into a satisfied smile. Samara threw her head back and released a throaty laugh as she leaned back in her chair, and something inside me eased at hearing that laugh. I'd been dreading this conversation, not only because talking about it was painful, but I'd been worried Samara wouldn't be comfortable discussing one of my past lovers.

Our relationship still felt so new and fragile that I didn't want to do anything to jeopardize it, but I never should have doubted Sam. She and Alaric were my best friends and had always supported me through anything without judgment.

Okay, well, Alaric could be a judgey bastard, but Sam never was, and eventually, Alaric would get over his opinion of me and Sam being in a relationship. I had a few ideas to help with that and get him to admit what his real problem was . . .

"So what happened?" she asked gently after sitting upright in her chair once more. "Because I could feel the tension between you two earlier."

"For almost a year, I made regular visits to the Sovereign House." I rubbed my face in a vain attempt to make the words come out easier. "Sometimes, he would show up at the outposts I was staying at. I don't know how he did it, but somehow, he'd get into my room without anyone seeing him. We talked. He'd tell me about his life, all the things no one saw, and I talked about mine. What it was like growing up at House Corvinus and moving here. It was nice," I confessed. "Talking to him was just . . . easy. Having someone on the outside of it all to talk to about everything. I think he felt the same."

Samara nodded in understanding. "My relationship with Draven prior to all of this was different than yours, and I wouldn't exactly say we were friends." She paused and thought about it a little more. "No, that's not right—we were definitely friends. We never spoke outside of times when I would visit the Sovereign House or the few times he would come to House Harker, never traded messages via striker or anything like that, but anytime we were in the same place, he would just appear like magic. It didn't matter if we hadn't seen each other in months or even years. The camaraderie was there, and falling into conversation with him always felt so natural."

"You should know . . ." I inhaled a deep breath. "I talked about you with him. About how I felt about you. The way we flirted with each other nonstop growing up. How you marrying Demetri devastated me. He knows all of that." Part of me wondered if that'd been what he'd wanted all along. That everything between us had been a lie and he'd just wanted information on Samara.

But just like I'd been too scared to ask Samara to stay before she'd left for House Laurent, I hadn't been able to bring myself to confront Draven about it. Instead, I'd just let the humiliating thought fester in the back of my mind.

"I know what you're thinking." Samara narrowed her eyes at me. "That he was just using you for information."

"Your perceptiveness is annoying," I said wryly as guilt nipped at me. I should never have spoken to him.

"I'll repeat what I said earlier," she said, ignoring my comment. "I'm glad you had someone to talk to about all of this, because we both know Alaric would have been a prick about it." Then her eyes darkened, and something predatory looked out. "But if it turns out Draven *was* using you that whole time—which I don't think he was, but I could be wrong—I'll make him fucking regret it."

She would. I had absolutely no doubt about it. "I think we have bigger problems to worry about, but I appreciate the sentiment." My throat tightened around the words.

She sniffed. "You'll *always* be a priority to me, Kier."

I smiled widely at her. "And again, I really want to fuck you right now."

"Of course you do. I'm amazing." She waved a hand towards me, gesturing for me to continue. "How does this story end?"

"We were discreet about our relationship, but I did occasionally speak to him at parties held at the Sovereign House. Six months ago, I walked up to him and greeted him casually . . . too casually, considering he was a prince and I was just . . . me."

Samara's eyes flared in anger as I spoke about myself in such a dismissive manner, but she didn't interrupt, which I was grateful for. I hadn't told anyone about me and Draven, not even Alaric. He would have berated me for being so foolish to get involved with the Moroi Prince in such a way. More importantly, Alaric traveled in different circles than me. As one of Carmilla's personal advisors, there had been a very real chance that he would have been in the same room as Draven one day, seated at the same table, and Alaric had a problem keeping his fucking mouth shut. The last thing I needed was him getting into a verbal sparring match with Draven in front of the queen.

I closed my eyes as I pushed the words out. The ones that had cut a deep wound in my already scarred heart. "He looked at me with this cool, almost bored expression and said, *'It's been fun, but I'm bored now. Also, watch how you speak to me in the future, courtier.'* And then he just walked off to stand by his mother's side. He didn't look at me, but she did." My jaw tightened as I remembered the cruel, arrogant smile that had flashed across her face that night. "She must have learned about our relationship and didn't approve. So Draven ended it. Maybe he already had all the information he wanted . . . I don't know."

Samara stared out the window, her brows slightly creased. I knew that look. She was cycling through scenarios in her head, analyzing each possibility before moving on to the next. I also knew from experience that it was best to let her sort through her thoughts, so I snagged a biscuit off the plate and ate it slowly, savoring each sweet bite.

"We need to determine what exactly the deal is between Draven and his mother," she said thoughtfully. "Considering what he has said to you and the little hints I've seen, I think there is nothing but hate between them, but he clearly serves her. We need to know why."

"Do you want to find this out because it will actually help us, or so that I feel like less of a fool for getting involved with him in the first place?" I tossed the rest of my biscuit back onto the table. "Because I'm an adult, Sam. It pains me that I got played and that I let my feelings go too far. That I thought I might be in—" I yanked that word from my throat before it could slip past my lips and stomped on it. Then I inhaled and let out a deep breath. "Draven and I are in the past. I just wanted you to know because I will never hide anything from you, and because he will no doubt wield my past with him against us."

"He already tried to," she admitted, still staring out the window, half-lost in her thoughts. I bit my lip, toying with the question I wanted to ask.

"If things were different . . ." I cleared my throat. "If you didn't know Draven was mixed up with the wraiths and he came here to ask you to consider marrying him . . . would you?"

Samara's head whipped towards me, and she scowled before unwinding herself from the chair and closing the distance between us. My arms slipped around her as she slid onto my lap, and her fingers trailed up my chest before wrapping around my throat and squeezing lightly. I released a breathy exhale at the feeling of her nails digging into my skin.

"No, I would not consider marrying him," she said evenly, and I believed her. Maybe it made me the biggest fool in the world, but I had no doubt she meant every word. "I do admit that I've always found him attractive and . . . intriguing. Perhaps I would have let him into my bed." Her lips curved into a sinful grin. "*Our* bed. But I would have spoken to you about it first, and if you weren't okay with it, then I wouldn't have taken things any further with him."

Moonsdamn it all, but my cock hardened at the thought of Samara and Draven in bed together. With me. Without me. Either was hot. Even with everything he had done to me and what we knew about him now, my body still reacted to Draven completely of its own accord, the same way it reacted to Samara. The thought of both of them together?

Samara released my neck and let out a husky laugh. "Feeling excited, Kier?"

"You are all kinds of wicked." I shook my head ruefully, even as I smiled at her.

She shifted until her legs were dangling off the side of the chair, and she nuzzled my neck. "Dinner tonight is going to be intense." Warm, full lips brushed against my throat, and I let one of my hands slip down to her thigh, slipping underneath the high slit of her dress. "We should take this opportunity to blow off some steam," she murmured.

"Excellent idea." My fingers drifted upward, and Samara spread her legs a little further apart, causing a deep chuckle to rumble out of me. "Is there somewhere in particular you want my fingers to be?"

She nipped my neck before raising her head and glaring at me. "Don't even think of making me beg. Between Draven and Alaric, I've had more than enough frustration today."

"Oh?" Her breath hitched as my fingers just barely passed over her undergarments. So wet already. I wanted to rip them aside and feel the hot slickness beneath them but couldn't resist teasing her a little. "And what did our dear Alaric do to piss you off this time?"

I let my fingers brush harder against the soaked fabric, and Samara moaned, nestling further into me.

"The same as he always does," she said through panted breaths. "That me and you were a bad idea and that he knew it would end like this. I informed him that nothing had changed and that you were still mine and that he should stay out of our fucking business. I might have thrown a dagger at him to punctuate the point."

"The two of you are ridiculous." I slipped my fingers beneath the fabric, and we both groaned at the dripping heat I found. "I love how wet you get for me," I growled. "Even before I touch you."

"Show me how much." She arched her back, and I leaned down to capture her mouth with mine. Then I slowly pushed two fingers inside her while I continued to circle her clit with my thumb. Samara whimpered, and I smiled against her lips, loving the sounds she made when I was inside her. Maybe I could get some new ones out of her this time . . .

"I have another secret to tell you," I whispered. Alaric would probably punch me for this later, but I knew my friend. His way of handling emotions, particularly confusing ones, was to lash out. I'd given him the time he needed to come to terms with how he really felt about Sam, but he was still stubbornly fighting it. He'd never even admitted to me how much he wanted her. But I'd noticed every heated glance he sent her way when she wasn't looking and the way his heart had practically stopped beating when he'd walked in on us at the hot springs weeks before. Enough was enough.

"What?" Sam panted.

"He's so pissed off all the time"—I thrust my fingers in deep, and her hips bucked in demand—"because he wishes it were *his* fingers doing this to you right now."

Dark eyelashes fluttered as Sam took in my words. "He *hates* me."

"He doesn't." I pumped my fingers in and out, loving the way her pussy clenched around me. "He might wish he did sometimes."

"You can't tell me things like that when you're—" Her words choked off as I pushed down on her clit and she unraveled. "Fuck!"

I let out a dark laugh as she trembled in my lap before pulling my fingers out and licking them clean. "Delicious," I murmured. Sam watched every swipe of my tongue with dark, hungry eyes. "We'll continue this discussion later when you're a little less distracted. Up you go." I maneuvered her body until she was straddling me with her back to my chest. "I might have gotten these chairs with a certain position in mind."

"Of course you did." She laughed in a low, husky tone.

"What can I say?" I teased as I unlaced my pants and pulled my cock free. "Every time I see a piece of furniture, I think about the best way to fuck you on it."

I could feel her thighs quivering as my cock pushed against her entrance, and I felt a desperate need to be buried inside her. Originally, my plan had been to fuck her slow and tease her a bit, but I needed at least the first round to be hard and fast. Just as I was about to thrust all the way in, the door swung open. Shit. I'd forgotten to lock it.

Samara went completely still in my grip as Alaric's pissed off expression fell on the both of us.

CHAPTER FIVE

Samara

"What the fuck is with you two and not understanding how locks work?" Alaric slammed the door shut, his eyes blazing with anger as his gaze roamed down our bodies . . . and compromising positions.

But there was desire there too.

How had I never noticed that before? I mean, he'd looked at me earlier in my bedroom, but I had been standing there naked, taunting him, and his expression had mostly remained cold and detached. The only thing I'd picked up on was annoyance at my antics. However, that was definitely *not* what I was seeing in his eyes now.

He wanted me. Desperately.

A heady anticipation raced through me. Since returning to House Harker, I'd had more than one lust-filled thought about Alaric, but given that we had to work together and my apparently false assumption that he was in no way attracted to me, I'd done my best to ignore those feelings.

Every time I'd felt Alaric's body pushed against mine when we'd rode together or practiced archery, my core hd instantly tightened and my breath had hitched slightly.

My dress was twisted around a bit, but it was still covering all the important bits, and Kieran's hand was wrapped around his cock where he'd been teasing my entrance. I could feel the hot slickness running down my thighs, my anticipation high over him sliding into me. Alaric couldn't see any of this, but given the way I was straddling Kieran, it was pretty obvious what we'd been about to do.

"You're the one who didn't knock," Kieran drawled. "One might think you enjoy walking in on us like this. Now why might that be?"

Alaric's nostrils flared, and the light green of his eyes was completely swallowed by turquoise as his gaze dropped to the apex of my thighs. My legs trembled, and I leaned further back against Kieran, which caused his cock to slide into me a little.

I froze, even as a moan slipped from my lips. Alaric's gaze dropped, as if he could see past my dress to where Kieran's cock was pushing inside me, but he made no move to come closer to us or leave the room.

"All this time," I breathed out, "I thought you hated me, or at best, barely tolerated my existence."

Silence stretched between us for what felt like an eternity. For once, Kieran kept his mouth shut, as if he knew this moment had to play out at its own pace. Alaric's throat bobbed as he swallowed. "I've always tried very hard to hate you."

"And have you succeeded?"

More silence. With a slow, deliberate movement, Alaric reached out and turned the lock on the door with a loud *click*. It felt like every one of my nerves was on fire, and based on how tense Kieran was beneath me, I knew he felt the same. Then Alaric walked over to us and trailed his fingers along my jawline before dipping under my chin to tilt my head back, forcing me to look up at him.

I had to shift a little further back, which caused another inch of Kieran's cock to slide in. Both of us let out a strangled gasp as a close-lipped smile spread across Alaric's face. The bastard knew exactly what he was doing.

"I've been frustrated with you. Annoyed by your antics. Occasionally wanted to strangle you." His bright, oceanic blue eyes darkened as his fingers slid down and gripped my throat just this side of painful. My legs pushed harder against Kieran as I fought to keep myself from climaxing at the contact. I'd had more than one fantasy about Alaric, but I'd had no idea he'd ever felt the same towards me. I was half expecting to wake up from a dream at my desk with paper stuck to my face.

Alaric's smile widened, as if he knew every thought running through my mind. "But I've also wanted nothing more than to kiss you for longer than I care to remember. And ever since I walked in on you and Kieran at the hot springs, I haven't been able to stop thinking about what you taste like."

"What else?" I breathed out.

"I still believe this is a bad idea that will only lead to heartache for all of us."

"You're wrong," I said forcefully and let him see the conviction in my eyes. "I can make this work. *We* can make this work."

"Perhaps." He didn't seem convinced. Alaric might know me well, but I knew him too. He was starting to overthink this and was going to pull away from me. The question was . . . would I let him?

Alaric and I had been at each other's throats for basically our whole lives. It had only gotten worse when Kieran had arrived and we'd started to fight over him as well. Since coming back to House Harker though, I couldn't help but respect him. He was smart and cunning and pushed me to do better—more than anyone else did.

My attraction to Alaric went so far beyond just his body. I wanted him. All of him.

I let my lips quirk up into the arrogant, sinful smile that

always set him off. He released my throat and started to step back, but I grabbed his hand and slipped two of his fingers into my mouth at the same time I let myself sink completely onto Kieran's cock.

Kieran swore as I moaned around Alaric's fingers, sucking and licking the digits before releasing them with a throaty laugh as I ground myself further onto Kieran's lap. Alaric's breathing grew ragged as he watched me slowly unlace his pants.

Strong arms pulled me back before tugging my dress down and exposing my chest. "Not yet." Then Kieran's hands gripped each of my full breasts hard as he continued to whisper into my ear. "You're gonna pay for that little maneuver, and he's gonna watch."

Kieran thrust up into me, and I threw my head back against his shoulder as my pussy clamped down around his cock. With my back to his chest and his arms around me, I couldn't do anything to control the pace or angle. All I could do was take it as he rocked into me.

Alaric watched for a few minutes, his eyes glazing over as my tits bounced when Kieran released them to grasp my hips so he could fuck me harder. I never would have thought I would like someone watching, but as Alaric's expression grew hungrier, I realized I loved it. There wasn't a hint of jealousy on his face. Just raw need . . . and excitement.

When Kieran's fingers brushed against my clit before pushing down, it was all I needed to tip me over the edge. I screamed as the climax tore through me before collapsing limply against Kieran.

"You're not done yet," Kieran chided, trailing his fingers up my side to lazily play with my nipples. Every part of my body was so sensitive that I whimpered as he squeezed them gently. "It's time for you to show Alaric just how talented that mouth of yours is, and I'm not done with this perfect pussy yet."

I raised my head from his shoulder, and my mouth went dry as Alaric stroked himself in front of me. "See something you want, Sam?" he asked languidly, his hand gripping the base of his thick length.

All I could do was nod, and Alaric and Kieran chuckled.

"Use your words," Alaric ordered.

I finally ripped my gaze away from his cock, and he raised one haughty eyebrow at me.

"What I want"—I dropped my voice to a low, throaty purr—"is your cock in my mouth and your hands in my hair. I want both of you fucking me hard until I'm not capable of piecing together a coherent thought, and then I want both of you to come inside me so that you're all I can taste for the rest of the day while the proof of how much I belong to Kier is running down my thighs."

"*Fuck*," both of them swore.

"Is that clear enough for the two of you?" I rolled my hips against Kieran, who was still rock-hard inside me, and he groaned as his hands gripped my breasts again.

"Yeah, Sam." Alaric's molten eyes stared at me before he reached out and gripped my hair. "I think we can do that."

Kieran slid one of his hands down to my hip while the other pushed lightly on my back so that I was forced to pivot forward.

Right onto Alaric's cock.

My lips parted as I took in his hard thick length. The plan that had formed in my mind of teasing him slowly until he begged me to take him evaporated. I should have known that Kieran and Alaric together would be a dangerous combination. One of Alaric's hands was still gripping my hair while the other pushed down my head, forcing me to take every single inch of him.

I gagged, but instead of releasing me, he just pulled my head back before forcing me to take him again. And again. My eyes watered, but I wasn't a quitter, so I sucked him down each time, finding the rhythm in his movements.

Then Kieran's hips shot up, and I moaned as his cock buried inside me even deeper. My hands that had been gripping the chair shifted to Alaric, wrapping around his thighs for balance. I was completely at their mercy in this position, and they both knew it.

"Look at you taking both of our cocks so beautifully," Kieran purred. Another wave of liquid heat raced down my legs as I clenched around Kieran.

Alaric pulled my hair back, drawing my mouth away until his cock slid almost all the way out. My tongue swirled around his broad head, and I was able to tilt my head back just enough to catch the last of the green in his eyes before it gave way to blue. I slid my tongue over the thin slit at the tip of his cock, and Alaric jolted beneath me.

Then his fingers twisted my hair, slamming me back down onto him, fucking my mouth with an almost feral need. Kieran let out a low groan, and the hand that had been on my back moved to curl around my hips. I felt a sharp sting as his nails hardened into claws and bit into my skin. His hips pivoted up, harder and faster each time.

I could feel the pleasure building, the intensity so much, it was almost unbearable. Being between Kieran and Alaric like this felt so *right*, like it was always meant to be this way, and I relished every second of it.

Neither of them held back, and tears streamed down my cheeks as Alaric thrust harshly into my mouth, his breathing ragged. From this position, Kieran was able to bury himself deep, and I moaned every time he hit a particularly sensitive spot, which only drove Alaric wilder.

When Kieran's hand slipped over my clit, I started bucking

wildly. Too much. The sensation was too fucking much, but their grips on me only tightened. Neither of their thrusts faltered as they fucked me exactly as I'd told them to, until I was incapable of thinking.

I didn't know how much more I could take as my moans turned into half screams, my thighs trying to clench together only for Kieran to force them apart. A delicious, salty taste started to spread across my tongue as Alaric switched to pulling his cock most of the way out before sliding it back in and hitting the back of my throat.

"Kieran," Alaric growled.

"I know," Kieran ground out.

A whimper slipped from my lips when Alaric pulled me off his cock, and I watched him stroke it in front of me. Kieran switched to excruciatingly slow and deep thrusts, his fingers still teasing my clit.

"Please," I begged. "I'm so close."

Alaric's eyes simmered with need and possessiveness as he looked at me, and Kieran swore as my pussy clenched around him.

"You're gonna drink every last drop," Alaric said. "And then you can come."

"She's our girl." Kieran pushed even deeper inside of me, and my breath hitched. "She'll take everything we give her."

Fuck yes, I would, because I knew exactly what they would give me in return. I held Alaric's gaze as I leaned forward and ran my tongue around his head before sucking it into my mouth and taking him all the way to the hilt.

I pulled one hand away from where I'd been bracing myself on his body and cupped his balls as I worked him up and down. For a few seconds, he let me control the pace and groaned as he took in his pleasure. Then his fingers tightened around my hair once more before he slammed into my mouth. I hollowed out my cheeks, sucking him in with each thrust, and felt his balls tighten in my hand. His cock hit the back of my throat one last time, and he held my head in place as he came hard while I did as I was told and greedily swallowed it all down.

"My turn." Strong arms pulled me back, and Alaric's cock slid out of my mouth. I made sure to lick it on the way, and he trembled at the sensation before staggering back a few steps. I gave him a slightly dazed smirk, satisfied that he was reeling from this as much as I was.

"Kier," I moaned as he palmed both of my full breasts, running his thumb roughly over my nipples as he started to move inside me again.

"Put those hands to use."

It took me a moment to realize Kieran wasn't talking to me. My head had fallen back against his shoulder, and my eyes had closed as pleasure rippled through me. Fingers dipped to where Kieran's cock was sliding in and out of my wet pussy, and I opened my eyes to find Alaric leaning over us, one hand braced on the chair and the other swirling around in the slickness.

"You're dripping all over that chair." His eyes were locked on my pussy, watching his best friend fuck the life out of me. "And you're going to be dripping with Kieran's cum in a second."

Kieran swore and picked up the pace as Alaric's gaze drifted up to watch my face, his fingers moving to circle my clit. Swear words intertwined with moans tumbled from my mouth as Kieran thrust into me over and over again. His hands still squeezed my tits as he groaned, his lips finding my neck and dragging his fangs across it.

Fingers pressed down on my clit, and I exploded. It felt like my mind was unraveling. Then Kieran's fangs sank into my throat, and I came again, feeling him do the same. I was so full of him and so wet already that I could feel it gushing down my thighs.

The fingers that had been playing with my clit suddenly vanished, and I blinked at Alaric, who was now standing several feet away. He'd pulled his pants up and was tucking his cock, which was already hard again, back into them.

"Fuck." He looked at where Kieran was still drinking from my throat, and I saw the moment regret flashed across his face, hurt stabbing me from his reaction. The pleasure I'd been basking in evaporated in an instant. Sensing the change in mood, Kieran pulled his fangs free and looked over my shoulder at Alaric, who just stared at the blood trailing down my neck. His light green eyes flashed solid turquoise before he strode away from us and fled Kieran's study.

I sagged in Kieran's embrace, and he sighed before helping me up. His cum mixed with my pleasure slid down my thighs as he pulled his cock free, but that only made me feel worse, because Alaric wasn't here to see it.

"What just happened?" I asked weakly.

Kieran got up and grabbed a towel from a drawer behind his desk and started cleaning me up as I stood there numbly. Then he reclasped my chest band and pulled my dress back up before tucking my hair behind my ear.

"It's my fault," he said softly. "I shouldn't have bitten you in front of him. I got caught up in the moment and forgot about his . . . issues."

"What issues?" My voice sounded numb, even to myself.

"You'll need to ask him." Kieran glanced hesitantly at the door. "I'll just say that Alaric has concerns over his control. For his bloodlust," he clarified when I arched an eyebrow. Alaric was obsessively controlled about everything. Even when his cock had been in my mouth, he'd been in control. "Some of his fears are justified, but some of them, he's just overanalyzing."

"He regretted doing this." I stared at the door, hoping he would come back and explain but knowing he wouldn't. "I don't think he wants to feel the way he does about me."

He regrets me.

"Hey." Kieran tugged me to him and wrapped his arms around me. "It'll be okay. You've just gotten spoiled by how perfect I am that you've forgotten how difficult dealing with other people can be."

I snorted a laugh against his shoulder.

We stood there for a few minutes, and I just enjoyed the feeling of being in his arms and breathing in his scent. Maybe Alaric had been right and that had been a mistake. I had Kieran. We belonged to each other, body and soul, and Roth was mine too. I claimed them as such, and they seemed to enjoy this.

I mean, they hadn't exactly said that, but they hadn't not said it either, and their room was gradually starting to look more homey in that stacks of books kept appearing. So I was pretty confident Roth had decided to stay here and was okay with me keeping them forever.

Then there was the Draven problem . . .

I burrowed further into Kieran's shoulder. "Can we stay here for a while? I just want to hide from the world for another hour."

"Yeah, Sam." He led me over to the small settee that sat across from the chairs and sat down, tugging me with him so I was leaning on his chest. "Whatever you need, I got you."

CHAPTER SIX

Samara

"S<small>AMARA</small>?" a voice called from down the hallway, and I held back a groan. I had really been hoping to make it to my room without anyone bothering me. Kieran had offered to come back to my suite with me, but I'd told him to go after Alaric and calm him the fuck down. Truthfully though, I'd just needed some time to come to terms with everything as well. I didn't regret what we'd done, because being with Alaric and Kieran had felt right, but Alaric had basically fled from that room.

His expression—a mixture of anger, confusion, and regret—had hurt. I was no stranger to the pain caused by Alaric's words, but now I'd just given him a whole new way to hurt me if he decided he didn't want to be with me after all.

I wanted to stand under scalding hot water and let myself sob where no one could see me, because I was the Heir to House Harker. Crying in the halls over a boy was not an option.

Composing my face as best I could, I turned around to face the rapidly approaching footsteps. "Yes, Sofia?"

The fair-haired Moroi came to a halt, the smattering of

freckles across the bridge of her nose and cheeks standing out even more at the faint reddening across her pale skin. She gulped a few deep breaths before standing straighter, and I already dreaded whatever words were going to come out of her mouth.

Sofia was Yolanthe's protégé. The sharp-minded advisor had chosen her because the twenty-year-old girl was studious and reliable. Usually nothing rattled Sofia . . . and yet she looked like she'd run up the stairs with haste to find me. Giving up all pretense, she placed a hand on my shoulder and bent over, sucking in breaths.

I'd thought I was bad at running.

"Sofia, whatever you needed to tell me wasn't worth you passing out in the hallway," I huffed out with laughter.

Her hand tightened, and she straightened enough to stare at me, wide-eyed. "The House Heirs are here!"

"What?" My amusement instantly evaporated, and I glanced out the nearest window that faced the front of House Harker.

"Well, not all of them," she clarified as my gaze snapped back to her. "Neither Taivan nor Tamsen are here. Taivan isn't that big of a surprise—the Devereux rarely leave their House. Except for Roth of course, but that's . . ." Her hand slipped off my shoulder, and she straightened her dress. "I'm not sure why Tamsen didn't come. It's odd for House Corvinus to not insert themselves into any political situation. Ary and Aniela are in the small reception chamber just off the main tower entrance."

It was suspicious that Tamsen wasn't here, but I'd have to worry about that later because the Heirs of House Tepes and House Salvatore were downstairs.

I swore and headed towards the stairs that would lead down, all while checking my dress on the way to make sure everything was laced up right and running my fingers through my hair. Something told me there was no hiding the fact that

I'd just been thoroughly fucked, but I needed to find out why two of the Heirs had shown up unannounced. It almost certainly had to do with Draven's attendance.

"Also," Sofia said hastily as she tried to keep up with me, "you should probably know . . . I mean, just so you know what you're walking into . . ." We rounded the corner, and I ducked into the stairwell, picking up my dress as I hurried down the stairs. "If you want to take a moment and think about this, that's okay. You don't have to see him if you don't want to—"

I whirled on the step, and Sofia yelped as she barely managed to halt before crashing into me. "Don't have to see *who?*"

She swallowed nervously. "Demetri is here too. As the Laurent Heir, the guards at the gate couldn't deny him entry."

"Oh." I slumped against the wall. "Right." It really said something about my current mental state that it hadn't even occurred to me he'd be here despite the fact that he was an Heir.

I hadn't seen or spoken to my ex-husband since I'd stormed out of House Laurent two months ago. The anger had faded, mostly, and any love I'd felt towards him had evaporated over the years of our strained marriage. Now there was just . . . embarrassment? I'd let myself turn into a shadow of who I was at House Laurent, trying to fit their mold of what a perfect Moroi wife should be.

Demetri hadn't even tried to fight for me. House Laurent had signed the papers to dissolve the marriage with zero fuss, which I still found odd. Some part of me had thought Demetri would have apologized for his actions and maybe tried to fix things between us. I most likely would have said no, but it hurt a little that he hadn't bothered. Our three-year marriage really had been a joke.

But more strange was that his mother, Marvina, hadn't used the request to dissolve the marriage to get better trade agreements between our Houses. She had no doubt been happy to see me go, but it wasn't like her to waste such an opportunity. Since I was the one requesting the marriage to end, it would have been House Harker's responsibility to offer any compensation.

"Do you want me to get Yolanthe?" Sofia asked quietly. "We can cover for you if you're not ready to face him yet. No one will judge you for it."

"I would judge me." I gave her a small smile. "Besides, we both know Yolanthe is very calm until she's not, and there's a distinct possibility of her walking into that room and trying to tear Demetri's head off."

Sofia snorted. "True. She can be quite protective of those she cares about. I still have to handle any correspondence with House Devereux because she refuses to speak to Desmond even though her sister has told her she's fine with how things ended between them."

"Nobody holds a grudge like Yolanthe." I shook my head at the memory of listening to the advisor rant about all the things she was going to do to the House Devereux Heir's brother for how he had treated her sister. Most of the threats involved cutting his dick off in rather imaginative ways. For someone who was usually quite prim and proper, Yolanthe had a real mouth on her sometimes.

"I'll be fine." I pushed off from the wall and did my best to channel Carmilla. She was always confident and steadfast no matter the circumstance. I would be the same. "Do you know where Prince Draven is?"

Sofia shook her head. "I haven't seen him since this morning."

Well, that didn't bode well at all.

I drew in an even breath and willed myself to be calm. "Can you track down Alaric and Kieran and let them know what's going on?"

"Of course. Anything you need, Samara." She shot me a mischievous grin. "Even hiding the body of a certain piece of shit Heir."

A sharp bark of laughter leapt from my lips. "Appreciate the thought, but I don't think it'll come to that."

"Kieran might feel differently," Sofia said slyly before darting back up the stairs.

She was right. I had no idea how Kieran would react to Demetri's presence here. On one hand, he was better than me at hiding his true feelings behind all those masks of his, but on the other hand, he was fiercely protective of me. While I was happy to be back at House Harker and finally be with Kieran in the way I'd always wanted . . . Demetri's betrayal had still hurt.

The memory of walking down the hall that day towards the sound of pleasurable moans played in my mind. My fingers curled into fists as I remembered what it had felt like to see Demetri in bed with someone else, displaying so much more passion than he ever had with me, at least in the last year of the marriage.

It was starting to feel like the moon had cursed me. As if I didn't have enough problems just existing in Lunaria and trying to keep my House in order. Now I had to deal with a potential secret alliance between the wraiths and our queen, a wicked but ever so charming prince, and piling onto all of this were a bunch of Heirs who were no doubt here to push their own agendas. And they all may or may not have allied with the Moroi Queen and whatever she had going on with the wraiths.

"Love it," I muttered to myself as I started making my way back down the stairs. "Absolutely love the life as an Heir. I mean, sure, I could be living the simple life at one of the outposts, maybe the one with the hot springs, but who would choose sitting in perfectly heated water every night while you relaxed from the toils of the day over dealing with a bunch of backstabbing, spoiled bitches. I mean, that's not even a choi —fuck!"

"I mean, if you want to fuck, I'm not going to say no." Draven grinned from the step beneath me. I'd almost reached the bottom landing when he'd stepped into the stairwell and cut me off. "Given that I'm basically an Heir, just with a fancier title, do you lump me into the category of 'backstabbing, spoiled bitches?'"

"Yes." I narrowed my eyes at him. "You're basically their leader."

"Harsh." He gave me a wounded look that I didn't believe for one second. "May I escort you into the den of vipers?"

I stared at the arm he offered and raised my chin. "No, thanks. I can walk just fine on my own." Pushing by him, I exited the stairwell and made my way towards the front of the main tower. Everyone I passed shot me relieved smiles. It wasn't that everyone disliked dealing with the Heirs—all of the advisors had met with them at one time or another—but they'd come here without any warning, and with the Moroi Prince here, also unannounced, everyone knew a political game was underfoot, and none of them wanted to deal with it.

Sadly, that was my job since Carmilla wasn't here. Even if she were here, I would still be involved, but at least I would have been able to let her run the show and just provide support instead.

Draven drew even with me, an amused smile playing across his lips. "This is your fault, you know," I hissed under my breath at him, even as I kept a confident expression on my face. As the Harker Heir, it was important that I always presented a solid front, no matter the turmoil I was feeling inside.

"Whatever do you mean, my lovely betrothed?"

"Don't call me that." I ground my teeth. "They're here because *you're* here. It's rare for you to visit the other Houses.

At the Sovereign House, they have to contend with your mother, but now, they can get to you directly and whisper whatever they want into your ear, and they no doubt want to know why you came to House Harker so they can use that information in the future."

"Thanks to the friendship between your aunt and my mother, there's already an established relationship between our Houses." He shrugged. "It's not the first time I've visited your home."

We were almost to the room when I stopped and stared at him. "Did you tell anyone why you were coming here?"

"No." Draven cocked his head. "Would you like me to?"

"Absolutely not!" I lowered my voice after taking a deep breath. "Do not mention your ridiculous proposal. If the Heirs learn of it, they'll become determined to hammer through as many trade deals and arrangements as possible because they'll think my House will be directly tied to the Sovereign House. But since we are absolutely *not* getting married, this will all just be a waste of my time, because those deals will evaporate as soon as they learn the truth. And I do not. Have time. For this bullshit," I enunciated.

Draven just smiled at me, and I threw up my hands in frustration. "Argh! Do not speak," I ordered, knowing it was pointless because the prince would do whatever he wanted. He didn't follow me when I started walking again, but I somehow doubted he was just going to walk away. No doubt he was plotting something I wouldn't like.

I didn't allow myself any hesitation as I strode into the room, feeling three sets of eyes landing on me.

"To what does House Harker owe the pleasure of not one but three Heirs visiting?" I smiled sharply. "Unannounced as it may be."

Ary scoffed, his back to the painting he'd been pretending to admire. The Tepes Heir was a little unkempt from his likely fast ride here. House Tepes was in the northern part of the Moroi realm. His midnight black hair that was shaved on both sides was pulled back into a messy bun, and he was sporting some stubble on his usually clean-shaven face. It was a two-day ride if you hauled ass and rode through the night directly through the wilds instead of sticking to the safer roads. Ary was definitely crazy enough to do that, which meant he'd somehow caught wind of where Draven was heading before the Moroi Prince had arrived.

The same basically applied to the other Heirs. Salvatore was also a two-day ride, although there was a road that went directly from our House to theirs, so it was less treacherous. Laurent was fairly close to us, the ride easily done in a day. If I had to guess, I'd say Demetri had been waiting nearby for the other two Heirs to arrive. He'd probably suspected I would have thrown him out if he'd arrived on his own.

He wasn't wrong.

"Don't be coy, Samara," Ary said in a deep, decadent voice. His light violet eyes shone brightly against his rich brown skin. The Tepes bloodline was the only one that shared purple eyes with the Harkers. Although ours were so dark, they looked almost black in dim lighting. Ary's were light and reminded me of lavender blossoms.

The rough-natured Heir would have probably found the comparison amusing. I'd always thought he was more suited to be a ranger than an Heir with his wild personality. He was built more like Alaric, tall and lean rather than broad and bulky like Vail. When we'd been growing up, his relatively small frame had led other Moroi to underestimate the Tepes Heir and challenge him to fights.

Ary had walked away unscathed from every one. Usually while whistling a jaunty tune. If there were anyone better than me with knives, it was Ary. He was fast and lethal in a fight—and loved every second of it. Despite his ruthless nature, he had a sharp mind, and I couldn't afford to forget that.

"Okay." I bared my fangs at him. "What the fuck are you all doing here?"

"There she is." Aniela laughed.

Out of everyone here, the beautiful, red-haired Salvatore Heir was the one I was most wary of. I was fairly confident House Salvatore was not allied with Queen Velika and the wraiths, but I knew almost nothing about Aniela. While I'd been growing up, Selene—Aniela's cousin and Dominique's sister—had been the Heir, then Dominique's parents and sister had died, and she'd risen to be the ruler of House Salvatore. She didn't have any children of her own yet, so she'd named her cousin, Aniela, as Heir.

"I've got a lot on my mind right now, Aniela." I walked to the center of the room and took a seat in one of the high-backed chairs. "So how about we cut the bullshit and you all tell me why you're here? Then I can tell you that you wasted your time so you can leave and I can get on with my day."

It wasn't Aniela who answered. Instead, it was the Heir I'd been avoiding looking at since I'd entered the room.

"We're here because Prince Draven is," Demetri said smoothly, taking a seat directly across from me. He looked good, much to my annoyance, the sunlight beaming into the room lighting up the golden highlights of his chestnut brown hair. My former husband had always had a sensual elegance about him. It had appealed to me, but now, I just found it rather tedious.

"I admit," he continued, "that when I heard the news, I thought the prince was coming to court you, and yet here you sit"—his hazel eyes traveled possessively down my body—"reeking of two other males. Rather interesting, considering how harshly you judged me, wife."

"Not your wife anymore, Demetri," I said in a bored tone

while I held his accusing stare. "And the difference is that I'm not being unfaithful to anyone. I do this thing called being *honest*." Aniela snorted, and I amended. "In my personal relationships anyway. I think I've had my fill of marriage for a while."

"So you deny it then?" Demetri's reproachful, hazel eyes remained focused on me. "That the prince is here to ask for your hand?"

"Oh, I'm definitely here to marry Samara."

I squeezed my eyes shut and counted to ten in my head, hoping it would help.

It did not.

Draven strolled the rest of the way into the room and perched on the arm of my chair, leaning possessively into me. I glared up at him, but he just shot me a flirty grin.

"Prince Draven," Aniela purred, leaning forward enough to put her ample chest on display. "I had no idea you were interested in marriage."

"I'm interested in Samara," Draven said evenly.

Silence reigned while I fumed. Both because Draven just had to open his big mouth . . . and because I was pissed off at myself for the flash of jealousy I'd felt at Aniela flirting with him.

Aniela immediately turned her attention to me, not the least bit concerned about Draven's mild rebuff of her, which told me she had no real interest in him that way. Now she and Ary were both staring at me like I was a juicy piece of meat. Meanwhile, Demetri was staring daggers at Draven.

This was exactly what I didn't want. I'd been hoping to make it clear to all of them that there was nothing between me and Draven, and whatever they'd thought they'd come here for had been pointless. Now it'd be harder for me to get them to leave. As much as I wanted to, I couldn't just kick them out. Being blunt or rude was fine, all of the Heirs played our games with each other, but actually throwing them out would have political consequences. Every House controlled unique resources, and I couldn't afford to alienate any of them.

Plus some of them could be potential allies against the Sovereign House, assuming they weren't allied with them already.

Footsteps echoed down the hall, and we all turned towards the doorway to watch Kieran and Alaric burst into the room.

"Greetings, everyone!" Kieran cheered, holding up a bottle of wine. "What did we miss?"

CHAPTER SEVEN

Samara

I FIXED my features into a bemused, somewhat haughty expression as I entered the small dining hall several hours later. When it had become clear earlier that the Heirs wouldn't be leaving any time soon, I'd excused myself and left Kieran and Alaric to deal with them while I'd arranged rooms for them to stay in.

Really, as the Heir, that wasn't my responsibility—I should have asked Kieran to do that since he was a courtier of House Harker—but if I hadn't left that room, I likely would have stabbed either Demetri or Draven.

Or both.

Once the rooms were ready, I'd returned and directed everyone to where they would be staying and threw out a time for when dinner would start. I was sure they'd been conspiring with each other after I'd left them to it, or maybe chatting with whatever spies they had in my House, but I was tired, and there wasn't anything I could do about it at the moment.

Since then, I'd spent the remainder of the afternoon and early evening diving into all the paperwork that had piled up on my desk, enjoying the solitude and losing myself to the management of the House. Kieran had dropped off tea for me at one point but left me alone otherwise. I suspected he'd been busy speaking with Alaric, who had done his best to avoid looking at me.

I raised my eyebrow at Draven as I walked across the room. As the Moroi Prince, he should have chosen one of the seats at the head of the table, but instead, he'd chosen to sit to the right of it, with Alaric and Kieran sitting opposite. I'd invited Vail, but I wasn't surprised to see he wasn't here. He might have come if it had been just us and Draven, but once he'd learned the other Heirs would be joining us as well, he'd likely opted to stay away.

If only I had that option. I had no doubt this dinner was going to be a mixture of frustrating and awkward.

"Sorry, I'm late." I took a seat at the head of the table. "I got caught up in some reports from the Riverfell outpost and lost track of time." It wasn't a lie. House Harker had almost half a dozen outposts that fell under our responsibility to protect, and I took that seriously.

"It's fine. As you can see, the other Heirs are following the standard protocol of arriving at least ten minutes late to any social event," Draven said smoothly. "This just gave me and your friends an opportunity to chat."

"Oh?" I reached for a glass of wine. "Discuss anything interesting?"

"Just the standard topics that arise when running a House." He cocked his head, his eyes never leaving mine. "Did you get up to anything interesting this afternoon? Was your *rest* sufficient before the Heirs arrived?"

Both Kieran and Alaric snapped their gazes to the prince, but he just smiled.

"Would it kill you two to be less obvious?" I muttered.

Draven chuckled. "It seems when it comes to you, Kieran struggles to be subtle." His eyes flitted briefly to Alaric. "And it appears he has similar issues. The three of you should be aware of that. It's a weakness just waiting to be exploited, and you must know the other Heirs will jump at the chance."

The muscles hardened along Alaric's jawline as he swung to look back at me. I didn't need to have the ability to read minds, because I knew his thought was, *See? I told you this was a bad idea.*

"How kind of you to warn us. We'll make a note to practice our acting in the future." I turned to face Draven and held my wine glass up in salute. "After we *rest* of course. Very. Thoroughly. Rest."

"You're always a delight to play with." Draven grinned. "I can't wait to marry you."

"She's no—" Kieran started, but I cut him off with a glare, and his mouth clicked shut.

"As I said earlier, I'm considering your proposal, but you're going to have to convince me. Something you're not doing a very good job of at the moment."

"I'd let you keep them." Draven shrugged. His casual expression was betrayed by the way he carefully glanced at Kieran, who was currently looking at me. "Whatever makes you happy."

Kieran stiffened, as if he knew who those words were really directed at. Just as I opened my mouth to tell Draven where he could shove his offer, the other Heirs flowed into the room and took their seats at the table. Only Demetri slowed at seeing Draven sitting next to me instead of at one of the head seats. His eyes hardened as he sat next to Alaric. The other two Heirs sat across from him, with Aniella next to Draven and Ary next to her.

"Did you see the report from the Riverfell outpost, Ary?" I asked. Even though the outpost was in Harker territory, I knew the Tepes Heir liked to keep track of all monster attacks in the Moroi realm. A door swung open before he could answer, several members of the staff carrying in plates, setting them in front of us, and then leaving without a word. Though a dark-haired young girl caught my eye on the way out, arching an eyebrow before scurrying after the others.

I hid my grin. Olena. She absolutely loved to gossip and had probably been delighted to be working tonight. I'd need to find her tomorrow morning and see if there were any interesting rumors circulating about the prince's or Heirs' visits here.

"Fish." Draven sighed happily. "You coastal houses have it so lucky."

Alaric frowned at the slap of white fish meat on his plate. "You get sick of it after a while."

"No, you don't," Kieran and I said at the same time. Then we grinned at each other as Alaric rolled his eyes.

"I agree with Draven." Aniella shoved in a mouthful and closed her eyes as she thoughtfully chewed. "We never get fish so far inland. It's all root vegetables or questionable meat I choose not to think about. Maybe some fresh fruit in the summer months."

"To answer your previous question, Samara," Ary said, "I did see the report. I'm not sure if you've had a chance to review the history of that particular outpost, but—"

"They had similar incidents last year," I interrupted, "which means this problem isn't going to just go away."

Ary grunted and dug into his food with significantly less gusto than the rest of us. Clearly, he was also not a fan of fish. Draven sent me a questioning look.

"Spine-backed boars," I explained. "There aren't as many here as in the Velesians' realm, but they do occasionally make their way this far south. Riverfell is almost dead center in Moroi territory, and there are a lot of animal migration trails that go directly through it from the north."

"I know where it is," Draven said lightly. My fork stopped

halfway to my mouth for a split second before I continued the motion, fighting to keep my expression neutral as I chewed on the fish. It tasted like ashes on my tongue now. As the prince of the Sovereign House, it was expected that he knew all the outpost locations and some basic information about them, but Draven had always come across as more of a pretty figurehead. Did he know the location of this one because the wraiths were planning on attacking it?

My stomach churned. I'd need to find Vail after this and tell him to increase the rangers stationed there just in case. We could use the boar problem as a cover.

"The boars showed up late in the growing season last year." My voice came out smooth, not betraying even a hint of the panic blooming inside my chest. "The hope was that it was a fluke. Sometimes they venture a little further south than usual, but they always go back."

"The herd has almost tripled in size from what I've been told. That's a lot of meat," Ary mused and grinned at Alaric. "Think of all the *not* fish you could be eating."

"We need to take care of the herd for multiple reasons," Alaric replied. "They've almost annihilated half the crops of that outpost, which is one of our best-producing ones. Plus, where there is prey, there will be predators."

"Still, Ary raises a good point." I swirled my wineglass. "If we can slaughter a good portion of the herd, it'll make up for some of the lost crops." I'd looked at the numbers. We couldn't afford to lose any type of food resource. Most of our food these days came from the outposts, and we'd already lost almost a dozen of them to the wraiths. We'd be okay this year, but if the trend continued, things would get bad. Fast.

"Have any of you ever hunted spine-backed boars?" Draven glanced at each of us curiously. Alaric and Kieran shook their heads, but I just smiled.

"Seriously, Sam?" Kieran complained. "And you didn't bring me?"

"You're too pretty for hunts," I teased.

"She's right," Draven agreed, and Kieran's smile slid off his face. Something flashed across Draven's face, but it was gone before I could figure out what it had been. "I would love to hear this tale, Samara."

I took a sip of wine and felt Alaric's heavy gaze on me. When I met his eyes, he looked quickly at Kieran and Draven before focusing on me again. Ah. So he'd picked up on the weird tension between them. Usually, Alaric was . . . not great at reading people. It was why the two of us worked so well together on House responsibilities. He had a sharp mind and was better versed in the current state of things since I'd been away at House Laurent for years, but he often failed to take into account how people's emotions could impact their motivations and therefore influence trade negotiations.

Kieran was his friend, and while Alaric and I had our problems, he was a loyal and good friend to Kieran. I gave him the smallest shake of my head, and he looked away. It wasn't my story to tell, but I would try to convince Kieran to explain things to Alaric so Draven couldn't blindside him with the information the same way he'd done to me. I also suspected Alaric's reaction to Draven hurting his friend might be . . . explosive.

"Ary actually knows this story since he was there too," I said.

He laughed and raised his pint of ale. "True, but why don't you tell it and I'll help fill in the details? You were always a better storyteller than me." He winked at me, and suddenly Draven, Kieran, and Alaric were hyper-focused on the Tepes Heir. He just laughed under his breath and drank half of his honey ale in one gulp in response.

"I was visiting my friend, Rynn—"

"Of course you were," Kieran groaned, giving me a pointed look. Even Alaric cracked a grin, his death glare dropping away from Ary. "Any trouble you get up to always begins and ends with Rynn."

"That's not true," I said defensively. "Sometimes it's Cali's fault."

"Yeah, but I would never say that." Kieran's eyebrows shot up. "Calypso scares the shit out of everyone except you and Rynn."

"Calypso scares the shit out of everyone," Aniela agreed around a mouthful of fish. She'd almost cleared her plate, and I waved at the servant hovering inside the room to bring her a second helping.

"You're friends with Calypso Rayne?" Draven cocked his head at me.

"She's my best friend." I raised my chin and dared him to say anything about her. It'd been years since a Furie had lost themselves and turned on us all, but everyone remained wary of them and was more than happy they preferred to stay within their borders of the badlands.

Except Cali. She traveled all over Lunaria and practically flaunted her shadow magic.

My friend was from the most powerful of all the Furie bloodlines and the one most known for going insane, which would not be happening. I refused to lose her, and Rynn felt the same. If Cali ever lost herself to the rage she kept chained within her soul, we'd just drag her back with our fangs and claws.

"The Rayne bloodline—" he started to say carefully, but I cut him off with a wave of my hand.

Then I leaned forward on the table, placing both hands flat on the wood surface as I let a little more of my bloodlust out. I had no doubt my eyes had darkened to black pools as my nails grew and hardened until claws dug into the hard wood.

"Sam," Kieran warned, but I ignored him, not taking my eyes off the prince. Draven's eyes had turned almost completely bloodred as the predator in him watched me carefully.

"Calypso fucking Rayne has single-handledly turned the tide of more than one fight that would have ended in the slaughter of Moroi and Velesians if she hadn't stepped in," I snarled. "She's never asked for anything, and she doesn't say anything as you fucks whisper behind her back while also *begging* her to help. I will not tolerate you or anyone else talking shit about her."

I pointed a clawed finger at him in warning before sinking back into my chair and letting my bloodlust fall away, taking with it my claws and black eyes. I kept the fangs out though and flashed them at Draven before swiping my wineglass off the table and taking a deep drink.

Ary snickered. He was used to me letting my bloodlust loose and often did the same. Aniella was eying me curiously, no doubt noting how easily I could slip in and out of bloodlust. I didn't bother looking at Demetri. He would no doubt be horrified.

The red faded from Draven's eyes as he picked up his own glass. "I was going to say, before you interrupted, that the Rayne bloodline is a powerful ally to have." He raised his glass. "And that your powerful alliances are just another reason why the marriage between us makes so much sense."

"Perhaps you should work harder on convincing me what you would bring to the marriage." I raised my own glass in salute. "Other than your pretty looks."

Someone, I was pretty sure it was Aniella, choked on a laugh.

"Well, at least you acknowledge that I'm pretty." He smiled, and fuck me, it was a very nice smile. Too bad the Moroi it was attached to was responsible for so many innocent deaths. Even if his mother were the mastermind behind all of this, he still went along with it.

"It's hard for me to picture Rynn hunting spine-backed boars," Alaric said, and it took me a minute to realize he was steering us back to the original conversation. "She's so . . ." He furrowed his brows, as if searching for the right word. "She's just Rynn. Soft-spoken and thoughtful Rynn."

I laughed. "That she is, but our dear, sweet Rynn shifts into a nearly five-hundred-pound wolf whose bite will give you nightmares. Have you ever seen her lycanthrope form?"

Alaric shook his head. "I haven't actually been around many Velesians in their shifted forms."

"It's impressive. They're all ridiculously large but can move with absolute silence. As if the wilds favor them over every other creature that wanders the forests." A small, playful grin tugged at my lips. "Rynn, in particular, is very good at sneaking around. When the three of us were at Drudonia, we'd often sneak out at night and play our own version of hide-and-seek in the forests. Two of us would hide, and the third would hunt. It would drive Cali insane because Rynn always won. We could never find her if she didn't want to be found, and she'd always find us unless Cali cheated and took to the air where we couldn't follow."

"The three of you went into the woods at night on your own?" Draven stared at me in disbelief. Apparently, I'd finally managed to surprise him.

"The wilds surrounding Drudonia are heavily patrolled." I shrugged. "It's rare for any of the beasts to get close, and avoiding the rangers only made it more fun." I glanced at Alaric and then Kieran in panic. "Don't tell Vail."

"You're asking us to lie?" Kieran's expression was full of mock horror. "To our beloved Marshal?"

"Feels like we should get something for putting ourselves in such potential peril," Alaric chimed in. "Lying to Vail is a risk. Even a lie of omission. So what would you offer us, Samara?"

My mouth hung open in what I was sure was a very unattractive way, but I couldn't help it. Alaric was joking. With me. About sex. Maybe there was hope for us after all.

Ary and Aniela were watching the exchange with amused expressions, no doubt filing all this information away in case it was useful later, while Demetri's gaze kept bouncing between Kieran and Alaric, like he couldn't decide which one of them he hated more.

"I'll think of something worth your while." I finally recovered and winked at Alaric, and the corners of his lips quirked into the barest of smiles.

Maybe whatever conversation he'd had with Kieran this afternoon had helped him come to terms with us. A little bit of hope filled me.

"Sometimes, Rynn would help me avoid Cali while we played this game of hers, so I was used to being around her when she was in her wolf form. I was visiting her in Narchis territory when a hunt was declared, and she invited me along. Well . . . I invited myself along, but she went with it."

"And you?" Draven looked at Ary. "How did you get involved in this?"

Ary smiled politely. "I like to get a bit of exercise now and then. Since Tepes' lands border Narchis' ones, they occasionally invite me on hunts."

I snorted. Currently, Ary was dressed in a beautiful, deep red tunic with gold threads, and glittering rings lined his fingers. He'd taken the time to shave and clean up before dinner, and now he appeared as nothing more than a handsome and well-kept Heir . . . but I knew he was far more comfortable covered in blood with his claws buried in the gut of a monster.

The Velesians loved to go hunting with Ary. He was insane

and feared nothing. I really hoped he wasn't mixed up in this wraith business, because he was not someone I wanted to have as an enemy. If I could sway him to our side though . . . he'd be an excellent ally.

"It was invigorating hunting under the moonlight." I smiled at the memory. "Rynn's birth pack was hunting that night, so it was mostly lycanthropes with a few ailuranthropes mixed in, but the panthers stuck to the trees, and I rarely saw them."

"How did they bring the boars down?" Draven rose and grabbed the wine bottle at the center of the table to refill his glass before walking around to refill mine. He glanced at Alaric, who shook his head, sticking with his honey ale. Kieran pointedly ignored Draven, who eventually sighed and returned to his seat.

"Easiest way is to get them on their backs—their bellies are their weak spot," Ary explained.

"I'm sure that's not hard at all," Draven quipped.

I huffed a laugh. A full-grown boar weighed close to eight hundred pounds. They were named for the nearly foot-long spikes they could raise down their spine, but those spikes actually covered most of their body, shorter below the spine but every bit as sharp. Their legs and belly were vulnerable though, and if you got too close, they would basically throw their body at you, relying on both their weight and spines to inflict damage.

Boars might technically be prey animals who preferred to root around for nuts and berries rather than tear flesh from bone, but they were ill-tempered and highly aggressive. Lunaria was a land of monsters. Some of those monsters just happened to be herbivores.

"The pack would split up," I explained. "Half of them would get the boars into a panic so they would run, then the other half would run at them head-on and slam their bodies against their sides. It takes careful timing, and the angle has to be perfect, but if you hit the boars right, you can flatten the spikes back down against their body to avoid getting impaled and cause them to stumble, ideally falling completely."

"Exposing their undersides," Draven mused. "Clever."

"And what were you doing?" Alaric cocked his head.

"She was being insane." Ary lifted his wine glass to me, and I raised mine back, a wicked grin on my face.

"There is another weak spot you can exploit. The spines that run along their back and neck are longer but less dense than the rest of the ones on their body. If you shoot an arrow at the base of their neck, you can sever the vertebrae and take them down in a second."

Alaric frowned. "You'd have to shoot at the same angle as the spikes, which means you'd need to be both behind and above them."

"There are dried-up riverbeds all over their territory, and they create narrow channels. Rynn convinced a few pack members to chase some of the boars down them. I would run along the edges and leap across to the other side. At the apex of my jump, I'd have the perfect angle. Could bring down three or four each time," I said smugly.

"You're good with a crossbow?" Draven asked.

Alaric and Kieran snorted, but it was Kieran who answered. "Samara isn't *good* with a crossbow. She's excellent. Pretty sure she's a better shot than any of our rangers, Vail included."

"And let's not forget the bloody knives," Alaric muttered, drawing a grin out of me.

"There are no helpful riverbeds down here, so it'll be difficult for me to pull out that trick," I said.

"I could throw you." Ary sent me a heated look. "It's not exactly how I've always wanted to get my hands on you, but I'll take what I can get. Perhaps offer to rub down your muscles after the hunt . . ."

"You should stick to hunting, Ary." Aniela laughed. "Your flirtations continue to be awful."

"They worked on you." He arched a thick, dark brow at her.

My eyes widened as I looked at the two Heirs who I'd always thought hated each other. "Did you know that?" I gave Kieran a wide-eyed stare.

He shrugged. "Old news. Happened two years ago, not long after Aniela was named Heir." He looked at the beautiful Moroi female who wore a simple, emerald green dress that did wonders for her red hair. "Summer equinox, if I remember correctly. You'd just been dumped by that cute blond boy you'd been seeing all spring."

Aniela glared at him. "He wasn't *cute*, he was *hot*, and I wasn't dumped. We mutually agreed to end things."

"Of course." Kieran smiled, which only pissed Aniela off more.

"So," I cut in and waved my hand between Aniela and Ary, "hate fuck then?"

They looked at each other for a long moment before nodding and saying, "Hate fuck."

Everyone at the table laughed, and some of the tension dispelled. I didn't think anyone else caught how Ary's gaze lingered on Aniela for several seconds after she'd already looked away.

I thought about asking some probing questions to start feeling out where everyone might stand on the wraith situation, but it would be easier if I could talk to them one-on-one. Before I could think of anything to say, Demetri leaned forward and caught my eye.

"Perhaps we should try it?" he suggested.

"Try what?" I arched an eyebrow.

"Hate fucking." He smiled. "It might do wonders to repair our relationship."

Ary looked at Aniela. "Okay, compared to him, you have to admit that I'm charming as fuck."

I took a sip of wine, keeping my expression relaxed even as I fumed internally at Demetri's words. The audacity of that male. Beside me, Draven, Kieran, and Alaric had all gone completely still. I needed to play this down before they did something foolish. As the Moroi Prince, Draven could do whatever he wanted, but if Alaric or Kieran did anything against the Heir of another House, there would be consequences.

"The only relationship we have is the one that exists between all Heirs," I drawled. "There is nothing beyond that, and despite what antics some might engage in"—I glanced pointedly at Aniela and Ary—"I have no interest in hate fucking any of the Heirs." I slid my hand across the table, and Kieran immediately grabbed it, intertwining our fingers. "As you pointed out earlier, I'm already getting quite thoroughly fucked. There is no reason for me to slum it anymore."

"You're fucking a courtier who was a throwaway from House Corvinus and an advisor who came from *nothing*." Demetri sneered. "The Lockwoods are outpost trash who have no business living in a House, let alone advising one."

My fingers curled around the knife next to my plate, but Draven's hand found mine before I could do anything with it, and Kieran's fingers tightened around my other hand so all I could do was glower at my ex-husband and envision slicing his throat open. It wasn't enough. I opened my mouth to tell him off, but Alaric beat me to it.

"House Laurent is going to run out of malachite by the end of the year," Alaric said calmly. "Which means you'll have to rely on other crystals to power your wards, ones that won't last nearly as long. Since you foolishly didn't pursue Samara's proposal of trading with the Velesians—who have malachite in abundance—you have no reliable way of getting more." He took another sip of wine. "She sent that proposal to the Order of Narchis as soon as she returned here, by the way. So House Harker now has one of the best trade deals for malachite in all of the Moroi realm."

"I'd love to speak with you about that tomorrow," Aniela cut in. "I believe House Salvatore can offer favorable terms in exchange for some malachite."

"Of course." Alaric nodded at her. "We can speak after breakfast."

Demetri's hate-filled gaze tore from Alaric to land on Aniela, but she just sent him a polite smile in return. I found myself liking the Salvatore Heir more and more.

"Your House"—Alaric returned his cool, even gaze to Demetri—"thinks of itself as better than everyone else. You forget the reality of our situation, perhaps because you live far enough down the southern coast that you rarely have to fight off any monster attacks. Because we do it for you. The Velesians do it for you as well. As do the Furies. At the end of the day, House Laurent is nothing but a bunch of free-loaders. And when your House falls, and it absolutely will fall, a new line will rise. Perhaps one from an outpost. Most will forget you ever existed. But don't worry." Alaric raised his wineglass in salute. "The Lockwoods will remember you and present you as an example of the terrible fate of mediocrity."

Demetri's face turned bright red, rage simmering in his eyes while Aniela cackled and Ary started to slow clap. Draven and Kieran released me so they could join in on the clapping.

I let out a husky laugh, and Alaric's gaze flicked to mine. "Honestly, Alaric," I purred, "I could fuck you right here."

"I'd watch," Kieran offered.

"Same." Draven sent me a heated look.

Alaric cleared his throat and looked away, focusing on the

wineglass in his hand, but I saw the corners of his mouth curl upward.

"This was definitely worth the frantic ride here." Aniela raised her wineglass to Ary, and he bumped it with his.

"Fuck all of you." Demetri shoved his chair back and rose, sending me one last glare. "You and I aren't done." Then he stormed out, and we all watched him go.

"I'm confused," Aniela said after he left. "From everything I've heard, he didn't put up much of a fight after you left House Laurent. So why is he pursuing you now?"

"No idea." I frowned in the direction Demetri had run off to. "Our marriage has been officially dissolved."

She hummed thoughtfully as she sipped her wine. "Well, he's doing a shitty job of wooing you back, which is good for me because it means one less House for us to compete against for your affections."

"You want my affections too, Aniela?" I asked dryly.

She tilted her head back and let out a musical laugh. Interest flashed across Ary's face before he hid it behind a mask of indifference. Maybe there was more than just hate fucking there after all.

"You're beautiful, Samara, but I don't swing that way. My House needs malachite and a few other things. I believe we can make you a good offer."

"Wonderful," I said truthfully. "Perhaps I can come visit your House soon. It's been a while since I've spoken to Dominique in person."

"She would enjoy that." Aniela smiled. "Our closest neighbor, aside from the Sovereign House, is House Devereux, and they're not exactly chatty."

"I'll speak with your Marshal tomorrow about the boars," Ary wiped his mouth with the back of his hand after taking a long drink of wine. "They almost certainly went through our territory to get to yours, which means they could easily turn back and wreak havoc at one of our outposts. We'll help with the hunt."

"Thank you." I gave him a nod. "I'm sure Vail will appreciate that. We'll split the meat of course."

"Something must have driven the boars out of their territory. They prefer the thicker forests of the Velesian realm," Ary mused and looked at Draven. "Wraith activity is definitely increasing. Does the Sovereign House have any information about that? I'm assuming the increasing attacks on our outposts have been your main priority lately."

"It's all my mother and her consort work on," Draven said evenly. "I know she's seeking Carmilla's wisdom on the matter as well. There hasn't been much I've been able to do to help. I'm not a particularly gifted fighter nor was I ever a good student." He gave me a self-deprecating smile. "Not all of us were considered a prized pupil by the scholars at Drudonia."

"You're definitely gifted at bullshitting," Kieran drawled. Instead of being insulted, Draven just looked happy that Kieran had said something to him.

"Vail and a good amount of House Harker's resources have been focused on solving the issue of the increased attacks on our outposts." I fixed my expression into one of concern, which wasn't exactly hard considering that's how I felt. It was slightly more challenging to keep the suspicion hidden away. "But we haven't learned much, and the attacks only seem to be increasing. Has the Sovereign House learned *anything* useful?"

Draven shrugged. "I'm sure you know more than I do at this point. We'll figure it out eventually."

I set my wineglass down so I wouldn't shatter it in my hand. "Eventually isn't good enough. Entire fucking outposts died." *And you played a hand in that*, I thought but kept that to myself. "We need to stop these attacks now."

The charming mask slid off Draven's face, and something dark and predatory replaced it. "This is Lunaria. People die every day. Often in horrible ways." I opened my mouth to argue, but the red bleeding through his deep blue eyes silenced me. "We might be monsters, Samara, but we're far from the biggest or the baddest. You'd be wise to be selective with who you choose to protect, because you can't save them all."

"And you'd be wise to not tell me what I'm capable of," I said coldly. "Some of us can do things you only dream of."

Draven looked at me for a long moment. That feral, predatory gleam still in his eyes. "That's what you've got wrong, Heir. I know nothing of dreams. The only thing I've ever known are nightmares."

CHAPTER EIGHT

Samara

"THERE YOU ARE."

Startled, I jumped slightly where I'd been sitting on the low balcony wall, but a strong hand grasped my arm, steadying me. My heart beat painfully, as it'd practically leapt into my throat as I glanced to the ground far beneath us. I looked over my shoulder and scowled at the prince. "I thought you were trying to court me, not scare me into falling to my death."

His lips twitched, and I had the sneaking suspicion he was trying not to laugh at me. "Sorry. That wasn't my intention. I've been sneaking around for the last hour looking for you, trying to avoid the other Heirs and everyone else who *'just wants a moment of my time.'*"

Slowly, he released his grip on my arm, trailing his fingers down it as if he wanted to prolong the contact before stepping back.

"Fair enough. I was just coming to find you anyway."

Roth wanted to do some research in the library, and Alaric was going to help them while Kieran chatted up the rangers who had traveled with the Heirs to see if he could glean anything useful. I was responsible for distracting Draven and keeping him out of everyone's way.

I spun around on the balcony wall to hop down. Demetri had left early this morning, but Ary and Aniela had stuck around. I'd already met with them both over breakfast and was growing more confident that they were not allied with the Sovereign House and the wraiths. Even if I trusted them though, it didn't mean someone in their House wasn't our enemy. We'd have to tread carefully if we wanted to bring them into the fold, and I wasn't ready to do that just yet.

"It's not every day the Moroi Prince graces us with his presence. You can't blame them for trying to get your support on whatever their latest scheme is."

"They're welcome to schedule time with me in the mornings while you're busy with House business." He extended an elbow to me. "But I'd prefer to spend time alone with you for the rest of the day . . . and night."

I did my best to ignore the flicker of excitement that raced through me. Mentally, I knew Draven could not be trusted. He was clearly working with the wraiths, which made him our enemy, but I'd known him for so long, and he was an attractive bastard, and when he said things like that, my body practically screamed, *Yes, please!* I gave him a bemused grin instead and slipped my arm around his. "You can have me . . . for the day."

"We'll see." His eyes roamed over the scenery. "Quite the view up here."

"It is," I agreed. "My study has a good view of the beach, but nothing beats this." I swept my free hand out towards the vast forest that covered the lands before us. "It's one of my favorite places to come and think, and play with the strikers of course."

A low-pitched trill filled the air, and I made a clicking sound with my tongue, keeping my hand extended. Seconds later, a bright red striker landed on my hand, its long talons wrapping around my fingers, the sharp points pushing against my skin but not breaking it.

"Good boy," I cooed. The creature shook its narrow, elongated head, a forked tongue darting out from its blunt beak. "You'll be flying further around here in no time."

Draven reached out and scratched the striker's back, and it flapped its leathery wings before releasing deep chirps of pleasure. "They're cute little monsters."

"I adore them. This one struggled a bit early on. I had to hand-feed it after it hatched because the others kept bullying it, so he's gotten rather attached to me."

"Something he and I have in common it seems."

I rolled my eyes. "Smooth."

"Thank you." Draven grinned.

"Come on." I tugged him towards the large, open-air structure we'd built to house the strikers. "Let's get him settled, and I'll take you on a tour of House Harker."

He groaned. "Did I not mention how I've been trying to avoid talking to people for the last hour?"

The striker hopped off my hand onto a free perch, and I gave him one more scratch behind the head before heading towards the stairs, dragging Draven with me. "Don't worry about it. I have a plan."

"Alright." He gave me a sly look. "But for every person who stops us, you have to spend an hour with me after dinner."

"Deal," I said confidently.

The winding stairwell was too narrow for us to walk side by side, so I slipped my arm free from his as we made our way down. It didn't take long for voices to reach us. This was one of the busier towers and where most of the advisors and courtiers spent their time during the day.

"Given the amount of people we're about to run into, I think you'll be spending all night with me, Samara." The way he said my name was indecent, and it sent a shiver down my spine, but I could play this game too.

I stopped and whirled around. Draven froze as I placed my hand on his chest, a coy smile twisting my lips. His eyes were locked on mine as I raised my other hand to my lips and used my fang to slice the tip of my index finger. A few drops of blood swelled, and Draven's nostrils flared. Without looking, I stretched my bloody finger to the wall, the dormant magic of the glyph engraved on one of the stones calling to me. As soon as my blood touched it, a portion of the wall simply disappeared, revealing a hidden stairwell.

Surprise flickered in his eyes, and I let out a husky laugh before licking the remaining blood off my finger. The red threads in Draven's eyes widened at the sight, and I was pretty sure he had stopped breathing. I licked my lips and leaned forward, one hand still on his chest. "Looks like you won't be getting that night with me after all, Draven."

"Fuck," he muttered as I slipped into the darkness. As soon as he crossed the threshold, I pushed on another glyph, and the wall reappeared, plunging us into absolute darkness. Our night vision was excellent, better than the Velesians or Furies, but even we needed some light to see by, and there was none here. "No Fae lanterns?" Draven asked.

"No." I shook my head, even though I knew he couldn't see it, and reached for his hand. My fingers bumped into his arm, and I slid them down until our hands were clasped. The contact was both intimate and innocent at the same time, and I was suddenly acutely aware of how warm his hand felt in mine. How right it felt. "They don't work anymore, and I never bothered to fix them, but I know the way. Trust me."

His fingers tightened around mine. "Lead the way, Heir."

I started carefully walking down the steps. Draven followed, not slipping once despite not being able to see anything or having my familiarity with the hidden stairs.

"How did you find this?" he asked after a few minutes.

Silence filled the air as I thought about how to answer. What truths to reveal and which to hide. Finally, I decided it was easier to go with the truth when possible—fewer lies to keep track of.

"After my parents died, I started to spend more time visiting the strikers. It became my safe place, especially since I wasn't old enough to leave the House grounds on my own. A week after"—the words caught in my throat—"their death, I was coming down, and I heard Carmilla talking to Alaric's parents. They were discussing the future of the House and their concerns about how I was handling things. I didn't want to face them, so I spun to run back up the stairs and tripped. It was pure luck that I noticed the glyph on the wall."

"I'm sorry," he said roughly. "I don't think I ever told you that, but I'm so sorry about how your parents died. They were always kind to me."

For the first time since we'd entered the darkened stairwell, I felt off-balance and had to concentrate on where my feet fell, despite having walked down these steps dozens of times before. I rarely spoke about my parents. The wound left behind by their deaths hadn't healed, it'd just festered in my soul over the years. I didn't know what to make of Draven's words. There was a raw edge to them that felt genuine.

But my parents had been killed by wraiths, and now Draven was working with them. Was that why he felt so guilty over this? He was only a couple of years older than me, which meant he'd been a teenager when they'd died, so I doubted he'd been working with them then. The urge to turn around and shake him until he told me what the fuck was going on was overwhelming, but I shoved that feeling down.

I had another hundred steps to get my emotions under control. Too much was riding on this for me to stumble now.

While Alaric and Kieran were helping Roth in the library, I should seize this opportunity to carefully question Draven.

"Thank you," I said tightly. "My parents were excellent rulers of House Harker. I only hope to live up to their legacy someday." Clearing my throat, I redirected the conversation. "Speaking of living up to legacies . . . it's been a while since I visited the Sovereign House. How are things between you and your mother these days?"

His fingers loosened around mine, and for a moment, I thought he would release my hand. But then they tightened once more. "Same as always. She's delighted about our engagement—*sorry*—potential engagement." He'd slipped back into his charming prince mode.

We continued our trek down, and I listened while Draven recounted some of the events that had transpired over the past couple of years at the Sovereign House. About how he was bored and had very little to do these days.

I listened to him lie to me for one hundred and eight steps.

OUR FOOTSTEPS ECHOED across the large, empty room we'd entered after leaving the hidden stairwell. Dinner was still hours away, and I needed to come up with something to do with Draven during that time so the others could continue their work unhindered.

Maybe we could go for a ride or something. Although, if Vail found out I'd left House Harker alone with the prince, he'd probably strangle me.

"What is this place?" Draven asked as he glanced around curiously.

"We're right beneath the main tower." I pointed to an iron and wood door across the room. "That leads to the kitchen. We're not sure what the Fae originally built this room for.

When they abandoned this place, they took almost everything with them except the furniture. We use it for storage now."

"Hmm." Instead of heading towards the door that led upstairs, he started aimlessly wandering around, studying the walls. "Seems weird they went through the effort of building a secret stairwell only to have it lead to the kitchen pantry, right?"

There was more than one secret passage that led to this room. After stumbling across the one in the upper stairwell when I was a kid, I'd made it my mission to find others. I'd found six in this tower alone, plus another dozen short ones that linked the hidden staircase together. There were more in the other buildings and towers that made up House Harker as well. I didn't understand why they'd done it. There was nothing special about this room, but the Fae had spent an awful lot of time planning a way for anyone to secretly get to this place.

I wouldn't be telling Draven any of that though. I probably shouldn't have even shown him the room we were in. It'd been careless of me, and I couldn't afford to be like that around him. The prince was not my friend, despite our history and how I felt about him. He was our enemy, and he'd hurt Kieran.

I should have pushed him down those fucking stairs. The sensation of his hand in mine and how right it had felt came rushing back. The way his voice had sounded so sorrowful when he'd said he was sorry for the loss of my parents. I ruthlessly grabbed the feeling and shoved it into the same box where I stored my grief for my parents' deaths.

"They built everything out of stone despite wood being far more abundant and easy to move. Paintings of places that don't exist around here adorn the ceiling of every bedroom, and the vast majority of books we've found written by Fae hands . . . is *poetry*," I said in a bored tone as I walked towards where Draven was standing and staring at the dark grey stones of the wall. "Not where they came from, how they ended up here, or why there was such hatred between the Seelie and Unseelie. And then they vanished practically overnight, never to be heard from again."

"Your point?" Draven didn't so much as look at me as his eyes continued scanning the stone surface. Was he looking for something? I started skimming the walls to see if there was something here I had missed this whole time.

"My *point* is that they did a bunch of shady shit." Nothing stood out on the smooth stone surface, but I kept searching. "The secret passages are just another thing on that long list."

"Passages?"

Shit. I hadn't meant to say that.

I felt his gaze on me and turned away from the wall I'd been studying to meet his stare. He cocked his head, causing his long hair to fall over his shoulder in a shimmering curtain. "There's more than one?"

"I hate you."

He chuckled. "I think that's the first truthful thing you've said to me all day."

"Exaggeration," I muttered and turned back to the wall, heaving a sigh of frustration. There wasn't anything here. "Let's get out of here. I need some fresh air."

"Wait." Draven's hand shot out, and his fingers wrapped around my wrist when I turned towards the exit. "Have you ever noticed this glyph before?"

All the thoughts in my mind scattered at the sudden contact. I didn't even look at the wall where Draven was pointing with his other hand. Instead, all my focus was on where his fingers were wrapped around me. Draven stilled, and we stood there for a long moment. Then he gently stroked his thumb over my pulse, and my heart sped up.

Moonsdamn it all. I needed to get ahold of myself.

"Let me take a look." I pulled my arm free and took a step

closer to the wall. My heart continued to race, but now it was because I was looking at a Fae glyph that had been created in a way I'd never seen before.

I traced the barely visible glyph. It wasn't all that surprising that nobody had ever noticed it. The glyph was a simple one, just a circle with a straight line running vertically through it, but normally, when glyphs were etched into stone, the lines were a lighter color and they caused a slight dip in the surface.

My finger skimmed over the glyph. The surface remained the same, there was no dip, and parts of the glyph were lighter, while other sections were darker. It was as if the Fae had moved around the natural minerals within the stone to create the glyph. I'd had no idea they could do that.

"How did you even find this?" My brows furrowed. Unless you were looking for it, your eyes would slip over it as just a natural discoloration. I mean, I was looking directly at it, and even now, it was easy to dismiss as nothing.

"Just lucky." Draven shrugged when I glanced at him. "Seemed odd for the stairwell to lead down here, and after you showed me that glyph upstairs, I was on the lookout for another one."

Plausible, but absolute horseshit. He'd been searching the walls as soon as we'd set foot in this room and I'd told him where it was located. He'd known this glyph would be here. Maybe not in this exact spot, but somewhere in this room. I was very curious about how he'd known about it. I was even more interested in why he wanted *me* to know about it.

"Do you know what it means?" Draven asked over my shoulder.

"Safe," I whispered. "It means safe."

I sucked in a breath as a deliciously wicked scent filled the air when Draven moved close enough for his chest to rest against my back. He reached towards the stone with bloody fingertips.

"Are you out of your mind?" I slapped his hand away before he could make contact with the glyph and spun around to smack him on the chest. "We have no idea what that spell was actually used for!"

"You said it means safe." He grinned at me, and I wanted to strangle him . . . and kiss him. Argh.

"Forgive me for not trusting the fucking Fae's definition of safe!" I shoved him away from me and the wall. Distance. That was the key to dealing with Draven—keeping a good amount of space between us so I could keep my unruly thoughts under control.

Unfortunately, Draven was not on board with this unspoken plan because he immediately stepped further into my space, reclaiming the distance I'd put between us. I stepped away until my back was against the wall, and a wolfish grin stretched across his lips as he boxed me in, placing one arm on either side of me. I had to tilt my head back to look at him, my heart thumping wildly as he leaned down to whisper in my ear. "Come on, Heir. It's fun to be dangerous sometimes."

The rational part of my brain was drowned out by the heat dancing across my skin as his lips trailed down my neck. Fangs grazed my pulse, and I didn't know what I would do if he tried to bite me. I knew what I should do. I should push him away again. Fuck, I should be doing that right fucking now.

Draven chuckled darkly against my skin. "You overthink things, Sam."

He raised his left hand and slammed it against the wall directly over my shoulder before I could stop him. The bastard had been distracting me. As soon as his blood made contact with the glyph, magic sparked, and the floor fell out from beneath us.

CHAPTER NINE

Draven

I fucked up.

Plummeting into darkness wasn't what I had expected to happen when I'd activated the glyph. I'd known to look for it because we had an identical room in the Sovereign House with the exact same glyph. Though when I'd activated that one, it'd been like being gently picked up and placed in a different room before getting a nice pat on the head.

This had felt like the floor cracking under us and a giant reaching up and jerking our bodies down. I was pretty sure my organs were no longer in the right positions, and I was fighting the urge to hurl my guts up.

On the plus side, Samara was clinging to me tenaciously. Her arms were wrapped around me, and she tucked her head against my chest. If she'd had time to think about it, she never would have done it, but in a moment of panic, she thought I was safe. Someone she could trust to see her through this.

I wasn't.

That fact hurt far more than the way she practically flung herself away from me when we stopped moving, hissing a bunch of words in dead languages that I had no doubt were promises of doing very nasty things to certain parts of my body. I let her get it out while I looked around, getting our bearings. Grateful the nausea had vanished almost instantly after the magic had finished transporting us.

It was foolish of me to turn my back on Samara when she was pissed. I knew from past experience that she had a fiery temper.

"Fuck!" I rubbed the back of my head, where something hard and blunt had just slammed into it. I turned at the pinging sound of something metal bouncing off the floor and I bent down to swipe up the dagger. Given that Sam had just thrown a blade at my head, and I didn't know if she'd meant for the sharp end to hit me, I should've probably been pissed off at her. Instead, I wanted to pass the weapon back to her so she could hold it at my throat while I fucked her against the wall.

Something told me she wouldn't like that though, or more accurately, she wouldn't be willing to admit how much she would like that. I hadn't missed all the conflicting expressions on her face over the past hour. Samara wanted me, and she hated herself for it.

Couldn't exactly fault her for that. I hated myself a little too.

Samara stalked over to me and held her hand out demandingly as black threads wound through her purple eyes. Okay, she was a little more than pissed.

She grabbed the dagger from me and thrust it back into a sheath that was hidden up her sleeve. "Next time you disobey me," she growled, "it'll be the dagger end that goes through your thick fucking skull!"

Guess that answered the question of if she'd intended to hit me with the handle. Apparently, she hadn't been bragging at the dinner table when she'd spoken about how good she was with projectile weapons.

Fuck, Samara got hotter by the minute.

Before I could stop myself, I reached out and ran my fingers down the thick braid that snaked over her shoulder, then trailed my fingers along the top of her chest.

"I can think of some better ways for you to punish me for my disobedience." For a split second, desire lit up Samara's eyes before she ruthlessly stamped it out. It was reckless of me to tease her like this, but I couldn't help it. I'd felt the same about Kieran, and he'd almost died because of it. Not that he had the faintest idea. His hatred of me hurt, but all I cared about was that he was alive.

Samara and her friends had only scratched the surface of how completely fucked Lunaria was. My mother had always been a power-hungry bitch, but now she had strong allies who could make all her dark and twisted dreams come true. Sooner or later, she'd decide I wasn't worth keeping around, and my life would be over. So I might as well flirt with Samara while I could. Thanks to her status as the Harker Heir, even my mother would hesitate to go after her. Kieran hadn't been so lucky.

"What is this place?" Samara stepped away from me as she peered around the dimly lit room. A few Fae lanterns had lit up, but they must have been running out of magic because their blue flames were nothing more than small flickers. I strode over to one of them and sliced the back of my hand, dipped my fingertips into the blood, and then brushed them against the flame symbol at the base of the silver lantern. The flames immediately burned brighter and chased more of the darkness away.

I went to the next lantern and repeated the process, the glyph greedily absorbing the magic in my blood. Samara strode to the wall opposite me and did the same on the lanterns on that side. It didn't take long to light up the enormous room.

"These walls are made out of the same stone as the rest of

House Harker," Samara mused as she ran her hand along the dark grey stonework. Then she slowly walked back to the center of the room, her steps echoing across the empty space. "What the fuck is this?"

"There's a door." I pointed to what was likely the one and only exit. So far, the layout of the place was the same as the one I'd explored before. "Maybe we'll find some answers through there."

Samara pursed her lips as she glared at the door like it had personally offended her. I bit back my laugh, not wanting to have another dagger thrown in my direction. On one hand, she was still pissed off over how all of this had played out—Samara liked to be in control and do things in a logical manner—but I also knew she had a bit of a wild streak and was obsessed with learning more about the Fae.

Despite her rant a few minutes ago about the Fae and their shady history, Samara would latch onto any opportunity to figure out more of the history of Lunaria, which meant diving into all the strange things the Fae had left behind, and this whole situation definitely qualified as weird, shady Fae shit.

I was a little disappointed this room was empty just like the one beneath the Sovereign House. Not because I'd expected to find anything that could help me, since my fate was already sealed, but because it would have made Samara happy to find some new piece of history.

"Let's go look," she said with a sigh, but she walked quickly, excitement practically dripping off her. I let myself smile now that her back was to me and I wasn't at risk of sharp, flying objects. She swung the door open and stopped with a sharp intake of breath.

I quickly closed the distance between us, my arm slinking around her waist, ready to pull her back from any potential threat. Another room stretched out before us, significantly larger than the one we'd just been in. The Fae lanterns in this one hadn't weakened, the entire area brightly lit, and neat rows of beds took up most of the space. Unlike the more elaborate beds that had been left behind in the fortresses, these ones were of a simple but functional make. Each one had a bottom and top mattress and blankets and pillows still tucked into place.

I released her so she could explore. This was indeed exactly like the room under the Sovereign House. And just like that one, this one only provided more questions instead of answers, it seemed.

"It's a shelter . . ." Samara walked slowly between the rows, eyes skimming over the room. "Did they never use it? Or did they retreat here and then leave?" I kept my mouth shut since I didn't have an answer and it was clear she was mostly talking to herself at this point.

She stopped by one of the beds and plucked at a blanket, raising it a few inches before letting it drop, a frown stretching across her beautiful face. "Something frightened the Fae enough that they built secret passages leading to a room that held some type of magical doorway to a bunker." Her eyes raised to the ceiling. "I think we're underground, directly below the fortress. If they planned for all this, they must have assumed that the fortress, despite all its wards, could be compromised. They wouldn't trap themselves down here." She looked away from the ceiling and started scanning the rest of the room. "There must be an exit somewhere that leads off the grounds."

"What do you think happened to the Fae?" I asked as we resumed our walk around the unused beds. The stillness of the room bothered me. It was like we were walking through a graveyard that had never actually been used.

Samara glanced over her shoulder at me. "I think the theory about the Unseelie losing control of their shadow magic is the most likely. It would explain the wraiths. From the books we've managed to find, everything indicates the arrival of the wraiths coincided with the disappearance of the Fae. It seems highly unlikely that there isn't a connection between the shadow monsters and the Unseelie. We know they hated the Seelie. We just don't know why."

She turned away and hurried down the row, something drawing her attention. I clenched my hands at my sides as I watched her go, a dull ache forming at the base of my skull. The promise of pain was a reminder of the geas. My mother had a lot of control over me, but even she couldn't compel me not to speak of her secrets.

Erendriel could.

Which meant I couldn't scream at Samara that she was wrong. Even just thinking about doing so was ratcheting up the pain. I paused by one of the beds and pretended to look at something as I leaned against it and pulled in several deep breaths. It'd taken me a while to figure out how to calm my thoughts and empty my mind, but it was the only way I managed to hold onto my sanity. Something that greatly disappointed my mother when she'd tried so hard to break me.

I didn't know why she hated me so much, but there were many things I'd never understood about her. In the end, it didn't matter. I was a weapon for her to wield until she no longer deemed me useful, and that day was coming soon.

All I cared about now was figuring out a way to keep Samara and Kieran safe. There was no saving Lunaria, but perhaps they could be protected. Not if they kept going down this path though. I knew Samara had been at that temple. When I'd returned with Erendriel and smelled her blood at the entrance, I'd felt the same terror I had the night my mother had looked at Kieran and smiled.

Erendriel had raged as we scoured the area, but there had been no sign of the wraiths we'd left behind. To my relief, Samara had already been gone, but it'd been difficult to maintain a steady heartbeat as the scent of her blood had hit me. I'd smelled the blood of at least three others as well, but I hadn't recognized who it belonged to. Erendriel had stared at the bloodsoaked ground, but the Fae didn't have a particularly sensitive sense of smell. He couldn't even tell it was Moroi blood, let alone who it belonged to.

Lying to Erendriel was tricky. I wasn't sure if all Fae could detect a lie or if he could only tell when I lied because of the geas he'd placed on me. Fortunately for me, I'd grown up in the Moroi courts and was quite skilled in misleading words and partial truths. When he'd demanded to know who the blood belonged to, I'd purposely knelt by a puddle of blood that did not belong to Samara. So I had been truthful when I'd claimed not to know who had been there.

My gambit had only bought Samara and her friends a little bit of time. The proposed marriage between Samara and me was real. Currently, my mother thought the Harker Heir could be controlled. If Samara would just agree to marry me, then the queen would be satisfied for a while. It would provide me an opportunity to figure out how to keep her and Kieran safe long-term and make it easier for me to keep track of them, because where Samara went, Kieran would surely follow.

I couldn't let them go back to that temple or stumble into any other areas where the wraiths frequented. They had no idea just how much the world was falling apart around them, and I couldn't let them walk into it blindly, but I couldn't tell them either.

If my mother found out just how much Samara knew . . . she'd make sure Samara met an unfortunate end, likely at the hands of wraiths. She'd also make sure anyone Samara might have told would be killed off as well. The Moroi Queen did not like loose ends.

Carmilla was the wild card in all this. The best I could tell, she was truly just friends with my mother and wasn't caught up in the plot with Erendriel and the wraiths, but I'd been wrong before about people and paid dearly for it. The only two people in the world I trusted were Samara and Kieran, and they both thought I was the villain in all this.

Which I supposed I was. An unwilling one, but a villain all the same.

I started to turn in the direction Samara had headed when the light from the Fae lanterns glinted off something nestled in the blankets of one of the beds. It appeared something had been left behind after all. I strode over to the bed and pulled back the blanket. A perfect glass sphere sat there, a swirl of dark blue and purple with thick white markings that reminded me of clouds cutting through the color.

A Fae memory ball.

Excitement coursed through me, and I picked it up, concentrating on the magic within. But the hope I'd been feeling faded. Empty. Someone had brought it here but had never stashed a memory in it. Looked like whoever had used this safe room before would continue to remain a mystery to us.

I glanced to where Samara was standing at the other end of the room, facing the wall, and hurried after her. There might be another one of those weird portal spells here, and I didn't want to risk her activating it without me.

"Find something?" I asked when I neared her.

"A book. Poetry." She held up a slim, leather-bound book, not taking her eyes off the wall. "And another glyph. I don't know this one."

My arm brushed against hers as I leaned in closer, but she was so engrossed by her discovery that she didn't seem to notice. Unlike the glyph in the other room, this one was carved into the stone and easier to spot. It was a triangle with three horizontal lines slashed through it.

"Never seen one like this before." A mischievous smile curled on my lips as I reached out to touch it.

"Damn it, Drav!" She gripped my wrist and tugged my hand away. "Quit touching shit you don't understand!"

As soon as Samara realized she was still holding me, she released her fingers almost reluctantly. My grin transformed into a self-satisfied smile. She *liked* touching me. Despite everything she knew—or thought she knew— about me, Samara wanted me. I needed to use that to my advantage if I was going to convince her to marry me.

"Where did you find the book?"

"Over there." She pointed towards an empty bookcase tucked into the corner. "I didn't find anything else. Either they never actually used this space, or they cleared everything out when they . . . left."

"Trade you." I tossed her the memory ball, and she snatched it out of the air with one hand. I saw the exact moment disappointment hit her when she realized it contained no memories.

I tugged the book out of her other hand and started flipping through the pages. "Unseelie," I noted, which made sense because, based on the style of murals I'd seen on some of the walls and ceilings here, this had been an Unseelie stronghold. "Didn't know you were a fan of poetry."

Samara's cheeks darkened, and she hastily took the book back, clutching it to her chest. "I'm intrigued by anything they left behind. You know that. Plus . . . I have a friend who . . . umm . . ." Samara stammered, and I cocked my head at her as she continued to struggle. "They like it when I read Fae poetry to them, and this book has a bunch of poems I've never read before."

I had absolutely no idea what was making Samara blush like crazy, but it was highly amusing.

"Here." She handed me back the memory ball. "You found it, so it's yours."

I took the Fae artifact from her and pondered it for a

moment. Perhaps it was reckless of me, but if things went bad —which I strongly suspected they would—I wanted her to have at least one good memory of me. Kieran too. Maybe someday, they could view me as someone other than the villain.

"What are you doing?" Samara asked, tension flooding her voice as I sliced open my thumb on my fang and swiped the blood over the glass orb.

My blood vanished, and I felt the tug on my mind as a copy of the memory I'd chosen slipped into the orb.

"Here." I held the glass sphere out to her. "A memory just for you. Might I suggest listening to it at night . . . when you're alone in bed."

Her gaze narrowed on me, and I let my lips curl into a sinful smile. I was rewarded by her cheeks flushing before she scowled. "It'll make a beautiful paperweight."

I laughed before waving a hand at the rest of the room. "Do you want to look around more?" Not that there was much to see. I was curious about what the glyph on the wall did, probably an escape route of some kind, but I could return later and explore.

"No." Samara shook her head, dark eyes darting back to the glyph. She knew something about it. Something she didn't want to share with me. Turning her attention away from the wall, she gave me a brilliant smile that caused my heart to skip a beat. The way her eyes laughed at me, I knew that had been her intention. Samara never had any problem wielding her beauty to knock others off their game. "This place is depressing. Let's go walk on the beach for a bit. I want to feel the sun on my skin."

"Anything for you, Sam." I let my voice drop low so it was more of a raspy purr than anything, and Samara's smile slipped for a fraction of a second, her breath hitching before she rolled her eyes at me and took my arm as I extended it to her. "Hopefully the glyph that got us down here can also get us back up to that room."

That was how the one beneath the Sovereign House worked, so I assumed this one did as well, despite it's magic being a little fucked up. Samara just hummed her agreement as we walked back down the aisle, arm in arm, neither of us speaking.

CHAPTER TEN

Samara

"FUCK!" Kieran yelled as I buried my fangs into his neck. His thrusts became harsher, and my thighs trembled while I matched his pace as I straddled him on the couch in my suite. One hand was tightly wound up in my hair, and the other gripped my ass so hard, I knew I'd have bruises. A delicious heat was building in my core as his breathing grew ragged, and I knew we were close.

He'd already made me come several times with his fingers and tongue, but I just couldn't get enough of him. I pulled away from his neck, blood dripping down my chin, and arched my back. Kieran released my hair, both hands moving to grip my hips as he pounded into me. Then he leaned forward, kissing and licking my breast before sucking a nipple into his mouth.

I let myself lean back as far as I could, trusting Kieran to not let me fall, and reached one hand down, brushing over my already sensitive clit as a breathy moan slipped from my lips.

"That's it, gorgeous," Kieran growled. "Play with that clit for me while I fuck this amazing pussy of yours." His words had me practically coming as my fingers swirled through my hot slickness and pushed down on my clit.

"Harder, Kier!" I screamed.

He let go of my breast and leaned back against the cushions, his grip punishing as he did as I commanded, the new angle allowing him to reach even deeper. I couldn't stop the scream that erupted out of me as I came hard all over his cock, and Kieran bellowed as he came with me.

With trembling muscles, I leaned forward and slumped against his chest. "First part of the plan, done," I panted.

Kieran laughed as his arms wrapped around me. "I don't know. Maybe we should go again just so everyone knows for sure where we are and what we're doing."

"That's what you said an hour ago," I mumbled into his chest. "Besides, I'm running out of dirty things to scream."

He tightened his arms around me. "Just please be careful, Sam."

I raised my head enough to meet his gaze. "I will, I promise. It's probably nothing anyway, but I know I saw that glyph in the caves by the beach. I think it's just an escape route, but the Fae might have left something there, and we need to find it before Draven does." I pursed my lips. "He suspected I was holding something back earlier about the symbol. I know he did."

"He's always been annoyingly observant," Kieran said tightly.

"You okay?" I asked, searching his face for the answer. "I know it's got to be difficult being around him again, and I'm sorry I have to spend so much time with him."

"It's okay," Kieran assured me. "Is it fucked up that I'm kind of glad he's here? I should hate him. After everything that's happened between me and him, and us knowing what we do about him and the wraiths . . . plus him trying to marry you for probably bullshit reasons. But . . ." He trailed off.

I kissed him gently. "You missed him."

"This is all kinds of fucked." He blew out a breath. "I'm still *inside* you and I'm thinking about *him*."

"Lucky for you, my ego is unshakable." I bit down on his bottom lip hard enough to draw blood, and he groaned. "I'm equally fucked, because I was thinking about him too, and Alaric."

The glass ball containing a memory from Draven was currently sitting on the table in front of my settee, nestled amidst books and paperwork. I hadn't scrounged up the courage to see what he'd transferred to it and didn't know if I'd ever be able to.

"We are *fantastic* at complicated relationships." Kieran brushed my hair back over my shoulder, gold streaking through his brown eyes. "I love you, Sam. Whatever happens with the others, you have me forever."

"I love you too, Kier." I snuggled back down against his chest and breathed in his scent. Kieran always reminded me of dawn on a spring day. If I closed my eyes, I could almost picture the dewdrops hanging off the tulips that bloomed early in our garden. "We'll figure the rest of it out."

"The rest being the evil prince who we both have the hots for, the Marshal who may or may not kill you, and my asshole best friend who is absolutely in love with you and refusing to admit it?"

"Yes. That." I let out a husky laugh. "I'm reasonably sure Vail isn't going to kill me. At this point, he's had two chances, and both times, he's ended up saving me instead."

"After trying to kill you," Kieran pointed out.

"I mean, he didn't try that hard." Reluctantly, I raised myself off Kieran, both of us groaning as he slid out of me. "If Vail truly wanted me dead, then I'd be dead."

"Was that meant to be comforting?" He gave me a flat

look. "Because given that you're about to go traipsing around in a cave with him, I'm gonna let you know it's not."

I cleaned myself off with a towel before pulling on some clothes. Not much point in rinsing off, considering where I was headed. "Alaric will be there too." I quickly braided my hair and then wrapped it up in a bun.

Kieran walked over to where I was standing by the window, concern stamped all over his face. "Don't say anything to piss off Alaric. He might shove you into the water, and then you'll come back smelling like seaweed."

"No promises. I exist to piss that man off."

"That is definitely what Alaric believes."

We both snickered as I unlatched the window and swung it open. This was the trickiest part of my plan. I needed to climb down the wall to the courtyard and then quickly make my way out of House Harker. Draven had said he was retiring to his room after dinner, but I doubted that. Ary and Aniela were also still here, and I wouldn't put it past them to do a little sleuthing before they left tomorrow morning. Luckily, this window opened up to one of the smaller courtyards near the outer wall. There was a secret tunnel on this side that we could use to get outside the walls so we didn't have to go through the main gate.

I just needed to climb down without drawing attention. Or falling.

The cool night breeze danced across my skin as I peered down. My living quarters were towards the top of the tower, and it was a long way to the ground, but it wasn't fear racing through me right now. Exhilaration lit up my skin as I breathed in the crisp air and admired the cloudless and starry night.

We might currently live our lives by day, but it was night that made us feel truly alive. Even tonight, when the moon was barely a sliver in the sky.

Moroi. Velesian. Furie. We were all Moon Blessed.

I sat on the windowsill and swung my legs until they dangled over the edge, Kieran's lips quirking as he watched me.

"You're kind of insane. You know that, right?"

"It's one of the many reasons you love me." With a sharp inhale, I let my bloodlust rise. It was easy to control during the day, but beneath the moonlit sky, it surged forward, and I had to claw it back so I could stay focused.

Kieran's brown eyes studied me, noting the change in my eye color and how my nails had lengthened into claws. There were other small changes, ones I couldn't see but could feel, like the killing instincts that slumbered beneath my skin coming out to play.

Not the least bit afraid, Kieran leaned down and claimed my mouth with his, gold sparks dancing in his eyes when he pulled back. "I want to feel those claws running down my back later as I bury my cock inside you again."

"Have I ever told you that you're excellent at providing motivation?" I smirked before twisting off the window and letting myself fall, my clawed fingertips instantly finding purchase between the bricks. I tilted my head back as much as I could to meet Kieran's stare from where he was leaning out the window and shaking his head at me. "You better be naked when I get back."

He laughed quietly and continued to watch as I hugged the wall and quickly scaled down towards the ground. It'd been a while since I'd done this, but I used to all the time when I'd been a kid. My parents hadn't liked me roaming around at night, but I loved walking on the beach under a full moon, so I'd sneak out without them knowing.

Or try to.

More often than not, my mother would be waiting for me at the bottom of the tower, fighting back an amused grin while she tried to lecture me about the dangers of climbing down a tower wall. Then she'd take me on a moonlit ride.

Of course, back then, my chest had been considerably smaller. I should have wrapped my breasts tighter. Aside from being cumbersome and making it difficult to cling to the wall, they weren't exactly comfortable. As soon as my feet hit the ground, I gently placed my hands over my breasts while I silently apologized to them.

"What are you doing?" Alaric hissed in a low voice from where he was standing with Vail in the shadows.

"Apologizing to my tits for dragging them against the bricks for the last two minutes," I snapped back as quietly as I could, the two of us glaring at each other.

"I'd say fuck and get it over with, but you already did that," Vail grumbled. "We doing this or what?" He didn't wait for an answer, just strode off down the narrow passage that stretched between the main tower and two of the smaller ones.

Alaric started to follow after him, but my hand shot out, and I gripped his arm, letting my claws sink into his flesh. Not a flicker of pain appeared on his face as he took in my predatory black eyes. I knew he didn't like it when I let my bloodlust ride high like this because it reminded him of the cousin who had turned Strigoi when they had been kids. While I understood why he felt this way, I didn't agree with it. Our bloodlust made us stronger, and it could be controlled. Even Moroi who didn't belong to the House bloodlines could do so with careful practice. Alaric was deliberately inhibiting himself by denying his true nature.

"How does he know about us?" Alaric was hardly the type to kiss and tell, and he certainly wouldn't where I was concerned.

"There is no *us*," he growled and yanked his arm out of my grip. His rejection stung, but I refused to let him see that. Alaric clenched his jaw and looked away when I merely arched an eyebrow. "I ran into him after I left your study. He could smell you on me."

"Great." I blew out a breath. "Now he's going to be even more of an asshole." I let my claws shrink back into nails but didn't bother trying to pull my bloodlust back any more than that. This close to the House, it was unlikely there would be any nasty beasties, but it was still nighttime in Lunaria, so one could never be too careful.

Alaric huffed out a laugh. "Can we go now?"

"Lead the way." I gestured dramatically down the alleyway, and Alaric just rolled his eyes before stalking away. Vail had accused me of sleeping with both Kieran and Alaric before, and now he knew it was true. I didn't fully understand Vail's problem with me, but for someone who claimed to hate me, he acted awfully jealous of my lovers.

The Marshal of House Harker was waiting for us at the end of the passage. The sides of his head were freshly shaved, and he'd pulled his shoulder-length, brown hair back into a bun. He'd trimmed his beard back quite a bit and ditched the bones that he often braided into it. Only Vail could still look half-feral despite the cleaned-up appearance.

The silver streaks in his dark grey eyes glinted at my approach. He'd been avoiding me the last couple of days, Alaric having to track him down and inform him of this plan. While Alaric was unnerved by my eyes full of bloodlust, Vail's reaction was the slight flaring of his nostrils and a hard look at my neck. The silver in his eyes expanded before he turned away and flattened his hand on the outer wall, activating the glyph on it. A section large enough for us to pass through vanished from the thick stonework, and the three of us quickly slid through. Within seconds, the hole vanished, and the wall was once again solid.

It was a shame the Fae were gone, because their magic was truly extraordinary.

Not gone, I reminded myself. The wraiths were Unseelie, and now they were using that extraordinary magic of theirs to reclaim what they'd lost. At the cost of our lives.

"Let me scout it out first," Vail said from where we stood at the mouth of the cave. The entrance was enormous, towering far above us. Water rushed in, surging around the jagged rocks that broke the surface here and there. It was low tide, which would make things a little easier for us. Vail hesitated before glancing at me. "You remember the path we used on the right side?"

"Yes." I nodded. "My memory is a little foggy about where I saw that glyph, but I think it's behind the large, flat rock."

"Alright. Listen for my call, and then follow in after me." He slipped away into the darkness, the moonlight reflecting off the large sword strapped to his back. We'd never encountered any monsters when we'd explored the cave system as kids. Given its location on the beach and the tide rolling in and out, it wasn't particularly appealing to the beasts that roamed the woods.

"I forget sometimes . . . that you and Vail were friends," Alaric said quietly.

"Yeah." A bone-weary sigh slipped past my lips. "He was my first friend, really. You always hated me, and Kieran didn't show up until we were teenagers."

"I never hated you, Samara."

"Really?" My gaze cut to his, and I saw desperation and need in his eyes before he quickly turned away. Frustration filled me. Maybe it would be me pushing him into the seawater, but if I didn't ask him, I knew I'd regret it. "What do you feel for me, Alaric?"

Big surprise, he didn't answer. I rolled my eyes, lacking

the patience to deal with Alaric's bullshit right now, and returned my attention to the cave. Occasionally, I'd feel his attention on me and thought he might say something, but he never did. After a few minutes, Vail's sharp whistle cut through the air.

"Let's go." I headed towards the right side, watching my step as we moved from the sandy shore to the slick, algae-covered rocks. "Step where I step. This path was challenging a decade ago, and it's probably gotten worse. I really don't want to go for a swim tonight to save your ass if you fall in."

"You just don't want to get your hair covered in seawater," he sniped back.

I looked over my shoulder at the hair he kept closely cropped to his head. "You don't know what it's like to care for long hair. There's a bunch of algae and seaweed in the cave. I'd probably just cut my hair off rather than deal with the grossness of it."

"No," he said quickly.

"No?" I stopped and turned more to face him.

Alaric stared at me for a long moment, his lips pressed tightly together like he was debating something huge before finally saying, "I like your hair."

"You mean you liked having your hand fisted in it while I sucked your co—"

"Samara!" he growled. I laughed and resumed walking towards the path. He made it too easy.

Silvery beams of moonlight lit up the cavern, courtesy of the random holes in the ceiling. Vail and I used to stare at them and try to figure out what had caused them. Something about them didn't seem natural, but we'd never been able to figure out what.

Bioluminescent algae shimmered in the water as the waves rolled in. There wasn't much of it this time of year, but in late summer, the entire shoreline practically glowed an impossibly

A Court of Bones and Sorrow

bright blue. Right now, it was more like little gems sparkling in the dark.

After telling Alaric to be cautious, of course *I* was the one to slip on a loose rock while admiring the water. A strong arm wrapped around my midsection before he tugged me back against his warm chest.

"Careful," Alaric whispered in my ear. Then he flexed his fingers, his thumb brushing the underside of my breast before he stepped back.

I immediately mourned the loss of heat, even as I wanted to growl at him for being so indecisive. He wanted me, that was certain, but one minute he was determined to deny that feeling, and the next he was running his hands over my body.

Once again, I debated pushing him into the water. It'd serve him right.

With a frustrated exhale, I continued forward, being extra aware of where I was stepping. It didn't take long for Vail to come into view. The cavern basically went straight back before the rest of the tunnel plunged under the water. There wasn't actually that much to explore, it was just precarious to do so because the few rocks that rose above the water level were always damp and slippery. During high tide, it was impossible to get to the back without getting wet.

Vail waited for us on a large, circular, flat rock. It was the only part of the cavern that was never submerged. Just as I was about to jump from our path to join him, something below caught my attention, and I stopped to peer into the depths. The water directly in front of the rock Vail was standing on was cast in shadow, and it was difficult to see anything.

"Samara?" Alaric asked from behind me.

"I thought I saw something," I murmured, my eyes still scouring the water but finding nothing. "Maybe it was just some seaweed."

"Scared, Heir?" Vail taunted, and I glared at him before

launching myself across the open water to the large rock, Alaric landing gracefully behind me a second later.

I brushed past Vail and headed towards the back of the rock but couldn't resist looking up to the sky above us. This section of the cavern had the most damage to the ceiling. When we'd been kids, I would beg Vail to sneak out with me to come here at night. We'd lie on our backs and stare up at the stars while the waves crashed around the rocks beneath us. Vail would point out all the constellations to me, and I'd hang on his every word.

Then our parents had died, and everything had changed. I'd only come back here once after the night the wraiths had attacked and changed both our worlds forever. Part of me wanted to ask Vail if this was his first time returning to this cave since then, but I couldn't bring myself to utter the words.

"I remember it being somewhere back here. Be careful around the edges, Alaric," I said over my shoulder. "This rock doesn't extend entirely to the wall, so it's possible to fall through the crack."

The three of us started searching the cave wall for any sign of the glyph, but because of the constant moisture, algae grew in patches on the rocky surface, making it challenging to see what was beneath. I started running my fingers across the surface instead of relying only on my eyes. Even when glyphs were completely tapped out of magic, something about them still called to the magic in our blood.

Minutes ticked by, and I started to lose hope when I felt it, the slight tingle across my fingertips when they went over a rough patch of rock. I slid my dagger out of my thigh holster and scraped the algae aside, a triangle with three horizontal lines through it greeting me.

"Found it!" I called out.

Vail and Alaric moved towards me, but I didn't wait. I dragged the blade across the back of my hand and dipped my fingers into the blood that welled. Magic pulsed as I pressed my bloody fingertips against the glyph, a static charge filling the air. I barely felt it across my skin, but two pained grunts sounded from behind me.

"What the fuck was that?" Alaric cursed.

"I don't know," I said, frowning at the glyph. "It didn't hurt me though. I felt it brush across my skin, but that's it."

Before we could debate it more, the rocky surface shimmered and vanished. As soon as I stepped across the threshold, Fae lanterns blazed to life, painting the large room in a warm, soft glow. It wasn't nearly as big as the space I'd explored with Draven earlier, but it was more than the simple tunnel I'd been worried we'd find. The walls were lined with shelves, most empty . . . but not all.

I moved to a section that had several shelves full of books and carefully pulled one from the shelf. Just like in the previous room, no dust covered the leather-bound book. Whatever spell the Fae had used to keep this room clean was still working, along with the lanterns.

Alaric appeared at my side, pulling a different book from the shelf while Vail moved around somewhere behind me, but I couldn't pull my eyes from the page, not believing what I was seeing.

"This wasn't written by the Fae," I whispered.

"What?" Alaric's fingers froze mid-page flip.

I swallowed. "This is my mother's handwriting."

CHAPTER ELEVEN

Samara

"Your mother?" Alaric leaned closer to look at the book I held open with trembling hands. "What language is that?"

"Ours." Heat built behind my eyes, and I blinked several times to clear away the gathering tears. "My mother liked to use it for personal things she didn't want anyone else reading. She taught it to me."

Alaric glanced between my book and his. "The handwriting in this one is different. Look." He held the book out to me, and I compared the writing to my mother's. He was right. It was written in the same language, I recognized that, but the handwriting was completely different, and the pages looked older.

I carefully set my mother's book back onto the shelf and took the book from Alaric, flipping to the front. "Rosalyn Harker," I read the name out loud. "This is the journal of my ancestor. Rosalyn and her daughter were part of the original ritual that changed us from human to Moroi."

The Velesians and Furies had been born from the same ritual. We still didn't understand exactly how they'd done it or why there were three distinct branches of magic. All we knew was that the ritual had been connected to the moon, and that was why we considered ourselves Moon Blessed. Aside from that, we'd only been able to find part of the wording for the ritual.

"We will give our lives for the blood."
"We will yield our fates in the wild."
"We will lose our souls to the fury."

I hadn't realized Rosalyn had clawed back enough of her humanity to be able to write. Most of that first generation had been completely lost to their bloodlust. They had basically been Strigoi.

The small amount of writings we'd found from that time period suggested the House bloodlines had been the first to come back to themselves, but I didn't think it'd been to this extent. There were at least three dozen journals here. Did they belong to all the Harkers who had come before me? Why hadn't my mother ever told me about this place?

Metal groaned, and I winced when a particularly high-pitched sound echoed across the chamber.

"Sorry," Vail grunted from where he stood before a dark hallway. "This must be the tunnel that connects this room to the one you found earlier." He disappeared into the darkness, and I set the journal down on the shelf before wandering over to inspect the tunnel myself.

I had to step back when Vail appeared again, almost bumping into me. "It's completely caved in." He shook his head. "Unclear if it was an intentional cave-in or if it just happened on its own, but there's no getting through it now."

"Do you think it's worth clearing out?" I looked around him into the inky darkness. "It would give us an escape tunnel if we ever needed it, but it also means someone would have a way to sneak into House Harker."

"I'll think about it." Vail's stormy grey eyes once again fell to my neck, and I suddenly became aware of just how close I was standing to him. I took a small step back, and the silver bled through his eyes until they were like bright moons.

"You good?" I asked warily. Usually, the rangers were pretty good about wielding their bloodlust as a tool. It was rare for any of them to turn Strigoi, but that didn't mean they didn't occasionally lose control for small amounts of time, like Vail had in the temple. My fingers slid down to rest on the handle of the dagger at my thigh.

Vail's gaze dipped down to the blade, and his lips curled in distaste. "Like I would ever want the taste of your blood in my mouth again." He stalked forward, forcing me to jump out of his way, even as a dull ache rose inside my chest. Apparently, being back in this cave didn't bring back fond memories of our friendship for him the way it did for me.

I tucked away the pain of Vail's words—I really should have been used to it by now—and walked over to where Alaric was studying something on the wall. Vail stopped to stand at Alaric's right, so I stood by his left, needing some space between me and the Marshal.

"Map of Lunaria," I murmured. Though calling it a map was a bit of an exaggeration. Someone had scraped landmarks into the stone wall. I recognized Drudonia at the center and some other landmarks, but it was rudimentary at best. We had far better maps than this.

Vail stepped forward and brushed two fingers against a marking that looked like an *X*. Now that I'd noticed that one, more jumped out at me.

"Someone was looking for something, and they didn't want anyone to know about it." I glanced over my shoulder at the shelves where the journals rested. "I don't think it was the Fae."

"Where is this?" Alaric pointed to what looked like a lake with a circle around it.

The three of us leaned in closer to examine the markings.

"If that's Drudonia"—Vail pointed to the blocky buildings that looked like a fortress—"then the only large body of water there is Lake Malov."

I chewed on my bottom lip. "What if there is another secret room like this one around there? Maybe that's what whoever made this map was searching for?" I suspected it had been my mother, but what I didn't understand was why she had been keeping it a secret, and did Carmilla know about this?

"Do we care?" Alaric stepped back and crossed his arms. "While I acknowledge that all of this is fascinating, we have some more pressing concerns."

"Agreed," Vail said. "This feels like a waste of time."

"We don't know that," I argued. "Generations of Harkers kept this place a secret. They wouldn't have done that for nothing." My mother wouldn't have done that for nothing. My throat seized as I thought about her sneaking down here and writing in that journal. Had she been planning on telling me eventually? Maybe this would have been something she passed down to me? Part of the Harker legacy. Unfortunately, death claimed her first. "Let me read through some of the journals. Maybe there is something in them that explains this." I waved at the wall.

"However you want to waste your time isn't my problem." Vail shrugged.

"Helpful as always," I snapped. "Where's the bag you brought?"

He flicked his fingers towards the entryway we'd passed through from the cave, which was once again solid. I stalked over to the leather bag lying on the ground. It wouldn't fit all the journals, but I could bring at least half a dozen back with me. Alaric joined me as I debated which ones to grab.

My mother's were definitely the most recent and the likeliest to have relevant information. My heart clenched at the idea of reading her words and getting a glimpse into what she'd been feeling. I checked through the bottom shelf and figured out where her journals started. There were five of them, which I carefully stuffed into the sack before eying the shelf.

It was unlikely Rosalyn had written anything that would help us, but I couldn't resist knowing. I grabbed the first journal on the shelf and placed it with the others before adjusting the strap of the bag on my shoulder.

"Do you think we should come back later for the rest?" I asked no one in particular.

"They're probably safer here than anywhere else," Alaric said. "No one knows about this place, and if Draven goes back to that room the two of you found and tries to use the passage, he'll find it blocked."

I couldn't argue with that logic, even if I didn't love the idea of leaving the rest of the journals here, but if I asked Vail to have some of his rangers guard this place, that would only draw attention to it. The journals had been here for multiple generations, so unless I came up with a better solution, I'd just have to trust that they'd continue to be safe in this room.

"Let's head back." I gave one last reluctant look at the rest of the journals before activating the glyph on the wall again and slipping back into the cave. Now that I knew where the glyph on this side was located, I felt like it would be obvious to anyone.

As if reading my mind, Vail rapped his knuckles against the damp rock. "This type of algae grows fast. That glyph will be covered again in less than a day."

I nodded. Vail might be an asshole to me, but he knew what he was talking about. The only one who had a reason to visit this cave was Draven, and that was only if he tried to map out where the escape tunnel might lead to. Yet another reason for us to keep an extra close eye on him. I couldn't let him find those journals. It was unlikely he'd be able to understand the language, but he'd almost certainly remove them.

A warning whispered across my skin, my instincts picking up on something while I'd been lost in thought, and I halted halfway to the path that led out of the cave. Vail instantly went still beside me, but Alaric continued walking, oblivious to the danger that had crept in while we'd been examining the hidden room.

"Alaric," I said in a low but commanding tone. He froze where he'd been about to jump across to the rocky path before slowly taking a few steps back.

Clouds must have rolled in recently, because the previously moonlit cave was now shadowed in darkness. Only the flat rock we stood on was still mostly lit up, and even that light was filtering in and out.

Something was moving in the shadows. A lot of somethings.

"Vail?" My fingers wrapped around the dagger as I slid it free. It was the only weapon I had with me. Swords had never been my strong suit—I was much better with ranged weapons but hadn't bothered bringing a crossbow because it wouldn't have been that useful here. Now I was kind of wishing I had. If I threw my dagger, I'd have nothing.

"Not sure," Vail murmured, his silver eyes tracking the movement across the walls. "I think whatever they are, they came from the sea. They're moving . . . strangely."

Great. We'd managed to find a monster even Vail hadn't come across. Alaric made his way back to my side, a wicked, cruel dagger in his hand. Of the three of us, he was the most disadvantaged, because he suppressed his bloodlust so ruthlessly. Aside from our fangs and claws only making an appearance when we let our bloodlust rise, we were also stronger and faster when we leaned into it.

Frustration warred with concern inside me. If Alaric got

himself hurt because of his stubbornness, I'd beat the shit out of him later.

The hair rose on the back of my neck, and I sidestepped so my back was to Vail and looked at the wall behind us. "Fuck. It. All." My heart raced as I watched dozens of creatures silently crawl down the rocky surface from where they'd been traveling across the ceiling. They vaguely resembled the occasional starfish I'd find while walking along the shore, which would be fine . . . except for the six eyes arranged in a perfect circle and the eight serpentine tentacles that stretched out.

"Can someone explain why the fucking starfish look like spiders?" Alaric cursed.

"Because Lunaria, that's why. Of course we'd have fucked-up arachnid starfish." I glanced up at the ceiling, which was teeming with hundreds of them. "If these things fall on us, I'm going to scream."

I wasn't kidding. There were a lot of things I could deal with. Spiders were not one of them.

"We make our way to the same path as before," Vail said calmly. "Samara, take the lead. Alaric in the middle. I'll cover you both."

"I should go first." Alaric glared at Vail. "Samara is the Heir of House Harker."

"Samara can handle herself just fine," Vail growled.

"Or maybe you're thinking third time's the charm in getting her killed?" Alaric narrowed his eyes at Vail, who was looking at the leaner-built Moroi like he was debating chucking him into the water as bait while we got away.

"It's fine, Alaric." I placed a hand on his forearm, and he glanced at where we were touching before meeting my gaze, a sharp, close-lipped smile stretching across my face. "I'd rather have you at my back anyway."

Vail stiffened, but before he could say anything, I stepped towards the path, my gaze bouncing between the wall writhing with monsters and the slippery rocks. Now was really *not* the time to fall.

I slid to the side just as the air shifted, and a creature slammed into the rock where I'd been standing a second ago. It landed on its back, giving me a view of the center of its underbelly, where five triangular teeth mashed together in its circular mouth. I barely managed to bite back my shriek. Its nearly two-foot-long tentacles slid across the ground, and it started to flip itself over. As soon as its back was to me and the tentacles were pointed in the opposite direction, I kicked out as hard as I could.

A loud splash sounded from where it had landed, but I could hardly make out the rocks two feet in front of me. The rest of the cavern was nothing but inky blackness. Sure would be nice for the moon to come back right about now.

The sound of hundreds of tentacles sliding across the algae-covered wall echoed around us, and I stepped closer to the edge of the rock. Slender tentacles stretched out from the wall towards me, and three more fell from the ceiling around us. I raised the strap of the bag over my head so that it rested diagonally across my chest before tucking the dagger back into the holster on my thigh.

More monsters fell from the ceiling, and one of them hit my shoulder and bounced off, its tentacles grazing my skin. Alaric hissed behind me as several of the starfish critters began to fall on the other side. I'd be jumping straight into them, but right now, there were only half a dozen on the ground. We needed to go before all of them fell off the ceiling.

I backed up a few steps, bumping into Alaric, then ran towards the edge and leapt across, but something wrapped around my ankle just before my feet hit the other side and yanked me back. My scream was cut off as my upper body slammed into the rocky ledge before I was dragged backwards. Tentacles grabbed me from all sides as I desperately dug in with my clawed fingers, trying to find purchase, but the rock was too hard and slick.

"Vail!" I cried as I went over the edge. Water splashed below as several starfish lost their grip on me and fell. Every muscle in my body screamed as my fingers gripped the edge of the rock. Whatever was wrapped around my ankle pulled harder, and pain raced down my arm as one of the smaller monsters wrapped all of its tentacles around me and flattened its circular mouth full of sharp teeth against my bicep.

My fingers started to slip when another tentacle wrapped around my waist, and I felt something pull on the bag. "VAIL!"

Two sets of hands gripped my arms, Alaric grunting where he was flat on his stomach above me, hands wrapped around my left forearm while Vail held my right arm, bright silver eyes shining with determination. "Don't look down."

A low, trembling, keening sound came from beneath me, and I couldn't help but look. Never in my life had I ever so immensely regretted disobeying a command. A shriek tore from my lungs. "Pull me up! Pull me up!"

"We're trying!" Vail ground out.

The enormous, spidery starfish beneath me pulled harder. It had to be at least twenty feet wide, and its eyes glowed a sickly yellow. I could feel something cutting into my skin where its tentacles had wrapped around me, and pained whimpers slipped from my throat. The rock to my right shook as it slammed another tentacle there, and I saw the flash of small, curved barbs on the underside.

Just when I thought things couldn't get worse, the starfish clinging to the ceiling started to drop even more. Alaric's and Vail's grips slipped, and I dropped another inch. "I don't want to get eaten by a fucking starfish!"

"Don't let go!" Alaric ordered. Several starfish chose that exact moment to fall on his back, and he bellowed, fingers digging into me as he tried to hold on. Vail hissed when one fell on his shoulder and latched onto his flesh.

"I've got her," Vail growled. "Keep these fucking things off us. Otherwise, we're all going to die here!"

"Fuck!" Alaric bellowed, tearing himself away to deal with the monsters ripping into him and Vail. The loss of his grip on my arm sent me swinging, and Vail's claws dug into my arm, skin tearing as I was wrenched into an awkward angle. The tentacle around my right ankle was pulling me to the side, while the one around the bag was pulling straight down.

My body pivoted until I was looking down at the beast once more. Terror drenched me at the small bulges moving across its body, unfurling their tentacles before gliding off into the water. That must have been how they'd all gotten here. This was their mother, and she'd carried them on her back.

Blood ran down my arm from where Vail held onto me. Despite his efforts, his grip had slipped to my wrist, and I knew he couldn't hold on much longer. I gritted my teeth and swung my free hand towards the dagger on my thigh, agony shooting through my back. It felt like I was being torn in two, but I freed the blade from its sheath.

I had one chance. If I missed, I would fall. To fall was to die.

Vail grunted as the creature pulled harder on my ankle. I used the momentum of being twisted to the side to my advantage and focused on the closest of the large, yellow eyes. The weak point. No matter the beast, eyes were something to be protected.

"Get ready, Vail." I panted before flipping the dagger in my hand and hurling it a second later. It whistled through the air, the spinning blade catching the small patches of moonlight and reflecting them back before sinking home, straight into the starfish's eye.

Water churned as the tentacled beast thrashed and the

tentacle around my ankle slipped away. Vail heaved me up, but I only made it halfway before the tentacle around the bag tightened and pulled me back down.

"Slip the bag off!" Vail commanded.

"No!" I screamed. We needed the information in these journals, and they had belonged to my mother. I couldn't let this part of her go, not without knowing what it meant.

"Damn it, Sam!" Vail clung to me, desperately trying to pull me up. "It's not worth your life!"

The strap snapped, and I barely managed to grab hold of the leather bag before it fell into the water. The tentacle around it tightened while another one tried to pry the dagger out of its eye.

"So fucking stubborn." Silver flashed inches from my face before a blade sunk into the tentacle gripping the bag. The dark, rubbery appendage flinched but didn't let go. Another dagger. Another twitch. Two more daggers joined the others before the beast finally decided this amount of pain and effort wasn't worth it. Water thrashed below as the starfish pulled back its tentacle and retreated further into the water.

A deep vibration I felt in my bones erupted throughout the cavern as Vail pulled me up and the smaller starfish slid towards the edge of the rock before falling into the water. The starfish still making a meal out of my bicep was ripped off, but in my pained haze, I barely noticed. Rough hands yanked me forward, dragging me as I clutched the bag and my shredded arm to my chest.

My ankle didn't feel like it was in much better shape, and by the time we made it to the sandy beach just outside the cave, I was barely capable of limping. I collapsed, my trembling muscles finally giving out, and I pulled aside what was left of my shredded pants to examine the damage . . . and immediately regretted it.

"Fuck," I hissed as I saw white bone peeking through the

ripped flesh. I was lucky I hadn't lost my damn foot, because those barbs ripped entire chunks out. Clenching my jaw, I stretched my hand towards the wound to draw the healing glyph, but large fingers wrapped around mine before pulling them back.

"I'll do it," Vail practically growled at me. Apparently, he was still pissed, which was fine. I was used to Vail being pissed at me.

He reached over his shoulder and rubbed his back where the freaky little starfish had fallen on him. His fingers came back bloody. I winced as he drew the healing glyph on a small patch of mostly undamaged skin. The burning, itchy sensation was immediate, and I let out a low hiss, turning my head away from the bloody disaster that was my lower leg.

Alaric gave me a flat look as he knelt beside me. "You should have let go of that fucking bag," he said coldly. Vail grunted in agreement as he looked over the rest of my leg.

"I—"

"Shut the fuck up, Sam," Alaric snarled, and I snapped my mouth shut. I didn't regret what I'd done, so I wasn't going to argue with him or Vail over it. The two of them could just be pissy together. My leg jerked involuntarily as some of the muscles pieced themselves back together. The healing spell might have been incredibly useful and sometimes lifesaving, but it fucking hurt.

Even worse, as the adrenaline continued to wear off, I could feel the rest of the smaller wounds spread over my body. I held my forearm out in front of me and grimaced at the deep grooves Vail's claws had left behind while he'd been clinging to me.

With more tenderness than I thought him capable of, Alaric grasped my arm and tugged it towards him, resting the back of my hand in his palm as he drew the healing glyph right below my elbow. Technically, once the healing glyph was drawn on a body, it would heal all wounds, but it always started with the closest ones.

My breaths came out in rapid bursts as the two healing glyphs worked in tandem. A distraction. That's what I needed. Vail was still busy examining me for any other major wounds that needed immediate attention, which I was a little surprised he cared about but was not willing to bring it up and get into it with him. Instead, I focused on Alaric, who had settled back into a crouching position after starting the healing on my arm.

Dozens of wounds covered his arms, ranging from shallow to alarming based on how much blood was still dripping out of them. Chunks of his tunic had been torn away, and I could see more bite wounds on his chest.

"Come here," I said firmly. Alaric glared at me for a moment before leaning forward again. I brushed my fingers across some wet blood on my arm and pulled his tunic down, revealing more of his chest. He wasn't nearly as large and muscular as Vail, but Alaric was in excellent shape. Like Kieran, he sparred regularly with the rangers and found it relaxing to go on daily runs.

Personally, I only ran if my life was on the line.

I felt his heavy stare on me as I traced the glyph over his heart. It was the best solution when there were multiple wounds like this and none were life-threatening. Our natural healing was impressive, and we could survive almost any wound as long as our heads remained attached and the blood loss wasn't too severe, but it was nowhere near as fast as the healing glyph and could only fix wounds inflicted by non-magic means.

Alaric winced before leaning back and closing his eyes as the magic coursed through his body, and I frowned when he looked on the verge of passing out. While he had a lot of wounds, none of them looked particularly serious. Our blood was necessary to initiate the glyph, but the magic behind the healing spell basically used the magic within our body, just at an accelerated rate. It was why, in life-threatening situations, an injured Moroi was usually given blood to drink as well.

"Here." I stretched my mostly uninjured arm out to Alaric. Every part of me ached, and I was pretty sure I would pass out any second, but he looked worse than me. "Drink."

Alaric reeled back like I'd struck him and leapt to his feet, swaying slightly before stiffening his back. "Absolutely not."

"Don't be a stubborn ass!" I snapped. "It's just blood, Alaric. You clearly need it."

"I'm fine," he ground out, even as turquoise bled through his green eyes as he stared hungrily at my still extended arm. Realizing what he was doing, he tore his gaze away and spun around, stalking away from me. "Get her back safely, Vail."

"Alaric!" I called after him, but he ignored me and kept walking. It wasn't that long of a trip back to House Harker, just down the beach a quarter mile before cutting up a trail. The chances of him running into anything nasty between here and there were slim . . . but I also hadn't expected to find terrifying, spider-like starfish in that fucking cave.

Arachnistar? Arachstar? Starachi?

As far as I was concerned, since I'd found them, I got to name them. I'd have to think of something good. Hopefully they wouldn't make that cave their new home. Otherwise, getting back into that room would not be fun. Then again, they would make an excellent deterrent for anyone who tried to explore the cave . . .

Vail stood up, apparently satisfied that I had no other wounds that required immediate attention. I struggled to my feet and sucked in a breath as aching muscles barked at me. The skin on my arm and leg was smooth and unblemished, but it still felt like my body had been through a meat grinder. I pursed my lips as I stared at the long stretch of beach before us. This would not be a pleasant walk back. I had no idea how I was going to climb back into my room either.

That was a problem for future Samara. For now, I set out at a slow but steady pace. Vail trailed silently behind me, and it set my teeth on edge not being able to see him but knowing he was there all the same. I made it two minutes before I snapped.

"Can you please just walk beside me?"

He sighed and moved to my side, and I started walking again, fighting the blackness that was starting to encroach on my vision. Just ten more minutes on this beach, another ten-minute hike up a fairly steep hill, then all I had to do was scale up the tower wall that led to my bedroom.

Piece of cake.

"Should have just slept in that room," I muttered, and Vail laughed under his breath. It had a deep, raspy quality to it. He might be a Moroi, but Vail's voice had always reminded me of a wolf shifter with its gravelly edge. "I'm glad we didn't run into those things as kids," I said lightly, checking his expression from the corner of my eye.

Vail liked to pretend our childhood friendship hadn't existed, but for once, he didn't bite my head off. Instead, a rueful smile played across his lips. "That definitely would have put a damper on our stargazing. Plus, your screaming was a lot higher-pitched back then. Would have blown out my eardrums."

"Ass." I shoved his shoulder, but the movement proved too much for my body when everything went dark for a second. The world tilted, and suddenly, my head was leaning against something warm and hard. I blinked several times, trying to bring the world back into focus, but ended up peering into Vail's face.

"Rest, Samara." His gaze flickered down to mine before quickly pulling away. "I've got you."

"Please don't feed me to the monsters," I mumbled before

burrowing further against his chest. "You've had three chances to kill me now and failed each time. Is this your way of saying you like me again?"

"Sam?"

"Yes?" I answered sleepily.

"Shut up."

The world went black.

CHAPTER TWELVE

Vail

SAMARA'S EYELIDS FLUTTERED RAPIDLY. She'd been dreaming for the last hour, and I had yet to figure out if it was a good or bad dream. Her midnight black hair was fanned out across my bed, and she'd been snuggling into my pillows and blankets since I'd laid her here hours ago.

I'd only hesitated for a moment last night before bringing her back to my room. She'd passed out hard, her body shutting down so it could finish healing. The wound on her leg hadn't smelled right when I'd been examining it. I couldn't say for sure, but I suspected there'd been some type of toxin in the barbs of that fucking gigantic starfish. Luckily the smaller ones had yet to develop those barbs; otherwise, all three of us would have been in serious trouble. As it was, Samara had taken the worst of it.

An echo of the fear I'd felt when she'd been dangling off that rock ledge raced through me, followed quickly by rage at remembering how she'd refused to let go of that fucking bag. Not for the first time, I wished Samara had never returned to House Harker. It'd been easy to hate her when she'd been

A Court of Bones and Sorrow

gone, playing the dutiful wife at House Laurent, but that piece of shit Demetri just had to fuck things up.

My fingers clenched into fists, and I felt my nails harden enough to bite into my skin. I'd thrown the failed marriage in Samara's face when she'd come back. It had been an asshole thing to do, even by my standards, but Samara always took my hatred in stride, which only pissed me off more.

No matter what I did, she never broke.

The blanket slipped down as Samara rolled onto her side, burrowing further into the pillow and letting out a breathy sigh. Satisfaction rolled over me at seeing her in one of my shirts, and my mood instantly soured. I didn't like Samara at all and definitely not like *that*. It was just an instinctual response I'd have to any beautiful woman in my bed wearing my clothing.

Covered in my scent.

Fuck. My nostrils flared, and I stalked over to the window. Unlike Samara, I didn't have a large suite. My living quarters only consisted of a bedroom and a small washroom. Carmilla had repeatedly offered me a place in the main tower that had larger and fancier accommodations, but I preferred to be in the barracks with the rest of the rangers.

Samara's spicy and intoxicating scent intertwined with my own drifted over, and I squeezed my eyes shut. I couldn't fucking escape her.

Moroi were possessive. We might have lax views when it came to sex, but once we claimed a long-term partner, we were ruthless about it. There were exceptions, but polyamorous relationships were far more common amongst the Velesians. It was why I found Samara's relationship with Kieran and Roth so confusing. And I'd always known Alaric had a thing for her too despite his attempts to hide it.

More often than not, I found Alaric Lockwood irritating to deal with, but I still had a begrudging respect for him. He was incredibly smart and used his brains to help House Harker instead of the social ladder climbing many of the higher-ranking officials attempted. And now he and I had something in common: we were both struggling to deal with our shifting emotions when it came to Samara.

The anger I felt towards her was still there. Always burning under my skin. The night all our parents had been attacked—the night they'd died—I'd gotten Samara to safety, and when I'd tried to go back and help my parents, Samara had knocked me out. She claimed she'd done it to save my life, but I knew that was bullshit. She just hadn't wanted to be left alone. It was her life she'd been worried about. No one else's.

In the months and years after that night, I'd never seen Samara cry once. She acted like the death of her parents didn't matter and had obsessed over House politics instead. It didn't take her long to secure an advantageous marriage. She'd gone to Drudonia to study and then flittered off to House Laurent to be yet another pampered Heir.

Carmilla had tried to make excuses for Samara's behavior to me, but more than once, she'd confessed she wasn't comfortable grieving her sister around Samara because of how little her niece seemed to care. While Samara had been away, it'd been easy to believe the worst about her, and that hadn't changed after she'd returned.

It was why I'd left her to die when that kùsu had attacked us weeks ago. When the long, insectoid beast had slid between us, its pinchers snapping in excitement at finding its prey, I'd felt a savage relief. Like Samara had been getting what she was owed for costing me everything.

Then I'd seen the flash of betrayal on her face before she turned and raced away from the monster. Away from me. An almost blind panic had overtaken me as I'd chased after her to fix what I had done, to save her, and I had, barely getting there in time but saving her all the same. She knew what I had done though, and now it lay there like an ugly truth between us.

Now I had to live with this simmering hatred and also the memory of how much she'd once meant to me. Samara had been my only real friend growing up. There'd been nothing romantic there, we'd been far too young for that, but the friendship . . . it'd been real.

As soon as we had set foot in that cavern last night, the memories had come flooding back. Us sneaking out under the always watchful eyes of our parents. Laughing as we ran across the beach. Carefully climbing those rocks until we collapsed onto our backs and watched the stars flickering across the sky.

I hadn't just lost my parents the night the wraiths had attacked our caravan. I'd also lost my best friend.

Now that best friend had grown up into the most beautiful woman I'd ever seen and was sleeping in my bed. *In my fucking shirt.*

Blood dripped from my knuckles, and I forced myself to take a slow, deep breath while I unclenched my fists. I wanted to leave, go into the wilds for a few months, hunt some monsters, and clear my head. However, now that we knew Prince Draven, and likely the Sovereign House, was involved with the wraiths, I couldn't leave. Not that I was particularly useful—subterfuge and subtleness were not in my skill set.

The inability to act was killing me, and there were brief moments when I thought about just slitting the prince's throat and dumping his body in the ocean for the sea monsters to feed on. That wouldn't solve anything though and would only draw the attention of that Fae we saw in the temple, Erendriel, and, of course, the Moroi Queen herself. I might not be good at playing this bullshit political game, but even I knew that would be foolish.

Adding to my frustrations was the fact that Carmilla was at the Sovereign House and, as far as I was concerned, in the hands of our enemies, even if she didn't know it. Growing up, Carmilla had been like an aunt to me. When my parents had died, she'd stepped in as both mother and father, ensuring I had someone to talk to and supporting me as I rose through the ranger ranks to take up the mantle of Marshal.

I didn't have any blood relatives left, so Carmilla was basically my only family. After everything she'd done for me, I couldn't let anything happen to her.

Samara stirred again on the bed, drawing my attention. I scowled at her before silently walking over to my washroom and rinsing the blood from my hands. The wounds had already healed, but I could feel the undercurrent of exhaustion in my bones.

I needed to consume blood. Soon.

Like most adult Moroi, I associated drinking blood with sex, but since I was the Marshal, I wasn't comfortable sleeping with any of the other rangers because of the difference in power. More than a few had made passes at me, but I'd always turned them down. Instead, I had some regular partners in various outposts who were more than happy to let me bury my fangs in their flesh while I fucked them senseless. It was a good arrangement that left everyone happy.

Even some of the Velesians I knew were game, although their blood wasn't as fulfilling as another Moroi's. We might all be Moon Blessed, but the magic between the three groups was different enough that it didn't always play nicely together.

Plus I couldn't leave to visit any of them now. I frowned at my now healed palm. Maybe I could ask Adrienne or Emil, two of my most trusted rangers. Not for the sex part, just a little top up of blood. I couldn't afford to be slower or weaker right now.

Just as I was about to step back into the bedroom, a low, throaty moan slipped from Samara's lips. I froze in the doorway. *You've got to be fucking kidding me.* Was she having a damn dirty dream in my bed? I watched as Samara twisted around in the bed, more of the blankets slipping away. The way she was lying caused my shirt to pull tight around her full breasts, giving me a full view of her erect nipples pushing against the fabric.

Then she let out another breathy noise that went straight to my dick.

I'd faced countless monsters in my life. Wraiths. Howlers. Kùsu. Every single one of those encounters I'd survived because I never hesitated.

Yet I had no fucking clue what to do at this moment.

Should I wake her up? That wouldn't be awkward at all. Her moaning turned into quickened breaths as one of her hands started to slip beneath the covers.

Oh, fuck me.

I rubbed a hand roughly against my beard. Leave. That was the best option, because if Samara ever learned of this, she wouldn't be embarrassed. Instead, she'd tease me about it mercilessly, and my feelings for her were complicated enough as it was. I'd just wait outside until she was . . . finished.

Angry banging sounded on the door before I'd made it halfway across the room. Samara bolted upright in bed, her cheeks flushed, and looked around in confusion. Her dark purple eyes landed on me, and her brows furrowed. She glanced down and plucked at the light tan shirt before looking back at me in question.

More banging came from the door.

"Vail!" Kieran yelled. "What the fuck are you doing?"

Samara leapt from the bed and raced to the door while I stood there like an idiot. She flipped the lock and yanked the door open, grabbed Kieran by the front of his tunic, and pulled him inside. He stumbled a few steps before catching himself while she closed the door and crossed her arms.

"Could you be any louder, Kieran? Or did you forget we're trying *not* to draw the attention of Draven?"

"I didn't know where you were!" he said urgently, barely managing to keep his voice down as he glowered at me. If he expected me to tremble before him, he was dumber than I'd thought. I had at least six inches on him and outweighed him by quite a bit. The bright turquoise and gold outfit he was wearing really didn't help the intimidation factor either.

I gave the pretty peacock a flat stare. *Honestly, what does Samara see in him?*

"Alaric told me what happened and that you were with Vail. He said you were fine and then passed out on the settee," Kieran explained as he gave up on staring me down and looked Samara over instead. His eyes widened when he took in what she was wearing. "Why are you in his shirt?" he demanded.

"Oh, this old thing?" she drawled as she twirled the edges of the shirt that dangled by her mid-thigh, and I looked away as it lifted up. "You'd have to ask him."

Kieran whirled around to face me, and for a second, I thought he might punch me. "Try it." I shrugged. "Could use a good laugh."

He actually took a step forward, but Samara was there in an instant, standing between us with her hands on his chest. "How about we use our words instead of our fists?" Kieran looked like he'd bit into something sour but wrapped his arms around Samara when she twisted so her back was against his chest. I kept my eyes focused on hers, refusing to let them drop to where Kieran's arms were now resting across her stomach. "Care to fill us in on what happened last night? All I remember is walking back on the beach with you, and then . . . you caught me when I fell."

"The barbs in those giant tentacles had some type of venom. Probably something to neutralize prey. You passed out, so I carried you back." I crossed my arms. "It was pretty clear you weren't making that climb back into your room, so I figured the barracks were the best place for you to sleep it off."

"So you just stripped her down when she was unconscious?" Kieran looked at me coldly.

"You're lucky she's here—otherwise, I'd break your jaw for what you're implying." My arms dropped to my sides and my fingers curled as I imagined grabbing him by the neck and slamming his head into the wall. "She was covered in dried blood and her clothes were torn to shreds. As soon as I got her into my room, I retrieved Adrienne. *She* was the one who cleaned Samara up. We used my shirt because it's large and baggy and agreed it would be most comfortable for her to sleep in. I slept on the floor."

Samara's eyes cut to the small space between the bed and wall. "You didn't have to do that," she said softly.

I shifted on my feet. "It's fine. I've slept in worse conditions." Her eyes lingered on me, and the discomfort I'd been feeling only increased. I could deal with Samara when she was annoyed or frustrated at me. I could even tolerate her when she was being obnoxious and flirty, but when she looked at me like she genuinely cared about my well-being . . .

"I've wasted too much time babysitting you," I growled. "Your pretty boy can fetch you other clothes. Close my door when you leave."

Before she could argue, I brushed past the two of them and fled into the hallway, and as soon as the door closed behind me, I let out a deep breath.

"Went that well, huh?" a bright, cheery, feminine voice asked.

"Adrienne," I groaned. "It's too early for your bullshit."

The blonde ranger fell into step beside me. She was tall for a woman, only a couple of inches below six feet, but I still towered over her. As the Marshal, I was in charge of all the rangers who belonged to House Harker, but I also had my own unit who traveled with me regularly. Adrienne had been part of that unit since the beginning, so I knew her well. Everything about her reminded me of sunshine. It should have been annoying, but somehow, it just worked for her.

"The sun has been up for hours," she pointed out. "I got here five minutes ago because I was worried Samara might have murdered you for being a prick."

"And you were going to avenge me?" I slid a glance at her.

"Fuck no." She laughed. "Was gonna help her hide the body."

"Your loyalty could use some work," I grunted.

Adrienne gave me a wide-eyed look. "She's the Heir of House Harker. Who else could I possibly be loyal to?" Thick eyelashes blinked rapidly over her bright blue eyes, where only the faintest lines of gold could be seen.

"I'm gonna tell Emil to pummel you in sparring today."

She grinned wickedly. "Please, I could beat that old man with one arm tied behind my back."

We both knew that was bullshit. Emil was older—he was one of the only fourth-generation Moroi who was still an active ranger. Despite being in his late eighties, he still looked and acted like he was in his forties. Even I had a hard time bringing Emil down. As good as Adrienne was, she was still nowhere near Emil's level.

But he had a soft spot for her, so he always went a little easy on her.

We traded barbs back and forth, and some of the tension eased out of me. A few rangers passed us and waved in greeting, but most were already outside or still sleeping if they'd been on night shift. We reached the stairs at the end of the hall and headed down. The barracks were a long, rectangular building that had four levels above ground and two underneath. We weren't sure what the Fae had used the building for, but the original rooms had been much larger before it had been repurposed for the rangers. Now the rooms were small but comfortable with a mix of singles and doubles. There were a few large enough for six or more, as visiting rangers from other Houses sometimes preferred to bunk together.

"Anything to report?" I asked as we stepped out into the bright, midmorning sun. Emil might be a better fighter, but Adrienne was more skilled at dealing with people, so she served as my right-hand. If she ever needed advice, she'd go to Emil. The arrangement had worked well for us for years.

"One of the units is back from investigating some type of burrowing creature on the badlands border. I think you'll be interested in what they have to say." Something about her tone gave me pause, like she was amused, but if she hadn't said it outright, then there was no convincing her to say it now. I'd just have to speak to the rangers and see what they had to say. "Also . . . Nyx has decided they're fully recovered, and they are currently in the sparring ring."

"It's been a week," I said slowly. "They were healed days ago."

"That wraith broke over a dozen bones in their body, including some of the vertebrae in their spine." She clenched her jaw as her cheeriness faded. We were all protective of Nyx because they were like a younger sibling to us, but neither I nor Emil had any actual siblings. Adrienne had a younger brother who had died when they'd been teenagers. I didn't know the specifics of it, only that it was one of the reasons she'd left her original House and came to Harker. "They should take another week off."

"Adrienne." I stopped and waited until she faced me. "Nyx is fine. They're frustrated that the wraith got the jump on them." The sound of bones snapping echoed through my mind as I remembered Nyx slamming into that wall at the temple. It was Samara who'd made sure Nyx got out. She'd prioritized the young ranger over her own safety. It was a surprising move for the Heir of a House. Foolish even.

Yet it had thawed a little more of my hatred towards her.

"Emil will make sure Nyx takes it easy." I rested a hand on Adrienne's shoulder. "And I'll make sure they don't go out on any missions any time soon."

"No missions without my approval," Adrienne pushed. "And they have to go with you, me, or Emil."

"Okay," I agreed, my lips twitching as I fought back a smile I knew she'd punch me for. "But try to limit your hovering. Nyx's confidence in their abilities is in the shitter, and you being a mother hen isn't going to help with that."

She slapped my hand off her shoulder. "I'm going back to my babysitting duties. Not that Roth ever leaves their room." Adrienne frowned. "Actually, maybe I'll stop in the kitchen and grab them something. They didn't eat any of their dinner last night." My lips curved upwards. "I'm not a mother hen!" Adrienne yelled before stalking off in the direction of the main tower, and I laughed under my breath at her retreating form.

"She's a fiery one."

For the second time this morning, I froze, the prince strolling up to stand beside me. It'd been a long time since someone had been able to sneak up on me. Adrienne and I had stopped in one of the small alleyways that led between the barracks and one of the smaller towers. Sound tended to echo against the stone walls, and yet I hadn't heard a single footstep.

"Draven." I didn't bother making my tone friendly. Adrienne and I had been talking quietly enough before her outburst that I was certain he hadn't overheard anything. She would have seen him if he'd been behind me, which meant he'd been lurking somewhere nearby and waiting for her to leave. "Something I can help you with?"

"Not going to fawn all over me the way everyone else does?" He smirked.

"No." For once, I wished Samara were here. She was clever with her words and would have no problem conversing with the traitor. Meanwhile, I was struggling not to bury my dagger in his gut.

"Man of few words." His blue eyes glinted with amusement. "I find that rather refreshing."

"I'm happy for you." I started walking. "You'll have to find someone else to entertain you though. I've got things to do."

"Is Samara one of them? She stayed in your room last night." Moonsdamn it. I stopped and slowly turned back around. "Although . . ." He tapped a finger against his chin. "She was with Kieran early on in the night, and she didn't leave her room through the door. Only other option was the window." Draven cocked his head and suddenly looked less like the charming, harmless prince and more like a cruel predator. "Does Kieran know she's going behind his back to fuck you?"

There was an edge to his voice I didn't quite understand. It sounded like he was more concerned about Kieran than anyone else. If I denied sleeping with Samara, he might wonder why else she would have snuck out of her room. Fuck.

"Kieran is aware of our relationship," I ground out. "But given her role as Heir and mine as Marshal, we prefer to keep things quiet." There. A totally believable lie.

"You might be an impressive ranger, but you're a terrible liar." The faint lines of red in Draven's eyes started to thicken as he looked at me like I was a bug he couldn't figure out. "She flaunts her relationship with Kieran, who is a courtier and technically below her station. Rumor is she's involved with some scholar from Drudonia—I'm assuming that's the person who's been holed up in that room you have your lovely, fiery ranger guarding. And clearly, there is something between her and Alaric."

"We're a complicated lot." I eyed him warily. There was something . . . not right about him. I was used to being around

Moroi who channeled their bloodlust—that was part of it, but not all.

"That is the truth." He stepped closer to me, more red bleeding into his eyes. "I find it strange that Samara would fall into your bed though. It's not exactly a secret how much you hate the Harker Heir."

In a heartbeat, I closed the distance between us until we were almost touching. Draven didn't back down an inch. We were almost the same height, but he wasn't built as broadly. "You know nothing about me," I said coldly. "And you sure as fuck don't know anything about me and Samara."

I looked at him through silver eyes, my bloodlust rising to meet his as he let out a dark laugh. "You'd be surprised about the things I know." The red faded from his eyes until it was barely visible, and the foolishly charming prince persona slid back into place as he gave me a lopsided grin. "Good chat. We should do this again sometime."

Then he stepped around me and whistled as he walked away, leaving me wondering what the fuck had just happened.

CHAPTER THIRTEEN

Samara

THE HALLWAY of the barracks was empty when I slipped out of Vail's room, for which I was thankful. I really didn't want to explain to anyone what I'd been doing there. Adrienne knew the truth, and I knew she wouldn't breathe a word of it. Personally, I didn't really care about who people speculated I was sleeping with, but I knew it would piss off Vail. Despite his opinion of me, I didn't actually strive to find new ways to make him despise me more. Thank fuck Ary and Aniela had left, because the Heirs would have had a field day with this.

It'd taken some persuasion on my part, but I'd convinced Kieran to go check on Alaric and preferably get him to feed. I knew Alaric wouldn't listen to me, but maybe he'd listen to his best friend. I also knew Draven would likely be lurking somewhere in the main tower, and I wasn't ready to face him just yet. My mind was still racing from what we'd discovered last night, and my body was tired from healing. I couldn't afford to be off in any capacity around Draven.

Although, I could afford to spend an hour throwing some daggers in the rangers' training area while I thought through some options. Plus, I could check on Nyx, which I hadn't done since we'd returned. They'd still been healing from the wraith attack on our trek back from the badlands, but Adrienne had assured me they were doing okay.

Warm and floral spring air greeted me as I exited the barracks. Summer would officially be here in a few weeks, and the days were already getting hot. I pulled my hair up into a bun as I walked and turned to duck through one of the small alleyways that led to the training grounds before pulling up short.

"Vail?" I took a few unsure steps towards him. He was standing in the middle of the alleyway with his back to me, but I knew he must have heard me approach. Stealthy, I was not.

"The prince knows you were in my room," he said quietly when I reached his side.

"Fuck," I cursed.

"My thoughts exactly." He turned his head to gaze down at me, and I saw frustration in them. "He believes we're sleeping with each other. I didn't correct him. Figured it was better to have him think that than start asking questions about why else you may have been there."

"Okay, not ideal, but I can work with this." I chewed on the inside of my lip as I absently stared off to the side. Vail clearly wasn't happy, considering the tension radiating off him, but this could be to our advantage. I'd reaffirm that Vail and I were sleeping together next time I spoke with Draven. On the plus side, if Vail and I had to look into anything, we could use this fake relationship as a cover.

Vail remained silent as I thought through all of this. His eyes were mostly silver, so something had triggered his blood-lust, but I didn't think it was solely because of this turn of events. "Did something else happen?" I scanned his face, looking for clues but discovering nothing besides the frustration and general anger I seemed to always find in his eyes. "You seem a little intense. Even more so than usual."

The silver receded until only thin tendrils of it wound amidst the dark grey. "There is something off about the prince. I don't know what . . . but he is more than he seems."

"I know," I said quietly. "Even though I've known Draven for most of my life, this past week has made me realize that I actually know and understand very little about him. The prince is full of secrets."

"You sure we shouldn't kill him?"

I honestly couldn't tell if he was joking or not. Knowing Vail . . . not joking.

"Not right now." If I was looking at this from a purely logical standpoint, Draven being dead could solve some problems. Even thinking that caused something inside my chest to tighten, but if the Moroi Prince truly was the villain in all of this . . . could I really put the future of our people at risk because Kieran and I had feelings for him?

No, I couldn't. It would break something inside me, but if Draven truly was choosing to harm other Moroi of his own accord . . . then I'd bury a dagger in his heart myself.

Draven's words from our dinner earlier in the week floated through my mind. *"The only thing I've ever known are nightmares."* There was more to this than I was seeing. "Until we understand his role in all this . . . we don't harm the prince."

Vail studied me for a long moment. "You like him."

"It's complicated." Sensing an argument, I started to walk away. It may have been late in the morning, but I hadn't had any tea yet, so Vail would just have to wait to tear into me.

My escape was short-lived though because Vail gripped my arm and moved me back roughly. I hissed as he shoved me up against the wall, boxing me in with his large body.

"Do I need to remind you that he brought guards with him that night at the temple? That he offered them up to that Fae bastard like they were nothing?" Vail kept his voice low, but it vibrated with rage. "Or of the Moroi, including *children*, who have been slaughtered in the outposts by wraiths?"

"My memory is just fine," I said icily.

Vail leaned in closer until his face was only inches from mine. "Then think with something besides your greedy fucking cunt for once."

"Fuck. You." I shoved my hands against his chest, letting my nails lengthen and harden until they were claws that sliced through his leather and into his flesh. "I am beyond sick of your shit, Vail. You hate me, I get it, but you don't have a problem with any of your rangers sleeping around, and you have a fuck buddy in almost every outpost. So why exactly are you so concerned about *my fucking cunt?*" I let my last few words turn into more of a throaty purr at the end, solely because I knew it would slip under his skin and enrage him even more.

In a blink, Vail ripped my hands away from his chest and pinned them above my head. The position forced his body to press against mine, and I could barely shift my head back enough to glare up at him. The scent of his blood filled the air, and if my fingers were within reach, I would have licked the blood off them. I'd been delirious at the temple, but I still remembered how delicious his blood had been.

I could be pissed off at him and want his blood at the same time. Nothing messed up about that at all.

"Keep it up, Samara"—Vail's eyes dropped to the throbbing pulse on my neck—"and I'll dump your body and the prince's in that fucking cave for the monsters to dine on."

"Vail." I smirked at him when his gaze snapped to my mouth and the way my lips had curved. "If you want a taste, all you have to do is ask. Although, if someone walks by and catches us, the rumor about you fucking the Harker Heir will spread like wildfire, which I suppose will help our cover story."

A sharp exhale flew out of my lungs as Vail shoved himself off me and backtracked until he was several feet away. I casually raised my fingers to my lips and licked the blood off, then I let out a deep chuckle when silver flared in his eyes before they hardened. "Honestly, Vail, you make it too easy."

He took a step towards me, fingers curling into fists before spinning and stalking down the alleyway. Even when he was pissed, he moved quietly. I waited until he was gone before sagging against the wall. "Well, that was a little terrifying," I muttered.

I knew it was a bad idea to antagonize Vail. Although, I was mostly sure he wouldn't actually kill me. He'd had his chance to get rid of me several times at this point and hadn't seized it, or had seized it and then changed his mind in the case of the kùsu attack. He could be such a fucking prick sometimes, and like Alaric, his barbed insults always hit home.

It hurt. I should have been used to it after all these years of being at the receiving end of his vitriol, but I just couldn't bring myself to hate Vail the way he hated me.

The scent of his blood was still in the air, and I couldn't stop myself from inhaling deeply. He seemed to want another taste of me as badly as I wanted his delicious blood splashing across my tongue again.

Vail also seemed very confused about how to deal with me. Another thing he had in common with Alaric. Maybe they should start a club? I snickered, trying to picture the two of them in a room together. They'd probably just sit there and glower stoically.

I was still laughing under my breath minutes later when I entered the main training courtyard. There was a narrow passage on the other side with a dead end that was often used for target practice. It was perfect for what I had in mind, I just needed to grab some daggers first.

Emil waved at me from where he was speaking with a group of rangers, and I returned the gesture. Vail might be an asshole, but I liked his rangers. The heavy, wooden door of the weapons storage building creaked open, and I took two steps inside before being engulfed in a crushing grip.

"SAMARA!" a voice boomed. I would have clapped my hands over my ears, but my arms were pinned to my sides.

"Hey, Rokai," I squeaked as the impossibly large ranger crushed me against his chest in a jubilant hug. "Too. Tight."

"Oh!" My feet thumped to the ground, and large hands gripped my shoulders until I was steady. "I was just really excited to see you." Rokai's light brown eyes practically sparkled with joy against his pale skin. "I was just telling Vail about what you did for us!"

Well, shit. I tore my gaze away from Rokai's cheerful round face and found Vail's glittering hard stare on me. Definitely still pissed. I was hoping to give him at least a few hours to cool off before tracking him down again. Unfortunately for me, one of the many plans I was working on would require Vail's help, which meant I would need to catch him in a good mood at some point.

This was definitely not that point.

"I'm glad to see you made it back okay, Rokai." I reached up to pat his shoulder. Rokai was the only Moroi I'd ever met who was larger than Vail. Everyone regularly joked that he must be half-Velesian, but that couldn't be true because he was far too happy. "Maybe we can catch up later? I was actually just hoping to grab some dag— oh!"

Rokai tugged me over to where several other rangers were standing with Vail, and I nodded at each of them in greeting. They all smiled at me, and a few murmured their thanks, although not as aggressively as Rokai, who had me clamped to his side in a one-armed hug.

Vail was currently eying that arm like he wanted to rip it

off. A couple of rangers noticed where Vail's attention was, but Rokai continued to chatter on, completely oblivious. "We were investigating reports of some burrowing creatures in the badlands just south of Drudonia, and we fell into a collapsed tunnel. Luckily, the beasties were somewhat shy. They looked like giant grubs." Rokai shuddered. "We killed one of them and the rest backed off, but we couldn't get out."

I snuck another look at Vail. He'd stopped glowering at Rokai's arm like it was offending him and was instead looking at the ranger with a blank expression. I didn't know if that was better or worse.

"It was pure dumb luck that I spotted Samara's striker flying above us, and it came when I called."

"He came because you spoiled the shit out of him every time you stopped by House Laurent," I said pointedly, trying to give Rokai a stern look and failing completely.

"I won't apologize for giving that cute little bastard extra scraps."

Vail's patience finally snapped. "Explain," he barked.

Rokai stood a little straighter, finally sensing Vail's dark mood, and swallowed. "I was on escort duty for most of the last few years and regularly stopped at House Laurent." He glanced at me, unsure, and I nodded encouragingly. "They're . . . uhhh . . . a little unfriendly there, so I never stayed long, but Samara and I would always catch up. We usually went up to where the strikers were housed because nobody ever hung out there."

The poor big softie of a ranger seemed to be wilting under Vail's hostile gaze, so I jumped in. "My striker had been returning from delivering a message to Cali. There are large, flying predators in that section of the badlands, so the strikers usually fly close to the ground so they can duck and cover if they need to. Rokai got the attention of the striker, used his blood to draw their location on the back of the scroll Cali sent me, and I sent some rangers to investigate."

"And saved our asses." Rokai beamed. "We might have had to eat one of those worms if we were in there much longer, and I don't think I would have recovered from that."

"Personally, I would have chosen to starve," another ranger chimed in.

"Well, I'm glad no one had to make the decision between starving or eating an overgrown worm for dinner." I wiggled out from under Rokai's arm and patted him on the cheek. "Good to see you as always. Tell your mother I said hello and that we should have tea soon."

"Of course." He grinned playfully. "And I'll be sure to pay the strikers a visit and give them all treats."

"Obviously." I gave him a wry smile before skirting past the rangers towards the small room in the back, where I knew there were always throwing daggers. The rangers continued the conversation about the new monsters they'd discovered, but I felt Vail's gaze burning a hole in my back the entire way. He was probably pissed off at me for interfering with House Harker business when I'd been at House Laurent, but what was I supposed to have done? Ignored Rokai's plea for help? Sent a message to House Harker and hoped they sent a rescue party in time?

I was fairly confident that no matter what action I had taken, Vail would have found fault with it. Whatever. He could stew in his pissy attitude as much as he wanted. I grabbed half a dozen daggers and headed outside towards the alleyway, which was thankfully empty.

The training courtyard was situated towards the back of the walled fortress of House Harker. The end of the alleyway was the outer wall, and two of the smaller towers made up the side walls. For targets, the rangers had cut down a large tree and sliced the trunk, hanging the circular chunks of wood on

A Court of Bones and Sorrow

the wall. A few of the more creative rangers had used their artistic abilities to paint monsters on them. Once the wood was too chewed up for the blades to stick in, they were swapped out.

I flipped a dagger a few times in my right hand, getting a feel for it before throwing it at the center target. A loud *thunk* sounded as it landed dead center. I sunk into a pattern, aiming for different sections of the targets, trying to be as precise as possible. Daggers weren't entirely practical weapons. The damage they inflicted was too small and rarely fatal for the monsters roaming Lunaria, but sometimes there were specific areas of a body that could be exploited. Even if it didn't result in a fatal wound, it might injure the beast enough for someone else to take it down. Eyes were always a good target. The other problem with daggers was once I threw them, I no longer had a weapon, which I had been reminded of in the cave incident.

I retrieved all the daggers for a third time and set them on a workbench near the front of the alleyway. Then I had a thought: Roth could control their ribbons with blood magic—maybe I could do something similar with a dagger? I thought through a few of the glyphs that might work and then sliced open a shallow cut on my forearm and used my finger to paint one on the hilt of the blade. If I figured out something that worked, I could carve the glyph into the handle to make it more permanent.

After surveying my work one last time, I stepped to the center of the alley and hurled the dagger at the target. The blade dug into the wood, and I took a deep breath, trying to center my focus. No one had been around to teach us how to use our magic, so we'd had to figure it out on our own. Magic worked differently between the Moroi, Velesians, and Furies, but the one thing it all had in common was that intentions mattered.

Moroi couldn't just carve a glyph into something and

expect it to work. We had to imbue that glyph with our intent; otherwise, it was just a scratching on a wall. The purpose of the glyphs was to help us channel our intention and keep it there. It was a tricky thing to learn, which was why simple spells were the easiest. I used to tinker around with different glyphs when I'd been at Drudonia, but it'd been a long time since I'd tried to create something new.

Holding my hand out to the side, I tugged on the link I'd formed with the dagger, and an invisible force ripped the blade from the wood before it spun in the air. I had a brief, exhilarated moment of triumph before a sharp pain sliced into my hand.

"AHH! FUCK!" I gripped my wrist with my other hand and clenched my jaw at the pain. The spell had definitely worked, because the dagger had returned to me. Unfortunately, it had returned point-first, and the dagger was now buried hilt-deep into my palm, the bloody blade sticking out the back of my hand.

"Brilliant move," Vail said from where he was leaning against the wall at the alleyway opening. I had no idea how long he'd been standing there, and embarrassment flooded me. He'd once made fun of me when I'd bragged about being good with knives, and here I was, injuring myself with my own moonsdamned dagger.

"Shut up," I growled.

He sighed, walked over, and gripped the handle. Dark grey eyes met mine before I jerked my head in a nod, and I hissed when he quickly but smoothly pulled the blade free. Clearly, I needed to adjust the spell a little bit. Warm blood leaked from my hand as I held my palm out and used my fingers to draw the healing glyph on it.

"Thanks," I mumbled to Vail.

He grunted and studied the glyph I'd drawn on the dagger.

"I'm impressed you were able to get it to return to you on the first try."

"I used a similar spell at Drudonia." Trying to ignore the pain radiating from my hand as the wound stitched itself back together, I moved towards the remaining knives on the workbench. "I used that spell to close the window in my room because I always forgot to shut it at night and then didn't want to get out of bed because it was cold. The tricky part of that one was it had to pull the window panels shut without breaking the glass." I winced at both the memory and a particularly painful spot of my hand being healed. Tendons always sucked for some reason. "Might have taken a couple of tries. Rynn and Cali helped me fix the window before anyone noticed."

"Nothing about that surprises me." The amusement I heard in his voice made me look over my shoulder at him. He was still focused on the knife, but I could just make out the ghost of a smile dancing across his lips. "You hate the cold."

I pressed my lips back together before returning my attention to the daggers. Vail was officially more confusing than Alaric.

After some consideration, I tried a few different modifications of the glyph on three of the daggers. This time when I recalled them to me, I was a little more careful. One of the glyphs didn't work at all, another made the dagger only wobble enough to fall out of the target, and the third did come flying back at me, but it was still coming blade-first.

The aim was off, and instead of going towards my palm, it headed straight for my face. I yelped and barely managed to duck out of its way as Vail snatched the blade out of the air without comment.

"Damn it. I really thought that last one would work." I stomped back over to the workbench and scowled at the remaining daggers. Maybe I needed to use a completely different type of glyph. I was using a modification of one that meant summon.

Warmth brushed against my arm as Vail moved to stand next to me. He set the first dagger down, my blood still coating the blade. "What if you use the same spell, but add something to the blade for 'away?'"

"I've never tried to use two glyphs in unison like that." I chewed on my lip as I looked at the original dagger. "In theory, I think it would work."

"Worst case"—Vail swiped the dagger up once more and passed it to me—"you get a repeat performance of getting a blade through the palm."

"Hilarious." I grabbed the edge of Vail's tunic and used it to clean the blade. Then I grabbed another dagger and etched a glyph onto the tip of the original one so it wouldn't get rubbed off when it sank into the wood. I pinched my fingers together where I'd wiped my blood on Vail's tunic and then smeared it over the glyph, letting it absorb the magic.

Flipping the dagger in my hand and focusing my intent, I flung it towards the targets. As soon as it hit the center of one, I called it back to me. The worn handle smacked into my hand seconds later, and my fingers closed around it, a wide grin on my face.

I'd forgotten how good it felt to figure out a new spell, and this would be even more useful than closing a window on a cold night.

"It worked!" I threw the dagger at the targets again but called it back midair, the handle slapping against my palm. I could already feel the magic in the glyph getting depleted. Roth periodically soaked their ribbons in blood to charge up the spell. I'd need to embed a gemstone in the daggers to keep it charged up, but I'd at least figured out the hard part.

I looked to Vail to find him staring at me, that same faint smile on his lips. It slid away as soon as he saw my attention on him though. "Thank you for helping my rangers. You didn't need to, but you did anyway."

Ah, so that was why he was here.

"My loyalty has always been to House Harker. That didn't change when I married into House Laurent. It will never change." I flipped the dagger a few times in my hand. "Don't ever forget that."

Vail stared at me for a few seconds before giving me a nod. "I won't."

CHAPTER FOURTEEN

Samara

THE WORN, brown, leather satchel I'd been carrying around all morning sat next to my curled-up legs. It seemed so innocuous, but the journals resting inside it were anything but harmless. My mother had a whole other part of her life that I knew nothing about. Granted, I'd been young when she'd died, but not *that* young. Was what she wrote in those journals so bad or dangerous that she hadn't wanted to share it with me? Had my father known?

I'd probably find at least some of those answers in them . . . if I could bring myself to pick one up and start reading. Five more minutes. I'd give myself five more minutes to enjoy this tranquility before I dove into my mother's secrets.

Two minutes into my respite, I let out a sigh and raised my head from where it'd been leaning against the tree. Someone was coming—their footsteps were light, but I still heard them. Like most of the Fae fortresses, House Harker was made up of multiple towers with courtyards and gardens interspersed between them. There wasn't space for any serious agriculture, so most of our gardens only had flowers, herbs, and a few easy-growing fruits and vegetables.

I'd chosen to sit in this particular one because it was the least popular of all the gardens. It was nestled in a space behind the main tower and received very little direct sunlight, so it was mostly neglected.

Lavender grew freely and was doing its best to take over the small patch of dirt, though one lone tree sat in the center. We had no idea what type of tree it was, but there was one at every Fae fortress, so everyone just referred to them as the Fae trees.

They bore fruit every year just before summer ended. The palish pink fruit was hard and bitter with bright purple seeds at its center. Aside from tasting horrible, they were highly toxic. One bite, and you'd be hating your life for at least two days. They didn't kill us, but the pain was unimaginable. Or so I'd been told. We discarded the fruit once it fell from the trees to prevent any mishaps.

Maybe the Fae had a different reaction to the toxin. They must have had some reason for growing the trees.

"Oh." Nyx rounded the corner and halted when they saw me. "Sorry, Samara. I'm not used to anyone else being here."

My brows rose. I'd observed Nyx around all the other rangers since I'd moved back to House Harker. Everyone liked them, and they seemed to enjoy the company of others. It was surprising to me that they'd seek out a quiet place like this.

"It's been a little challenging for me to find solitude the past few days." I patted the ground next to me. "Come join me. I wouldn't mind getting out of my own head for a bit."

Nyx grinned and sauntered over towards me. I'd been worried about them since we'd returned, but with everything going on, I hadn't been able to check on them myself. Nyx was a few years younger than me, and I'd known them briefly at Drudonia before they'd disappeared and become a ranger instead of pursuing the scholarly path. I hadn't seen them again until they'd shown up on Vail's personal squad of rangers.

It'd been a little awkward at first because we'd been sort of friends before they'd vanished. Everyone knew things between me and Vail were a little tense, so I hadn't blamed them for being unsure of how to act around me while also remaining loyal to Vail, but it hadn't taken us long to fall back into a friendship of sorts.

My eyes traveled over every inch of their body as they walked across the garden, looking for any hints of lingering damage from the fight at the temple. They'd clearly been working out before heading over here because their light brown shirt was soaked in sweat and loose-fitting black pants were covered in dirt. To my relief, they appeared completely fine now.

"You and Adrienne are ridiculous." Nyx rolled their eyes before dropping down next to me. Then they stretched their long legs out and leaned back on their hands. "Usually I'd be very excited about having the attention of two beautiful women on me. Except I know for a fact neither of you look at me that way and you're just convinced I'm going to collapse at any moment. As if my ego didn't take a big enough hit being sidelined so quickly by those fucking wraiths."

"Sorry." I winced. "To be fair, this is the first time I've seen you in person since we got back. Everyone told me you were fine, but I just needed to see it for myself."

"I promise I'm okay." They shot me an easy grin. "Only thing that's still bruised is my pride."

"None of us did particularly well in that fight."

"Yeah, but I've been working hard to prove myself to Vail." Nyx let their head fall back, and their eyes stared up at the sky that reflected back the exact same shade of blue. "He took a chance on not only letting me join the rangers but also taking me on to serve in his own unit."

I picked up a broken twig and started twirling it between

my fingers. "Why did you?" I asked. "Leave House Corvinus to join House Harker? As a ranger no less?"

Nyx's older sister, Tamsen, was the Heir to House Corvinus. She was the reason Nyx had been at Drudonia in the first place. They'd been training to be an advisor to support her and House Corvinus as a whole. I'd always wondered why they'd left. When I'd inquired about their disappearance to House Corvinus, I'd received a letter from Tamsen herself telling me to leave it be and that Nyx was happy.

When Nyx didn't answer right away, I worried I'd stepped too far. Normally, I would have had more tact in asking such questions, but the journals sitting between me and Nyx were messing with my head and making me sloppy. I'd need to get it together before I conversed with Draven again.

"You don't have to answer." I dropped the twig and glanced at Nyx, who was still staring at the sky. "Carmilla approved of you joining our House, and Vail obviously accepted you into the rangers. I meant no offense by the question, I was just . . . curious."

"It's fine." They sighed. "I kind of owe you anyway for how I handled leaving Drudonia and ignoring all your attempts to contact me afterwards."

"That was kind of an asshole move," I agreed.

Nyx laughed and shifted until they were lying down and then let their head flop to the side to face me. "I'm guessing you went through the standard training all Heirs and other high-ranking Moroi go through when arranged marriages are in their future?"

"Yep. Although starting my sex education at twenty was a little late," I said wryly. "Pretty sure I showed the instructors some things that made them blush."

"Somehow that doesn't surprise me."

I did some quick calculations in my head. Nyx was several years younger than me, twenty to my twenty-four. They'd arrived at Drudonia a little over midway through my time there, so I'd been, what? Eighteen?

Only the Moroi engaged in this practice of "marriage training," and it was only for high-ranking arranged marriages, typically those of House bloodlines. The tradition had started with the fourth generation and continued as our inner House politics only grew more complicated. Some of the early arranged marriages had failed, and this had been the solution for correcting that.

The training wasn't *just* about sex and making your future spouse happy in the bedroom. More tailored instruction was created for each person based on the potential Houses they might be married into and the customs within them, but the sex aspect of it was what most people got hung up on. Cali and Rynn had been horrified when I'd first told them about it, but when I'd made it clear I was fine with it, we'd used it as a source of entertainment. Every time I came back from a session, they'd ask for all the details and how many times I'd embarrassed my instructor.

Well, Cali did. Rynn was mostly still mortified by the whole thing but couldn't stop asking follow-up questions.

"How old were you when the training started?" I asked carefully, dreading their answer. As far as I knew, most Moroi didn't start the sexual aspects of the training until they were at least eighteen. I'd been on the later side at twenty, but that wasn't uncommon.

"Seventeen." When Nyx saw my dark expression, they gave me a close-lipped smile. "Tamsen fought with our parents about it—they wanted me to start at sixteen. Seventeen was the compromise."

"You should have told us." I scowled. Rynn and Cali had taken Nyx under their wings too and wouldn't have been happy about this.

"So the three of you could cause a political nightmare by

going up against my parents?" Nyx shook their head ruefully. "The only thing that would have accomplished was further fracturing the alliances between the Moroi Houses and making things even more tense between the Moon Blessed."

"We would have figured something out," I said tightly. Since I was an Heir, it was my business to know the history, strengths, and weaknesses of all the other Houses. Kieran was also from House Corvinus, and while he rarely spoke about what it was like growing up there, I knew it hadn't been enjoyable. They were a smaller House that was obsessed with moving up the ranks, and they viewed their children as pawns.

To some extent, all of the Houses were like this, but I'd had a choice in my future. Carmilla never would have forced me to marry Demetri or any of the other Heirs. If I'd told her I didn't want to go through the standard training prior to a marriage, she would have accepted that. I'd assumed other Houses were the same. Clearly, House Corvinus was not.

"Tamsen would have paid the price if there had been any interference," Nyx said. "It didn't take long for our parents to figure out that the best way to control us was to threaten the other."

I'd met Tamsen several times. We weren't friends, but I respected her. Even more so now that I knew she'd at least tried to protect Nyx. She hadn't come with the Heirs to see Prince Draven, and it was likely House Corvinus was working with Velika. But that didn't necessarily mean Tamsen was in on it. She was Heir, but her parents still ruled the House. It was also possible they were forcing her cooperation by promising to harm Nyx if she disobeyed their orders.

Nyx and Tamsen's parents were fourth-generation like Carmilla, which meant they were in their eighties, but that meant nothing anymore. Carmilla was ninety-five years old but had looked like she was in her mid-forties for as long as I could remember. The Moroi were still evolving with each generation, and none of us knew how long we would live anymore.

If Tamsen was to rule anytime soon, her parents would have to meet an untimely end . . .

"Samara." Nyx rapped their knuckles against my leg.

"Hmm?" I blinked down at them.

"Stop plotting the death of my parents."

My hand flew to my chest, and I widened my eyes. "I would *never*."

Nyx chuckled. "You absolutely would, and don't think it hasn't crossed Tamsen's mind too. To say we're not close to our parents is a bit of an understatement." Nyx folded their hands behind their head and rested back on them to gaze up at the sky again. "There were a lot of reasons I wasn't happy at House Corvinus. My parents raised me as a boy and then expected me to fulfill my duties as a Corvinus male, but that never suited me. I didn't really understand why as I was growing up. Then I met Roth at Drudonia, and I realized maybe the reason I felt like I was always crawling out of my own skin was because I was trying to be something I wasn't."

"Never met any chirlin Velesians growing up?" I asked curiously, using the Fae word for those who didn't fall in the categories of male or female. Technically, the word chirlin meant either all of something or none of something. Either way, it seemed fitting, and the Velesians had been using it for some time. It was slowly catching on around the Moroi and Furies as well.

"Are you kidding?" Nyx's brows rose. "My parents can't go five minutes without talking shit about shifters. Rynn was the first Velesian I met."

"House Corvinus is even more fucked than I realized." I hesitated before asking, "Did you go through with the training?"

"No. I tried for the sake of my sister, but I couldn't do it."

Nyx rubbed their face. "I didn't have any experience before the training. I mean, I hadn't . . . There hadn't been anyone I'd . . . done things with." They caught my eyebrows creeping towards my forehead and laughed. "I know that's crazy, considering most Moroi start humping everything in sight as soon as they hit sixteen if not earlier, but I've never really felt inclined to stick my cock into everything that moves. Add to the fact that physically, I'd matured quickly and looked like this"—Nyx gestured at their handsome, masculine face and broad shoulders—"so everyone treated me like I was a typical male, which only added to internal confusion and ensured my sex drive was nonexistent."

I winced. What a shitty experience. My first time hadn't been amazing, but it'd been my choice, and it'd been with a courtier who was just as inexperienced. We'd stumbled through it together with clumsy fingers and panted breaths. Nyx had been quiet at Drudonia, but I'd had no idea they'd been dealing with all this.

"My instructors took things slow, but I panicked two weeks into the training, just as things started to get serious. I grabbed a horse and ran, not even caring which direction I was going as long as it was away from everything." They snorted, a wry grin playing across their lips. "Ran straight into Vail fighting off a pack of howlers. Helped him out, and the rest is history."

"You do seem happier now," I said. "It was the main reason I didn't tear your head off when I saw you for the first time with Vail. I was pissed off at how you just disappeared on us like that, but none of that matters if you're happy."

"Ah. I was wondering why I didn't get the typical *Samara Chewing Out*."

I shoved my knee out to the side so it dug into their hip. "Don't worry, it's still coming. I'm just letting it stew a little bit more."

"Thank you." Nyx's eyes flicked to mine. "For being my friend then and for being my friend now."

"Always." I wrinkled my nose. "Still think you had poor taste in choosing your ranger unit though."

"We've all decided to not touch what's going on between you and Vail with a ten-foot pole." They shot me a pointed look.

"Can I take that option too?" I dropped my head back against the tree.

"Sadly, I don't think you can." Nyx nudged the leather satchel between us. "Did you steal some books from Roth? Because I'll protect you from a lot of things, but there is zero chance of me getting between you and them if books are involved."

My lips quirked. "I'd never ask you to do such a thing. Besides . . . I kind of like Roth's idea of punishment."

A light flush streaked across Nyx's cheeks, and they squeezed their eyes shut. "I really need to get laid soon." We both laughed, and after a moment, they peeked one eye open at me. "Is Cali . . . involved with anyone?"

"Nyx Corvinus, do you have a crush on Calypso Rayne?" I gaped down at them, and their blush deepened as they quickly squeezed their eyes shut with a wince. "Oh my gods, you do!"

"I swear to the moon and all that she gives us, if you tell Cali, I will bury your corpse beneath this Fae tree."

The threat would have landed better if Nyx hadn't covered their face with their hands and half-mumbled the words.

"Wow." I cackled. "To answer your question, Cali isn't involved with anyone." I thought about it a little more. "Not seriously anyway. You know how Furies are. No serious relationships and all that."

Nyx made a noise of agreement and tucked their hands behind their head. "Do you mind if I nap here? I'm feeling a little tired, and if I go back to the barracks, Adrienne will somehow find out, and it'll only make her worry about me more."

"Sure." I eyed the leather satchel. "I have some reading I was going to do."

"Perfect."

I waited until Nyx's breathing evened out, and then I pulled out my mother's most recent journal. With trembling fingers, I cracked the spine open and started reading the secrets of the dead.

WE'RE CLOSE. *I feel it with every fiber of my being.*

Kasem is worried, and I don't blame him. The last two sites we searched were completely empty, yet it felt like we were being watched the entire time. Lunaria has never been safe, but the wraiths are acting strangely now. They're less feral than they were before. That should be a good thing, except I can feel them lurking in the shadows, waiting. For what, I don't know, but every time we leave the safe walls of House Harker, I feel death following in our wake.

But we can't stop now. We must find it before Velika does. Otherwise, our fates will be far worse than a grisly death.

I wish we had allies, but I don't know who we can trust aside from Inés and Edric. It feels wrong to lie to Carmilla. Despite all our disagreements, she's my sister and I love her, but our mother entrusted me with this legacy. I'd always intended to tell Carmilla eventually. About the journals. The crown. All of it. But then she became friends with Velika. I can't risk it. No matter how much it pains me, our people must come first.

We're leaving to visit one of the Velesian packs tomorrow. I didn't want to stop our search, but Kasem insisted, saying it's been too long since we've visited any of the Velesians, and he's concerned about the rising tensions between our people and theirs. I only agreed to his request because the next site I want to explore is somewhere around Lake Molov, and we'll need permission from the Narchis Order to go there.

Samara is coming with us, as is Inés and Edric's son, Vail. Part of me wants to keep Samara forever tucked away in House Harker behind the wards, but Kasem is right. She's the Harker Heir and needs to see more of Lunaria. I'm sure it'll be fine. We're taking a main road, and Inés and Edric are the fiercest warriors I've ever met—aside from Kasem of course. It'll be fine. Plus, it will give me some time to spend with Sam. My daughter is a wonder, and she's going to change the world one day. I just know it.

I'm going to try to sneak back into bed without waking Kasem. It never works, but it's fun trying, and I enjoy what he does when he catches me. Maybe when all this is over, we can give Samara a younger sibling. Because we will survive this. I won't accept anything else.

HEAT POOLED BEHIND MY EYES, and I slammed the book shut. She hadn't survived. This was the last entry of the journal. Three days after this, she'd been killed by wraiths along with my father and Vail's parents. Nyx's light snores filled the air, and I concentrated on their rhythmic breathing as I bottled up everything I was feeling and shoved it down.

I couldn't afford to lose it now. The wraiths were the lost Fae, the Sovereigns were betraying all of the Moroi and working with them, and there was a wicked prince in my home, courting me for marriage. I didn't have the luxury of losing my shit right now.

After a few minutes of steady breathing, I reviewed the facts. My parents had known Velika had been plotting something, though nothing indicated they'd known she was working with the wraiths. Carmilla didn't know about the journals or what my parents had been searching for because my mother had been concerned about how close Carmilla was with Velika.

And finally . . . they'd never made it to Lake Molov.

I'd already been planning on going there. It was what I

needed to talk with Vail and Rynn about. What I hadn't been sure of was if I should prioritize it or not. I had my answer now. Whatever my parents had been searching for had to have been important, and Velika had wanted it too. I needed to go to Lake Molov. Perhaps, Velika had already gone there . . . but maybe she hadn't. Or maybe she'd gone but hadn't been able to find what was hidden there. In either case, I felt I owed it to my parents to finish what they'd started.

The small journal felt heavy in my hands. I'd deliberately started with the last entry because the more recent ones were more likely to have information relevant to our current situation. Maybe some of the earlier entries would mention what exactly my mother had been hunting for.

Fortifying my nerves, I opened the book again and started scanning the pages. I didn't let myself linger on any of the sweet moments she mentioned between herself and my father, and I entirely skipped over the one where she talked about my eighth birthday and how she'd worked with Leora all morning to make me the perfect cake because she wanted to have a hand in it too instead of just passing it off to someone else.

Most of the entries covered their failed search attempts and some mentions of increased wraith or other monster activity. Then I found it, and it was like a snake had reared from the page and sunk its fangs into me.

I HAD an odd encounter with Velika today. Something about her has always bothered me—I have never been able to describe what it is, and the few times I've mentioned it to Carmilla, she's waved me off as being paranoid, which, to be fair, I am. There is a sickness running through the Moroi. Everyone judges the Furies, but it's not like they choose to lose their minds and slaughter all around them. The Moroi are consciously choosing to harm each other in nefarious ways.

The Moroi Queen is one of those nefarious souls.

She hides it well—the rest of the Moroi practically worship her like she's one of the old gods the Fae prayed to—but this time when we met, she wore a crown. Velika's so vain, it was perfectly within character for her. Especially since she's determined to bring back the old ways of how we believe Fae courts worked. It's foolish. We're barely surviving in this fucked-up land and she wants to hold balls and wear fancy dresses.

But when Velika wears jewelry, it is always dripping in gems. This crown had been so simple. Just a simple silver band with delicate carvings. Parts of it had even appeared broken. Still, something about it had bothered me. I could feel the magic in it, which was odd because I saw no glyphs and it held no gems that would have stored magic.

I couldn't resist asking Velika about it, but I stumbled over the words. Carmilla is so much better at wordplay than me. I'm sure I tipped my hand about my suspicions. Velika just laughed it off as something she had made recently and acted like she didn't particularly care for it, but I didn't miss the way her fingers caressed the silver.

The Moroi Queen has a Fae artifact. I am sure of it.

There must be more out there, and we need to find them before she does.

"Fuck," I breathed out. What if Velika had collected more Fae artifacts since my parents had died? Or maybe she was still searching for them and that was why she had allied with the wraiths? Were they helping her find them in exchange for Velika assisting them in reclaiming their true Fae forms? Once again, I felt like the few answers I got only led to more questions.

I glanced down at a still sleeping Nyx. My parents had given their lives to stop Velika's mad quest for power.

My daughter is a wonder, and she's going to change the world one day.

I would not let them down.

CHAPTER FIFTEEN

Samara

"THIS IS MAGICAL, LEORA," I groaned around a mouthful of tart berry deliciousness. After spending a couple of hours beneath the Fae tree, pillaging the journals for any other bit of information, I'd been in desperate need of a break and something sweet. "I think you're one of the gods in those old Fae stories. That's the only rational explanation."

Leora huffed a laugh and waved off my compliment. I'd missed both her and her delicious baked goods while I'd been at House Laurent. The Moroi who ran the kitchen staff there weren't nearly as friendly nor as talented.

"Agreed," Nora said from where she sat across from me at the small table tucked into the corner of the kitchen. She worked in the gardens with her husband and had been taking a break when I'd stumbled into the kitchen, following the scent of freshly baked goodies. The young, pretty Moroi eyed the plate filled with the spring berry pastries. "I think I need one more to get the taste of that tea out of my mouth."

I nudged the plate towards her. "You definitely do." I flashed her a look of sympathy as her lip curled at the now empty teacup resting next to the pastries. The spelled brew prevented pregnancy. It lasted until we had our cycle, and then it had to be taken again. Apparently, our human ancestors had gone through their cycle every month. When we'd become Moroi, that had changed to every four months, and our bleeding only lasted for two or three days.

Unfortunately, those two or three days were absolute agony. I had no idea if the monthly cycle of the humans had been as bad as ours was. If it had been . . . then the humans who had gone through it had been tougher than we gave them credit for.

The tea was an old Fae spell that for some reason worked for us too. It tasted absolutely vile, like milk that had gone sour, and it coated your tongue and throat, the taste lingering long after. Nora had slammed the tea back in several gulps and then powered through three pastries. I didn't blame her at all. My cycle was due in the next few weeks, and I was very much not looking forward to it.

"So you and Floran aren't going to try for a little one now that you're an old married couple?" I teased Nora, and she blushed faintly. While our cycle was painful, the week that followed was also . . . intense. It was jokingly referred to as the mating frenzy. Couples tended to hide away for days at a time, and single Moroi would often find someone, or several some-ones, to shack up with. The tea would prevent pregnancy but did nothing to lessen our lust-addled minds.

"No plans for any young ones yet." Nora smiled, and the blush deepened across her cheeks. I was about to tease her again when her smile faded and a crease formed in her brows. She picked at the corner of her pastry as her eyes flicked to mine hesitantly. "We've heard the rumors about the outposts . . . about some of them falling to wraiths. I know Lunaria is never technically safe, but it feels a little more volatile right now. We both agreed now isn't a good time to bring a child into it."

Shit. It had only been a matter of time before rumors started spreading about outposts being wiped out by wraiths, but since most of the ones that had been targeted were more remote, I'd really been hoping we'd have at least another couple of months before it became common knowledge.

"I can't say I disagree with your assessment," I said quietly. Leora continued humming to herself as she alternated between kneading dough and checking the bread baking in the brick oven. I knew she could hear every word we said, but I also knew she would keep it to herself. Leora was happy to gossip about harmless things, but she'd never repeat anything serious, especially if it came from me. "Would you mind sharing how you heard about the attacks? The Sovereign House has been trying to keep it quiet."

Nora paled at the mention of the Sovereign House. "I haven't told anyone," she said quickly and then winced. "Other than mentioning it to you just now."

"It's fine," I assured her. "Personally, I have mixed feelings about keeping this information from the remaining outposts, but I can't go against the Sovereign House. So I'm trying to solve the issue as quickly as possible, but if people start to panic . . ."

"I don't think many people know." Nora twisted the end of her long, blonde braid in her fingers. "Floran's older brother is a tracker. He was training to be a ranger, but it didn't work out. There was a girl he was sweet on at one of the outposts that was . . ." She swallowed. "He went to check on her one day and found the outpost empty and some rangers investigating. They didn't give him the specifics, but wraiths were mentioned. I don't think he's told anyone else, and I'll make sure he doesn't." Nora's breathing quickened, and I reached out and laid my hand over hers.

"It's okay, Nora. It'd be a good idea to let him know that,

simply so he doesn't run afoul of the Sovereign House, but neither of you did anything wrong."

"Okay." She smiled weakly.

"We'll figure this out, I promise." I removed my hand from hers and tapped the rim of the empty teacup. "And then you can skip drinking this tea for a little while. If that's what the two of you want of course."

She laughed. "Floran wants to have six kids. I thought we could start with one and see how it goes."

"You always were the wiser one," I said, drawing a laugh out of Leora as she plopped a plate of muffins down in front of us.

"I knew I'd find you here as soon as I caught wind of the freshly baked deliciousness." Kieran breezed into the kitchen and kissed Leora on the cheek and then Nora before pulling up a chair beside me and grabbing one of the berry muffins. Alaric followed a second later and nodded at Leora and Nora but opted to stand awkwardly a few feet away from us. "A certain cranky scholar would like to see you. They're in the library."

My eyes darted to Nora, who grinned and grabbed a muffin as she rose. "I'll leave the three of you to your scheming."

Alaric watched her go before sliding into her seat, then his eyes briefly flicked to mine before falling back to a spot on the table midway between us. I glanced at Kieran, who just shook his head and rolled his eyes. So he hadn't had any luck convincing Alaric to drink either. Wonderful. Alaric was cranky and difficult on a good day. I somehow doubted he'd be more pleasant when he was running low on magic and refusing to do anything about it.

Argh.

"Where's Draven?" I asked quietly.

"He's with Yolanthe," Alaric answered, still not looking at

me. "I met with him earlier. He's probably going to look for you as soon as he's done. Something seemed to be bothering him earlier—he was distracted, which is unlike him."

Probably because he thought I was sleeping with Vail. Another lie I'd have to maintain. Speaking of . . . might as well get that out of the way.

"He's just being pissy because I spent last night with Vail." Something slammed into the wood counter behind us, and I looked over to find Leora gawking at me, her discarded rolling pin halfway across the surface. "Apparently, the prince doesn't like the idea of sharing with the Marshal."

"That makes two of us," Kieran muttered, drawing my attention away from Leora's surprised face. Alaric was staring at me intently, his full mouth flattened into a hard line, but he didn't voice any objections.

It annoyed me that he didn't, and then it bothered me further that I cared what he thought.

"It's not real," I said quietly as Leora took a few steps closer to us, abandoning her dough as she sent me a questioning look. "But Draven needs to believe it for now."

Leora studied me for a long moment. "Are you sure about this, dear?"

Reluctantly, I nodded. Leora could help spread the rumor, giving more legitimacy to the claim. I didn't like that it would be yet another complication between Vail and me. He wouldn't like it either and would take out his frustrations on me, but it's not like that would be anything new.

Pushing Vail out of my mind for now, I refocused on our immediate problem.

"We need to distract Draven." I thrummed my fingers against the table. "Whatever Roth has discovered shouldn't be heard by him, and I have something I want to discuss as well."

I twirled the ring on my pinkie, the two embedded gems shining bright against the dark silver band. Rynn, Cali, and I were long overdue for a chat anyway, and I wanted to make sure they were caught up on all the latest developments. Plus . . . Rynn was an important part of what I was planning, as was Vail.

Neither of them were going to like it. In fact, nobody was going to like it, but I was confident I could convince them to go along with it. Mostly.

"Maybe we should wait until late tonight?" Alaric suggested.

"No." I shook my head. "Draven is clearly keeping an eye on my nighttime habits. We're lucky he didn't follow us to the cave, but going forward, he'll likely be monitoring my whereabouts more closely." Kieran didn't say anything, which I thought was odd. I studied his expression as he slowly nibbled on the muffin. He seemed relaxed; there were no lines of tension, and the corners of his mouth were quirked upward slightly. Even his eyes were bright.

It was a lie. I knew that mask. It was the one he slipped on when he knew he'd have to do something he didn't want to. Usually, I saw it when he made the rare journey home to visit his parents.

"Kier?"

His eyes flicked to mine, and he sighed before putting down the half-eaten muffin. "I'll distract him."

"No," I said immediately. "You don't have to do that."

"Well, I'm not planning on doing *that*." His lips twitched into a wry grin. "You know there are other ways to distract people, right?"

I pursed my lips stubbornly. "You don't have to do this—whatever this is—if you don't want to. We can find another way."

"This makes the most sense." He shrugged with a casualness that made me want to scream. I knew this plan bothered him, and I hated that he was trying to hide it. "You don't need me for whatever conversation you all want to have."

"I always need you."

Kieran's eyes softened. "While I have many skills, we all know the three of you are far smarter than I am. My skills are suited towards being a decoy, and if I ask Draven to go for a ride with me, he'll go."

"I bet he will," I grumbled, still not liking this one bit. It wasn't that I was jealous of anything that might happen between them, but Draven was a complication, and while I suspected there was more going on than we were seeing, he was technically the enemy right now. One who had betrayed our people.

He'd hurt Kieran before as well. I loved Kier with all my soul but he was also the most kindhearted person I'd ever met. It was difficult for him to trust people, but once he did, he did so absolutely. Draven had broken that trust and his heart. Kieran would forgive him for it though, whether the prince deserved it or not. I just didn't want to see him hurt again.

"Will one of you please tell me what is going on?" Alaric finally asked, raising his gaze from the table to glance back and forth between me and Kieran.

"I'll explain later." Kieran grimaced before rising and grabbing one of the folded-up towels Leora kept stacked throughout the kitchen, then he stuck a few muffins in it. "How much longer do you think he'll be meeting with Yolanthe?" he asked Alaric.

"They've been talking for almost an hour already, but you know Yolanthe, she'll go on forever. Could be thirty minutes, could be another hour." Alaric stared at his friend for a long moment. "Are you okay?"

"You know me." Kieran shrugged. "I'm always okay."

Alaric narrowed his eyes. He knew just as well as I did that Kieran had a tendency to suppress his feelings around us, like we would think less of him if he presented anything but a strong, confident front.

"I need to get some things from my room." Kieran leaned down to kiss me on the cheek before straightening and looking at Alaric. "I'm guessing they're meeting in Yolanthe's study?"

Alaric nodded, still studying his friend, trying to figure out what was going on that he was missing. Kieran ignored his best friend's gaze and headed towards the back stairwell, his bundle of muffins in tow, and left without another word. I wasn't any happier about this than Alaric, but I had to trust that Kieran knew what he was doing.

"Let's give him some time to get Draven out of here. We can meet in two hours." I snatched up Kieran's discarded muffin and tore off a chunk full of berries. Mmm . . . so tart and yummy. The spring berries didn't last long. They flowered, grew, and ripened over a two-week period, and that was it until the next year, but they were the first fruit of the season to grow and always marked that spring was in full swing. Hence the name. "Any chance you can find Vail and bring him with you to the library for the meeting?"

Alaric frowned. "Why can't you do it?"

"Because Vail isn't in the best of moods and will probably say no just because it's me asking." I let out a bone-weary sigh. "Given that we want the rumor of Vail and me sleeping together to spread, him rejecting a simple request from me in public would be less than ideal."

I shoved the rest of the muffin into my mouth and closed my eyes while I savored the flavor.

"Fine," Alaric ground out. "But I don't appreciate being blindsided by this plan. You're playing it up like it's all pretend, but I haven't missed the heated looks Vail has sent you since returning from the temple, and I know there is something else going on with Kieran that the two of you are keeping from me. I'm tired of being kept in the dark."

"Oh?" I cracked an eye open from my pastry-derived bliss. "Care to enlighten me as to why you're refusing to drink blood then?"

"I'm not refusing."

Pastry bliss officially over.

I leaned across the table and extended my arm to him, my wrist facing up. "Then have a drink." Turquoise flashed across Alaric's light green eyes so fast, I barely caught it. When he made no move to take my offer, I withdrew and crossed my arms. "Kieran will tell you when he's ready. I'm not telling you his secrets, just as I wouldn't tell him yours."

"Fair enough." Muscles flexed along his jawline. "And Vail?"

"Honestly . . . I don't understand what's going on between me and Vail. He might actually be more confusing and frustrating than you at this point." Alaric snorted, and I gave him a tired smile. "It'll just be easier if you ask him. Trust me."

"Alright." Alaric stood and straightened his midnight blue tunic. "We'll meet you in the library in a bit."

I nodded, my thoughts already drifting to my plans and what Roth might have discovered. It took me a minute to realize Alaric was still standing there and looking . . . nervous. I couldn't remember the last time I'd seen Alaric look nervous. In fact, I wasn't sure if I ever had. "Is there something else?"

"If . . ." He trailed off and swallowed. "If the offer of your . . . blood . . . is still on the table later . . ." Alaric released the buttons he'd been fidgeting with and met my eyes. "I'll take you up on it."

I blinked. "Really?"

"Yes," he rushed on. "But it has to be somewhere private."

"Damn," I drawled. "There go my plans of straddling you in the hallway of the main tower entrance."

"Samara," he said warningly, and I grinned as some of the tension eased from his face.

"Whatever you need, Alaric," I said before he could change his mind. "We can do it after the meeting if you'd like."

He hesitated for a moment before jerking his head in agreement. "Alright."

I watched as he practically fled from the kitchen, and then I rose and wandered over to Leora, who had returned to the large workstation and was rolling out dough in perfect rectangles. She shot me an amused glance before passing me a bowl of raspberry jelly. "Spread this in a thin layer while I roll out the next one."

"Sure." I set to work, spreading the thick, dark purple filling across the dough. Leora had been in charge of the kitchens of House Harker for longer than I'd been alive, and I always enjoyed coming in here. Not just to sneak treats but because there was something relaxing about helping her cook and bake things. Sometimes I'd be here for hours and we'd barely talk. I knew others did the same. There was just something calming about being in Leora's kitchen.

"Any advice?" I asked after I'd moved on to the third rectangle of dough.

Leora smiled as she started rolling up the first piece and then sliced it into thick discs. "You really did go out of your way to get yourself a complicated assortment of lovers."

I huffed a laugh. "Exactly how many lovers do you think I have? Because last I checked, it was *actually* only two." I thought about Alaric joining me and Kieran in my study. "Two and a half."

The older Moroi slid me a sly glance. "Trust me, it's a solid three. He just hasn't realized it yet."

"We'll see." I scraped out the last of the filling, put the bowl aside, and started rolling up the dough. I could never get it as perfectly even as Leora, but it'd still taste fine.

"Alaric will come around." Leora paused, and I felt her concerned gaze on me, so I glanced up from my less than perfect rolled out dough. "It's the Marshal and the prince who worry me."

"Leora—" I started, but she waved her hand in the air, cutting me off.

"I know you can take care of yourself." She patted me on the cheek. "But you always worry about everyone else, Samara. Many of us care deeply for you, my darling girl. So we'll worry about you too."

She went back to rolling her dough, and I did the same. When I finished, we moved on to the next round. "I can't help but notice that wasn't advice," I pointed out.

Leora laughed. "That's because I don't have any, and I was hoping you wouldn't notice. I think you're fucked in more ways than one."

"Thanks." I shook my head ruefully because she was probably right.

MY DAMP HAIR soaked into my robe as I contemplated all the things we needed to discuss at the upcoming meeting. I'd returned to my suite to rinse off because I'd somehow managed to get flour all over me and raspberry jelly in my hair.

I glanced at the large, upright clock that rested between my book cases. Thirty minutes to go. Draven's meeting would be wrapping up soon, and Kieran was waiting to intercept him and get him out of our way for a while. I still wasn't thrilled about that plan, but if Kieran said he could handle it, then I trusted him.

A few scenarios of just how Kieran could keep the prince distracted flashed through my mind. Great. Now I was anxious and horny.

Then again, they would probably just ride around the

property. Kieran was really pissed off at Draven. As much as he wanted him, I wasn't sure if he'd be willing to let anything happen between them. Once again, concern for Kier bloomed in my chest. I didn't want him to get hurt, and Draven had already caused him such pain.

"What the fuck are you up to, Drav?" I muttered.

We knew he was working with the wraiths—whether he was only doing so because he was being forced was still something we had to figure out. But that didn't explain why he'd treated Kieran the way he had. I'd known Drav for most of my life, and while he could occasionally be short with people and was excellent at delivering well-crafted insults, I'd never known him to be cruel.

And what he'd done to Kieran had absolutely been cruel. Once again, I wondered if I was letting my attraction to him and our past friendship blind me to the truth.

My gaze fell on the memory ball still resting on the table in my sitting area. What memory had he planted in it? I glanced at the clock . . . I did still have time. And I could always pull out if it was taking too long.

Before I could second guess myself, I strode over to the table and picked up the glass sphere before plopping down on the settee. I leaned back and rested the ball in one palm with the other lying across the top. Memory balls like this one weren't exactly common, but all the Houses had at least a few in their possession. None of them contained Fae memories, but they were useful for recording meetings and other information.

Typically, we locked those memories to our blood so no one else could access them. But I could feel Draven's memory floating inside this one, trying to tug me under. He'd deliberately left it unlocked so I could access it without him.

I closed my eyes and let myself be pulled into it.

"When I said I wanted to escape the party for a while and you said you knew just the place, this wasn't what I was expecting." I held a

warning finger up at the chestnut stallion, who laid his ears back in the stall on the left. The horse snorted like he wasn't the least bit impressed before trying to bite me.

No. Not me. Draven. I was seeing this memory from Draven's point of view. Well, this was a bit disorientating. Normally, when we used memory balls, we just recorded our voices. But Draven had included so much more than that. I could make out some of his thoughts—although many were muddled and I couldn't understand them. But I could get a sense of what he was feeling.

Longing and confliction. Some contentment. He enjoyed my company. But also . . . fear.

Why had he chosen this memory? And why was he afraid?

I tuned back in, letting myself fall back into the echo of Draven's psyche.

"Quit antagonizing him." Samara held up a warning finger in the same way I had just done to the stallion. When I snapped my teeth at her, she laughed and spun away, sending her dark hair flying. That moons-damned laugh stole my breath. Hearing it was like coming home after being lost in a storm for weeks.

She'd be married to that asshole from House Laurent in a few weeks. Truthfully, I didn't actually know much about him. Only that Samara was too good for him. But it's not like I could marry her. Samara had no idea how I truly felt about her and Demetri . . . Demetri was the safer option.

"I'm just saying"—I followed after where Samara had moved deeper into the stables—"we could have swiped a bottle of wine and been up on the roof right now."

"We can do that after," she tossed over her shoulder. "I wanted to see them first."

"Them?"

Samara stopped in front of a stall and leaned over the door. "Them," she said in a soft voice.

I stepped up beside her, letting my arm graze hers briefly before resting it on the door. A black mare eyed us warily but didn't move from where she was standing over two identical dark bay foals. Both were passed out and sprawled across the straw bedding.

"One of the servants told me about them earlier," Samara whispered, her dark purple eyes full of wonder. "It's a miracle they survived."

"They look very small. Ranger mounts have to be strong and robust. The weak don't survive." A hint of bitterness crept into my voice, and I winced. Samara loved horses—I should let her have this moment of happiness instead of bringing my dreariness into it.

"So they'll be quick and resilient," Samara shot back. "There's more than one way to survive in Lunaria. Don't count them out yet."

I smiled. "You're right of course."

She slid me a cocky glance. "I know."

We both backed away from the door to let the foals sleep in peace. Samara went to each stall, giving every horse a scratch behind the ears—even the ornery chestnut stallion, who was more than willing to let Samara pet him while giving me the evil eye.

"Would you like one of the foals?" I blurted out.

Samara looked over her shoulder at me, dark eyebrows raised. "I would never separate them. And even if you gave me both, it'll be years before they're old enough to ride." A hint of sadness crept into her expression. "I'll be in need of a mount sooner than that. Mine passed away last year from old age. He had a good, long life, but I miss him. I've been using temporary ones, but I'll need to figure out a more regular solution when I move to House Laurent." Something flickered across her face—too fast for me to catch what it had been—then she shrugged. "I'm sure they'll have something there that will work."

"What would your dream horse be?" I asked, unable to stop myself.

She turned around to face me, leaning her back against the stall door. The chestnut stallion nudged her shoulder, and she absently stroked his cheek. "Dark like the storm clouds. With a loyal spirit and a fiery temper." She grinned. "And fast enough to outrun death itself."

"That's a tall order." I smiled back at her.

"You said dream horse." She leaned over and kissed the stallion on the nose. "*I suppose we should get back to the party. My aunt is probably wondering where I slipped off to.*"

"*Of course.*" *We walked out of the stables, but I halted after a couple of steps.* "*Actually, I need to check in with the rangers about something. I'll see you back at the party.*"

"*Okay . . .*" *Samara eyed me suspiciously. I couldn't say I blamed her, it was rare that I did anything that looked like work around her. Usually, we would just split a bottle of wine or two and talk about random things. Well, I'd ask Samara about her life and then redirect the conversation anytime she asked something about mine.*

With a wave, Samara set off towards the main tower of the Sovereign House, where the party was no doubt still in full swing. I waited until she was out of sight before doubling back to the small building behind the stables and rapping my knuckles against the door.

An older-looking Moroi male swung the door open. His light grey hair hung loose around his shoulders. "*My prince!*" *His bushy eyebrows shot up.* "*I, uhh—*" *he brushed some crumbs off his shirt, and his posture went ramrod straight.* "*My apologies. I was just having dinner and wasn't expecting company—definitely not you. Not that you're not welcome her—*"

"*My apologies for interrupting your meal, Stablemaster.*" *I held my hands up in an apologetic gesture.* "*I was hoping to intrude on you for just a few minutes and ask for a favor.*"

"*Oh?*" *A puzzled crease formed between his eyes.* "*I mean, of course!*" *He held the door open and waved me inside.* "*Whatever you need.*"

I stepped into his simple but clean home, his interrupted meal still on the table. "*I'm looking for a particular horse, and I was wondering if you could reach out to the stablemasters of the other Houses to see what they have available—and arrange for me to go see them. I'll need to inspect all the options myself.*"

"*Sure.*" *He nodded slowly.* "*What type of horse are you looking for?*"

I gave him a small smile. "*One made of dreams.*"

The memory faded, and I was vaguely aware of the glass

sphere slipping out of my hands to land with a thud on the carpet before rolling away.

Zosa. My hot-tempered and beloved grey mare. Demetri had given her to me as a wedding present, but I'd always suspected he hadn't been the one to find her. That he had just told the House Laurent Stablemaster to find me a horse, and they had done as commanded.

I'd forgotten all about that conversation in the stables with Draven. The weeks leading up to my marriage had been a blur, and then I'd been busy fighting to make space for myself at House Laurent. Not to mention missing Kieran terribly.

One of the few things that had kept me sane had been riding Zosa on the beach. Draven had given me the horse of my dreams. And until now, he'd never said one word about it.

I stared at the Fae memory ball as it slowly rolled across the floor before coming to a stop against the clock. That memory hadn't been at all what I'd expected, and I didn't understand why he had chosen it. Part of me wanted to track down wherever he was with Kieran and demand answers—but another part of me was scared of what he might say.

Because I was absolutely falling in love with Draven . . . but I still didn't trust him.

CHAPTER SIXTEEN

Kieran

IN GENERAL, I prided myself on having nothing but good ideas. Convincing Alaric to stop working for a few hours so we could spar instead? Good idea. Telling Leora she should practice her new pastry ideas and I would sample each one? Great idea. That time I convinced Samara to sneak some honey from the kitchen so I could drizzle it all over her body and lick it off?

Fucking. *Fantastic*. Idea.

Telling the others I could distract Draven for a few hours by taking him out for a ride? Bad idea. Like, epically terrible idea.

The look of surprise on Draven's face when he'd walked out of Yolanthe's study and I'd immediately asked him to come for a ride with me had almost made it worth it. But now we were alone in the woods surrounding House Harker, and the reality of my situation came crashing down on me.

I blamed Samara and Alaric for not doing a better job of talking me out of this. They were the smart ones, and it was their responsibility to point out the stupidity of my ideas. Both of them would be getting an earful when I got back.

"Something the matter?" Draven slowed his enormous

black stallion until it was riding next to Zosa. I barely managed to rein her in when the grey mare snaked her head out and tried to take a chunk out of the other horse's neck. She snorted and danced angrily beneath me. I don't know what had possessed me to take Sam's horse out. The stable boy had paled when I'd led her from the stall, but when I'd told him I had Samara's permission, he just jerked his head in a nod and practically ran away, muttering something about me having to saddle the ornery mare myself.

"Everything's fine," I said tightly, steering Zosa a little further away from Draven. Distance. That was what I needed. Just a little space between the two of us.

Once I had Zosa under control—or at least out of biting range—I glanced back at Draven. He was staring at the grey mare with a strange expression I couldn't read. "If you're thinking about saying something nasty about my mount, you should know this is Samara's mare and she doesn't take kindly to anyone talking shit about her horse."

Draven smiled faintly. "I wouldn't dream of it. Just surprised you're riding such a magnificently vicious creature instead of a flashy, even-tempered mount." His smile grew wider. "Maybe something with a chestnut coat that glistens like polished copper in sunlight."

Damn it. My normal mount—Aelix—*was* a chestnut mare.

The fact that he knew me so well was frustrating. She loved to prance around with her flaxen-colored tail raised as if she knew perfectly well how glorious she was.

Zosa was a storm cloud who absolutely loved Samara and barely tolerated anyone else, but today, I'd needed her strength over Aelix's beauty, so I'd bribed her with an extra ration of grain in hopes she wouldn't throw me.

I felt Draven's heavy stare on me when I didn't answer. In my head, I'd convinced myself this would be easier. Just a nice little ride around the woods full of monsters. No big deal. I gripped the reins tighter, and Zosa tossed her head in annoyance.

"Come on," Draven said suddenly and spurred his horse forward before I could argue. Zosa didn't need any encouragement from me and immediately raced after them, nearly unseating me in the process. Gods, no wonder Samara loved her. This mare was lightning made flesh.

When we pulled even with Draven, I had to tug Zosa back so she didn't take the lead, since I didn't know where Draven wanted to go. I didn't even know why I was following him in the first place. This ride had been my idea—I was the one who was supposed to be leading him around. Plus, I was far more familiar with the area than he was, but this always happened when I was with him. It had felt nice to let someone else take charge, and I'd trusted Draven back then. I didn't trust him now.

Then why are you following him so blindly? The irritating thought surfaced in my mind, and I gritted my teeth, determined not to think about the answer.

After ten minutes, Draven gradually slowed his mount to a walk, and I did the same. It took me a second to recognize where we were, and I'd never felt so much excitement and dread at the same moment. How the fuck did he even know about this place?

We ducked under some branches, and I noted some bright sapphire gems dangling from the trees. Faint magic pulsed from them, a little dimmer than the last time I had been here. They'd need to be replaced within the next two months. This type of ward wasn't as powerful as the ones we used to protect the outposts, but most of the monsters crawling around this area of the forest were harmless to us because the rangers kept all the serious threats away. Once in a while, a pack of howlers would wander this way, but the sapphire-powered ward was enough to keep them out.

A twisted, green vine with bloodred leaves wound around a tree, trembling as we passed it, and I eyed it warily. In a few months, it would grow delicate, white blossoms that had some beneficial medicinal uses. Unfortunately, the leaves were coated in a fine powder that would not only make one break out in a rash, but they'd make one's skin itch for weeks. Not just a minor itch either. It was a deep, burning feeling, like something was crawling beneath one's skin. Anyone who was afflicted had to be tied down to keep them from tearing their own flesh off.

Lunaria, a land of nightmarish monsters, where even the plants wanted to kill you.

What in the fuck had the Fae done to be banished here? Or had they come here voluntarily? And why had they brought humans with them? Most of the time, I left the wondering of our history to people like Roth and Samara. Like Alaric, I was more of a forward-thinking person, and knowing those answers was unlikely to help with our immediate concerns of surviving, but sometimes, even I couldn't help but wonder what had happened five hundred years ago to set all this in motion.

The underbrush started to thin out and the tree line abruptly ended, revealing the reason for the ward, a crystal-clear pool of water in the middle of the clearing. Draven dismounted and loosely tied his mount's reins around a tree. I did the same, although I put a healthy amount of space between them since Zosa didn't look like she would tolerate any of the stallion's bullshit.

"How'd you even know about this place?" I didn't bother keeping the suspicion out of my voice. This little oasis was a hidden gem of House Harker that we didn't tell outsiders about. The water wasn't hot like the springs I'd taken Samara to in that outpost, but it wasn't exactly cold either. An underground stream fed the pool, and wherever that water came from, it was hot. Warm currents lazily circled around the pool, which helped with the overall temperature. On top of that, the bottom was made of black stones that soaked up the heat of the sun. There weren't any stones like that around here naturally, so it was assumed that some enterprising humans or Fae had taken advantage of the fairly shallow and crystal clear water to help increase the temperature a little bit.

"Samara mentioned it years ago." Draven shrugged. "We passed the markers for it a while back, and I wanted to see it for myself."

I frowned. Samara had never come here with me when we'd been growing up and had given me the impression she didn't like this place. I never understood why, because Sam *loved* water. If there was an inch of it, especially if it was warm water, she would crawl into it. She knew this place existed, but I didn't know why she would have talked to Draven about it.

Seeing my confusion, Draven smiled faintly. "Samara and I used to confide all sorts of things to each other. This place was in one of her confessions. You used to bring a lot of girls here when the two of you were growing up before she left for Drudonia. It hurt her greatly."

"Oh." I squeezed my eyes shut as regret at unintentionally causing Samara pain curled in my gut. "We couldn't be together back then—she was promised to Demetri, and even then, despite our young age, we knew nothing between us would ever be casual. I brought any dalliances I had here because I didn't want to rub Samara's face in them."

"She knew you were trying to protect her feelings," Draven assured me. "That's why she never mentioned it to you and told me instead."

Before I could ask him what his confession in return had been, Draven pulled his shirt over his head, and any words I'd been about to speak died in my throat. Fuck, I'd forgotten he was built like that. He might look like a spoiled prince with his well-tailored clothes and easygoing smile, but his body told a different story. I hadn't even known it was possible to have abs that well-defined.

"You're drooling, Kier."

My eyes darted up to his, and I snapped my mouth shut. "Am not."

He laughed and unlatched the coiled whip with bloodred, serrated edges from his belt before setting it next to the edge of the pool. I'd asked him once why he didn't carry a sword, as that seemed like a more practical and effective weapon. He'd simply said he didn't like them, but I hadn't missed the flash of pain and fear across his face when he'd answered.

The only other time I'd seen something close to fear on his face was when he'd pleaded with me to leave the Moroi realm days ago. Samara was convinced there was something else to Draven we weren't seeing. That he wasn't the villain all the evidence suggested he was. I wanted to believe her, but Sam's past with Draven was different than mine. She hadn't had her heart ripped out by him.

The heated desire that had been winding through my body at seeing Draven strip instantly cooled at the reminder. He hadn't just ended things between us. I was an adult, and while it would have hurt, I would have dealt with it, but he'd humiliated me and used his knowledge of my past and my private thoughts I'd shared with him to hurt me. I so rarely trusted people, and he'd known that.

His words had been calculated and cruel.

"It's been fun, but I'm bored now. Also, watch how you speak to me in the future, courtier."

Rationally, I knew this lended more support to Samara's idea that Draven was being controlled somehow by his mother, or at least wasn't the complete villain she'd initially thought. He'd even claimed that he'd said those things to protect me. None of that erased the pain though.

I glanced at Zosa, wanting to jump onto her and ride out

of here, but I'd promised Samara I'd keep Draven occupied for a few hours. She'd understand if I bailed, but Roth wouldn't have called a meeting if it hadn't been important. They needed time to talk and plan, and I would give them that time.

Angrily, I tore off my clothing, not even bothering to fold it, just dumping it all in a pile before stomping over to the pool and striding in. Pleasantly cool water greeted me as I swam out to the center where it was deepest and I couldn't reach the bottom. I treaded water while facing away from Draven, only turning around when I heard him enter the pool. The last thing I needed was to see him fully naked.

Every inch of that man was perfection, and I still remembered what it felt like to have his cock moving inside me. My resolve at keeping my hands to myself and maintaining distance would likely crumble if I saw all of him. I'd never really understood the appeal of hate fucking before, but that glimpse of his muscled chest earlier had definitely made me reevaluate my stance on that.

"You're thinking about hate fucking me, aren't you?" Draven drifted in front of me, a smirk stamped on his lips and his striking black-and-silver hair floating around him in the water.

"No," I said lightly. "I was thinking about drowning you, but then your ugly corpse would mess up my favorite swimming hole."

"Please." He smiled. "We both know my corpse would be gorgeous."

I laughed before I could stop myself, and his smile widened.

Then something flickered across his face faster than I could catch it before his smile faded and he swallowed. "I know you have every reason to distrust me. To hate me."

"I do." I watched him warily as we treaded water around each other.

"You need to know that—" He cut off his words as he winced sharply, as if he'd been struck by something.

"Drav?" Concerned filled me as I swam closer to him, sweeping some of his hair away from where it had been plastered to his face.

Bottomless blue eyes watched me with such sadness that I wanted to shake the truth out of him. The anger, the hurt, the fear, all of it fell away in an instant as I stared at him in this moment.

"Everything about me is a lie, Kier," he said desperately. "Half the words out of my mouth are lies. My past, present, and future are all lies crafted by *her*, but this"—he placed his hand over my heart—"this was always real."

Then he yanked me to him, and our mouths crashed against each other. I didn't even try to fight it; I just tangled my fingers in his hair and clutched him to me, our legs kicking in the water to keep us afloat. Draven parted his lips, and my tongue delved in. Fuck, I'd missed the way he tasted.

There'd always been something wild about Draven, different from other Moroi. He reminded me of the woods on a dark night. Dark and powerful and a little terrifying.

He groaned into my mouth when I pulled his hair a little rougher, then I felt his hard cock against my stomach, and when his hand slipped under the water to grip mine, my legs faltered and I almost slipped under. He chuckled and directed me over to the edge of the pool where several flat rocks rested in the water.

I intended to flip us so Draven was sitting on the stairs because I wanted to feel him come apart on my tongue, but just as my fingers gripped his hard length, stroking it once, he growled, "I want you first."

"You don't get everything you want, princeling." I snorted and tried to shove him up onto the stones, but the bastard twisted out of my grip and lifted me out of the water. Before I could slide back down, he jerked my legs apart and slid my cock into his mouth.

No teasing. No playful licking. He just swallowed me whole.

"FUCK!" I screamed as my dick hit the back of his throat and his claws dug into my thighs. How had I forgotten Drav had zero gag reflex? I raised my head so I could watch him draw back. This time, he did swirl his tongue around my head before licking off the bit of precum that'd already formed.

His wet hair hung around him, the silver more of a dark grey now, looking every inch the wicked prince that he was, and it made my cock twitch in his grip.

"I love it when you look at me like that," he purred.

"Like what?" I said in a strained tone as he sucked the tip of my cock back into his mouth and released it with a *pop*.

"Like you *see* me." Thin red lines raced through his deep blue eyes. "And want me anyway."

He didn't wait for me to respond, and I moaned as he took me all the way into his mouth again. My fingers twisted around that gorgeous hair, and I bucked my hips as I shoved his head down. His grip tightened on my thighs as he spurred me on, loving the brutal pace I was setting for him.

I watched his head bob up and down on my cock, and when his teeth lightly grazed my skin, I saw stars for a moment as my balls started to tighten.

"Fuck, Drav," I ground out. "I'm close."

My words only encouraged him as he hollowed out his cheeks until it felt like I was halfway down his throat. Then one of his hands left my thigh and cupped my balls a second later, fingers rubbing against them exactly the way I liked.

I threw my head back as I thrust up into Draven's perfect mouth and came down his throat. He sucked down every last drop before sliding up and down my cock a few more times as I continued to tremble in his grasp.

"Moonsdamn it all." I panted and let my head fall back as

he finally released me. "This was not what I'd planned when I asked you to come for a ride."

"Oh?" I could practically hear the smirk in his voice as he climbed up my body until he was above me and staring into my eyes. "And what type of *ride* were you hoping for?"

I raised my head and kissed him, enjoying tasting myself on his lips. "I don't regret this . . . but it doesn't change anything either, does it?"

Sadness crept back into Draven's face. For whatever reason, he wouldn't or couldn't tell us what was going on and why he was working with the wraiths and helping them attack Moroi outposts. Regardless, he was working with our enemy, which made him our enemy.

"No," he said in defeat. "It doesn't change anything. You and Samara might have my heart, but the Sovereign owns my soul."

CHAPTER SEVENTEEN

Samara

As I slipped through the double doors of the library, I was still reeling from what I'd seen in Draven's memory. But I tucked that away for later once I saw the scene before me. Roth was the only one there, and they were pacing.

Roth did *not* pace.

They sat perfectly still with a book in their hand, absorbing all the knowledge it contained before moving on to the next one. In fact, Roth would regularly yell at us for so much as breathing too loud while they were reading.

"Roth." I closed the distance between us until I stood in front of them. Roth stopped, orange fractures winding through their hazel eyes like fire. Usually, Roth's dark red hair was tidily swept back and they kept the sides closely shaved. Today, it just sort of flopped over to one side. I brushed my fingers beneath it, feeling the overgrown sides. "You're due for a shave," I mused.

I wasn't sure if it was possible to have more polar opposites than Kieran and Roth. While I'd known them both for a long time, it was easier to slip into a relationship with Kieran. He was cuddly and usually open with his emotions. Roth and I had known each other at Drudonia, but this romantic aspect of our relationship was new, and I was still learning how to navigate it. Roth did *not* cuddle. They also didn't tell me how they were feeling or whisper sweet nothings.

But they looked at me like I was a treasure when I recited Fae poetry, and they asked me my opinions on translations or history. Roth desired my mind as much as my body, maybe even more so, and I loved being consumed by them.

"Where are the others?" Roth rasped.

"They'll be here soon," I soothed before leading them over to a chair. They thunked down into it and wrapped the soft, dark blue shawl I'd gotten them a little tighter around their tunic. Roth was somehow always cold. They'd mumbled a thanks when I'd given it to them but had proceeded to wear it every single day since.

I brushed my fingers against the two embedded gems on the dark silver ring I wore on my pinky, letting Cali and Rynn know we needed to talk. If they weren't available now, I'd have to fill them in later, but Rynn was vital to my plan, so it'd make this a lot easier if she could join now.

"What are those?" Roth eyed the leather satchel I'd set on the table, the flap open and revealing the journals inside.

"Journals written by my mother." I pulled one of the books out and passed it to them. "There are more. We found them last night in a secret room in a cave down by the beach, all written by Harkers."

"What language is this?" They carefully flipped through the pages.

"I don't know," I said softly. "But my mother taught it to me. She said her mother taught it to her."

"I've never encountered it in any other writings." Roth frowned. "But some of these words . . . they're familiar. We use them in our common tongue."

Before we could dive further into the odd linguistics of the

Lunarian language, the library doors swept open, and Vail, followed by Alaric, stalked in. I glanced back and forth between them. Alaric's expression was flat, and his fingers were curled at his sides like he was imagining strangling someone. Thin lines of silver raced through Vail's eyes as menace practically poured off him.

Okay. Clearly they were pissed at each other. What exactly had Alaric said to get Vail to come here?

I decided it was not my problem because they were both here and I was used to dealing with them in pissy moods anyway. I pressed down on the gems on my ring again to get Rynn's and Cali's attention.

"What?" Cali snarled, her shadowy form appearing suddenly in the middle of the library. Alaric jumped, and even Vail looked a little unnerved. All Furies had shadow magic, which put everyone on edge because it made them very wraithlike. The more talented ones could appear in shadow form like Cali, but unlike her, others' forms were less defined and it was hard for them to hold any type of shape.

Cali appeared before us exactly as she looked in real life, only made of shadows instead of flesh.

Darkness billowed outward as she spread her wings wide, causing the individual strands of her hair to flutter around. There was another secret about Cali that only Rynn and I knew. She could also turn corporeal for small snatches of time, something that no other Furie could do . . . but all wraiths could.

"I wouldn't have annoyed you if this wasn't important," I told her. "Are you okay?"

Cali's lips hardened into a flat line. "I'm fine. Don't worry about it."

As if that were possible. "Okay," I said instead. "We'll give Rynn a few minutes, and if she can't make it, we'll ge—"

Shadows swirled next to Cali, and Rynn's lean frame

appeared a second later. Her shadowy form was a little less well-defined than Cali's since she was using a spell Cali had crafted specifically for her. But I could still make out her expression enough to see Rynn was worried.

That in itself wasn't unusual, because Rynn constantly worried about everything, but she was also in the thick of some complicated Velesian politics that she was trying to shield from me. This also meant my request was going to make her life even more difficult, but I didn't see any way around it.

"Good, we're all here." I grimaced and leaned my butt against the table where Roth was sitting, the others standing around in front of me. "We have a lot to go over. First, Rynn, Cali, let me catch you up on our special guest here at House Harker."

Ten minutes later, I'd told both of them everything about Prince Draven. How he'd been waiting for us when we'd gotten back from the temple, the suspicious marriage proposal, and every conversation we'd had with him since he'd been here. I left out his relationship with Kieran because I didn't feel right discussing that without Kier here, but sooner or later, that would have to be brought up as well. As much as I wanted to leave Kieran's personal life out of this, his history with Draven was relevant.

"Why the fuck didn't you tell us sooner?" Cali exploded. The shadows responded to her tension and skittered across the room.

Rynn's head turned sharply. "Calm down, Cali," she ordered. The pissed-off Furie whipped around to glare at her, but Rynn didn't back down. Dominance radiated from her as if she was in her considerably larger and more lethal lycanthrope form instead of her current lithe human skin. "Samara wouldn't have repeatedly summoned us like this for no reason. Find your center, take a few deep breaths, and settle down."

"Fuck you and your peaceful Velesian bullshit," Cali grumbled, but I could see her shoulders dropping a little as she concentrated on her breathing. The Velesians were the only ones of the Moon Blessed who actually transformed into predators, yet in many ways, they remained the most human of all of us.

While Cali reined herself in, Rynn looked at me. "I agree with your assessment that there is more to Draven than it appears. I've only met him twice, but both times, his soul was . . ." Rynn cocked her head in a purely lupine gesture. "He was unsettled."

I nodded in understanding. Most of the Moroi discounted the Velesians because they had little magic of their own. But they could shift into their beast forms and were in tune with the environment to a sometimes eerie degree. A Velesian might be able to sense if the growing season would be poor and the crops wouldn't be bountiful, or sense predators nearby, but they couldn't give you any concrete facts. Only feelings.

The Velesians trusted their instincts, while the Moroi scorned them for it.

They also occasionally had visions, but because of the increasing tensions between our people, they were less inclined to share those visions with us. It was one of the many ways the divide between the Moon Blessed was hurting us all.

"Roth has some things to share," I explained. "And then I have more to tell you all, in addition to what I think our next step should be."

"You mean your scheme," Cali muttered, but she appeared less feral, so I let it slide.

"I've discovered two things." Roth swept a hand through their hair. "Those black stones the humans used for the ritual aren't originally from Lunaria. The Fae did something to either bring them here or summoned creatures who could create them."

They flipped open a book, pulled out a folded piece of paper, and started reading.

> *Once they were doom*
> *Now they are salvation*
> *At great sacrifice we called*
> *They answered with death*
> *From fire and chaos*
> *A glittering dark was born*
> *Stones lead to home*
> *Where vengeance calls*

"I bet that sounded a lot prettier in the original Fae," I grumbled.

"Not all of us are fluent in those languages." Alaric slid me an amused look before focusing on Roth. "If the Fae went through some 'great sacrifice' to get those stones created, then they must be important to them."

"We already knew that." Vail shrugged, unimpressed. "It's clear that's what they're looking for in the outposts they're raiding."

"True," Roth acknowledged with a dip of their head. "This is merely confirmation that there is something important about those stones, and also, more can't be made, at least not easily. I wasn't able to find anything else about what the Fae did to acquire them in the first place, but whatever it was isn't something that can be easily repeated."

"It's in our best interest then to make sure they don't get their hands on any more than they already have." I looked at Rynn. "You were the one who noticed they were raiding old human towns. Can you work with Roth to come up with a list of all known settlements, and we'll try to get to them before the wraiths do?"

"We'll have to do it quietly," Vail said. "If they realize what we're doing, they'll increase their attacks."

I nodded. "We'll get the list to you and trust your judgment on that."

"There probably aren't many settlements in the badlands, but I can take care of any of those," Cali said. "And if there are any in the Northern Ridge, I can take those as well."

Rynn frowned. "That's Avala territory. The Alpha Pack won't like you poking around there."

"It's amazing how much I simply don't care." Cali's wings stretched out further before snapping inward. "Besides, they won't even know I'm there."

Rynn didn't look convinced but didn't argue, instead, she just shot me a concerned glance. I gave her a barely perceptible nod in return. Cali was always a little wild, but she wasn't usually this antagonistic, definitely not towards us. There was zero chance of us getting her to tell us what was wrong with other people around though. We'd have to corner her about it later.

"What else did you find out, Roth?" I asked. The information they'd shared so far was useful, but I didn't think it was what had them so worked up.

"The other day, when you were reading an Unseelie poem, one of the words stuck in my head. Since I was a little distracted at the time"—their eyes darted to me, orange fractures flashing across the light brown for a second—"I didn't fully realize why that word had jumped out at me until later. Based on the context in which it was used in the poem, I realized we have been translating it wrong this whole time."

Roth raised a book with a dark red covering and gold foiling off the desk. A Fae poetry book. Human books were always bound with simple leather. Roth flipped through the pages and then turned the book around so it faced us. On one page was the illustration of a crown. It looked like two bands that had been joined together, and a short poem was written in Unseelie on the opposing page.

"Most of the poem is so vague that it's hard to follow, but I think the Fae brought this crown with them from wherever they came from," Roth explained. "It's described as follows, '*A crown of two parts. Glittering gold and frosted silver. One half to see a soul. Another half to bind it.*'"

"Well, that's not good." Rynn sighed.

The others started talking about what this could mean, but I was trying to control my growing panic as I remembered my mother's words from the journal.

"This crown had been so simple. Just a simple silver band with delicate carvings. Parts of it had even appeared broken."

"Samara?"

I snapped out of my spiraling dread to meet Alaric's steady gaze. "I think Velika has the crown. Half of it anyway."

"What?" Roth paled even further. "What makes you think that?"

"That was the part I was going to tell all of you." I waved a hand at my bag and the journals it contained. "I read through some of my mother's journals. She talks about Velika wearing a simple silver crown with odd magic. My mother suspected it was a Fae artifact, and she was searching these lands to find more before Velika did."

"Did she mention anything specific about the crown?" Rynn asked. "Or about Erendriel or the wraiths being Fae? About Velika's alliance with them?"

"No." I shook my head. "Every hidden Fae hideout she and my father found was empty. She mentioned the wraiths acting strangely, but I don't think she knew they were the Fae, and she made no mention of an alliance between them and Velika. I think she only had strong suspicions about the Sovereign House but no actual proof."

"We need to tell Carmilla," Vail said firmly.

I pursed my lips, trying to think of how to phrase this so Vail wouldn't tear my head off. He was fiercely loyal to my aunt, and so was I, but unlike Vail, I could separate my own personal feelings from the situation at hand. "We need to make sure Carmilla is safe," I said carefully. "But we can't tell her any of this yet. First, she's at the Sovereign House, and we can't risk alerting Velika to what we know. If Velika's half of the crown gives her the ability to bind a soul to her, then there is a chance Carmilla is compromised."

The very idea of my aunt's will being taken away from her made me sick. But Carmilla trusted me to keep House Harker safe, which meant I had to consider the possibility that Velika would use her as a weapon against us.

"No." That one word so full of fury echoed in the space between me and Vail as he took a step closer to me. Cali immediately slid between us, and I had no doubt that if Vail continued towards me, she'd solidify enough to tear out his throat. He bared his teeth at her and his eyes bled silver.

She gave him a wicked grin in return, and I could practically see her eyes daring him to do something about it.

"Enough!" I snapped and slid around Cali to stand in front of Vail. I was reasonably sure Vail wouldn't attack me . . . and I couldn't let him know Cali had the ability to become corporeal. I knew Vail already considered her a potential threat based on the calculating way he watched her, looking for weaknesses. He had treated Cali with respect on account of how many times she had saved rangers, but if she ever changed from potential threat to actual threat . . . I had no doubt Vail would do his best to destroy her.

Or try to, at least. My money was on my friend, but I'd rather avoid that fight altogether, which meant keeping him away from Cali so she didn't do something stupid and give herself away. Seriously, what was she thinking antagonizing him like this?

A low growl rumbled from Cali's chest, and the hairs on the back of my neck rose, but I didn't turn around to look at her. No matter how strange she was acting right now, I had to believe she would never harm me. I would keep my friend sane through sheer force of my own will if I had to.

"There is nothing I won't do to protect Carmilla." I met Vail's unrelenting, predatory stare. "She is my aunt and the only family I have left, but if we storm the Sovereign House and tear her out of it, Velika will retaliate, and we have no idea what that crown can actually do. If she's already bound Carmilla to her, we don't know how to break it. We need answers, and we have to find them before showing our hand."

"And where exactly do you propose we find these answers?" Vail crossed his arms and took a few steps back.

Tension still wound through him, but the silver faded until it was only a sliver against the dark grey. Better. I let out a breath and moved to stand next to Cali, who was still staring at Vail like she was imagining carving him apart with her talons.

"My parents were planning on searching another Fae site before they were killed." Grief briefly rose to the surface before I ruthlessly suppressed it once more, keeping my voice even, if a little flat. "That trip took to Velesian territory wasn't just to try to repair relations between them and the Moroi. My mother wanted to get permission to search around Lake Malov."

"Shit," Rynn spat. "That's going to be a problem."

"I know." I gave her an apologetic look. "But we have to go there. The wraiths have avoided that area too, so there is a real chance that if something is there, they haven't found it either."

Rynn frowned but didn't disagree.

"What's so special about Lake Malov?" Roth's piercing

stare locked on Rynn. "I've heard the rumors—it's not just the wraiths that avoid it, other monsters do too. In some ways, it's the safest place in all of Lunaria. Yet the Narchis Order steers clear of it and forbids anyone from going there. I've searched through every text and book I could find, but nothing explains why."

"We don't know exactly." Rynn shifted back and forth on her feet. "Velesians may not have blood or shadow magic, but we feel things. The land whispers to us, and we've learned to always listen to what it tells us."

"And what does the land around Lake Malov tell you?" Alaric asked.

"To stay the fuck away." Rynn shook her head, appearing to be genuinely rattled at even discussing the lake.

"We can't." I sighed. "Maybe the other half of the crown is there and that's what's causing the discontent? My mother said she could feel the magic from Velika's half of the crown and that it felt wrong."

Rynn rubbed her face, causing the shadows to lose their form slightly. "There is a gathering of the packs in one week. All the Orders will be there, and my pack is hosting it in Fervis territory. Lake Malov is only an hour from us. That will be our best opportunity to slip past the patrols unnoticed, but we'll have to be quick."

"All the Orders?" I raised an eyebrow. The Velesians were broken up into three Orders: the Narchis, the Fervis, and the Avala. The Alpha Pack was of the Avala Order and was the one Rynn was to join to further the alliance between them and her birth Order, Narchis.

The Fervis Order was the most volatile of the three, and anytime all of the Orders met up, it was almost guaranteed to result in bloodshed, which meant it would definitely be the perfect opportunity for us to explore.

"All of them," Rynn confirmed, moving restlessly again and causing tendrils of shadows to swirl around her. "Cade made it very clear they're all expected to come."

Ah. That was why she was so uncomfortable. Cade was the leader of the Alpha Pack and the one who had negotiated for Rynn to join their pack. He was also the one Rynn corresponded with the most—and most of those conversations were fraught with tension.

"Alright, that's our best opportunity then," I said evenly. "We'll have to figure out the exact timing, but once we do, whoever goes can meet Rynn and Cali near Lake Malov."

Everyone nodded in reluctant agreement except Cali. "I can't go there," she said in a low, haunted voice and wrapped her wings around her body, shadows dripping off them. With mournful eyes she met my stare. "Something in that place . . . calls to me. All Furies feel it, but I seem to feel it more than any other. If I go there, I will lose myself."

Even from her shadowy form, I could see the genuine fear in her eyes. I knew then that whatever was going on with my friend, she was aware of it, and it terrified her.

Fuck it.

Without giving a shit what the others thought, I moved towards Cali and wrapped my arms around her shadowy form. I could sense her wavering for a moment before the shadows became solid and my friend hugged me back.

Alaric sucked in a breath, but Vail and Roth kept quiet.

"Whatever is going on with you, Cal, we have your back," I whispered. "We'll survive this, and then we'll figure out how to help you."

"Our ties are eternal." Rynn moved closer, her hand hovering around Cali as if she wished she could join in on the hug.

Cali shuddered beneath me, and for a second, darkness spread throughout the room before being sucked back into her.

I felt it the moment she became nothing but shadows again, the dark wisps tickling my skin as they pulled away.

"Me, Vail, and Rynn will go," I declared.

"No." Alaric shook his head. "I'll go with you, and you know Kieran will want to come too."

Roth was looking at all of us, a torn expression on their face. They'd spent the majority of their life behind the wards of Houses or Drudonia. Roth wasn't a fighter by any stretch of the imagination, but even they didn't seem keen on me going out into the wilds with only Vail at my side until we met up with Rynn.

"You have to stay, Alaric," I said softly. "House Harker needs someone to run things while both Carmilla and I are away. And I won't risk Kieran."

"That's not your decision to make." Alaric's eyes flashed a brilliant turquoise before fading back to light green.

"She's the Heir," Vail growled. "It *is* her right."

"You would say that," Alaric snapped and stepped towards Vail. "Maybe the third time will be the charm and you'll actually claim her life on your next attempt."

The Marshal of House Harker straightened as he met Alaric's accusatory stare, and then he looked at me, his expression the same as when I'd told him to never doubt my devotion to House Harker. I hadn't been able to decipher it then, but now I could see the emotions brimming in his eyes. Respect. Yearning. Confliction.

Once again, I was confused by Vail's reactions. Even worse . . . my feelings for him were getting confounding as well. Waking up surrounded by his scent this morning had been nice, really nice, and that was an absolutely insane feeling to have about someone who'd tried to kill me recently.

I didn't think he would try to kill me again, but I hadn't thought that the previous times either. The situation in the temple wasn't entirely his fault—it was his bloodlust that had been driving him. Even if I wasn't sure I was safe around him, he was the only option I had to get me through the wilds quickly to Lake Malov.

Vail watched me steadily, and I got the impression he understood every conflicted thought that had just raced through my mind.

"I pledge on the grave of my parents that I will protect Samara with my life." I inhaled sharply as a muscle in Alaric's cheek twitched. He knew the Marshal was speaking the truth, but he still didn't like it.

"It'll be okay, Alaric." I laid a hand on his forearm. "We have to do this, and you know it makes sense for the three of us to go. Vail can get me there safely, and Rynn is the most familiar with the area."

He tore his gaze away from Vail to look at Rynn. "Do you? Know the area, I mean?"

"Yes." Rynn nodded confidently. "It's not a pleasant region to be around, but I wandered there often when I was a child. It was one of the few places I could be alone." She worried her bottom lip. "Lately, I've found myself going back there for the same reason."

This time, it was Cali who looked at me with concern. The three of us all had our issues. Cali struggled with her rage and magic, I struggled balancing being the resilient Heir of House Harker while also processing the grief of losing the two most important people in the world to me, and our sweet Rynn, she struggled with being used as a political pawn her entire life and never knowing who she could truly trust amongst her own people. I had no doubt her parents cared for her in their own ways, but that hadn't stopped them from agreeing to send her away to join the Alpha Pack when she'd come of age.

"What about the prince?" Alaric grimaced. "We won't be able to cover your absence for so long."

"We have at least a few days to figure that out," I said.

"We'll just need to keep him occupied for a few hours after we leave so we can create some distance. Maybe mention that more of the spine-backed boars have been spotted and I wanted to investigate myself. Let him know he's welcome to stay here and wait for my return."

Alaric snorted. "That'll go over well."

"It doesn't matter." I shrugged. "Vail and I will keep off the main roads and won't stay at any of the outposts. He won't be able to track us."

"I'll review the list of old human settlements. There may be some close enough that I can investigate them before we have to leave. I need to update Emil as well so he can help with the searches." Vail strode towards the door to leave but stopped when I called out to him.

"Vail, if you find any, tell me. I want to see them for myself." The hand at his side bunched into a fist at the command in my voice, but he turned his head slightly and jerked it in a short nod before leaving.

"I'll find out more about the meeting so I can determine the best time for us to do this, as well as the patrols in the area. They'll no doubt be increased with all the Orders gathering in one place." Rynn waved goodbye and vanished.

Cali stared at the space she'd been standing in before swiveling her head towards me in a movement that felt distinctly predatory. "Be careful."

In a blink, she was gone, a few shadows swirling in the air before dissipating.

"Do we need to worry about Cali?" Alaric asked in a calm, measured tone.

"She's fine," I said with a confidence I didn't entirely feel.

Alaric looked at me for a long moment, and I could see the doubt in his eyes, but he didn't voice his concerns. "I'll be in my study whenever you're ready," he finally said before he too left.

It took me a moment to remember he'd agreed to feed from me. I was a little surprised that not only had he not changed his mind but that he'd reminded me.

"I'll do some research on Furies while you're away," Roth said quietly. "We understand them the least out of all the Moon Blessed, but I have a few scrolls that detail cases of Furies losing themselves. Perhaps I'll find something useful."

They wouldn't. Rynn and I had poured through every scroll, book, and scrap of information we could find over the years. Nobody knew why the Furies were so volatile, but I appreciated the sentiment all the same.

"Stay with me tonight?" I swallowed, feeling a little unsure of my request. Roth's eyes flicked up from the book they'd already started reading, and they arched an eyebrow. "If you grab whatever books you want and head to my suite now, the prince won't see. He's out with Kieran. I'll tell Kier he has to sleep in his room tonight."

I wasn't exactly sure where Roth stood in regards to Kieran. They obviously had no problem with me being in a relationship with him, but as far as I knew, Roth wasn't attracted to Kieran. Even if all we did was sleep, I didn't know if they would be comfortable sharing a bed with him as well.

One corner of Roth's mouth quirked up into the barest hint of a smile. "You will return to your room after dinner," they ordered, and a thrill ran up my spine. "I will have you until midnight, then the pretty one and the grumpy one can come. You'll be passed out by then because I plan on being quite thorough, but they can at least sleep next to you. Want me to take these back with me?"

It took my mind a second to focus on the leather satchel Roth was holding up, the one that contained the Harker journals.

"Yes." I cleared my throat. "Thank you."

Roth swung the bag over their shoulder and flicked their

left arm towards the table, the bloodred ribbons they kept wrapped around their forearms unwinding and maneuvering around the stack of books until they were in a neat little bundle. Then Roth winked at me before sauntering towards the door with their ribbons tugging the bundle of books behind them. "See you in a few hours."

CHAPTER EIGHTEEN

Samara

My steps were quick as I made my way to Alaric's study from mine. His was also on the third floor of the main tower but on the complete opposite side. I'd wanted to go there directly from the library, but instead, I'd forced myself to go to my own study and get some work done. Then I'd met with Yolanthe and a few other advisors.

I hadn't told anyone I'd be gone for a few days soon because I couldn't risk Draven getting tipped off, but I made sure to deal with any issues that needed my attention. And there had been many. Surviving in Lunaria wasn't easy, even when there weren't nefarious plots threatening to damn us all. The wards that protected our Houses and outposts were powered by gems, which we seemed to always be running low on. And then those fucking boars had wiped out more crops. We'd be fine unless something went wrong with the summer crops. If that happened, the upcoming winter would be a lean one.

"Couldn't the Fae have picked a nicer place to drag us all?" I muttered, although I doubted they had come here voluntarily, which begged the question, who was powerful enough to force the Fae to do anything?

I was still musing this over when I reached Alaric's study. The door was open a crack, so I pushed it and stepped inside. Alaric's eyes rose from the letter he was reading, watching as I closed the door behind me and flipped the lock. Then I brushed the glyph on the wall, activating the silencing spell before walking towards his desk. I wasn't sure exactly what was going to happen in the next few minutes, but I was pretty sure we wouldn't want anyone to overhear or interrupt us.

"You came." He leaned back in his chair, a tightness around the corners of his eyes.

"I told you I'd let you feed from me." I moved behind the desk and sat on it, scooting over until I was sitting directly in front of him. As usual, Alaric's desk was perfectly organized, and I was careful not to knock over the stacks of letters and scrolls. "Did you think I would change my mind?"

Alaric's gaze fell to where the high slit of my dress revealed a large amount of skin. Then he swallowed as impossible blue lines flashed across his light green eyes. I could feel the bloodlust rising within him as he wrestled it, and my heart raced a little faster as I leaned back on the desk, the movement causing even more of my thigh to be on display.

I still remembered quite vividly how he had tasted in my mouth. I wanted to feel his fangs in my neck as he buried his cock inside me. He'd been so demanding before, and I wanted him to give in to that urge again, but something told me that if I pushed him on this, he'd pull away. So I forced myself to wait.

"My family has a history of turning Strigoi." The heart hammering inside my chest froze, and Alaric looked at me with an almost mournful expression. "It wasn't just my cousin, Faolan, who turned."

"Who else?" I asked softly, even as my mind was racing,

trying to remember anything else about Alaric's family. Aside from his parents coming from one of our outposts, I couldn't think of anything useful.

He looked away, staring at a spot on his desk. "Maternal grandmother—she turned after my grandfather was killed by wraiths—and both grandparents on the paternal side. Best I can tell, over half on my father's side have turned Strigoi, and my mother's side isn't that much better. It's one of the reasons my parents were so relieved to be offered high-ranking positions here."

Because they could regularly drink from Carmilla. Partaking in the blood of any of the House families significantly reduced one's chances of becoming Strigoi. So much so that drinking from the House bloodlines had been the norm for a while, but now there were too many Moroi for that to be feasible. Parents would bring their young children to whichever House they belonged to shortly after they were born so the child could be given House blood, but that was it.

My generation had been the most stable so far, only a few instances of Moroi losing themselves completely in bloodlust and becoming Strigoi, but it did happen. I suspected, with the increased wraith attacks, it had happened more in the past few months and we just didn't know yet. When facing certain death, some Moroi would relinquish their hold on humanity in an attempt to survive. Who knew how many more Strigoi were prowling the wilds after all the outpost attacks?

I mentally added that to the long list of problems we were facing and refocused on the one in front of me. Alaric's cousin, Faolan, had turned, and I knew he'd been there to witness it. It wasn't all that surprising that he'd been scarred by that.

"You won't become Strigoi." It was both a command and a promise. I leaned forward and tipped Alaric's face up with my fingertips. "You are *mine*."

His green eyes turned solid turquoise, and he released a low growl that had me clenching my thighs together.

"I can feel it every time my bloodlust rises, the all-consuming hunger. It's only a matter of time." His eyes fell to the pulse on my neck before he forced himself to look away and stare blankly at the wall. "There is a courtier who I have an arrangement with. She visits every couple of months, and I feed from her then. I only drink a little, and we do it at midday, when the sun is the strongest over the moon."

Because the moon called to our bloodlust. All of our senses were heightened at night, but letting our bloodlust rise under the light of the moon was intoxicating.

The rangers often hunted at night because of it. They'd point themselves in the directions of the monsters and let themselves go, reclaiming their humanity in the morning. They spent years practicing that ability though, always keeping the smallest hold on themselves so they weren't lost forever.

"I almost lost it last time she came." Alaric rubbed his mouth like he could still taste the blood on it. Some part of me raged at the idea of him feeding from someone else, but I bit back the growl that crept up my throat. There was a time and place for territorial bullshit, and this wasn't it.

"When's the last time you fed?" I asked softly.

"Almost four months ago."

Fuck. Our bodies needed food, but our magic needed blood. Most Moroi drank once a month, more often if they'd used a lot of magic for spellcasting or healing. Alaric's control over his bloodlust had to be ironclad if he was still holding it together.

But even he had a breaking point.

"You're only hurting yourself. Harker blood will help you."

"I don't want to hurt you," he rasped as he turned his gaze away from the wall and back to me.

"You won't." I let my bloodlust rise until I knew my eyes were black. "Trust me, I can hold my own."

Alaric went still as he took me in. "What . . ." Then his eyes dropped to my fangs peeking through my parted lips. "What does it feel like to you? You almost never put it away anymore, not entirely."

I thought about it. "Everything is just . . . more. The scents in the air. The colors in the flowers." Slowly, I reached out and trailed my fingers along his jawline, my heart skipping as he turned his head slightly to inhale my scent better. "Your skin beneath my touch."

A few beats passed between us before he looked at me with bottomless eyes. "And the hunger?"

"There," I admitted. "Always there, but it's like an impatient friend I've learned to live with and occasionally throw a bone to." Something shuddered in his expression, prompting me to ask, "What does it feel like for you?"

"Mindless and cruel," he said without hesitation. "Whatever it is that prowls beneath my skin . . . it isn't me. It feels like it wants to devour everything I am until nothing remains but itself. The monster."

I understood that I was part of the small group of Moroi who were exceptions to the rule. Something about us was different, our bloodlust integrated more with who we were, but Vail and the other rangers weren't like me, and they could harness their bloodlust just fine. It was possible for any Moroi.

Alaric was letting his fear override everything else, and that was making things so much worse. There was no separating a Moroi from their bloodlust. It was something that had to be accepted. Alaric was trying to deny an intrinsic part of himself, and it was going to be the death of him someday.

Panic wrapped around my heart and squeezed when a little green came back into Alaric's eyes, and I could tell he was pulling away. If things had been different, I would have let him. I understood now why he was so paranoid and obsessed with control. His perfectly organized office. The clothing that was never out of place. Why he was so annoyed at me every time I got him to lose his temper.

Alaric lived every day terrified he was going to lose control of his bloodlust. Given his family history, his concerns were valid, but starving himself wasn't going to help—he had to know that. His fear was winning over his logic. I was leaving tomorrow, and he was still weak from the monster attack in the cave. He needed to feed, and I refused to leave this office until he was sated.

With slow, deliberate movements, I slid off the desk until I was straddling his lap. Alaric went completely still, his hands hovering around me but not touching.

"Samara," he warned.

"You're not healing the way you should be because you've waited too long to drink," I said calmly. "I'm worried about you, and that means I'll be distracted when Vail and I leave tomorrow. Do you really want me wandering around the woods with this weighing heavily on me instead of fully concentrating on my surroundings?"

He narrowed his eyes. "You won't convince me with logic."

I smiled, completely undeterred.

"There are two ways we can do this." My hair fell in a dark curtain as I pulled it aside and bared my neck to him. "You can drink from me and *only* drink, or"—I rolled my hips, feeling his hard erection, and he groaned—"you drink and fuck me at the same time. The choice is yours, but you have to drink, Alaric."

Blue and green warred in his eyes like waves crashing against each other. Then his lips parted, revealing sharp fangs, but he still didn't move.

"I don't believe you'll hurt me." He shivered as I trailed a finger along his jawline. "But I am capable of defending myself and will do so if I have to."

"Promise me." Alaric reached around me and pulled a drawer open before a silver blade appeared between us. "Promise you'll use this if things get out of hand."

I took the dagger, wrapping my fingers around the handle. His eyes bore into mine, and I knew he would not relent on this. If this was what it took to make him willingly drink from me, then I'd do it, even if my stomach rolled at the idea of hurting him.

My grip tightened. "I promise."

Alaric studied me for a long moment before wrapping one hand around the back of my neck. He was giving me time to change my mind, which was kind of sweet, but I was officially out of patience.

I let my hand holding the dagger fall loosely to my side but slid the other one behind Alaric's head and yanked him towards my neck. His chest vibrated with a deep growl, and the possessiveness in it had my toes curling.

Fingers dug into the ridge of my hip as his hand on the back of my neck squeezed harder. A throaty moan slipped from my lips as I ground against him. If he didn't bite or fuck me soon, I was going to burst. Lips brushed against my neck, the touch delicate compared to the punishing grip of his hands. Then he kissed my neck again before I felt the sharp sting of his fangs sinking into my flesh.

"Yes," I breathed out as the brief moment of pain gave way to pure pleasure.

Alaric drank deeply but still pulled away too soon, and warm blood slid down my neck as I looked into bright turquoise eyes. Quick, shallow pants escaped through his lips, and I could feel how taut his body was beneath mine. He needed more.

I licked my bottom lip, and his eyes snagged on the movement. "You're still hungry," I purred, "so we're not done here." I sucked in my bottom lip and bit down, piercing it with my own fang. Blood dribbled down my chin, and Alaric was there in an instant, his mouth crashing against mine.

The knife almost slipped from my grasp when he suddenly rose out of the chair, taking me with him, but I kept my hold on it. I'd promised him I'd watch out for myself, and while I didn't believe I'd need to, it was important to him. He didn't trust himself yet to not lose control, and that knife was his safe word.

Alaric sucked on my bottom lip before kissing me deeply as he sat me down on the edge of his desk, my legs spread wide on either side of him. Fingers wrapped around my hair to wrench my head back, and I writhed in Alaric's grip when he struck at my neck, leaning me further back on the desk. The neat stack of papers went flying, and I barely managed to slam my hand down on a pile of books to keep them from crashing to the floor too.

Fingers slipped between my thighs and roughly tugged my undergarments to the side before plunging into my slick center, and Alaric gave an approving growl at how wet I was for him. A strangled moan escaped me as he slowly pulled his fingers out, rubbing them over my clit before thrusting them back in. The climax was instant and brutal. I barely managed to keep from slamming my head back onto the desk as my body clamped down around his fingers, the books tumbling to the floor.

Alaric's fangs slipped from my neck as he raised his head and eyed the mess we were making of his desk. He glanced at my hand that was still awkwardly holding the dagger to the side because I really didn't want to accidentally stab myself or him. My mind was still reeling from the orgasm, so I was only faintly aware of him plucking the dagger from my grip before he slammed it into the desk. The blade sunk a few inches into the wood, still upright and within my reach.

I extended my hand to grab Alaric's tunic, wanting to see

more of him, but apparently he had the same idea because he ripped the front of my dress in half. I moaned as his mouth found my nipple and sucked hard, his hand gripping my other breast, then I arched my hips up, trying to grind against him. I wanted to feel his hard cock in my hands, but I wasn't in a position to reach it.

Alaric laughed against my skin as he twirled his tongue around my sensitive nipple. "You're very needy," he said roughly before sucking my nipple back into his mouth. "I want to taste you everywhere."

"Fuck!" I cried out when his fangs sank into the swell of my breast, causing me to buck upward. I slipped my hands under the back of his tunic and felt the hard, corded muscles of his back flexing beneath my touch.

Then the hand that had been playing with my breast trailed down my stomach, fingers dipping and rising over every one of my curves until they disappeared between my thighs once more. I felt his nails harden into claws that he slid lightly across my skin before tearing my undergarments away.

Sliding his fangs free, he hovered above me, hunger still shining in his bright turquoise eyes. There wasn't a hint of green to be seen, his bloodlust riding high. The sound of more fabric being torn rang throughout the room, and then I felt his cock nudge at my entrance. Alaric went predatorily still as he took me in, splayed out beneath him, and hesitation flickered in his eyes.

I stretched my hand up and cupped his cheek. "You're still you, Alaric. This is part of who you are, and I want all of it."

My words were his undoing, and a scream tore out of my throat as he slammed into me. There was no easing into it. No going slow. Alaric's fingers dug into my hips as he fucked me hard and fast, and the tension that had been building between my thighs erupted. Alaric didn't slow down a bit, just fucked me through it as I saw stars. I gripped my bouncing tits to keep them in place, and when I saw Alaric's eyes burn with desire, I squeezed them a little harder.

This time, his eyes glazed over, and I let out a husky laugh. One hand left my hip to rub my clit, and my pleasure-laden laughter turned into a strangled scream as his damn fingers played with the already overstimulated bundle of nerves.

"So fucking wet," Alaric growled. "I could smell how turned on you were when Kieran was fucking your cunt and I was thrusting my cock in and out of that perfect fucking mouth." Strong hands gripped my legs, raising them up until the tops of my thighs brushed my stomach. "You enjoyed taking every inch of our cocks, didn't you?"

Fuck. My pussy clenched around him as he continued to hammer into me. I never would have guessed Alaric would be a dirty talker, but I was fucking here for it.

He thrust into me hard one more time, and the desk slid a few inches. My eyes stared into his, and I saw the same desperate need reflected in them. A possessive growl rippled up his throat as he lowered my legs and took a step back, his cock sliding out of me. I let out a whimpered cry at the loss but then yelped when Alaric flipped me over so I was bent over the desk.

"Option two," he breathed into my ear, his chest against my back. I felt him rubbing the head of his thick cock against my slick folds. "You said I could feed from you, or feed from you *and* fuck you at the same time. *Option fucking two, Sam.*"

"Fuck yes," I pleaded in a tone that I'd probably be embarrassed about later, but holy fuck, I hadn't expected Alaric to be like this. I'd expected him to be amazing but in a calm and thorough kind of way, not whispering dirty words into my ear while roughly using my body however he wanted.

His chest rumbled against me as he let out another deep laugh, and I couldn't resist grinding my ass against him. In a second, his body vanished from where he'd been pinning me down, and then a loud slap sounded. I let out a sharp exhale when he slapped my ass again.

Hard.

Wet heat spread down my inner thighs, and Alaric swirled his cock in it as his fingers rubbed the spot on my ass he'd slapped. "You like to play rough, don't you?" I clenched my thighs together, and he chuckled darkly. "When you get back, Kieran and I are sharing you again, and this"—he slapped my ass again—"is *mine*."

"Sure," I breathed out, my entire body trembling in anticipation. "Just fuck me now please."

"I think that's the first time you've ever said please to me in your life." He nudged my legs further apart so I was even more bared to him and leaned over me again. I moaned as his fingers slipped over my clit before he pushed them slowly inside me. "Grab the desk," he ordered roughly.

Alaric withdrew his fingers, and I grabbed the edge of the desk. Then he kissed my neck over the place he'd bitten me when we'd started all this. The broad head of his cock pushed through my slickness, and he buried himself inside me at the same moment his fangs sank into my flesh.

My fingers dug into the wood as Alaric pounded me into the desk, his grip on my hair almost punishing as he wrenched my head back further and drank deeply. One of his hands seized my left leg and lifted it until my knee was on the desk.

"Oh fuck!" I screamed as the adjusted position allowed him even deeper access, the intensity of it all sending me spiraling as waves of pleasure slammed into me. Alaric's grip on my hair tightened for a second before he ripped his fangs free from my neck and bellowed as he followed me over the edge.

Neither of us moved for a few minutes. Alaric just released my hair and pressed his head to the back of my neck while we panted and trembled as the remnants of our orgasms passed.

Finally, Alaric straightened, and we both groaned as his

cock slid free. I winced a little as I stood, feeling tender . . . everywhere. I had an indent on my thigh where it'd been pinned against the desk, my head and neck were sore from the hair pulling, and my poor pussy had taken a beating.

Alaric looked at me carefully, as if he was noting all of this and feeling a little unsure about what we'd just done.

"I loved every second of that, so wipe that look off your face." I grinned at him. "Didn't know you had it in you, Alaric. Want to bet we can break the desk next time?"

"You're a menace." He shook his head even as a smile crept across his lips. "We're using your study next time. It's always a disaster zone anyway."

"Rude." I looked around the floor surrounding his desk that was now covered with paperwork, scrolls, and everything else that had been neatly stacked. "Better idea—we use Kier's study."

Alaric laughed. "Look at that. You and I are capable of negotiating and agreeing on something."

"Keep fucking me like that and I think you'll find I'm a lot more agreeable." I sent him a sly look.

"I think I can do that," he murmured and pulled the dagger free from the desk. Then he studied it for a long moment before raising his gaze to me. "This comes out every time, just in case."

"Okay," I agreed softly, even though I didn't believe we'd ever need it. "Whatever you need, Alaric. Just don't pull away from me if you get scared, because I'm all in on this and I can't watch you walk away again."

He tossed the knife back onto the desk and wrapped his arms around me. "Never again, Sam. I promise. You are all I need."

CHAPTER NINETEEN

Roth

I BLEW out a frustrated breath and slammed the book closed. Another dead end. So far, I had a long list of problems and very few solutions, and that list was only growing.

Solving problems was my thing. I enjoyed it and was good at it, but usually the problems I was trying to solve were things I could look at from an abstract viewpoint. If I couldn't solve them, I would be annoyed, but I'd just move on to something else and forget about them in a few days.

It was harder to do that though when my lover, who was a fucking Heir, was counting on me. I didn't want to let her down.

I glanced around the suite and the absolute chaos it contained. For someone who always appeared so well put together, Samara's rooms were a bit of a shock. I'd only been here a handful of times because she almost always came to my room. I had a tendency to lose track of time, and Samara often felt compelled to hunt me down and make sure I was eating and sleeping enough.

At first, it had annoyed me, but after ensuring I ate or drank something, Samara would flop onto my bed and pick up a book. No other demands. No questions. She'd simply wanted to make sure I was okay and, once she'd done that, purely enjoy my company.

Nobody in my life had ever given a shit about me this way, and I didn't exactly know what to do about that, or the fact that I'd been at House Harker for such a short time and already couldn't imagine my life anywhere else with anyone else.

I scowled at the book in my hand for daring to not have the answers before tossing it onto the table in front of me. When it slid across the surface and stopped just before some books that Samara had placed haphazardly into a tall, teetering stack, I winced. I didn't quite understand how it hadn't fallen over yet, but I was worried that if I so much as breathed in its direction, it would collapse. So I'd left it alone and hoped it continued to defy its destiny.

I'd barely gotten into a book again when the door opened and Samara strolled in looking a little . . . disheveled.

The scent of blood, sweat, and lingering lust filled the air.

"You and Alaric are still working things out, I see." I raised an eyebrow at her, and Samara just smirked before heading towards the washroom, stripping as she went.

"I think we've worked past all the hard bits."

"I bet," I said dryly, lips curling up slightly. It was good to see Samara happy, given everything that was going on.

She paused halfway across the room and whirled around in nothing but her panties, giving me a concerned look. "Are you . . . okay about me being with Alaric? I know you're fine with Kieran, but I just realized I never specifically talked to you about Alaric." The smile that had been plastered across her face fell, and her brows bunched in concern. "Fuck, I'm sorry, Roth. Things kind of happened fast between me and Alaric. I wasn't expecting it to be honest, but that's no excuse. I should have talked to you about this sooner and—"

"Samara," I cut her off, a bemused look on my face. It wasn't often that I saw the supremely confident Heir of House Harker looking unsure about anything. "As long as he treats you well and makes you happy, I have no problem with any of it."

"Okay." She chewed her bottom lip. "You're absolutely sure?"

I rolled my eyes before standing from the settee and walking over to her to kiss her lightly on the lips. "Babe." I kissed her again. "It's fine. I appreciate you taking my feelings into account." Another kiss. "But it is impossible for me to take you and this conversation seriously when you're standing there basically naked and chewing on your lip like that."

"Oh!" Samara looked down at herself like she'd just remembered she was in nothing but panties. Then she gave me a sheepish grin as color darkened her cheeks. "I . . . ummm . . . usually start stripping as soon as I'm back in my rooms. Given the option, I prefer to just lounge around naked or maybe in an oversized shirt if it's cold."

"I'm going to be in your rooms a lot more now." The left corner of my mouth tilted up. Samara usually came to my room, and the few times I'd been in her room had been because she'd dragged me here from the library. We hadn't exactly wasted any time getting each other naked. I'd never just . . . hung out with Samara in her rooms. This was new territory for me, and I fought to keep from running my hand through my hair.

"Okay," she said again, this time, a little mischievous spark lighting up her dark purple eyes. "You called me *babe*."

Some of the tension bled out of me. She was so adorable sometimes.

"Sure did. Now go rinse off." Then I leaned forward to whisper into her ear, "*Babe*."

She grinned and sauntered off to the washroom,

swinging her hips with a ridiculous exaggeration. I watched every second of it before retreating to the settee and diving into the books once more. A stupid smile stretched across my face, but I didn't care because there wasn't anyone here to see it.

Ten minutes later, a thoroughly clean Samara sat down next to me, towel drying her wet hair as she scanned the books I'd brought with me. Despite the messy state of her room, I had no doubt Samara knew exactly where everything was and easily identified my items.

Her eyes lingered on the neat stack of clothing sitting on one of the chairs. I'd brought not only clothes for tonight, but extra clothes to keep here for whenever I stayed over. She didn't comment on the clothing, but I didn't miss the pleased expression that flashed across her face.

Samara liked me being in her rooms. This wasn't a passing fancy for her, and it sure as shit wasn't for me. She had brought up Alaric and apologized for that misstep, even though I truly didn't care since it had been clear to anyone with eyes that those two were headed in that direction, so it was time for me to come clean too.

"I got kicked out of Drudonia," I blurted out. *Smooth, Roth. Couldn't have come up with a better way to phrase that?*

Once again, the happy expression vanished from her face, and I squeezed my eyes shut with a wince. Why was I so terrible at talking like a normal person?

Oh, right, because I'd barely spoken to anyone for the first ten years of my life.

"What I meant to say—" The words died on my lips when I opened my eyes and met Samara's solid black ones.

A tightly contained fury rolled off her in waves, and she flexed her now claw-tipped fingers. "Was this your House's doing? Their way of forcing you to go back to them?"

"What?" I asked in shock. "No, they don't care—"

"Because I will tear House Devereux apart brick by brick," Samara snarled. "You are *mine*."

"I am." My hands gently wrapped around hers, and I raised her right hand to sit over my heart, not flinching as her claws pierced my thin shirt to sink lightly into the flesh below. "House Devereux doesn't want me either." I tried and failed to keep my tone light. "So it's good that you're a fan of my tongue and reading comprehension because otherwise, things would not be looking too good for me right now."

Samara took in a deep breath, and I felt her claws slide free before she pulled her hand away and winced at her bloody fingertips. "Sorry." She sighed. "I haven't bothered to tuck the bloodlust completely away since getting back. With Draven here, I'd rather keep it close." Purple bled back into her eyes as the black threads receded until they were just thin, dark jagged lines, a reminder of the monster always lurking under the surface.

"The fangs haven't escaped my notice." I gave her a reassuring grin that I wasn't frightened of her. Every Moroi treated their bloodlust differently. Some viewed it a weapon to wield. Others would only let it out when they were feeding or fucking. Usually both.

But Samara let her bloodlust out frequently, and there was barely a difference in her personality. This was the first time I'd seen a flash of anything else, and even then, I hadn't been the least bit scared. If anything, I'd wanted to shove her down on the settee and let those claws rip off my pants while I sat on her face.

I squeezed my thighs together as a pleasant heat started to build. Definitely an idea for later.

When she saw I wasn't the least bit disturbed by her outburst, Samara licked my blood from her fingers and then moved to rest her head on my lap. I stared at her wide-eyed for a moment before settling back against the cushions and running my fingers through her still-damp hair.

"Why did Drudonia kick you out? You're brilliant," Samara said. "They were lucky to have someone like you there."

"This may shock you, but I'm not exactly good with other people." I shrugged. Honestly, I didn't know how Samara and Kieran did it. They were both so good at navigating social niceties. Most people were dumb and not worth my time.

She pursed her lips into a hard, flat line. "You're just direct is all."

I snorted. "Well, my *directness* managed to piss off every scholar at Drudonia over the last few years. They couldn't actually kick me out because, despite my estrangement from my House, I *am* still a Devereux, but when I told them I was coming here, they made it very clear that they would prefer I remain here."

Samara didn't say anything for a long moment, and I concentrated on getting some tangles out of her hair.

"Roth," she said slowly, "have you been obsessing over finding answers because you're worried that if you don't, I'll kick you out?"

My fingers froze on a tangle, and I slid my gaze to Samara's. One perfectly sculpted eyebrow was raised as she gave me an exasperated look.

"To borrow some of your directness, don't be an idiot. I adore you, Roth. If all you ever do is sit in my room with me and play with my hair while I read, I'm fine with that. You do not have to earn a place here. You already have it." She snuggled further into my lap, and suddenly, I felt heat building behind my eyes.

No. Absolutely not. I would not cry.

As if sensing my internal struggle, Samara closed her eyes and gave me a few minutes to get a hold of myself. I finished getting the tangle out and moved on to another, the heat behind my eyes gradually lessening.

"I won't ever push you about your family," Samara said, still keeping her eyes closed, "but do you think we need to worry about them allying with Velika? Taivan is one of the only Heirs who didn't come here earlier this week, not that House Devereux is particularly social."

Understatement of the year. While most of the Houses were constantly jockeying for better positions, especially in proving their worth to the Sovereign House, Devereux was happy to remain in the shadows. We were on the southern coast, the border of the badlands to our west and the ocean lapping at our doors to the south. Most of the other Houses were situated on or near the main roads for travel. There was no reason to travel to our territory unless you wanted to visit us.

And House Devereux was not welcoming to outsiders.

"That House is loyal to itself and only itself," I said evenly. "Thessalia and the rest of the Devereux, my parents included, are reclusive, paranoid, and obsessed with enforcing their borders."

"You talk about them as if you aren't a part of their House," she noted.

"I was the youngest of three, and my parents really didn't know what to do with someone who would rather pick up a book than a sword."

So they did nothing. I couldn't stop the bitter thought from surfacing. I wasn't entirely sure they had even noticed when I'd left for Drudonia and never returned.

"Rynn thought you might have stayed at Drudonia after you finished your studies because your Hou—" Samara quickly corrected herself, "because House Devereux was pushing you to do something you didn't want, like a marriage or stepping into a higher-ranking position."

"What?" I frowned. "No, they barely acknowledged me when I briefly returned to collect the rest of my things. Taivan forced me to pack some daggers and other things to bring back to Drudonia, but we barely exchanged a few words. He's the oldest of us, and I think he just feels obligated to act like a protective brother."

"Brother . . ." Samara's eyes flew open, and she gawked at me. "Taivan is your brother!"

"Yes." I stared down at her in confusion. "I thought you knew that."

"So Severen and Celestina are your parents?"

"And Taivan and Desmond, my older brothers." I cocked my head at her wide-eyed expression. "Did you really not know who I was?"

"I mean, I knew you were a Devereux, but you never spoke about your family, and they never mentioned you." She winced. "Everyone has always assumed you were a distant cousin or something, not that your father was the brother of the current ruler of House Devereux."

"Like I said"—I shrugged nonchalantly—"they never really paid attention to me, so I'm not surprised I was never mentioned."

"I'm sorry, Roth." Her expression softened. "That couldn't have been easy growing up."

"It was lonely and frustrating," I admitted. "But it could have been worse. They were never intentionally cruel, and no one has demanded that I return. Though if you're hoping I can help improve relations between House Harker and House Devereux, I don't think I'll be of much help."

"That's fine," Samara said. "I'm leaving House Devereux as a bit of a wild card in all this but leaning towards them not being allied with Velika. Though they likely won't help us against her either."

"I think that is a correct assessment to take for now. If . . ."

I swallowed. "If you'd like me to reach out to my parents to arrange a meeting, I can do so."

"Thank you." Samara reached for one of my hands and pulled it away from her hair so she could kiss my palm. "I don't think that's necessary right now, but we'll see what the future brings. But I will never ask you to do anything you're uncomfortable with."

She released my hand and eyed the pen that was resting next to some notes I'd been taking. "Can you show me how you enchanted your pen? I'd like to do the same. It'll help with translating the Harker journals."

I leaned over her and picked up the pen, turning it so Samara could see the tiny glyph carved into the wood and the small sapphire gem embedded into the pen just above the glyph. "It's a combination of 'recite' and 'write.' You can use this one. Just feed it some of your blood, and when you push your intention into it, keep in mind the language you're dictating. The casting itself is simple—the harder part is keeping track of your thoughts and only pushing out the ones you want written down."

"Got it." She took the pen from me, lifting her head out of my lap, and sat on the edge of the settee as she reached into her bag and pulled out a journal. I closed my eyes as she snagged a book off the top of the leaning stack I'd been eying earlier, but when no crash sounded, I cracked one eye open to make sure it still stood.

Samara chuckled as she flipped open the book she had grabbed to reveal a blank page. "You know, Alaric has that same exact expression on his face more often than not when he's in here."

"I can only imagine," I said dryly. Alaric loved order while Samara apparently loved chaos. Their relationship was going to be interesting, especially with Kieran involved, because he enjoyed causing trouble.

Where I fit in, I wasn't exactly sure yet, but I was finding myself more and more curious to figure that out.

"Which journal are you starting with?" I asked, opening both eyes and squinting at the book.

"Rosalyn Harker's," Samara said. "I've already scanned through most of my mother's journals." Her voice tightened for a moment before she steadied herself. "Any important information we need to know, I've compiled into notes, but I'm not ready to dictate it word by word just yet. I need some . . . space. So I thought I would start at the beginning."

I didn't know how to comfort her. Samara had rarely spoken about her parents when we'd been at Drudonia. I didn't talk about my parents because we weren't close and our relationship was one of distance and frustration, but Samara didn't speak of her parents even though she had loved them with her entire heart, and I had no doubt they had felt the same. I had no idea what that type of love was like.

Or how to comfort someone who had lost it.

What would Kieran do?

I raised my hand and patted her on the back. Awkwardly. How did he do this in a non-awkward manner? Was that even possible?

"What are you doing?" Samara looked over her shoulder at me, her fingers resting on the page she'd opened.

"You were sad," I said helplessly. "I was making you feel better."

I patted her on the back again.

She smiled, and I let out a breath. *Look at me. I did it.*

"Thank you." Samara leaned back to kiss me on the cheek before returning to the journal.

"What does that say?" I peered over her shoulder. Not only was it written in a language I wasn't familiar with, but the words were mangled, sometimes crushed together. Other times, they were spread far apart, but I was fairly certain it was the same two words written over and over again.

Samara raised a finger to her mouth and dragged it over a fang, then let the drop of blood that welled fall onto the glyph etched into my pen. It immediately absorbed the blood, and she released the pen so it hovered over the blank page of the other book as she wrestled with her thoughts.

"This is the first page. There are no dates on any of the pages, so I have no idea how long Rosalyn was lost in her early days as a Moroi before she regained enough of her humanity to write, but the first half of this journal is just these two words written over and over again."

After a few seconds, the pen slowly started to move, and two words in the common tongue appeared on the page.

I hunger.

CHAPTER TWENTY

Samara

"You seem troubled."

I tried not to jump from where I was sitting on a grassy overlook just above the beach as Draven appeared at my side, seemingly out of nowhere. If it weren't for the fact that it was still daylight, I would have sworn it was shadow magic.

"Next time you sneak up on me, I'm stabbing you." I shot him an irritated look.

He just grinned. "Don't tease me with a good time."

"You're ridiculous." I shook my head even as my lips twitched in amusement.

"What's bothering the lovely Heir of House Harker today?" he asked lightly.

You, I thought. Trying to reconcile the prince who always managed to make me smile with the traitor who was responsible for killing our people was mentally exhausting. Constantly having to stop myself from falling back into our easy friendship and accidentally saying the wrong thing. Giving away everything we knew about him, his mother, and the wraiths.

Or at least what we thought we knew, because it all felt like jagged pieces that didn't exactly fit together.

Kieran was struggling even more than me. He'd confessed what had happened between him and Draven immediately when we'd met up before dinner last night. He'd been avoiding the prince ever since. Based on how Alaric had been outright glaring at Draven every time he was in a room with him now, I suspected Kieran had also told him what had transpired between them in the Sovereign House.

Everyone in House Harker knew something was going on, and there was an underlying tension now in every room I walked into.

On top of that, I'd stayed up late last night translating the first journal Rosalyn Harker had written. Reading as she'd gotten pieces of her humanity back had been heartbreaking. The hunger gave way to grief as she remembered the husband and daughter she had lost.

There were some entries where it alternated between begging the moon and cursing it for giving her back the humanity she'd apparently been only too happy to lose. Most of the first generation of humans who had changed to Moroi had become Strigoi immediately and remained that way for years. Some of them had never regained their humanity. Only the Harkers and a handful of others—most of which made up the current House bloodlines—had changed back to Moroi within a matter of months.

The fact that any of them had eventually recovered enough of their humanity to become Moroi again was impressive. As far as I knew, only the original ones had ever pulled that off. Nowadays if someone became Strigoi—they stayed that way.

For reasons I didn't fully understand, Rosalyn had been pissed off about that. She had tried repeatedly to lose her humanity by completely giving in to her bloodlust and ripping into monsters every night, but by the morning, her bloodlust had always faded.

After a few meetings this morning, I'd been desperate to get out of House Harker, if only for an hour. I couldn't afford to falter now, but I'd needed an hour to settle my mind away from everything that was threatening to tear it apart.

But it's not like I could tell Draven any of that. I thought briefly about asking him why he'd found Zosa for me. And why he'd felt compelled to share the memory.

The questions were on the tip of my tongue, but I bit them back. Whatever his answer might be . . . I knew it wouldn't be something I could handle right now. Not on top of everything else.

"I'm fine, Prince," I said instead.

He raised a dark eyebrow. "You should improve your lying skills, Heir."

I held his gaze. "We can't all be as good as you."

Draven stiffened for just a second before leaning back on his hands and tilting his face up towards the sun. He'd left his hair loose today, and it fell in a dark wave down his back, the silver streaks glistening in the sun.

I wanted to run my fingers through it almost as much as I wanted to trace his jawline and those entirely too kissable full lips.

Instead, I turned away and watched the waves gently roll in and out. It was good swimming weather. Unfortunately, as inviting as the bright turquoise water looked, monsters swam beneath those waves.

A shudder ran through me as I remembered the cave encounter with those damn spider-like starfish. We were trapped on a small continent full of monsters by an ocean that was full of them as well.

Fucking Lunaria.

Draven didn't try to get me to talk again, just sat there like the hot, evil prince he was and soaked in the sunshine. Just when I was about to get up and return to reality, a flash of vibrant green caught my attention.

Raising a hand to shield my eyes against the sun, I watched as an emerald green striker circled above us. I held my arm to the side, and it immediately dove down to perch on it. I barely winced as its claws flexed in and out of my flesh, leaving behind little droplets of blood.

Draven shifted and leaned forward to eye the striker, his nostrils flaring slightly as the scent of my blood filled the air.

"Whose?" he asked.

Some strikers didn't belong to one person in particular, those ones were trained to simply travel to one particular location and back again, but most of us had at least a few strikers that we trained ourselves. It took more work, but we could teach them to deliver messages to specific people and not just locations.

I thought about lying about who this one belonged to, but the red tips on this striker's tail were easily recognizable, and if Draven asked around, someone would tell him.

"Ary's," I said and gave the creature a scratch under her chin. She nipped at me with her blunt beak but didn't break the skin, just a warning. Ary's favorite striker was such an ornery thing.

I plucked the message from the pocket on the back of her harness, and she immediately took off to fly back home. My eyes skimmed Ary's neat handwriting, and I worked hard to keep my expression blank.

"Problems?" Draven asked. I was holding the letter at an angle so he couldn't read it.

"No." I folded up the paper and slipped it into my pocket. "He was just thanking me for hosting him here earlier this week and inviting me to visit him at House Tepes," I lied through my teeth.

"Interesting," he drawled. "Ary doesn't usually bother with such polite words and invitations."

"Perhaps he just finds me a delight to be around." I rose to my feet and brushed some dried grass and dirt from my deep purple dress, the letter burning a hole in my pocket. I needed to find Vail. Immediately.

"No doubt," Draven murmured as he plucked a pink wildflower and rolled to his feet until he was standing right in front of me. My breath hitched as he pulled my long braid over my shoulder and wound the stem of the wildflower into it. "Everything about you is delightful. That's why I'm going to marry you." He winked before tugging on the end of my braid and leaning in to kiss me on the cheek.

"Still not marrying you," I said a little too breathlessly to be convincing. Damn it. Damn him. I cleared my throat. "I have some meetings to attend to. See you for dinner tonight, Prince?"

"Of course." He smiled. "Wouldn't miss it."

IT TOOK me a while to find Vail because he wasn't in any of the training yards. Emil had been the one to tell me Vail was inspecting some tracks that had been found in the woods nearby. Less than five minutes later, I had Zosa saddled up and was racing out of House Harker to find him, Emil's bay gelding hot on my heels.

Zosa nimbly leapt over fallen trees as we turned down one of the lesser-used trails that had never been cleared away after some of the winter storms. It didn't take long for me to spot the bright chestnut mare tied to a tree.

I jumped off Zosa and looped her reins around the saddle, loose enough that she could nibble on grass but wouldn't get tangled up in them, trusting her not to go far, then set off to where Vail was.

Emil was at my side a second later, sending me a curious look. When he kept staring, I glanced at him. "What?"

"I didn't tell you where Vail was," he said slowly. "Only that he was in the forests outside the House, but you seemed to know exactly where to go . . ."

I stopped dead in my tracks. He was right. I'd been so caught up on getting to Vail that I hadn't thought about it, but I'd been growing more and more desperate as I'd searched the House for him. Then Emil had told me he was in the woods and . . . I rested a hand against my chest.

A pull. I'd felt a pull and had just naturally followed it. This had happened before when we'd found the body outside one of the outposts that had been attacked, but I'd assumed that had been because of the blood magic involved and I was just more sensitive to that kind of thing because I'd experimented with it so much over the years.

I rubbed my chest as the pull intensified the more I focused on it. This . . . wasn't normal. I'd never read about anything like this in all my time at Drudonia.

"Okaaay." I drew out the word and dropped my hand from my chest. "We're going to add this to the 'Weird Shit We Need to Figure Out Once We're Not in Danger of Dying' list."

It probably said a lot about my life that strange, unexplainable magic happening in my own freaking body was far down on the list of mysteries I needed to solve. But here we were.

Emil grunted, and we started walking again. He let me take the lead since, apparently, I could magically find Vail now. "Kind of a long name, but I suppose it's accurate." His gaze cut my way again before focusing on the woods around us. "You gonna tell Vail?"

"Depends," I said lightly. "You gonna rat me out if I don't?"

Emil sighed. "I'm getting too old for this. Maybe I should listen to Adrienne and retire."

"Probably." I snorted.

"I'll leave it up to you to tell him," he said. "Unless something changes and I think it becomes important for him to know."

"Fair enough."

"So . . . are you going to tell him?"

"Tell me what?"

I jumped two feet into the air when Vail slid out from between two trees. His dark brown hair was pulled back into a bun, but pieces of it had slipped free and were plastered to his sweat-slicked skin. The light beige shirt he wore clung to his body, and for a second, my eyes snagged where he'd unlaced the top, giving me a good view of his chest.

The man was built like a mountain but could still move as quietly as a wraith. It was seriously hot, and his blood was positively divine.

No. Bad, Samara, I mentally chastised myself. No more complicated lovers. Absolutely not.

Emil snickered. "Apparently you'll need to practice a little more with your newfound talent."

Vail shot me a questioning look, but I shook my head. Given all the mixed messages he'd been sending me lately, I had no idea how he'd react to learning I could apparently *feel* him.

Probably not well.

There were bigger things to worry about. Besides, it was possible this was just a strange side effect of how much we'd been exchanging blood lately. I'd never heard of such a thing happening, but our magic did change slightly with each generation. Maybe this would start occurring more with other fifth-generation Moroi who had lovers they regularly exchanged blood with.

Not that Vail was my lover. My eyes drifted to his chest again. Damn it.

"We've got a problem," I said. Vail's enticing body and the issue of our new magic connection faded to the back of my mind as the urgency of what had sent me racing out here resurfaced. "Ary sent me a letter. He encountered a wraith last night just north of Lake Myalis."

"There's a human settlement there that we haven't investigated yet." Vail's expression hardened. "What happened with the wraith?"

"Ary managed to kill it, but he said it was definitely searching for something before he did." I glanced through the trees to the west and then up at the midday sun. "If we leave right now, we could get to that settlement not long after sunset."

"More wraiths will likely head there tonight to continue the search and possibly avenge their fallen friend if they know," Emil pointed out. "Dealing with one wraith is nasty enough, but if they come in numbers, you're walking into a death trap."

I remembered the three wraiths we battled in the temple and swallowed past the lump in my throat. "Like I said, if we leave now, we can get there just after night falls, do a quick search, and get out before they arrive."

Emil's brows creased, clearly not liking this idea, then he looked to Vail for the final decision.

"We search fast," Vail finally said. "Even if we haven't found anything, when I say we leave, *we leave*." He looked at me with an expression that brokered no argument.

I nodded in agreement. "We leave. I won't argue. I just want the chance to search while we have it."

Because more wraiths would definitely go to that settlement, and if there was still a piece of that strange obsidian stone there, we couldn't not take the chance of them getting it before we did.

"Did Ary provide the exact coordinates for where he saw the wraith?" Vail asked. "I want to make sure we're heading to the right place."

"Yes." I reached into my pocket to pull out the letter, and my blood went cold. Empty.

"Lose something, love?"

For the third time in an hour, I jumped.

By the time I'd landed back on my feet and whirled to look up into the tree behind me, Emil and Vail had already moved to stand beside me, swords drawn.

Draven continued to read the letter—*my letter*—from where he sat on a branch ten feet above us, one leg dangling casually off the side.

How the fuck had he gotten up there without any of us sensing him? And how had he gotten here ahead of us without anyone detecting him? It was one thing for him to slip past me, but Emil and Vail? I added this to the list of things that didn't make sense about the Moroi Prince.

I glanced at Vail's face. Based on how hard he was clenching his jaw and the way the scar that ran diagonally across his face was pulled tight, he definitely hadn't known the prince was there until he'd said something.

"Drav," I half growled.

His bright blue eyes finally looked away from the letter to arch an eyebrow at me. "Oh, we're back to Drav now?" He slid off the branch and dropped to the ground, landing lightly on the balls of his feet before strolling over to me. "I like it when I get to be Drav and not Prince."

"Will you like it when I strangle you?" I snatched the letter out of his hand.

"Probably." He grinned and then looked back and forth between the swords Vail and Emil still held. They weren't angling them towards the prince, but they'd only lowered them a couple of inches. "Are we having a sword measuring contest? I haven't lost one of those yet."

Vail took a step towards Draven, and red flashed through

the prince's eyes in challenge. Emil stepped away from me to give himself more space to work.

"We don't have time for this." I stepped between Vail and Draven with my hands held up as Emil paused to watch how this played out. Then I turned to fully face Draven. "Talk. Now."

"I'm coming with you."

CHAPTER TWENTY-ONE

Samara

IN WHAT FELT like the first time in ages, the moon smiled upon us. We'd gotten lucky. I slipped the three pieces of smooth, black stone into my pack before securing it on my back.

"Let's find the others and get out of here."

Emil nodded while Ary just scrutinized me from where he waited a few feet away.

The Tepes Heir had found us less than a mile from the remains of the human settlement. He'd claimed to be checking to see if the wraiths had returned while his rangers investigated a nearby monster nest, but I had little doubt he'd been waiting for us.

If he'd truly thought the wraiths would have made an appearance again, he would have kept his rangers with him. Ary was a cocky bastard, but even he wasn't crazy enough to tackle wraiths on his own. No. Ary suspected something was going on and that I was involved somehow. He could have easily sent that letter to House Salvatore or Laurent, both of whom were just as close as House Harker.

He'd sent it to me as a test. I needed to figure out what to tell him, and I needed to do it soon. We needed more allies, but I couldn't afford to trust the wrong person.

Ary wasn't the only addition to our search party. Nyx had found us while we'd been saddling our horses at House Harker and had insisted on coming. Vail had grumbled something about having to inform Adrienne, and then we'd set off.

Currently, Nyx and Vail were keeping an eye on the area around the old settlement in case the wraiths or some other beasts came prowling. I'd told Draven to stay with the horses because they were a tasty snack to most things that went bump in the night. To my surprise—and suspicion—he'd agreed. Unfortunately, none of us could tell the Tepes Heir what to do, so when our group had split up, he'd trailed after me and Emil.

"Shiny," a deep voice purred. "I like shiny things."

A golden-haired man nimbly leapt down from a tree that had grown out of the wreckage of collapsed building. He rose to his full height—which was easily over six feet—and cocked his head, his cat-like green eyes catching the moonlight, which caused a sheen to roll across them.

Emil had his swords free in a moment and pointed at the newcomer. His jaw hardened, probably in annoyance at not detecting the Velesian but it's not like I could blame him. Velesians had an uncanny knack at being undetectable in the woods. They were even more adept at sneaking up on others than Vail or Draven.

While Emil and I might have been caught off guard, it did not escape my attention that Ary didn't appear to be least bit surprised to see the handsome Velesian, who was currently smirking at all of us.

"Bastian," I said evenly. "What brings a member of the Alpha Pack to Moroi territory?"

"Just helping out our neighbors on a little friendly hunt." He grinned and two dimples formed in his cheeks, escalating him from handsome to charming... and a little wicked. "After all, the monsters don't really care about the borders between Moroi and Velesian lands."

My gaze cut to Ary. "Funny how you never mentioned the Alpha Pack being here in your letter."

He shrugged. "Like Bastian said—just a spur-of-the-moment hunt is all."

Spur-of-the-moment hunt my ass. The Alpha Pack usually stayed in the far north of the Velesian realm. While Ary was definitely on more friendly terms with the Velesians than many of the Moroi—thanks to his lands bordering theirs and the fact that he did love to go hunting with them—it wasn't like Bastian would have just happened to be in the area.

According to Rynn, the big meeting being hosted by her pack in Fervis territory near Lake Malov wasn't happening for another week. She would have mentioned if she'd heard of any of the Alpha Pack members coming sooner than that. Which meant they hadn't told her . . .

Bastian let out a low, raspy laugh. "So suspicious, Samara. I can practically hear you sussing out all the reasons for me being here in that pretty head of yours."

"Really?" I drawled. "Then you know the loudest thought in my head right now is me lamenting over the fact that I have to deal with you instead of Cade."

Cade was the leader of the Alpha Pack and the one I preferred to deal with. He was direct and to the point. It was refreshing, albeit a little frustrating at times because once he set his mind on something, it was difficult to steer him away from it.

Bastian was his second-in-command . I didn't know if it was his feline nature—he was an ailuranthrope, a panther shifter—that made him so aggravating to deal with or just his own personal nature.

But the fact that Bastian was here meant two things: there was something going on in the Velesian realm to draw the Alpha Pack south, and Ary was suspicious enough about other Moroi and what was going on in our own realm that he'd chosen to bring the Velesians in on it.

He must have had a better relationship with the Alpha Pack than I'd been aware of for Bastian to join him on this adventure. None of that mattered for the problem at hand though, and I could have punched Ary for complicating things so much.

The amused grin on the other Moroi's face told me he knew exactly how I was feeling and found my pain entertaining.

I couldn't tell Bastian—and therefore the Alpha Pack—about the stones or what was going on. Not yet at least. The Moroi Houses were all about keeping their secrets. Half of our trade deals were sweetened by offering an exchange of information. But the Velesians prided themselves on being more open about things.

If I brought the Alpha Pack in on this, they would feel compelled to tell the rest of Velesian packs. We already knew there were Moroi working with Erendriel, so there was no reason not to suspect some of the Velesians were as well.

And even if I could convince them to not tell the rest of the packs, that would present a problem down the line. Because sooner or later, it would get out that the Alpha Pack had known about Erendriel, Queen Velika, the truth about the wraiths . . . and hadn't told anyone.

Tensions between the Velesians were rising, and that could very well be the final blow that caused a war to erupt amongst the packs.

Rynn was promised to the Alpha Pack. She would be in the middle of it. I would sooner bring the wrath of the Alpha Pack down on me than put my friend in jeopardy.

"You'll have to admire my pretty face another time, Bastian," I said smoothly. "This is Moroi business."

The easy-going grin slid off his beautiful face. "You sure that's how you want to play this? You want me to return to Cade and tell him I saw you skulking around this old human settlement—where wraith activity has been spotted—and that you collected something from it?"

Tension bled between all of us, but I kept my expression even. "That's exactly what I'm saying."

Bastian shook his head. "You're making a mistake, Samara. Thought you were smarter than this."

Doing my best with the shitty options presented to me, furball.

"Duly noted." I flicked my gaze towards the forest behind us. "Time to leave."

He looked at me for a long moment before shrugging and turning around to stride towards the trees. "I'll give Rynn your regards," he tossed over his shoulder.

Before I could curse him, Bastian shed his clothing, shifted into a sleek black panther form, and took off through the trees.

That hadn't been a physical threat towards Rynn—he would never harm her, nor would any of the Alpha Pack. For all intents and purposes, they were good people. Well, as good as anyone could be in Lunaria. But that didn't mean they weren't cunning and devious at times.

Bastian's dig had been a reminder that they had a claim on Rynn.

I'd have to tell her about this encounter when we made it back and hope I hadn't just made her life infinitely harder.

"Interesting way of handling delicate political situations." Ary started walking towards me. "Not sure that's how I—oww!!! Motherfucker!"

He clutched his nose and backed away as blood flowed down the lower half of his face.

"I'll do more than break your nose if you ever ambush me like that again," I growled.

Vail chose that moment to stalk through the few buildings that still stood, Nyx right behind him. The two of them joined our group, and Vail's grey eyes took in Ary before glancing at Emil, who I'd shoved aside to punch the Tepes Heir.

"Ary here thought it would be a good idea to invite Bastian to visit this settlement." A wry smile played across the older Moroi's lips. "Samara was giving him feedback on that."

"Interesting," Nyx said. "I don't recall Drudonia teaching us that providing feedback involved our fists, but I did skip out on my lessons early."

"What did you tell the Alpha Pack?" Vail asked the Tepes Heir harshly.

Ary used the back of his hand to wipe more blood away before directing a hard stare at Vail and then me. "Wasn't much I could tell them, was there? You lot haven't told me anything. All I know is that there is something weird going on with the wraiths and you all know more about it than you're sharing. We all need allies. With the way things are going with the other Houses, I personally think the Alpha Pack is looking like a better choice every day."

We all glared at each other for a long moment before I sighed and stomped over to Ary, who eyed me warily. "You're not wrong." I gripped his nose before jerking it into place. "Come with us back to the outpost, and we'll tell you what we can there. We've already stayed here too long. The wraiths will be back."

The five of us headed in the direction of our mounts.

"Where's your horse?" Vail asked.

"Had to give it to one of my rangers," Ary replied. "I wasn't lying about them dealing with a monster nest. A pack of howlers grew too large, attacked us yesterday, killed two of our horses, and seriously injured a couple of us."

"You can have Samara's mount. She'll ride with me."

My head whipped towards Vail. "Oh, I will, will I?"

"Yes." He bared his teeth.

"Gods, you didn't bring Zosa did you?" Ary interrupted.

I tore my gaze away from Vail. "No, I wasn't sure how much we'd be riding at night and I didn't want to risk her."

Relief flickered through Ary's face. Apparently, the idea of riding my hot-tempered mare was more intimidating than traveling in the wilds of Lunaria at night.

As the horses came into view, concern flared in my chest. Draven wasn't there.

"Where's the prince?" Nyx asked.

Moons fucking damn it all. I slid one of my throwing daggers free from my thigh sheath as I searched the trees around us but saw no signs of Draven anywhere. Was this the moment he betrayed us?

My heart said Draven would never hurt me, but my brain offered up a myriad of ways that he could. I shifted on my feet as the forest around us took on a more ominous tone.

Ary's light violet eyes shone brightly even in the dark. He glanced at all of us before asking, "Are we going to search for him or . . ."

"You're welcome to look," Vail replied, "but we're getting the fuck out of here."

I balked when Vail and the rangers moved in the direction of the horses. What if Draven had gone to investigate something and had been attacked? What if he wasn't betraying us but was actually out in the woods injured?

"Samara," Vail growled, "you promised you would leave when I told you to."

"I know, but—"

"Don't make me force you to leave him."

My fingers tightened around the blade as I focused on taking steady breaths. I couldn't fight Vail. He'd just laugh at my attempt and throw me over his shoulder. Plus, I didn't want to argue with him. I had promised to follow his orders, and I knew he was right, but . . . I anxiously scanned the woods again for Draven but saw nothing.

"Alright," I said weakly and stepped forward only to be shoved back by Emil.

Three wraiths materialized around us, one between me and the others and two on either side of Vail. They'd clearly determined him to be the biggest threat, because neither of them wasted any time in their attack.

I screamed as their shadows stretched into towering, beastly forms, resembling nothing that had ever walked this land and only existed in nightmares. At least, that's where they belonged. The two wraiths struck out at Vail, letting the foot-long talons that tipped their monstrous hands materialize for a brief second.

Nyx moved faster than I could track and struck at the wraith on the left. Their gold and silver blade sliced through the wraith's wrist, and it screamed as the magic within the sword burned through its momentarily corporeal flesh.

I didn't see if Vail had managed to block the attack from the other wraith because the one in front of me snapped into the shadowy form of a serpent and lunged forward.

Another scream ripped from my throat as I slashed at the wraith, but my blade passed harmlessly through its shadow before hot, fiery pain tore through my shoulder as the wraith bit down.

Even through the pain, I still managed to stab at its eyes with my dagger, but my strike had been too slow, and the wraith was already nothing more than shadows again.

"Samara!" Nyx screamed from where they were still battling one of the other wraiths. Emil had joined them, and Ary was helping Vail.

Which meant I was on my own.

Twin rivers of blood coursed their way down my shoulder. I blocked out the pain before carefully gauging how much mobility I had, finding I could still move it easily. For the second time tonight, I'd gotten lucky. The snake's fangs had only punctured me, which meant, while it was painful, it was still a relatively minor wound.

The wraith shrank down into an amorphous form before becoming something more humanoid, the shape sharpening enough for me to make out delicate features . . . and tapered ears.

Fae.

A masculine chuckle filled the air as he raised his hand to his lips. The blood on my shoulder felt hotter as I watched him draw his fingers away and study them before looking at me. Then he cocked his head and smiled.

"Din tros." The words slithered into my ear, and the breath I'd just taken froze in my throat.

The words were mangled and corrupted by shadows, but I'd understood them well enough. He'd just called me *forgotten queen* in Seelie.

The wraiths weren't the Unseelie. They were the Seelie.

More whispered words flowed from the wraith's mouth faster than I could process, then his form stretched upward until he was once again a serpent, this time with a crown of horns extending from behind his head.

My dagger felt so small in my hand as I prepared myself to dive to the side and avoid those jaws that were considerably larger than the first time he'd bitten me.

The wraith struck impossibly fast, and I barely managed to leap aside. The dagger left my fingers a second before his tail slammed into me and sent me hurtling through the air, further into the forest and away from everyone else.

An eerie shriek filled the night air, and I felt a brief moment of satisfaction at knowing my aim had been true before I slammed into a tree.

Something crunched in my back, but I forced myself to my feet and held my hand up. A pulse of magic and a second later, my dagger flew through the air to my waiting palm. Blood so dark that it was almost black coated the blade.

Shadows wound through the trees and snapped back into the giant snake, the eye I'd ruptured already good as new. This time, I had nowhere to go. The underbrush on either side of the tree was too thick. I held my dagger up defiantly as the wraith opened its mouth, displaying long fangs dripping with shadows.

"Spitka e chof." The whispered words wrapped around me. *Come with me.*

"Not a fucking chance," I snarled as pain racked my body. Only pure rage and adrenaline kept me standing.

A high-pitched wail back towards the others announced the death of a wraith. One down, two to go. I just had to survive a little longer.

Just as I readied myself to try to dive forward to run past the wraith, a dark form fell from the trees to land at my side.

"Where the fuck have you been, Draven?" I snapped.

"These weren't the only wraiths," he said tightly. It was then I noticed he was covered in blood, some the dark purplish-red of the wraiths, but most of it was definitely his.

"Mikin," the wraith hissed.

Draven dove towards it, but the snake burst into a shapeless shadow before quickly disappearing into the trees. "FUCK!" he shouted and whirled to slam a fist into the trunk behind me.

I jumped, and he froze before slowly lowering his hand to his side and unclenching his fingers. The rage that had been on face a second before vanished, and now he just looked exhausted.

"Come on." He grabbed my hand and tugged me towards the others. "He'll be back with more help."

Thoughts raced through my mind as we ran back to Vail and the rest of our party. I'd read that word before—*mikin*—but the translation was escaping me. Then it hit me, and I almost stumbled.

Traitor.

AN HOUR LATER, the six of us were behind the relative safety of an outpost's wards and gathered around a table in the far corner of the tavern. Well, Vail was in a room upstairs, passed out in a healing sleep. He'd managed to kill the third wraith, but not before the damn thing had nearly disemboweled him.

Draven had thrown a fit when I'd slashed open my wrist and practically shoved it against Vail's mouth while tracing the healing glyph in the blood that coated his stomach. I hadn't even hesitated. Despite all the complications between us, all the pain and confusing animosity, Vail had been hurt, and all I'd cared about was making him better.

Even with the strength of my blood coursing through his veins, Vail had barely managed to stay conscious on the ride here. As soon as his head had hit the pillow, he'd passed out. Nyx and Emil had assured me he was fine and would be ready to leave by the time the sun rose.

We all sipped our honey ale as the local residents eyed us curiously. It wasn't unusual for the House Heirs to visit outposts, but it definitely wasn't a common occurrence for the Moroi Prince to stay at one.

The charming mask Draven usually wore as his public persona was nowhere to be seen, and the grim expression on his face was doing an excellent job of keeping everyone away.

Only the barkeep had approached us, and that was only to drop off some food and ale.

Ary took a long drink before setting his glass down and sliding a small, wooden square with the glyph for silence to the center of the table. He sliced his index finger open on his fang and let the blood drop onto the glyph.

"This glyph doesn't store much magic. We've got ten minutes." His gaze locked on mine. "Tell me what the fuck is going on, Samara."

Out of my peripheral vision, I saw Nyx and Emil stiffen, but it was Draven who spoke. "You don't give her orders, Tepes," he said in a quiet voice that promised all kinds of violence.

Ary didn't back down, and I saw a flicker of pain in his eyes. "My best friend's husband was in one of the outposts that fell to wraiths. The three of us grew up together. Nicholai was like a brother to me. These attacks aren't random. The wraith last night was searching for something." He leaned forward from where he sat directly across from me. "Something *you* found tonight."

I couldn't tell him everything, not with Draven here, but Ary wouldn't let this go. I had to give him at least some information, and then we could tell him everything later when it was safe to do so.

"You're right," I said, choosing my words carefully but quickly. "They're searching old human settlements for relics of the spell the humans used to turn themselves into the Moon Blessed. All the outposts that have been attacked have been ones built on those old towns and villages."

The muscles along Ary's jaw flexed. "Do you know how they're getting past the blood wards?"

"No." I forced myself to not look at Draven.

"Like passing through a waterfall," Draven said suddenly.

"What are you talking about?" Ary shot Draven a confused look.

"A curtain of water falling, drenching anyone who passes under." The odd cadence to Draven's tone had me looking to him, only to find him staring blankly at the table. "But if someone was to hold an outstretched arm through the water, another could pass underneath it to avoid the deluge."

Ary, Emil, and Nyx stared at him. The rangers didn't bother to hide the suspicion on their faces, but whatever Ary was thinking was behind a mask of cold indifference.

"That actually makes sense," I said slowly. "We're used to passing through the wards, so we don't feel it anymore, but there is a thin veil of magic rising from where we root them in the earth. Draven is suggesting"—my gaze darted to him to find him staring intently at me, as if urging me to continue my line of thinking—"that the wraiths aren't breaking the ward nor temporarily disabling it. They're finding a way to block the upward flow of magic in one specific place and slipping through."

"They can't interact with the wards at all," Emil pointed out.

"A Moroi could," Ary said, his voice hardening in understanding. "You think a Moroi is helping the wraiths. That's why you're being so secretive about all of this."

"Yes, but we don't know why someone would help them." I kept my tone even, but I didn't look away from Draven either. It had to be him. He was responsible for letting the monsters in. "Why would a Moroi turn on their own people? There were *children* in those outposts. Who could do something like that?"

The tension in the air increased until I could practically feel it on my skin. I didn't say anything else, just silently begged Draven to tell me I had this all wrong. That he wasn't responsible for the slaughter of thousands of innocent Moroi.

"A monster," he finally said, still never taking his eyes off me. "A well-trained monster."

I let my fangs slide a little further out of my gums. "Even a monster can refuse."

"Maybe they did." He flinched as if a phantom pain had raised up his back.

Hope and dread warred in my soul. If he had willingly helped the wraiths kill our people, I would never be able to forgive him for it, but if he'd refused . . . what had it cost him?

"How many times did the monster say no?" I asked quietly.

Draven opened his mouth to speak only to snap it shut with a hiss before he rubbed his temples. Ary's expression remained locked down, but Nyx and Emil continued to eye him warily. I just waited. Finally, he dropped his hand away, his eyes dark and bleak. "Who knows what monsters say or do? Does it matter? They're still monsters at the end of the day."

"Drav . . ." I trailed off, unsure what to say.

"I'm tired." He rose from the table. "I'm going to rest for a bit." Then he stepped away before pausing and turning his head slightly so I could just make out his profile. "I've never really liked waterfalls. Refused to go through them nine times. Turns out your body can still be used to block the water even if your soul is unwilling."

A sharp pain struck my chest as he walked away without another word. *A well-trained monster*. Maybe he wasn't so much well-trained as he was beaten down.

"What in the moonsdamned fuck have the lot of you been up to?" Ary stared after Draven, a hint of frustration leaking into his expression.

I pursed my lips together. We'd have to trust others eventually, and Ary had already seen too much tonight.

"Emil and Nyx will fill you in." I looked at both of the rangers. "Tell him everything. I'm going to check on Vail."

Nyx shifted uncomfortably. "You're sure?"

"Yes." I smiled at Ary. "If you betray us, I'll make you beg for death, and even then, I won't give it."

An actual smile blossomed on the Tepes Heir's face. "Honestly, threats like that are the only reason I both like and trust you."

"You're seriously fucked up."

He smiled wider. "It's more fun that way."

"We have two rooms, Samara," Emil said. "You should go rest in the other one after you check on Vail. If you're okay with it, Nyx can sleep on the floor in your room. The rest of us can stay with Vail. I don't think he'll wake, but in case he does, somebody should be there."

"I'll stay with him." The words rushed out before I could think better of it. Nyx arched an eyebrow, and Ary laughed under his breath. "Fuck you both," I muttered.

"Is that an actual offer?" Ary cocked his head and then let out a sharp exhale when Nyx elbowed him in the gut.

"No," I said wryly. "I'll see you all in the morning."

I walked away from the table. If Ary had anything else to say, I couldn't hear it thanks to the silencing spell still surrounding the table. After a few conversations with the locals to assure them that everything was fine, I made my way upstairs and slipped into the room where Vail was sleeping. I made it two feet from the door before I froze at the form sitting in the chair in the corner.

"Figured you'd sleep in the other room," I said to Draven before continuing to the bed to check on Vail. He was still fast asleep and barely stirred when I lifted the sheet to peek at his chest. An angry, pink scar snaked its way down his body, but considering he'd been holding in his intestines a couple of hours ago, this was nothing. He probably wouldn't even have a scar in the morning.

I brushed some loose strands of hair away from his face before tracing the jagged scar that ran across his right eyebrow down his cheek. He'd gotten it protecting me from the wraiths the night our parents had been killed. I'd been too panicked to heal it properly, and by the time we'd been rescued days later, it had been too late to do anything about the scar.

I could bury the emotions from that night deep inside myself, but Vail was reminded every time he looked in a mirror.

"I knew you'd come here," Draven said. "You're rather protective of those you love."

My fingers went still over Vail's skin. "I don't love him."

"Whatever you need to tell yourself, *tros*."

"I'm not a queen," I snapped. "We going to talk about that wraith calling you a traitor?"

Draven sighed. "Nothing has changed. There is still so much I can't tell you, and you still shouldn't trust me even though I can swear to you that I'm doing everything I can to keep you and Kieran safe."

"I believe you . . . but I don't know what to do with that," I said honestly.

"Two years ago, you came to the Sovereign House." Draven paused like he was remembering it. "After a rather stuffy dinner, Demetri fucked off with some of the courtiers, and you and I went up to the rooftop to stargaze."

"I remember." We hadn't done anything except stretch out on a blanket and talk, but it'd been nice. By that point, my marriage had become so rigid, it hadn't even felt strange to me that Demetri had decided to spend the night catching up with some courtiers rather than with me. I hadn't seen Kieran in over a year, and the only chats I'd had with Rynn and Cali were via shadow magic.

Lonely. I'd been so fucking lonely.

"What if, for the rest of the night, we just pretend we're back on that rooftop?" Draven asked. "I think we've both earned a few hours of peace."

"And you won't tell me anything else, right?" When he didn't answer, I sighed. Fuck it. I was tired, and I had already intended to stay in this room.

I stalked around the bed to where Draven was lounging in the oversized cushioned chair and eyed it. There was plenty of space for two people if he'd just move over.

When I opened my mouth to tell him that, his hand snapped out and grabbed my arm, pulling me forward. I yelped as I tumbled into the chair, but he smoothly maneuvered my body until I was lying snuggly across his lap.

I should have jumped off and shoved him aside to make room. That was definitely what I *should* have done. Instead, I instantly relaxed against his body like he was home and I'd been away for too long.

Then the asshole ruined it by tugging the corner of my shirt down off my shoulder so he could inspect where the wraith had bitten me. "For the tenth time, it's fine," I hissed as I slapped his hand away and pulled my shirt back up. He'd been fussy about it all night, even after I'd cleaned up the blood and changed into a clean shirt. "Puncture wounds always heal fast."

Draven just nodded numbly, still staring at my shoulder. The wraith that had attacked me had gotten away, no doubt to report back to Erendriel. I had no idea if that meant Velika would be informed as well. She and Erendriel were clearly allies, but that didn't mean they shared knowledge freely. Draven probably knew more specifics about how their relationship worked, but it was clear he wasn't going to tell me, or maybe *couldn't* tell me was more accurate.

I thought back to that peaceful night we'd shared under the stars and let my eyes drift closed. My body was tapped out thanks to the amount of blood I'd let Vail drink. Ary had offered to let me drink from him, but Draven's growl had practically made the walls vibrate, so I'd turned him down to keep a fight from breaking out.

"Do you need to drink?" Draven asked quietly.

My eyes flew open, and I blinked up at him. "Are you reading my mind? Is that a thing you do?"

He chuckled darkly. "You just snuggled your face into my neck and inhaled deeply. Pretty sure you licked me."

"I absolutely did not." I thought about it and the fact that I was tucked in against his neck. "Okay, I did smell you, but there was no licking." I grinned at him. "Trust me, you would know if I licked you."

He groaned, and I felt something very hard pressing into my backside. Then Draven's light purple eyes fell on Vail, sleeping only a few feet from us, before he squinted down at me. "How quiet can you be?"

"According to Kieran, I'm a bit of a screamer."

"Not helping, Sam." He leaned his head back against the chair and took a deep breath.

So I leaned forward and gently kissed the side of his neck before slipping off his lap. Instantly, he shot forward and grabbed my wrist. "Where are you going?"

"Bed." I gestured to the large mattress Vail was sprawled on. "It's not like I haven't shared a bed with him before, and I'm not going to be able to sleep in that chair."

"Wasn't really planning on sleeping," Draven muttered before ushering me forward so he could stand as well.

When he followed me over to the bed and stood there expectantly, I crawled into it and arched an eyebrow at him. "Something you need?"

"For you to move over."

"What?" I dropped my gaze to a sleeping Vail before looking back at Draven. Did he really mean to sleep with me when I was in bed with Vail? The chair wasn't big enough to sleep in, but I'd assumed he'd just sleep on the floor.

Draven leaned down until his lips were almost touching mine, and my breath caught in my throat at the intensity in his eyes. "Fucking you tonight isn't an option, because when I do, I want you to be able to scream until the walls shake." Then he kissed the corners of my mouth as I trembled slightly. "You should know that Kieran and I are a bit . . . competitive. If he makes you scream, I'll make you scream louder. If I make you come"—his hand slid down my body until he cupped me between the thighs—"then Kieran will make you come harder."

I clamped my legs around his hand as heat pooled between them. "Now who's not helping?" I growled.

His mouth crashed against mine as his fingers rubbed against the seam of my pants, creating a friction I'd been desperately craving.

Just as suddenly as he kissed me, he broke it off and shoved me further across the bed before sliding in behind me. Then his arm wrapped around my waist to tug me back against his chest. "I can't fuck you tonight, but I can ensure that you dream of me," he whispered into my ear, "while sleeping in a bed with *him*."

"Jealous?" I rasped, glancing at Vail to find him still asleep, but there was a crease between his brows now.

"He's not good for you," Draven said smoothly as his grip on me tightened.

"And you are?"

"No." The arm around me pulled back a little. "I suppose I'm not."

A gap formed between my back and his chest, and fear shot through me at him leaving. My hand clamped down on his arm, and Draven went still. "Stay."

Time stretched as the word hung between us. Finally, Draven settled back down beside me, and the knot that had been forming inside my chest loosened. He let out a long, shuddering breath and nestled his face into the back of my neck.

We lay like that until we both fell asleep. At some point in the night, I woke to find that Vail had rolled over and I was plastered against his chest, his arm wrapped around me. Draven was still tight against my back, his arm draped along my hip.

Nestled between two people who could very well be the death of me, I should have felt at least a hint of alarm. Instead, I just drifted off to sleep and dreamed of starry skies.

CHAPTER TWENTY-TWO

Roth

"You're absolutely certain he called you the forgotten queen?" I asked again from where I was sitting in one of the comfy chairs in Samara's living room. Alaric had claimed the chair across from me while Samara and Kieran were sprawled out on the settee.

Well, Kieran was sprawled out. Samara was hunched over the low table, translating the last of Rosalyn's journals.

"Yes, Roth," Samara said tiredly. She'd only returned an hour ago and had announced that there would be no group dinner this evening since everyone was tired from the journey.

I kept glancing at the door to her bedroom, expecting them to knock any second, but apparently, both the prince and Vail had made themselves scarce as soon as they'd stepped foot inside House Harker.

Alaric, Kieran, and I had gathered in her rooms, and she'd told us everything that had happened—although the details of them staying the night at the outpost had been a little sparse. I didn't think Samara was intentionally hiding anything from us. If anything, she seemed a little . . . confused?

I'd have to talk to Kieran about it when I could get him

alone. Alaric wasn't much better than me at reading people, but Kieran seemed to always know what was going on in Samara's head.

Was it bad that Alaric and I were likely going to have to depend on Kieran for relationship advice? I frowned and then shook my head. Kieran was pretty and had a praise kink. He'd appreciate being told he was useful, which meant he wouldn't give me too much shit about having no idea how relationships worked.

"He definitely called me that," Samara confirmed without looking up from the page. "And he wanted me to come with him."

"In Seelie?" Alaric asked. "You're absolutely sure he spoke in Seelie and not Unseelie?"

Samara finally looked up from the journal to arch a dark eyebrow at Alaric. "I realize you think I'm nothing more than a pretty face with air between my ears, but between all of us, I *am* the person most adept at Fae languages. So yes, I'm sure it was Seelie."

"I said that one time." Alaric rolled his eyes. "And it was almost a decade ago."

Samara sniffed. "It was on my sixteenth birthday, you ass. Ruined the whole party."

The smallest smile graced Alaric's lips as he looked at Samara with a heated intensity. "If I promise to make it up to you, will you let it go?"

I caught Kieran's eye, and he just grinned before we went back to listening to this unfolding drama like the juicy entertainment it was.

"Yes." Samara tilted her head as she continued to study Alaric. "I remember every nasty thing you've said to me though, just so you know."

A sliver of turquoise slid through Alaric's light green eyes. "Guess I'll be on my knees a lot in the future then."

"Fuck." Kieran slammed a book shut. "The two of you are making it really difficult to concentrate, which really isn't fair, considering I got yelled at for suggesting we relax before diving into work."

"Relax?" Samara laughed. "I believe your exact words were, 'Everyone, take your clothes off. I got a jar of honey and some ideas.'"

"I still have the honey." Kieran smirked at her.

"I'm with Kieran on this," I said, gently setting the book I'd been scanning onto the table before leaning back in my seat.

"You want the honey?" Alaric asked in confusion.

"No, I don't want the honey." I paused and thought about it before amending, "I don't want the honey *tonight*."

"I think what Roth is trying to say is that we actually do need to concentrate tonight," Samara said dryly. "Vail and I are leaving just before sunrise, and Draven has some meetings in the morning, so hopefully it will be at least a few hours before he realizes we're gone."

A weariness flashed across her face before she buried it. My beautiful forgotten queen was excellent at tucking away her emotions, which was a little concerning.

"We assumed the wraiths were the Unseelie Fae," Samara continued, her eyes dropping back down to the journal she'd been translating. "I don't know what it means that they're actually the Seelie, or how they got shadow magic. We don't even really know what the Seelie's original magic was because all the texts are kind of vague about it."

"The Seelie spent most of their time lamenting about how arrogant and devious the Unseelie were," I said. "Most of the writings we've found have been Seelie, so we're most familiar with their point of view. They rarely talked about themselves. And what we do have from the Unseelie is . . . not all that informative."

"Because it's all useless poetry," Alaric griped.

"I wouldn't say it's entirely useless." Samara's lips curved into a grin, and I felt mine doing the same.

"It is strange how little we have from the Unseelie," I mused. "Most of the Unseelie fortresses were entirely stripped of books and scrolls. Literally all that was left was poetry and a few other random texts."

"Maybe Vail and I will finally find some answers up north," Samara said. "Instead of just more questions."

"We'll keep researching while you're gone," I assured her. "Learning the wraiths are actually the Seelie is confusing . . . but at least we're no longer going down the wrong path."

Samara rubbed her face, and I could see the exhaustion of the last couple of days weighing heavily on her.

"I don't know what the queen comment meant," she admitted. "The House bloodlines are clearly different from most of the Moroi, but I've never come across anything to suggest the Harker line is more unique than the Tepes, Corvinus, or any of the others. The only queen we've ever had is Velika, and that was a self-appointed title."

"Maybe it's somehow connected to the crown?" Kieran suggested. "Seems like a strange coincidence for the wraith to refer to you as a queen while we're also searching for the other half of a Fae crown."

"Maybe," Samara said, but she didn't sound convinced. "I'm going to switch to translating my mother's journals. I think the odds are better of us finding something useful in them."

"I'll get us some snacks," Kieran offered. "Seems like it's going to be a long night."

"So you're who Samara has been keeping away from me."

I froze in my seat as Prince Draven appeared between the

bookstacks at the back of the library. How had he gotten in here without me knowing? My heart was racing at finding myself in such sudden close proximity to the Moroi Prince. I willed myself to rise casually from my chair, turning my head just enough so I could glance at the double doors. Still closed. I definitely would have heard them open. There were a couple of windows in the back, but I always kept them locked . . .

"Apologies, I'm not sure what you mean," I said tightly before adding, "my prince."

A small, knowing smile played across his lips as he strolled down the line of bookcases on the wall, his finger trailing across the shelves. I glanced at the clock on the wall and cursed inwardly. It was late afternoon. Alaric was supposed to have kept Draven busy in meetings all day, and then Kieran was going to make an excuse for why Samara wasn't at dinner. The hope was that we could delay Draven from knowing Samara had left until tomorrow.

I'd missed working in the library, so I had snuck in here this morning, even though I'd promised Samara I would stay in her suite while she was gone. My plan had been to only be here for a few hours and return to her rooms for lunch, but I'd lost track of time while researching.

And now I was trapped in a room alone with Draven, exactly what Samara had been trying to avoid.

Fuck. Me.

He turned away from the bookshelves and sauntered over to me, his hands in his pockets. He was like the dark mirror of Kieran with his perfectly combed hair and well-put-together outfit, but while Kieran had an easygoing charm, Draven had an intensity to him that had the hairs on the back of my neck rising.

Black and silver hair fell over his shoulder as he cocked his head and studied me. Then his eyes drifted over my features, lingering on my red hair and hazel eyes.

"You're a Devereux." Not a surprise he figured out my bloodline. Most of the House bloodlines had very distinctive appearances. Everyone in my family had pale skin, deep red hair, hazel eyes, and sharp features. If we were in a room together, there was no mistaking the fact that we were all related, whether I liked it or not. "Astaroth?" he guessed.

"Roth," I said stiffly, trying to hide my surprise. Maybe he knew my name because I was the only Devereux ever to go to Drudonia. "I go by Roth."

He smiled. "Pleasure to meet you, Roth. Do you prefer to be referred to as *them* as well?"

I blinked, not having expected the consideration, but nodded.

Draven shrugged. "I might have to kill you after this conversation, but there is no reason not to be polite about your preferences."

Once again, my eyes darted to the doors, and I took a tiny step towards them.

"You won't make it." Draven gestured towards the table I'd been sitting at when he'd arrived. "How about we have a chat?"

His tone was still light, but his eyes were hard as he walked over to the table and pulled two chairs free so they were facing each other. Fear clamped down on my heart. Draven knew Samara was gone, and he'd decided I was the weak link in finding out where she'd run off to. Stiffly, I walked over to the chair, resolution building with each step. He would get *nothing* from me.

My ribbons shifted slightly on my forearms. I just needed to bide my time. All I needed was a few seconds to make it out the door and down the stairwell. Draven had been careful to keep up the persona of the charming prince around others—he wouldn't pursue me in front of witnesses.

I hoped.

Draven folded his large frame into the chair opposite me. I looked him over quickly but didn't spot any weapons on him aside from a coiled whip at his hip. Seemed like an odd choice for a prince. It wasn't like he couldn't afford a flashy sword.

"How exactly did a Devereux find themselves in House Harker?" He tilted his head thoughtfully. "Your House isn't exactly known for playing nice with others."

"I met Samara at Drudonia, and she asked if I'd be interested in doing an extended stay here for the summer. The beaches are much nicer here than further south."

Draven glanced pointedly at my white skin that was so pale, it looked like I'd burn immediately if I stepped outside, which was accurate. More importantly, I would get freckles if I spent too much time in the sun, and I refused to have more freckles than the few I already had.

"Was Samara trying to keep you away from me because you're researching something for her?" Bloodred lines slowly bled into the deep blue of his eyes. "Or because I can still smell her on you?"

I barely restrained myself from brushing my fingers against my neck where Samara had fed from me this morning after Kieran and Alaric had left. At some point, we'd both ended up in the washroom together, but considering what we did afterwards, it wasn't surprising I still smelled like her.

Fuck it.

"Jealous that my tongue was deep in Samara's cunt while she sat on my face this morning?"

"Yes," he said matter-of-factly.

"She's not going to marry you." I raised my chin. "And I'm not going to tell you shit."

Red churned in his eyes like rivers of blood, the blue a distant memory. What unsettled me more was how calm he appeared. His bloodlust was running high, but he was lounging in the chair like he didn't have a care in the world. The only other person I'd seen who could control their bloodlust that well was Samara.

"I could make you tell me." A cruel smile stretched across his mouth. "Believe me when I say I'm quite good at getting people to spill their secrets."

My ribbons shifted along my forearms, the outer layer loosening a little more. "You don't frighten me."

His smile widened. "Lies. We both know I can hear your heart beating faster every second you're in my presence. Where has Samara gone? I know she's no longer within these walls, and I know that temperamental Marshal is with her."

"Maybe she just wanted to get away from you after being forced to see your hideous face every day for the past couple of weeks?" Almost ready. Strike. Run. Find Kieran and Alaric. Whatever game the prince had been playing this week was over.

"Alright." Draven raised a hand, flicking his fingers out to reveal nails that had hardened into sharp, black claws. "Let's see if you reconsider after I peel the skin from your bones. I think I'll start with the face."

Faster than lightning, my ribbons shot forward, aiming for his eyes. I bolted up but stumbled back when his whip leapt from his hip of its own accord to slap my ribbons aside. My hesitation cost me, because when I spun to take off towards the door, something yanked my feet out from under me, causing me to slam face-first into the floor, and I screamed when a snapping sound came from my wrist as I tried to break my fall.

Draven let out a disapproving sound, and I blinked through my tears just as his brown leather boots filled my vision. Then he nudged me over until I was lying on my back, my arm clutched against my chest as I stared up at him. The dark brown leather whip hovered in the air, coiled around my blood ribbons.

"Impressive." He toyed with the end of a ribbon before

grabbing them and balling them up in his fist. "Not the best choice for a weapon though. A whip is much better."

I bit back another scream, trembles racking my body as his whip lunged forward and its bloodred, pointed tip stopped less than an inch away from my eye.

"Tell me where she is," Draven purred.

"No." I clenched my jaw, pushing back the pain, and then met the prince's stare again. "Eat shit and die."

Something like respect flashed across his face before his eyes darted to the door. "You just had to scream, didn't you?" I let out a relieved breath as he summoned the whip away from my face.

The doors slammed open, revealing Alaric, Kieran, and Nyx—Adrienne and Emil behind them. The last two had been babysitting me the past week, and I could tell by their expressions that they were annoyed at me.

That was fair. I was annoyed at myself too.

They'd both had things they'd wanted to take care of and had told me to stay in Samara's room. I'd promised to do so, and I'd meant it at the time . . . but then I had remembered some books I wanted to reference in the library and had figured it wouldn't hurt to sneak out for an hour.

Alaric's eyes were flat and hard, and the rangers were looking at the prince like they were imagining ripping out his spine, but Kieran . . . he looked disappointed.

I laughed, wincing as the movement jostled my wrist. "You and the dark prince, eh? Didn't know you had it in you, pretty boy."

Kieran paled as all eyes fell on him.

"It's"—he swallowed hard—"complicated."

"Everything about you lot is complicated," Adrienne growled. "I still think we should kill him."

"Think you can?" Draven looked at her curiously, not the least bit concerned about being significantly outnumbered.

"Drav," Kieran said tiredly. To my surprise, the prince backed off. Emil and Alaric helped me to my feet while Adrienne and Nyx continued to glare at the prince.

We all watched warily as Draven paced back and forth, his whip gliding down to coil on his hip again. My ribbons were still bunched up in his hand, the ends of them dragging on the floor.

"FUCK!" Draven picked up a chair and slammed it onto the ground. It shattered into several pieces, and he threw what remained in his hand at the table before spinning around to face us. "Tell me where she is. *Now*."

The rangers stepped forward, swords in hand. There was so much tension in the room, I could feel my bloodlust rising.

Alaric was a rigid wall at my back, but Kieran moved until he was standing in front of Draven and cupped the prince's cheek with his hand. "Tell us why, Drav. I love you . . . but I can't trust you."

"Well, shit," I muttered. "I just thought they were fuckin'."

"My mother wants Samara," Draven admitted reluctantly. "She's run out of patience. I received a letter from her this morning telling me to bring the Heir to her."

"Why?" Kieran stiffened.

"I've been buying time, telling her Samara was considering the proposal." Draven stepped away from Kieran and resumed pacing while running a hand roughly through his hair. "She'll know Samara has left and she'll send her guards after her. And Erendriel—" Draven cut himself off as pain flashed across his face. He spoke the next few words carefully, like he was testing how much he could say. "The wraiths will be after her too. You have to tell me where she went, Kier."

"We'll go and get her," Nyx said.

Draven shook his head. "The woods will be crawling with wraiths soon, if they're not already. You'll be cut down before you ever reach her. It has to be me."

"Why do you stand a chance?" Emil asked.

The prince smiled. "I'm more than just a pretty face."

"My ribbons," I spat and held out my uninjured hand.

Draven glanced at me and then down at my ribbons still in his hand. Then he loosened his fingers, and my ribbons shot towards me before I pushed them back with a thought. Kieran yelled as one ribbon wrapped around the prince's neck and the other wrapped around the whip that instantly lunged up to defend the prince before wrapping it around a chair.

Magic flooded the room as the prince rose several feet into the air, his claws tearing into my ribbons, but I just coiled more length around his neck.

"Roth!" Kieran screamed. "Let him down!"

"Still think my ribbons are useless as weapons?" I snarled and flung my good hand out to the side. The prince crashed into an empty bookcase before collapsing to the floor. Then I called both ribbons back to me, and they swiftly wrapped around my forearms, looking a little worse for wear.

Draven slowly got to his feet, rubbing his neck with one hand while reaching the other for his whip, which instantly leapt to his hand. Kieran slid between me and him, a worried look on his face. The rangers raised their swords a little higher, and to my surprise, Alaric moved to stand in front of me too.

"Relax," Draven said smoothly, tucking his whip back to his side. "I'm not going to kill them. Samara would be pissed. She clearly likes the Devereux *outcast*."

My ribbons rustled on my forearms, and Alaric gave me a censuring look over his shoulder. I gave him a cool one in return, and his lips twitched in response.

I stepped around Alaric and moved towards Draven. "Tell us why we should tell you," I demanded. "We know you're hiding things from us, and while Samara and Kieran believe there's something redeemable in you, I remain unconvinced."

"Same," Alaric said as all three rangers muttered their agreement.

Draven regarded me for a long moment before stretching a hand to me, palm up. "May I?" His eyes lowered to my injured arm that was still pressed against my body. Slowly, I extended it until my wrist rested in his palm.

He held my gaze as he raised his other hand to his mouth and sliced open the tip of his finger. I watched as he drew the glyph for healing on my skin, surprised by how light his touch was. Then a sharp exhale rushed out of my lips when I felt the magic from his blood sink into my flesh.

"What are you?" I breathed out.

"Something that shouldn't exist," he said tightly. "My secrets are my own, but trust me when I say I am uniquely suited to fight against wraiths."

I pulled my arm away from him and tentatively flexed my wrist. It was a little stiff, but other than that, it was completely healed. There was something off about his magic though. I'd felt the magic of other Moroi before. Draven's was different. It was . . . more.

Powerful. Chaotic. Wicked.

"Swear it," I said. "Swear on your soul that you will protect Samara from whatever is coming."

Alaric started to object, but I held my hand up, cutting him off. I wouldn't shed any tears if Draven met an untimely end, but I suspected Samara would, and I didn't want her to be sad, because I felt . . . things about her. I scowled at Draven, and he smiled at me in understanding.

Ugh.

"I'm not a good person," he said evenly. "There are reasons I am the way I am and I've done the things I've done, but none of them truly excuse anything." His eyes, which were still more red than blue, held my own without wavering. "But I promise you with every piece of my broken soul that I only want to protect Samara from what is to come. I will do whatever I have to, to protect those I love."

I glanced at Kieran, who was staring at Draven like he wanted to wrap the dark prince in his arms and whisk him away from everyone. Adrienne had been right earlier. We were a complicated bunch.

"Lake Malov," I said. Alaric swore behind me, but I ignored him. "There is something important there, and if you care about Samara as much as I think you do, you'll let her and Vail find it. Keep the wraiths off their backs until then."

Draven's lips pursed together but he nodded. "I can do that."

"I'll come with you," Kieran said.

"No." The prince shook his head sharply. Hurt spread across Kieran's face, and Draven's expression softened slightly. "If you're there, my attention will be split between protecting you and protecting Samara."

Kieran's mouth flattened into a hard line, but he didn't argue.

"This is insane," Alaric cut in. "We can't trust him to protect Samara."

"Is it any crazier than trusting Vail to keep her safe?" Nyx asked softly. "He's almost killed her twice."

My head snapped around so quickly, it hurt. "What the fuck are you talking about?"

They blinked. "You didn't know? Vail left Samara to be monster food for the kúsu, and things got a little out of hand at the temple."

"He attacked her," Alaric growled.

"But he also saved her," Kieran said. "Both times."

Nyx rubbed their forehead. "Does it count as saving if he was the danger in the first place?"

I should have kept her tied up in bed. Samara would have been pissed about it, but at least she would have been safe.

"Go," I told Draven. "Protect her."

The prince traded glances with Kieran before striding towards the door, the rangers hesitating for a moment before stepping aside to let him pass.

"Prince?" Draven paused mid-step and looked over his shoulder at me. "I don't give a fuck what you are or what type of magic you have. If you betray Samara . . ." Alaric and Kieran moved to stand next to me as I let my own bloodlust rise, knowing it would turn my eyes into a fiery orange. "If you hurt her, we will make you suffer in ways you can't even dream of."

The Moroi Prince smiled. "Good."

CHAPTER TWENTY-THREE

Samara

"Sorry, girl." I patted Zosa's nose, and the grey mare tossed her head in irritation. "You'll be safe here, and I'll be back in a few days."

"I'll take good care of her," the stablehand promised, and I smiled thankfully at the young girl. Her parents were in charge of this outpost, and I knew they were all good people. I hated leaving Zosa behind, but Vail and I agreed that we had to go on foot from here.

The sun was setting, and we were in the last outpost in Moroi territory. We'd traveled straight up the coastline and made it here in less than two days, pushing the horses as hard as we could. The Velesian border was only two miles away and would be the more dangerous part of our trip. It'd be slower on foot, but we were traveling at night, and the horses would have attracted too much attention.

"Thanks, Nisha." I stroked Zosa's neck one last time before striding towards the front gates, where Vail was waiting for me. Shortly after we'd arrived, a striker with dark blue scales tinged with purple had landed on his shoulder. It wasn't one I'd recognized, but we had over a hundred strikers on active duty, so it wasn't like I knew all of them. It probably belonged to a ranger who was often in the field. Some of them traveled with their strikers, and the flying reptiles only left them to deliver messages.

Vail's brow had creased as he'd read the message, but when I'd asked about it, he'd just said it was a ranger thing he needed to take care of and instructed me to get the horses sorted and meet him at the gate.

The rangers posted at this outpost were standing next to him with frustrated expressions. They hadn't been happy to learn that their Marshal would be traveling into Velesian territory at night, and they'd been even more upset when Vail had refused to let any of them come with us.

"Let's go," he said as soon as I reached them.

My heart beat a little faster as the rangers opened the gate for us, and I followed Vail out of the relative safety of the outpost and its ward. The wraiths had figured out a way past the outpost wards, which weren't as strong as those that protected the Houses, but the outposts were still far safer than the wilds.

Especially the thick forests of Velesian territory.

"We'll stay on the road until we're closer to the border," Vail said quietly. "Then we'll have to move into the forests to avoid the patrols."

I nodded. Thanks to a glyph that would hide our scent and Rynn detailing where the patrol routes were, the odds were in our favor of slipping past the Velesians. I didn't love sneaking into their territory like this, especially after my latest encounter with Bastian. If we were caught, he would almost certainly get word about it, and he'd be only too delighted to take advantage of our situation.

But we didn't have time to get permission to search the area around Lake Malov either. So we'd just have to make sure we didn't get caught and avoided the Alpha Pack at all costs.

"Okay." I looked up at the last rays of sunlight streaking across the sky. "How long will it take us to reach the rendezvous spot?"

"Two days, unless we have to veer significantly off course."

I slid a glance towards Vail. We'd barely spoken since leaving House Harker. Granted, we'd been racing up the coastline so there hadn't really been any good opportunities to speak, but now we'd be traveling on foot and then hiding out together in what would no doubt be a small space.

As if reading my thoughts, he turned his head to look at me. "We'll need to be quiet. This isn't far from where I think the spine-backed boars were driven into the Moroi realm, which means something is creeping around these woods that we really don't want to mess with. The Velesians patrol this area less than the land west of the lake, so it'll be easier for us to slip past their patrols but also increases our chances of running into something nasty."

The fear that had been building inside me since we left the outpost surged forward. The last time I'd been out in the wilds at night, we'd been attacked by küsu and Vail had left me for dead. My gaze fell on the darkening shadows of the woods surrounding us. As bad as the küsu were, there were worse things roaming Lunaria than overgrown insects.

"I'll keep you safe," Vail said softly, his eyes on the forest around us. It was probably foolish of me, but I trusted him. When he extended a hand, I slipped mine into his without hesitation before we stepped off the main road into the midst of the trees. "We'll be at the border in ten minutes. Do not speak unless absolutely necessary. Our scents might be hidden, but the Velesians will easily pick up our voices."

I squeezed his hand in understanding, and we crept forward at a steady pace. The trees grew taller and wider as we moved until they blocked the sky. Vines writhed as if they were snakes, and some of the flowers bloomed as night fell, releasing sweet scents into the air to lure in unsuspecting prey. I felt the moment the sun fully set, giving way to night.

Strength flooded my limbs, and it was like a damper had been lifted from my senses. I could smell the creatures stalking the trees above us and hear leaves crunching to my left where something was slinking through the forest undergrowth. The night came alive around us, and despite my fear of what we might encounter, I couldn't help but love it a little.

We were children of the moon, and the night belonged to us as much as to the other monsters.

Knowing I might need every advantage tonight, I allowed my bloodlust to rise as well. Vail looked back at me over his shoulder, my hand still clasped in his, and his silver eyes practically glowed in the darkness. Looked like we were both embracing our inner monsters tonight.

Hours passed as I followed Vail's footsteps, stepping where he stepped and stopping when he stopped. A few times, he squeezed my hand in warning and would then look pointedly in one direction. I'd focus until I saw whatever it was he was pointing out.

A monstrous-looking flower devouring the canine corpse of a howler, some type of tree-dwelling mammal with four arms and hooked claws, and my personal favorite, a baby küsu. I'd almost screamed when I'd spotted the nearly six-foot-long beast curving its body around the trunk of a tree, its shiny, black scales reflecting the small amount of moonlight that peeked through the tree canopy when the wind caused the branches to sway, and it's too many legs propelling it forward as it climbed further up the tree.

Thanks for the nightmares, little buddy.

Vail stopped so suddenly, I ran into him, the hand that wasn't in his instinctively going up to steady myself, feeling the hard muscles of his lower back flexing underneath the leather vest. I immediately started scanning our surroundings while my ears strained to pick something up, but I saw nothing and only heard the insects chirping away in the night.

No. Wait. There. Dark shapes were slinking down the trees around us.

"What are they?" I asked tightly, wanting to know what we were up against. Whatever these creatures were, they clearly knew we were here, so our silence was pointless.

"*Beduv kodgeg.*" Vail released my hand to free his sword. "Moon devils."

Shivers ran down my spine, but I forced myself to remain calm before sliding my throwing daggers out from my thigh sheaths.

The branches above us creaked, and more moonlight danced across the trees, giving me a better look at the creatures. I'd never had the pleasure of seeing moon devils in the flesh before, only sketches from people who had survived encounters with them. They were one of the more reclusive predators in Lunaria, and what they lacked in size, they more than made up for in intelligence.

I had to admit, they had a certain beauty to them. Short black fur coated their sturdy, feline bodies, and silver dapples in the shape of crescent moons decorated their fur. My heart hammered inside my chest when one of them got halfway down a tree and unhinged its jaws to what seemed like an impossible degree, showcasing the six-inch fangs that jutted out on either side of its mouth.

"Do not get bit, Samara," Vail breathed out. "They will snap through bone like it's nothing, and if you can't run, we die."

We die, because Vail wouldn't leave me behind this time. He'd die protecting me.

I tightened my grip on the blades. "Plan?"

More devils climbed headfirst down the trees, and some remained crouched on the trunks while others slunk across the ground and began circling us. Low, throaty clicks echoed throughout the night air, and in the dark, several short barks rang in response, the clicking sounds growing more excited.

The panic I'd been feeling increased until my breaths were nothing but quick pants. There were too many. We were going to die here. They'd snap through our bones and tear the flesh from our bodies as they devoured us. There would be nothing left.

I would die here. In this forest. Far from friends and family. Vail would die with me. Part of me felt guilty at being glad I wouldn't die alone.

But I didn't want to die. Not here. I didn't want—

A steady hand closed around my forearm, cutting off my thoughts. "It's their magic," Vail said softly. "They can increase whatever emotion you're feeling. It's easier for them to take down panicked prey. We need to run before the rest of their pride gets here."

I concentrated on Vail's hand on me, then slowly felt for the foreign magic pushing itself into my mind and shoved it back. The chittering increased, an angrier edge to it now, and several sharp bellows boomed. We were running out of time.

"When I say go, you run towards the tree directly in front of us with the blue vine growing up it. Run past it and don't stop until you reach a dried-up creek bed, then turn west. There's a cave we can seek refuge in. I can find it if we make it to that creek bed." Vail pulled his hand away and shifted lightly on the balls of his feet, holding the sword loosely at his side. "If any of them get in front of us, throw your daggers at them. Don't worry about fatal wounds. We just need to keep them off us. I'll guard our backs."

"How far?" Sweat ran down the sides of my face despite the brisk night air.

"Five miles."

Fuck. Me.

"Don't be a whiny little Heir now, Sam." Vail shoved me forward before yelling, "RUN!"

I took off, darting under a low branch and past the tree Vail had pointed out. Sharp cries echoed around the forest as the devils immediately gave chase. Two shadows peeled off the trees ahead, one darting directly into our path. My daggers were soaring through the air a second later. One sunk into the flank of a devil, and it howled before leaping back into the trees. The other missed by a hair but still caused the feline monster to retreat.

The daggers flew back into my outstretched palms, and I immediately threw them again. More angry screams. The muscles in my thighs burned, but between embracing my bloodlust and it being nighttime, I was nowhere near my limit. Behind me, I heard Vail cut away anything that got too close to us.

For a few minutes, I thought we actually might make it, then my foot caught on a tree root and I stumbled. The moon devils seized the opportunity, and their magic flooded me again.

I stumbled once more and barely managed to right myself as sheer panic gripped me.

"If you can't run, we die."

Another raised root snagged my foot, but this time, I didn't recover fast enough. My shoulder hit the ground first, and I flipped over, barely managing to avoid stabbing myself with my own blades.

"Samara!" Vail bellowed.

The devils were there instantly. One snapped at my leg, and only Vail yanking me back kept me from losing a foot. Then he practically threw me forward, causing me to stagger a few steps before I spun around as he released a pain-filled snarl.

Blood poured from his thigh, but the devil was writhing on

the ground where Vail had pinned it with his sword. Another leapt for his back, aiming for his exposed neck, but my dagger sank into its throat instead. The dead weight still carried forward, and Vail grunted when the fifty-pound creature slammed into his back, almost taking him off his feet.

All around us, devils released sharp sounds—an eerie mix between a cough and bark—between those clicking sounds they clearly used to communicate. Blood filled the air, both ours and theirs, and I could feel their magic trying to seep into my mind again.

"FUCK OFF!" I screamed as the dagger slid free from the throat of the one I'd killed and landed back in my hand. We needed to move. Now. "Come on, Vail." I shoved one dagger back into my thigh sheath and grabbed his hand that wasn't holding the sword. "Time to go."

He took a step forward and faltered, blood soaking his entire right leg. I didn't think they'd broken any bones, but the devil had clearly torn through a lot of flesh. I could feel the excitement of the beasts around us as they slunk through the shadows. They'd temporarily backed off after we'd killed two of their own, but it was only a matter of time before they had another opportunity to strike.

"Go," Vail ordered, his face pale. "I'll only slow you down."

"Who's being whiny now, *Marshal?*" I snarled in his face. "We're a team, Vail. You go down, I go down."

Fury lit up his silver eyes, and I let my bloodlust fully off the chain, knowing my eyes were nothing but solid black pools.

"If we die, know that I'm going to beat the shit out of you in whatever afterlife awaits us," he promised.

"Deal." I moved to his injured side and gripped his arm. He was too tall for me to fully support him, which meant I could only throw with my left hand, but I couldn't risk him falling again. "Let's get the fuck out of here."

We ran, not nearly as fast as before, but we kept going. Anytime Vail stumbled, I used every ounce of my strength to keep him on his feet. Between his sword and my dagger, we kept the devils from biting us with their bone-crushing jaws. Unfortunately, they changed tactics and started swiping at our legs with their claws.

Panic and fear still nipped at the edges of my mind. Some of it was definitely mine, but I could feel their influence as well. Up ahead, I could see a break in the trees. *Please let that be the dry creek bed,* I sent up a prayer to the moon. We just needed to reach the damn cave.

Moon devils raced across the branches, chittering back and forth rapidly. They knew we were close to getting free of the forest, and they didn't want to lose the advantage of the trees. I swallowed a scream as one of them deeply dug its claws into my calf, yet I somehow managed to stay upright. Vail grunted when I almost went down, more weight going on his injured leg, but I surged up and kept us both running.

The distraction cost me though when two devils flew from the trees on either side of us. My dagger found one while Vail barely managed to knock the other with his sword. Neither of us saw the third one flying directly towards my side, its jaw stretched open wide to sink its fangs into my ribs.

A sound like thunder cracked through the dark forest, and the devil that had been flying through the air at me jerked and veered off course. Another thunderous boom sounded from behind us, and as one, the devils released a high-pitched, undulated wail before falling back. Whether they were converging on whatever was attacking them or just retreating, I didn't know and didn't care.

"Vail!" I shouted. "Creek bed! Where do we go?"

We crashed to a halt, both of us breathing hard as Vail whipped his head around, taking in our surroundings. "West. Half mile." He grimaced and tentatively pulled away from my support, testing his leg. "Let's go before they come back or something else is attracted to the blood."

For a moment, I stood there, bathed in moonlight, and looked back into the dark forest where I could hear the devils hunting whatever had saved us.

"Thanks, beastie," I whispered, "and good hunting."

TWENTY MINUTES LATER, Vail and I collapsed onto the floor of a small underground cave. The only reason it'd taken us so long to find it was because the sky had opened up and dumped what felt like a lake's worth of water on us. Visibility had been so poor that we'd walked past the cave and had to backtrack, the entrance barely noticeable.

I winced as I dipped my fingers into the bleeding wound on my calf before drawing the glyph for seal in the dirt and on each side of the narrow cave mouth. This spell wasn't particularly powerful—wraiths could have breezed on by it and it would shatter if it was physically hit too many times—but it would prevent anything from hearing or scenting us, and we'd been careful not to let any blood drip from our wounds close to the cave. I waited until I felt the magic lock into place before heading back towards Vail.

"I don't know how the Velesians deal with these sudden showers all the time." I shivered and tugged my cold, wet tunic away from my skin with a grimace. "There's no way these are going to dry in here."

"The sun will rise in a few hours." Vail set his sword next to where he was sitting on the floor, examining his leg. He'd pulled a small Fae lantern from his pack along with a canteen of water and some dried meat. "We'll use that time to heal and rest and then try to cover as much ground as possible during

A Court of Bones and Sorrow

the day, but we'll likely still need to travel at least a few hours at night if we're to reach Rynn on time."

I nodded and sat on the cool, hard floor, trying very hard not to think about the last time I'd been alone with Vail in a cave while I drew healing glyphs around my various wounds. It'd been easy to block that memory before because I'd been so focused on finding safety, but now we were here . . . and exactly like that night, we'd barely survived a monster attack and were covered in blood. At least this time, thanks to the rain, most of the blood had been washed away.

Of course that meant I was freezing, but I was still glad we didn't have to spend the rest of the night covered in sticky blood with no way of rinsing off. One of these days, when I wasn't busy just trying to survive or unravel nefarious plots, I'd figure out a glyph that could instantly clean and dry clothes.

Vail passed me a piece of dried meat.

"Thanks," I murmured before popping it into my mouth. Rabbit. My lips twisted in distaste, but I choked it down.

"Sorry." The corner of Vail's eyes crinkled in the barest hint of amusement as he handed me several more pieces. "Tried to find venison, but meat supplies are running low so rabbit was the only option."

I blinked, a little surprised he remembered my food preferences and my strong dislike for the gaminess of rabbit.

"It's fine," I said and scarfed down the rest of the gamey bits while sneaking glances at him, trying to gauge if the memory of that night was haunting him the way it was me.

At least once a month, I still woke up in cold sweats, remembering how terrified I'd been as the wind had howled outside that cave and we'd heard the shrieks of the wraiths as they'd searched the forests for us, not to mention the trauma of seeing my parents cut down before my eyes. As a child, I'd thought they'd been invincible. My mother had been so confident that nothing had ever rattled her, and my father had been a skilled fighter from a family of rangers.

The wraiths had gone for them immediately, bypassing other easier prey. I hadn't understood it then, but I did now. They'd known my parents had been searching for the other half of the soul crown. I wondered if Queen Velika had ordered the attack or if Erendriel had taken the initiative.

Vail and his parents had simply been at the wrong place at the wrong time. Maybe he was right to hate me a little. My family was the reason his were dead, and I'd stopped him from trying to save them.

"I was wrong."

"What?" I blinked and raised my gaze from where I'd been staring blankly at the floor to meet Vail's solemn expression.

"No one knows you better than me," he said evenly. "Not Kieran. Not Rynn or Cali. Me." He laid a hand over his chest. "You were my best friend long before you were any of theirs. I know every single one of your tells, and I know you better than I know myself."

"That was then. This is now." I shook my head, not knowing how to deal with this conversation. Being trapped with him in a fucking cave again was too much. Especially while hashing out our old pain. "You don't know me at all anymore."

"Oh yeah?" he challenged. "Tell me you're not thinking about the night our parents died. That you're not thinking your parents are responsible for looping my parents into protecting them? And that you're not feeling guilty about stopping me from running out of that cave like a fucking fool." He pulled his hand away from his chest and waved it in my direction, inviting me to argue as he bit out his next words. "Tell me, Samara. I fucking dare you."

I held his steely gaze, refusing to look away, but what the fuck could I say to that? He was right. It pissed me off that he was able to crack open my mind and see all my thoughts so easily.

He let out a humorless laugh. "Exactly."

"Your parents were only there that night because they were protecting mine," I said hotly. "And I did take away your choice, Vail. You were my friend, my only fucking friend, and I didn't want you to die too, but it wasn't my fucking choice to make, was it?" I choked off the last word before rubbing my face. If I could avoid caves for a while, that would be great. Clearly nothing good came of them.

"I was wrong," Vail repeated. "If you hadn't knocked me out and prevented me from running out of that cave, I would have died that night, and you would have too, because we both know you would have followed me out into the night."

He was right. I would have followed Vail anywhere back then. Fuck, I would follow him anywhere now, despite all the animosity between us. Apparently I was a fool too.

"You don't get to rewrite history, Samara." The kindness in his voice finally made me look at him again. It wasn't just the echoes of grief I saw reflected in his eyes. There was acceptance too. "My parents loved yours. It wasn't just a case of the Marshals being devoted to the rulers of a House. They were friends, and they died trying to protect each other, and us. The last thing my father told me to do was protect you."

"The last thing mine told me to do was protect you," I whispered and then shot him a contrite smile. "Sorry I had to hit you over the head with a rock to do it."

He shrugged. "Sorry I almost let a kùsu eat you a few weeks ago."

I laughed sharply. "That was a real asshole move. I'm going to have nightmares for the rest of my life about that overgrown centipede chasing me."

"I really am sorry." He winced. "I was just so angry at you. For so fucking long. I let it warp everything about us."

"Why, Vail?" I searched his face, trying to find the answer I'd been seeking for the last decade. "Why did you hate me so much? We both lost our parents that night, but you turned on me so quickly." I couldn't keep the soft desperation out of my voice.

"It's complicated." Vail's mouth hardened into a flat line, and he looked away from me.

Fuck that. He didn't get to get off this easily.

"You tried to feed me to an overgrown insect." I narrowed my eyes. "Explain it."

Vail's gaze snapped to mine, and I saw a hint of the accusing anger that I was used to in them. "You never mourned them. I was falling apart, and you carried on like nothing had happened."

"Carmilla told me I had to be strong." I swallowed, remembering the exact conversation with her and how distraught she'd been. "That I was the Heir of House Harker and that everyone was counting on me. I wasn't allowed to fall apart." He frowned like something about that didn't make sense, but I barreled on. "My entire life ended in one night, Vail, and when I finally snapped and snuck out of my room to find my best friend and tell him I was fucking breaking, he shoved me into the dirt and said he wished I'd died that night too."

"I'm sorry," he rasped. "I didn't know. I thought . . . Fuck, I don't know what I thought." Vail's brows bunched together before he slowly said, "Carmilla said that you got frustrated with her when she grieved about losing her sister around you."

"What?" I jerked back like I'd been struck. "Carmilla was concerned I was breaking down and that it would harm my future as the Harker Heir. Everything I did was to prove to her —and the House—that I was worthy of my parents' legacy, but even then, I never said anything cruel about her grieving."

Vail frowned. "Maybe I'm not remembering it right."

"Damn fucking right, you're not," I said through clenched teeth. There was no way Carmilla would have said such a thing. He must have been so caught up in his hatred that he'd seen or heard something that hadn't been there.

"All I knew was that I was hurting and you seemed . . . fine."

"Fine?" I repeated, my voice cracking as I shook my head ruefully. "I was falling apart and had no one to talk to. There wasn't anyone our age back then aside from Alaric, and we didn't exactly get along."

"You get along now," Vail muttered, and I didn't miss the hint of jealousy in his tone, which snapped me out of the heartache I was feeling and sent me straight into pissed-off territory. He was the one who had ended our friendship. He was the fucking one who had been flipping back and forth between hot and cold since I'd returned. One second damning me and the next saving me.

"After you decided I was no longer worthy of your friendship, I had no one, Vail!" My hands slammed against his chest as I gripped the front of his shirt. I didn't know if I wanted to shove him away from me or pull him closer. "It wasn't until Kieran came to live at House Harker that I had another friend, and things between us were always complicated. By the time I went to Drudonia and became close friends with Rynn and Cali—" The words got stuck in my throat as I struggled to get my emotions back in check. "The lie became the truth. Everyone believed I was fine, and I'd gotten really good at hiding the pain. Seemed easier to just go on like that."

Vail placed his large, warm hands over mine, and I stared at them for a long moment before raising my eyes to meet his, which were full of understanding, like he finally saw me, and something inside me settled. Then his lips curled into a lopsided smile. "We're both equally fucked."

"I suppose," I admitted and shivered as the dampness of my clothes sank into my bones.

"Truce?" Vail offered and squeezed my hands.

"You were the only one declaring war," I felt the need to point out.

"Please," Vail scoffed. "You used to prance around in those skimpy outfits every time you were back visiting from Drudonia."

I stared at him wide-eyed. "What are you talking about?"

Vail leaned forward, silver flickering in his eyes. "You know exactly what I'm talking about," he said in a deep voice that had my toes curling. "Every summer, you would come back for a few weeks, usually dragging Rynn and Cali with you, and the three of you would generate chaos around House Harker as you ran around basically naked."

"Oh." I tilted my head and thought about it. We'd started doing that when the three of us were eighteen. Three years before I was supposed to marry Demetri. I'd been going through a bit of a wild phase, and Cali and Rynn had only been too happy to participate. "Honestly, I was just trying to make Kieran jealous. It never worked because usually he had his tongue down the throat of some other girl."

"It definitely worked." Vail chuckled, and my heart skipped a beat. "As soon as you left, we'd all have to deal with Kieran's mood swings for months afterwards. Honestly, I'm surprised Alaric didn't drown him in the ocean. Or himself. I caught him staring after you more than once."

My lips curved into a victorious grin. "Good to know."

"You're ridiculous." Vail shook his head, a faint smile on his lips.

"Did you?" I asked.

"Did I what?" He quirked an eyebrow, and I raised mine in return.

"Ever get jealous?"

Vail looked at me for a long moment and then shrugged. "Of course. Rynn is pretty hot."

"Cade will kick your ass." I glared at him, ignoring the flare of jealousy I sensed and the fact that I actually had no idea how the leader of the Alpha Pack felt about Rynn.

"Unlikely." Vail bared his fangs at me even as light danced in his eyes. "I'm faster than that old bear."

"He's only a couple of decades older than us." I laughed.

Vail gave me an unimpressed look before releasing my hands and stretching out on the cave floor. I didn't think everything was completely fixed between us, but I felt . . . lighter? The painful history was still there, but for the first time, I thought that maybe Vail and I had a chance at something new.

No longer distracted by the conversation, I became very much aware of the cold, wet clothes clinging uncomfortably to my skin.

Sighing quietly, I started pulling them off. There was no way I was going to be able to fall asleep in them.

"What are you doing?" Vail asked in a rough tone as he stared at me with silver winding its way through his eyes.

"I'm not sleeping in wet clothes. At least this way, they'll hopefully be only damp in the morning." My fingers felt along the wall until I found some creases that I could tuck the edges of my tunic and pants into so they could hang. I left the thin shirt I wore under my tunic on along with my underwear, but I did turn my back to Vail and reach under my shirt to unlace the band I wore around my breasts.

A moan of relief slipped from my lips before I shoved the band into another crevice.

I heard Vail rise behind me, and when I glanced over my shoulder, my mouth went dry as he pulled off his wet vest and tunic. He had his back to me, and it had never occurred to me until this moment that well-defined back muscles were hot as hell. Even though scars littered his lightly tanned skin, my fingers itched to trail over each one and to feel his corded muscles beneath my touch. The healing glyphs hadn't been enough to fix the damage he'd taken over the years.

You're only feeling this way because you almost died an hour ago, I told myself, but when I'd returned to House Harker, I'd embraced a new motto.

Want something? Take something.

Vail could absolutely not be one of those things though. Alaric might be complicated, but I had no doubt he desired me. More than that, we had something that could work if we were both willing to try. Despite this heartfelt conversation with Vail, I didn't entirely know what he wanted, and more importantly, I didn't think he did either. Until he made that decision clear, I wouldn't allow him to break my heart more than he already had every time he'd spat on our friendship.

"How's your leg?"

I frowned as Vail tugged his pants off and then realized that by staring at his thigh, I was dangerously close to staring at something else that was hidden only by the thin fabric of his underwear.

Nope. Not going there. I jerked my gaze away and took a seat on the cavern floor again.

"It will be sore tomorrow, but I should be able to move okay." Either he hadn't noticed me almost staring at his dick, or he was choosing not to comment on it. I couldn't decide if I was disappointed by that.

"Do you . . . ah . . . need to drink?" My gaze hesitantly flicked to his as he took a seat across from me.

We both knew I wasn't talking about water.

"No," he said in a guarded tone, but his eyes still darted to my neck as silver flickered in them. "You should save your strength."

"I fed deeply from Roth and Kieran this morning." My eyes fell to his exposed thigh. The six-inch wound was mostly healed across the top, but the skin was still red and puffy. "If you're not at one hundred percent tomorrow, you'll slow us down," I pointed out.

Vail's even stare told me he wasn't swayed by my logic. I shook my head, but it was his choice, and if he said he was fine, then I'd drop it.

I stretched out across the hard dirt floor of the cave. It was a far cry from my soft bed at House Harker or even the lumpy but relatively comfortable one I'd slept in at the outpost on our way to the Velesian realm. Between our surroundings and Vail though, I couldn't help thinking again about those nights we'd hidden in the cave after the wraiths had attacked our caravan.

My already cold body shivered at the memory. I was mentally and physically exhausted from the encounter with the devils and our heartfelt conversation, but we had to keep going in a few hours, which meant I needed to rest. Unfortunately, it was very difficult to force my mind to let me sleep.

The dampness of the cave only burrowed further into my skin, and I began to shiver. I turned onto my side, hoping that less contact with the cold earth would help.

It did not. Neither did my long, wet hair.

I sighed, about to give up on getting any sleep, when a large arm wrapped around my waist and tugged me back against a broad chest.

"Your teeth were chattering," Vail said tightly as every part of me went absolutely still. "It was annoying. Body heat will help."

"Right," I half squeaked. Every part of Vail was pressed up against my back. He'd slid his other arm underneath my head and even threw a leg over mine. *Body heat. This was just about survival.* I was feeling warmer already. My teeth had stopped clacking against each other, and the shivering was mostly gone too.

I snuggled a little further into Vail's arms, and he seemed to stop breathing for a moment. Then the arm around my waist tightened slightly, and I felt his beard tickle the back of my neck. I tried to remind myself of all the reasons getting involved with Vail was a bad idea, but for every bad memory, there was a good one.

"Why is this so confusing?" I whispered.

"Because I should hate you." His breath danced across my skin. "But I can't. And you shouldn't trust me, but you do."

His hand slipped underneath my shirt and made lazy circles over my belly. Each circular motion drifted a little higher until his thumb brushed the underside of my breast. I gasped and pressed a little harder into him, his hard length pressing against my ass, only the thin fabric of our remaining clothing separating us.

"You were right earlier," he said in a soft voice. "I should drink."

Any attempts at being rational and maybe offering him my wrist instead of my neck fled as his teeth grazed my skin, not breaking it, just waiting for me to say yes.

Fuck it. I'd be rational in the morning.

"Drink," I commanded, and a shiver that had nothing to do with the cold ran through me when one hand cupped my breast while the other wrapped around my throat and squeezed lightly. "Fuck, Vail," I groaned and raised my hand so I could bury it in his hair, holding him tighter against me. My thighs clenched together, and an aching need started to build as he roughly rolled a thumb over my pebbled nipple.

The hand on my neck slid up, guiding my face to the side so he could get better access to my throat. Then teeth nipped at me before his beard rubbed roughly against my skin. My breathing quickened as he hungrily kissed my neck, still playing with my nipple, and raised his head enough to whisper in my ear, "Are you wet for me, Heir?"

"Find out for yourself, Marshal," I said huskily.

"I know you are." His hand moved to play with my other nipple, rolling it between his fingers and making me squirm against him. "I can smell it. Your cunt was dripping as soon as I touched you."

"Fuck, why are you all such dirty talkers?" I whimpered.

Vail tore his hand from my breast and shoved it between my legs, pushing my underwear to the side while using his leg to spread mine wider. "Don't"—he shoved two fingers inside me with zero warning, and I let out a strangled moan as he gripped me to him while harshly pumping his fingers in and out—"talk about the others when I'm inside you."

"You weren't," I panted, "inside me yet."

The hand around my chin pulled it further to the side before Vail struck, his fangs piercing my neck just as another finger joined the others that were fucking me hard. The sharp pain mixed with the building pleasure was too much, and I came all over his hand.

He pulled it free to flick my overly sensitive clit before rubbing it with two of his fingers that were slick from my arousal. I jerked in his grasp, but his arm tightened around me, keeping me flush against his body.

"Vail," I half whimpered and half moaned as he continued to tease me. His fangs slid out, and he laughed against my neck before sliding one of his legs between mine to rotate us until he was beneath me, my back still flat against his chest. The leg that was between mine leaned to the outside, making my legs spread even more.

"Next time we do this," he rumbled into my ear, "it'll be in front of a mirror. That way, we can watch me fuck you. Watch as my fingers disappear"—he thrust three fingers inside me, stretching me out, and I moaned from the fullness—"into this perfect, tight little pussy of yours."

Shivers coursed through me as he continued to pump his fingers in and out, his thumb occasionally brushing over the sensitive bundle of nerves, causing my hips to buck. Vail increased his pace until my entire body was trembling.

As if he could sense how close I was, his fangs grazed my neck again before slowly sinking in. He didn't drink, just bit down hard, as if he was pinning me in place, claiming me.

That was all it took to push me over the edge. My pussy clenched around his fingers as the orgasm rolled through me, and I screamed his name again before sagging against him in a boneless heap.

My eyes had shut at some point, but I heard him licking his fingers after he withdrew them. Then he shifted us until we were both on our sides once more. I could feel his erection pressed against me, but when I reached around to slip my hand into his undershorts, he stopped me and guided it back to rest on my hip.

"You need rest," he said roughly. "And if my cock gets inside you . . . I won't be able to stop for hours."

The reality of what we'd just done crashed into me. I was lying on a cave floor with the man who had once been my dearest friend, then became one of my worst enemies, and now . . . I didn't know where we stood or how much I could truly trust him.

CHAPTER TWENTY-FOUR

Samara

I'D EXPECTED things to be awkward between us in the morning, but they weren't. We didn't talk about what had happened, but things had definitely shifted between us.

Kieran would probably have mixed feelings about this new development. He was easygoing about a lot of things, but not when it came to people who had hurt me, and almost nobody had hurt me more than Vail. Considering I felt the same about him and Draven, I couldn't really fault him for that. I had no idea how Roth and Alaric would react to Vail potentially entering our . . . thing.

My lips quirked into a wry grin. I didn't know how the Velesians so easily navigated these multi-threaded relationships. Well, most Velesians. Poor Rynn was more lost than I was when it came to this type of thing.

"What are you thinking about?" Vail stretched out a hand to help me over a fallen log.

"Nothing." I slipped my hand into his and gave him a sunny smile. He narrowed his eyes but didn't call me out on my bullshit. It felt strange for him not to launch back a scathing remark. A girl could get used to this.

"If we're to make it to the southern tip of Lake Malov by tomorrow morning, we need to travel a little further tonight." We both looked up at the rapidly setting sun. "Rynn mentioned a cabin about twenty miles from here. It's warded, which means we'll have a safe place to stay tonight, and it'll put us only a few miles from where we're supposed to meet her."

I chewed on my bottom lip. "Do you think we'll run into the moon devils again?"

"No." He shook his head. "We should be out of their territory by now, and they're likely still recovering from whatever tore into them last night."

"What do you think that was?" I asked. While I was glad whatever it was had shown up when it had, that didn't mean I wasn't worried about there being a bigger and badder monster lurking out there—one that could be tracking us now.

Vail didn't answer right away, and I didn't push him as he pondered it. We wound our way through the trees that only grew thicker the further we pressed into Velesian land. The type of fauna changed as well. Along the coast, the trees were spread out a little more, and the other plants . . . well . . . they were devious. Particularly in the Moroi realm further south, everything was deceptively beautiful. The better to lure in unsuspecting prey so it could devour them.

The plant life of the Velesian realm hid nothing about its intentions though. We passed several trees that were weeping what looked like blood, and large, purple flowers stood upright from the ground—their six-foot-tall petals closed tight as something bulged in the center of them—likely digesting whatever they had caught last night with the black, thorny tentacles that slithered around their base.

Not for the first time, I was glad the Moroi had ended up where they had. The Velesian realm was twice the size of ours, but I was pretty sure my ass would have been eaten a long time ago if I lived here.

"Most of my concentration last night was spent on staying upright and not passing out." Vail finally spoke. "I heard several loud cracks, which makes me think that whatever attacked the devils was large. Maybe attacked from above and broke some branches on the way down?" He shook his head, clearly not buying his own theory, and looked at me. "You didn't see anything?"

"I was a little busy keeping your heavy ass moving." I waved a hand at him. "Do you really need all those muscles?"

A squeal leapt from my throat as Vail grabbed me and picked me up like I weighed nothing at all before pinning me to a tree. He was so much taller than me that my feet were nowhere near the ground, so I wrapped my legs around his waist.

"I think you can benefit quite nicely from my muscles." He grinned, and for a second, it took my breath away to see such a carefree look on his face instead of the usual scowl.

"Maybe you can show me later?" I gave him a heated smirk, and his eyes lit up. "We can see how sturdy the walls of that cabin are."

Something roared in the distance, and a chorus of wolf howls answered it. Both of our heads whipped in the direction the sounds had come from, and Vail slowly set me back onto my feet. "The wolves are probably Velesians," he said. "Most of the sentinels in this area are lycanthropes."

We had rangers, the Velesians had sentinels, and the Furies didn't have a dedicated fighting force. There simply weren't enough of them to justify it. Instead, every single Furie was trained to fight, and they were all lethal.

More howls sounded.

"We need to move. They're headed this way along with whatever they're fighting." He held his hand out, and I slipped mine into his once more. We took off at a steady jog, avoiding the more nefarious-looking fauna as we cut our way through the forest.

Only when the forest started to darken did we stop to rest. Unease rippled through me. I really didn't want to spend another night traveling through the wilds, but I also knew we didn't have a choice.

Vail tugged me to him and kissed me gently. I blinked up at him, still not used to this softer version of him, and part of me worried about how long it would last. Vail's temper was volatile. I was bound to do something that would piss him off again. It had been bad enough when our friendship had ended as kids—I didn't know how I would handle it now that we were more than just friends.

If Alaric were here, he would have lectured me. Kieran would have offered me chocolates to ease my concern while scowling at Vail, and Roth . . . They would tell me I was an idiot for getting involved with Vail and to sit on their face as punishment.

I missed them. All of them. My heart clenched. I'd almost died last night and could die tonight.

"Hey." Vail tipped my chin up until I met his gaze. "We'll get through this and I'll get you back to them."

"How'd you know I was thinking about them?" I rasped.

He smiled and kissed the corners of my mouth. "You're easier to read than you think, especially when you're thinking about the people you care about."

We looked at each other for a long moment, neither of us willing to say anything else on that subject. Finally, Vail pulled his sword free and nodded at the daggers on my thigh. "We made good time today and aren't too far now. The further inland we go, the less familiar I am with the terrain, but I think we have less than five miles until we reach the cabin."

"I'll have to take your word for it because I have no idea where we are right now," I admitted. Vail smiled faintly and tapped the tree closest to us with his sword. I looked at where the tip of his blade rested and saw several markings carved into it. A wolf's head followed by what looked like a lake with an arrow pointing in the direction we were facing. Below that, squiggly lines—waves maybe? That one had an arrow pointing back to where we'd come from.

Now that I knew it was there, it was incredibly helpful, but I never would have spotted it without Vail pointing it out.

"Lead the way." I swallowed past the lump in my throat as the shadows around us darkened and the forest became more sinister. I took in a steady breath as magic flooded me. The sun had fully set. We just had to survive tonight, and then we'd get our answers tomorrow. I refused to even entertain the possibility that this had all been for nothing.

We *would* find answers at Lake Malov, though I was less sure we would *like* those answers.

Unlike the previous night, the woods around us were eerily silent. Nothing moved in the trees above us or in the thick underbrush, there were no howls or barks in the distance, and even the insects had ceased their chirping.

Vail kept scanning our surroundings, because something was clearly out there, and whatever it was, none of the other monsters wanted to mess with it. I concentrated on keeping my breathing steady and my fingers loose around the daggers, ready to throw at a moment's notice.

It felt like we'd barely been walking more than a few minutes when Vail whirled and shoved me. Hard. I flew backwards, my back slamming into a tree before I fell to my knees. One dagger went flying from my hand, but I managed to hold on to the other. I staggered to my feet and froze when Vail's pissed-off snarl rang throughout the night and the scent of his blood hit me a second later.

Five Strigoi stood completely still between me and Vail. Two of them were facing me, and the other three were facing

Vail, one of which had blood dripping from long, jagged claws.

My heart clenched, and I wished we'd come across any other type of monster. Anything but Strigoi. I'd even take the more dangerous wraiths over this. I looked over the two who were focused on me, trying my best to keep my emotions in check. One of them had been a woman once. Her blonde hair hung in long, tangled knots down to her waist. Like the rest of them, she was completely naked, and her frame was so gaunt, I could almost count her ribs.

The one next to her was equally thin with dark brown hair. He looked like he'd turned when he'd been younger, eighteen at most.

At some point, they'd been living their lives just like me, trying to survive in this fucked-up world, when something had happened to make them lose their humanity and never find it again. Guilt bit at me. I didn't know when they had turned, but I was a member of a powerful House. We should have done more.

I should have done more.

"I'm sorry," I bit out. The words were meaningless, and they wouldn't understand them anyway, but they were all I could offer.

Both of them looked at me with empty eyes. The hunger was all they felt now.

"Blood," the blonde female rasped.

"Don't run," Vail commanded. He backed away, and the three Strigoi watching him stepped with him, further away from me. "Just stay alive. Whatever you have to do, Sam, fucking do it."

If I ran, they would chase me, and unlike many of the monsters that roamed Lunaria, they would catch me. Even if I embraced my bloodlust to its full potential, it wouldn't be enough. They were nothing *but* bloodlust. It made them stronger and faster than any Moroi. The blade felt so heavy in my hand, but I gripped it tighter, and the male Strigoi caught the movement, his lips curling in a silent snarl, revealing his long fangs.

They can't be brought back, I reminded myself. It still felt like I was killing my own kind, but we didn't have a choice. Either we kill them or they kill us.

And I wouldn't be dying here tonight.

With no warning, the female Strigoi dove forward, trying to slash my throat with her claws. I twisted to the side, barely avoiding her attack. My blade kissed her throat, and blood sprayed, but she didn't even notice.

My instincts screamed at me and I whirled, shoving my dagger forward, sinking it into the chest of the male Strigoi. He snarled inches from my face, and then something slammed into my side, ripping me away from the male Strigoi while also tearing the blade from my hand.

I landed on my back, the female Strigoi on top of me. She lunged forward, her fangs bared, and I shoved her to the side but not far enough—instead of her ripping out my throat, she bit deep into my shoulder. A scream ripped out of me as I tried to push her off me, but the male was there immediately. He wrenched my left arm to the side and then tore into my arm.

Bites from a Strigoi were nothing like the ones from a Moroi. These two were feral in the way they bit, their fangs constantly shifting and piercing my skin over and over as they greedily gulped down my blood. I could hear Vail roaring, trying to fight his way to me.

He wouldn't make it though, not before these two sucked me dry.

The male Strigoi still had my arm pinned down, but the female Strigoi had shifted to get a better angle, so my right arm was no longer pinned beneath her. I felt my own nails harden into claws, and I shoved my hips up as hard as I could. It did nothing to dislodge the male, but the female reared back and screamed into my face.

I shoved two fingers directly into her left eye.

She shrieked, and I fought the urge to clamp my hands over my ears. This time when I shoved her, she moved, crashing into the Strigoi who had been frantically drinking from my arm. The two of them went down in a snarling pile of fangs and tangled limbs.

I scrambled back and twisted, trying to shove myself up, but my arm gave out. Then my vision darkened as pain laced up my entire body. I tried again using only my right arm and managed to get to my feet. I blinked several times, trying to clear my vision, but it barely helped. Blood flowed from the wounds on my shoulder and arm. The Strigoi had really chewed the fuck out of me.

"Daggers," I mumbled. "Need weapons."

Before I took a step, both of the Strigoi were rising, still snapping at each other, but my hopes of them taking each other out vanished. The female Strigoi's left eye was nothing but a bloody socket, but her remaining one was locked on me.

I took a step back and swayed slightly. Shit. How much blood had I lost? Too much. The answer was too fucking much.

A flash of silver caught my attention, and I looked towards Vail's fight with the three Strigoi just in time to see the head of one of them slide off its shoulders. The smell of blood permeated the air, both ours and theirs. Something glinted in the moonlight on the ground to my right.

The dagger I had dropped at the beginning of the attack.

I started to move towards it before realizing how monumentally stupid I was being. Flinging my hands out to my sides, I called the daggers to me. Both of them obediently leapt to my palms, one still stained with the Strigoi's blood.

If we survived this, Vail was going to give me so much shit

for creating these fun little blood daggers and forgetting to fucking use them.

The male Strigoi cocked his head in a move that was so different from how Moroi moved, it sent chills down my spine. His nostrils flared wide as he breathed in my scent before he stalked towards me. The female Strigoi was struggling a little with depth perception, and her movements had lost some of their fluidity. She jerked forward, a low snarl vibrating from her throat.

My vision started to waver again, blackness seeping in at the edges.

Don't pass out. Don't pass out. Don't fucking pass out. I chanted the words over and over in my mind, the motto the only thing keeping me standing.

The two Strigoi moved farther apart, forcing me to split my attention.

I spun around slowly, trying to keep them both in my line of sight but they were on opposite sides now, so I couldn't guard against one without turning my back on the other.

Without any warning, the male Strigoi leapt at me, fangs bared and claws aimed at my neck. A snarl at my back told me the female was moving in too, and in that split second, I knew I was going to die. I raised the dagger to meet the male, wanting to at least take him out and give Vail a fighting chance at surviving all of this.

Then a whistling sound raced through the air, followed by two loud cracks. I dove to the side, and the two headless bodies of the Strigoi who'd been attacking me crashed into each other before falling to the ground, their heads spinning through the air before landing a few feet away.

Two long, dark, slender shapes moved on the ground, the last couple of feet of each lined with bloodred, serrated edges. I leapt to my feet from where I'd landed on my ass and stared at the tall figure wrapped in a black cloak.

Bright red eyes peered out from underneath the hood. They looked me over once, eyes glowing brighter at each of the wounds I bore, before he snarled and sprinted to where Vail was still squaring off against one Strigoi.

So this was the beast Draven hid beneath that charming prince exterior.

Another loud crack rang through the air. Then the *thud* of a body hitting the ground.

I looked down at the corpses of the Strigoi who had attacked me and offered them a silent prayer to find peace in whatever afterlife greeted them.

"What the fuck are you doing here?" Vail growled in a low, dangerous voice. Knowing exactly what that tone meant, I raced over and slid between the two males before they decided enough blood hadn't been spilt tonight.

I had a very logical argument prepared about how we needed to work together to get to safety. Unfortunately, my body realized we'd survived the fight, and the adrenaline started to fade. Blood coated every inch of my clothing, the wound on my shoulder and arm still bleeding profusely, and the darkness that had been trying to claim me for the last ten minutes finally won the battle.

The last thing I remembered before passing out was Draven snatching me before I hit the ground, his eyes still a sea of blood. "Don't worry, love. I'll always catch you."

CHAPTER TWENTY-FIVE

Samara

I WOKE UP WITH A START, the memory of hungry, vacant eyes, sharp fangs, and long, jagged claws plaguing my nightmares. Strigoi. We'd been attacked by Strigoi. I'd done my best to fight them off, but they'd overpowered me—fed on me. Vail hadn't been able to get there in time . . . but Draven had.

Draven had found us.

"It's okay. You're safe."

Speak of the devil.

I looked to my right to find Draven leaning casually against a wall. His posture was relaxed and almost bored, the same way he stood when attending the Sovereign House masquerades or all the meetings the Moroi Prince was expected to attend. His leisurely facade was ruined by the ominous, black cloak still wrapped around him, splattered with blood, and the whip coiled at his hip. I stared at it for a long moment. It only looked like one whip, but I was sure I had seen two earlier.

His hood was pulled down, revealing his black-and-silver-streaked hair braided back away from his face. I met his eyes, lapis lazuli blue cracks winding their way through the red. He hadn't fully released his bloodlust, which meant he was still expecting a fight.

"We're at the cabin." My head snapped to where Vail was standing to my left. I was pretty sure he hadn't been significantly injured during the fight, but I still methodically searched his broad frame, looking for any hints of injury.

"You're okay," I said with a relieved sigh and took his hand. Vail pulled me to my feet before directing me slightly behind him. My relief quickly turned to annoyance, and I stepped forward so I was at his side, Draven only a few feet away from us. "He saved my life, Vail. I'm not saying we have to tell him our deepest, darkest secrets, but I'm confident he's not going to hurt me."

A wicked grin lit up Draven's face. "And what would I have to do to get you to tell me such deep, dark secrets?"

I matched his carnal smile with one of my own. "I'll tell you mine if you tell me yours." He stiffened, and I laughed. "Thought so."

"How did you find us? Tell us," Vail asked. He didn't push me behind him again, but I could feel the tension rolling off him.

"I don't take orders from you," Draven drawled.

"Fine." Vail shrugged. "I wouldn't have believed anything you said anyway, but maybe after I beat the shit out of you, something akin to truth will dribble out of your broken jaw."

"Try it." Draven bared his teeth and I felt . . . something. Did the ground tremble?

I glanced down and saw that the cabin had no floor. It was just four walls and a roof over a fairly flat, dirt surface. Given that we were in Velesian territory, it made sense. They didn't like being apart from the earth, even when inside.

"There it is." Vail narrowed his eyes at the prince. "You have magic. More than just the blood magic of the Moroi." His steel-grey eyes fell to the bare floor. "It's earth magic, isn't it? Is that what you used to sneak up on me in that alley?"

Draven's face went carefully blank. "I don't know what you're talking about. Maybe you're just not as skilled as you think."

"Enough," I snapped. They continued to glower at each other, but they ceased with the threats. Good enough. I glanced at Vail. "How much time do we have?" *Before Rynn shows up and we all go sneaking around a forbidden lake looking for a lost Fae crown.* I left that part out but trusted Vail to understand what I was asking.

"You were passed out for two hours while you healed. I gave you some of my blood to speed it up, but the Strigoi tore through a lot of your flesh and you lost a lot of blood." Vail's voice turned raspy as he admitted how badly I'd been hurt. "We have less than an hour now."

Shit.

My eyes softened as I looked at Draven but I kept my voice strong and steady. "You've been trying to play both sides since you arrived at House Harker. Telling me and Kieran you care about us and only want to protect us but in the same breath saying we can't trust you. We can't continue like this. Either you're with us or you're not. Decide."

"It's not that simple." Pain flickered across his face along with something that looked a lot like fear.

"Make it that simple," I pushed. He had followed us here, and while I was grateful for him saving our lives, I couldn't let my feelings for him risk everything. All that mattered was keeping the other half of the crown out of Velika's grasp. Once we secured it, we'd have to figure out how to rescue Carmilla and get the second half of the crown.

"And if I refuse?"

I swallowed before steeling my nerves. "Then we'll make the choice for you."

"I'll happily carve into the Marshal." Draven pulled a blade from somewhere beneath his cloak, and Vail unsheathed the curved dagger he kept at his hip in response.

"What about me?" I stepped forward and gripped Draven's hand, moving it until the blade was at my throat. Vail let out a rumbling growl at my back, but I ignored him, and thankfully he didn't interfere. For now. "Will you cut through me to get to him?"

Draven paled and yanked the blade away. "I would never hurt you."

"I know," I said quietly. It was probably foolish of me, but I did trust Draven. Even more foolish of me was that I wanted him, and that desire I felt was so much more than just a passing fancy. I liked him.

I liked it when he was being a charming prince, I liked it when he was being a devilish rogue, and . . . I loved it when he was just being Draven. I suspected the latter was a side only Kieran and I got to see.

"Please, Drav," I begged. "Give us a reason to trust you."

Slowly, he reached up to stroke my cheek. "I've tried so hard to figure out a way to keep the two of you safe. I thought the best way to do that was to stay away."

Me and Kieran. I thought about how he always kept a careful distance between us when we were in public and how he had pushed Kieran away so cruelly. I was still pissed off about how he'd handled things with Kieran, but I also believed he must have felt he had no other option.

"I know," I said softly. "Tell me why. What are you keeping us safe from?"

We stared at each other for a long moment, and I could see the conflict he was battling within himself.

"Okay." He rubbed his face with clear reluctance before sliding the dagger back into sheath on his thigh. "I'll tell you what I can, but you have to understand that there are *some* things I *can't* speak of."

I cocked my head at how he emphasized two of the words. Magic of some kind. It had to be. I nodded. "Tell us what you can."

"You already know my mother has half of the soul crown and about her allies."

"Yes," I confirmed. "She has the half to bind a soul and is looking for the other piece to see souls, and she has an alliance with the Seelie Fae, who are the wraiths that plague our lands. They're using some type of spell that requires Moroi blood to regain their original shapes."

He looked at me for a long moment, a slight crease forming along the corners of his deep blue eyes, and then he winced. His hands flew to his head as he let out a sharp hiss.

"There are some things I can't speak of."

Something about what I'd said was related to that. Could he not even think about it without pain? What the fuck type of magic was that?

I reached out a hand and rested it on his forearm as we waited for him to continue, scared if I said anything else, it would only cause him to have more thoughts that would hurt him. I glanced over my shoulder at Vail, who was still studying the prince but had put his dagger away. His expression was unreadable, though if he was swayed by the pain Draven was in, he wasn't showing it.

After a couple of minutes, Draven straightened. I started to pull my hand away, but he rested his hand over it, keeping it trapped on his arm. I let him have it.

"Velika came into possession of the crown—half of it anyway—shortly before I was born. At first, she didn't understand how to use it, but she figured it out. Luckily for all of Lunaria, without both halves, the crown is only capable of half of its potential." I watched as his expression closed off until his feelings were hidden behind an emotionless mask that made dread pool in my gut. "But there are many wicked things she can do with that half . . . things she learned how to do by experimenting on me and those close to me."

"But she's your mother," I half whispered as the dread continued to grow.

Draven gave me a small smile that broke my heart. "She wishes she weren't. There is no one the Moroi Queen despises more than her own son."

"Why?"

He winced painfully. Clearly, this fell under things he couldn't speak of.

I squeezed his arm. "It's okay."

"What did she do?" Vail asked. "How does the crown work?"

"I'm not sure how the crown worked for the Fae, but for us, it seems there has to be some connection between who wears the crown and the person they want to bind. Velika is currently limited in only being able to control those whose blood she has taken and who have taken her blood in return. Because I am her son and of her flesh and blood, she has no restrictions in controlling me. I can fight it, but I will always lose.

"My mother had no interest in raising me. I always had caretakers," Draven continued in that monotonous voice, as if he was speaking of what he'd had for breakfast and not the horrors his own mother had inflicted upon him. "For the first five years, I rarely saw her. Then she started showing up to check on me. They were short visits, and she always left disappointed."

It didn't escape my notice that he hadn't mentioned his father once. Most people assumed Velika's consort, Lucian, was Draven's father. The Sovereign House had never confirmed one way or another. I always thought it strange since Draven didn't look like either of them with his strange, black-and-silver hair and vivid blue eyes with their secondary bloodred coloring. Both Velika and Lucian were fair-haired with pale skin.

"One of the people who helped raise me was an older Moroi woman. She was always kind to me. Some of the others were distant, but Selia would read me a story every night." His lips curved into a soft smile. "Pretty sure she made up most of them on the spot, because they didn't always make sense, but it was something I looked forward to every night before falling asleep."

"My parents would tell me stories too," I said. "It was nice. I'm glad you had someone like Selia in your life."

Draven's smile died, and I nearly wept at the loss because I knew I wouldn't like what was to come.

"When I was eight, my mother came for one of her visits. She had this . . . maniacal smile on her face." Draven shuddered beneath me and gripped my hand tighter. "When Selia arrived, my mother said we were going to play a game, and then she set the crown on her head . . . and handed daggers to me and Selia."

Unease swirled in my gut. It didn't feel right to make Draven relive this. As if sensing my thoughts, Draven looked down at me. "It's okay. You need to know what the crown is capable of."

I nodded reluctantly. He was right, we did need to know, but that didn't stop me from feeling sorrow about what Draven had experienced at the hand of someone who should have done everything she could have to protect him.

"She told Selia to slit my throat," Draven said, the barest hint of sadness leaking into his voice. "She told me my options were to defend myself or allow myself to get slaughtered and that she didn't really care one way or another." A hand cupped my jaw, and I met Draven's stare. "I appreciate how murderous you look right now, Sam, but you cannot ever go after Velika. Promise me."

"I won't," I said evenly.

Draven narrowed his eyes. "You promise you won't go after her? Or you won't promise me anything of the sort?"

When all I did was smile at him, he swore and looked over my shoulder to Vail for support.

I glanced back just in time to see Vail shrug. "Trust me when I say it's impossible to get Samara to agree to anything she doesn't want to do. Nobody is better at twisting words or offering beautiful, empty promises."

I turned back to Draven, not saying anything to counter Vail's words because they were the truth. Velika's days were numbered. I may not be the person who ended her life, but I had no doubt I would play a hand in it all the same. The sooner the better.

Seeing the resolution on my face, Draven sighed and dropped his hand away, admitting defeat, at least for now. I had no doubt he'd do everything in his power to keep me away from Velika, not because he cared about his mother's life, but because he cared about mine.

"What happened?" I finally asked, knowing I wouldn't like the answer but needing to know regardless.

"Selia and I both refused to hurt the other, which was exactly what my mother had wanted. She'd wanted to test just how strong the abilities of the crown were."

"She waited all those years for a bond to form between the two of you," Vail said, stepping closer to me. I stepped back enough so I could see both men. The prince to my right and the Marshal to my left. "Selia likely loved you like her own child at that point. Velika wanted to find out if the soul crown's magic could override that."

"She ordered Selia to kill me, and it was like a switch went off in her mind." Draven squeezed his eyes shut. "The woman who had raised me and read me stories every night plunged a knife into my chest. The only reason I didn't die was because she didn't hit anything vital. I tried to fight her off, and in the process, I stabbed her in the throat. It was enough to get her off me, and I scrambled away, bleeding from my own wound while I watched her bleed out on the floor. Even while dying, she attempted to crawl across the room to get to me. To kill me."

"Drav," I rasped, not knowing what to say. He opened his eyes to look at me, and they were so hollow.

"Velika didn't stop there." Draven's hands clenched into fists at his sides. "A day later, I had a new caretaker. I was so traumatized about what had happened to Selia that I didn't even want to speak to this one. I thought maybe if my mother thought I didn't care about her, then she wouldn't do that again, but I severely underestimated her cruelty."

"You were eight years old," I said softly. "No child should understand that level of cruelty, or any cruelty for that matter."

"I learned very quickly." Draven's expression hardened. "By the time I was ten, I'd lost track of how many people she'd ordered to kill me, and I . . . started defending myself. Towards the end, I would attempt to slit their throats as soon as my mother walked in with that crown. Seemed like the least painful option for all of us."

"You did what you had to in order to survive," I argued. "All of these needless deaths lie at your mother's feet."

Draven shrugged. "Doesn't help with the screams I hear every time I sleep."

"Has she used the crown's magic on you?" I asked. "Is that why you serve her despite everything she's done to you?"

"That's part of the reason." The muscles along his jaw flexed as he clenched his teeth. "I can fight against it, but only for a short amount of time. Less than a minute usually, until the pain becomes too intense."

"Is there any way to block the magic? Or better your odds of fighting it?" Vail asked.

"The crown has to be worn for the actual binding, but after that, you have to obey her, crown or not. The binding does fade and has to be renewed occasionally." Draven's lips twisted into a grimace. "The House bloodlines seem to have a greater tolerance to it."

"Why does it work on you then?" Vail voiced my question before I could.

"I'm not entirely sure, but I think it's because she's my mother and her blood is my blood," Draven said. "She hasn't exactly shared her thoughts about how the crown works, but I've been able to piece it together over the years." He swallowed before inhaling deeply. "For a while, she had someone of a House bloodline held captive and she tried to use the crown on them. She was frustrated by the results."

"Who?" I asked sharply. Someone from a House bloodline being killed or going missing would have been a big deal.

"Dominique's father didn't die in that attack," Draven said quietly.

"Oh fuck," I swore before shaking my head. "But they found the bodies!"

Draven looked away. "They found the bodies of her mother and sister . . . and part of her father's leg. Everyone assumed he'd been torn apart trying to keep his wife and daughter alive."

I rubbed my face. How was I going to tell Dominique that while she'd been grieving the loss of most of her family, her father had still been alive? Aniela had been close to him as well. Her own parents had died at a young age, and Dominique's had raised her after that. If they'd known he'd been alive, those two would have done anything to save him.

But they hadn't. So he'd died alone.

"What did *your mother* do to him?" Vail asked.

The muscles along Draven's jawline tensed at the reminder that the monster who was responsible for the death and torture of our own people was his own damn mother. I shot Vail a look that said to tone it down. It wasn't like Draven had a choice in who his parents were.

Vail's grey eyes darted to mine, and a crease formed between them before his lips flattened into a hard line and he returned his attention to the prince.

"She would spend hours working on him every day. Trying to bend his will to her own. Sometimes, she would force me to stand there and watch . . . Other times, she would order me to inflict physical pain on him to see if that would weaken his mind enough for her to seize control." Draven held Vail's heavy stare even as a hollowness entered his eyes. "He fought it with everything he had. Until his mind shattered and all that remained was bloodlust."

"You mean . . ." I stared at Draven in shock. The House bloodlines *did not* become Strigoi.

Draven gave me a pitying look.

"Fuck," I muttered "She can turn us Strigoi."

"What happened after he became Strigoi?" Vail pushed. I glanced back and forth between them, not understanding why Vail was being so hostile about this.

The prince raised his chin, defiance in his gaze as he focused on Vail. "I did what I hope anyone would do for me if I became a mindless killing machine under the complete control of Velika."

"You killed him."

"I saved him," Draven countered.

"Death isn't saving someone." Vail's eyes flashed silver.

Red bled into Draven's eyes, and for a moment, I thought he was going to go for Vail. I eased forward, ready to get between them, when the red vanished and Draven's charming prince mask fell back into place.

"You're right," he drawled. "I should have let Dominique

see her father one last time. I'm sure she would have appreciated it right before he tore out her throat."

"Enough," I snapped. Both men looked away from each other. Something was bothering Vail, even more so than usual, but I didn't understand what. Everything that had happened to the former head of House Salvatore was fucked up, but it hadn't been Draven's fault. And Draven was right, killing him had been a mercy.

None of us would want to live on as Strigoi, especially ones that could be used as weapons against our families.

A thought occurred to me. The wraiths might have been behind the attack, but someone would have had to take Dominique's father back to the Sovereign House and help keep him under control.

"Are all the rangers who serve the Sovereign House blood-bound to Velika? Or are they aware of what she's doing and serve her anyway?" I rasped.

Each House had their own rangers whose fealty they claimed. But there was also a loyalty that all rangers had for each other because they spent so much time in the wilds, more so than most Moroi. It was common for units from different Houses to team up together for missions.

It wasn't just Dominique's family that had been killed in that attack. All the rangers traveling with them had perished as well. For the Sovereign rangers to see that carnage and continue to serve Velika . . .

"The Sovereign Marshal and most of the high-ranking rangers know what Velika is up to and support her. I'm sure they're blood-bound to her as well because my mother is not a trusting person. Not after—" Draven winced as his words were cut off. "The crown cannot compel loyalty or emotion. Its effects are short-term. I suspect that will change if she gets her hands on the other half of the crown."

"So you are not under her control right now?" I asked.

"No." Frustration flared in his eyes. "*Her* control of me is tenuous and really only works if she's physically near."

"Then why haven't you run?" I half shouted. "Just don't go back! We can find the other half of the crown before she does and keep it out of her reach, then we'll figure out a way to take her down. You can be free of her once and for all." Draven remained silent during my outburst, which only increased my anger. "What else, Draven? What else are you hiding?"

He flinched. My beautiful and wicked prince *flinched*.

"You think I haven't run away before? The wraiths can always find me and drag me back, and then I'm punished for my insolence," he said with a grim acceptance that made me want to shake him. "My usefulness is running out. I thought maybe . . ." He looked away from me again and out the window. "She knows you were investigating the wraith outposts and wants you under her control. Since you're a Harker, she won't be able to use the crown on you. I thought that if you agreed to marry me, it would appease her, and between the two of us, we could protect Kieran. It would have bought us a little more time."

"Time for what?"

"To get out of Lunaria."

"There is no getting out of Lunaria, Drav." I shook my head. "The ocean surrounds us on all sides, and we have no means to build a boat that can travel far."

Attempts had been made, but enormous sea monsters dominated the waters off the shores. I didn't even know if it was possible to build a boat that was capable of withstanding their attacks. It didn't matter though since that was far outside of our capabilities. There was also the problem of us not knowing what lay beyond Lunaria. Who knew how long we would have to sail for before we reached land again?

"There is no stopping what's going to befall Lunaria," Draven argued. "You and Kier have to get out."

"What about you?"

"Like I said, the wraiths will always find me, and they won't let me go. I've already accepted that my days are numbered."

"Well, I don't!" I hissed and gripped his face in my hands. "And I'm pretty sure Kieran doesn't either!"

"Personally, I'm fine with it," Vail said calmly.

Draven laughed under his breath as he pulled away from me.

I glared at Vail, but he just gave me a dispassionate look. "He's still our enemy, an unwilling one, but an enemy all the same. He already knows too much. We should kill him now, and if he cares about you as much as he claims, he'd do it himself."

"Absolut—" I started, but Vail cut me off, his calculating eyes falling on Draven.

"The Moroi Queen can command you to answer her, can she not? Which means anything you know, she will know."

"Yes," Draven admitted, his expression shuttered. "I've gotten good at dodging her questions and answering as vaguely as possible. Sometimes there is enough wiggle room to mislead her, but if she suspects I'm hiding something, she'll continue to question me until I give her what she wants, and she definitely knows I'm hiding something when it comes to Samara."

I thought about how Draven had practically raced to House Harker after the temple incident.

"You knew it was us in the badlands," I said slowly. "You haven't returned to the Sovereign House because Velika will question you as soon as you do."

"She's not particularly happy with me at the moment," he said tightly. "I received a letter ordering me to bring you to her."

A low growl rumbled from Vail, but he stayed where he was against the wall. We both knew Draven had had plenty of opportunities to snatch me and return me to the Sovereign House, yet he hadn't.

"I can ignore her written orders, but I cannot go against any commands she gives me in person. If she told me to kill you, I'd fight it with everything inside me, but it wouldn't be enough. Eventually, my mind would snap the way Dominique's father's did. I would become a Strigoi—one who was completely in her control."

My blood ran cold at the thought of Draven becoming a mindless Strigoi. I refused to let that happen.

"I wish you had just told us all this at the start," I said softly. "You know we'll help you."

"That's partly why I didn't tell you. I didn't want you to waste time trying to keep me alive when you should be focusing on yourself and Kieran." He paused, eyes flicking to Vail. "And the others you care about. I might be a lost cause, but they're not."

"You don't get to tell me who I deem worth protecting, Prince," I said steadily, raising my chin a little.

"Apologies, Heir." He didn't look the least bit sorry. "There is also a lot I can't tell you, and I realize all you have is my word on that. I wasn't sure if you would believe me."

"I still don't believe you," Vail's grumbled.

"And I still doubt your loyalty to Samara." Red lines wound their way through Draven's eyes again, clashing against the deep blue as he cocked his head at the other male. "I would have preferred to share her with only Kieran. Alaric and Roth, I will tolerate, but her interest in you is the first time I've truly questioned her judgment."

"Technically, I'm not with either of you yet," I said lightly. "And if you keep up the possessive bullshit, it might stay that way."

Draven's piercing gaze landed on me, and my heart skipped a beat as more red bled into his eyes. "Want to bet I can change your mind, love? Tell me you haven't thought about being between me and Kieran. How much we'd make you scream."

"Too late." I gave him a breezy smile. "He and Alaric already did a good job of that, and Roth has some . . . interesting ideas for when I return. It seems I don't really need any more lovers. I'm more than satisfied as it is."

"That a challenge?" He arched an eyebrow at me, and I arched one back.

"Do you want it to be?"

Draven looked out the window to the lightening sky and then at Vail. "How much time do we have before the next part of your scheme comes into play?"

Silver eyes met red ones. Confliction flashed across Vail's face before he answered. "Thirty minutes."

"That's not nearly enough time." Draven prowled towards me, and suddenly I felt very much like prey. "But I'll make it work."

The whip at his waist uncoiled and wrapped around my wrists before I could react. I exhaled sharply as it yanked my arms above my head and held them there. I looked at where the end of the whip had wound itself around the beams running across the ceiling, then jolted at finding Draven in front of me.

"Not only do we not have time for this . . ." I fought to keep my voice even. "But we were discussing how to keep you safe." My words probably would have been more convincing if they hadn't come out so breathy.

I shivered as he trailed a sharp claw along my collarbone.

"It's Lunaria. Any of us could die at any moment, so we have to seize any opportunity we can, even the inopportune ones." Draven kept his eyes on mine as he tugged at the lacing that ran down the front of my tunic. "Perhaps after I've felt you come on my tongue, I'll be feeling more motivated to stay alive."

I opened my mouth to argue, but Draven captured it with his. There was nothing tender or coaxing about it. This kiss was demanding and possessive. I clicked my teeth shut, refusing to let him in, but his fingers finished unlacing the tunic. A second later, he'd tugged my shirt down, unhooked my chest band, and he circled my nipple with a claw. My lips parted in a gasp, and his tongue darted in.

Any remaining protests I had fled as his kiss seared me.

I kissed him back, my tongue playing with his, and I wished I could wrap my arms around him. Feel his hard muscles beneath my fingertips. He laughed darkly against my lips when I tugged hard on the whip.

"You were right earlier when you called me possessive, but that doesn't mean I don't know how to share." Draven spun me around so my back was to him, and I met Vail's heated stare from where he still stood across the room, watching. Draven kissed my neck before whispering into my ear, "Let's find out just how much the Marshal and I can make you scream."

CHAPTER TWENTY-SIX

Draven

THIS HAD BEEN A BAD IDEA, but the rational side of me had fled the minute Samara had taunted me with Kieran and Alaric fucking her together. I'd known she'd been with them in that way ever since she'd walked into the room where the Heirs had been waiting—with Alaric's and Kieran's scents woven around her. More than one night, I'd woken up with a raging hard-on because I'd been dreaming about Samara writhing between me and Kier.

Or Kier taking her while I took him.

My dick hardened further against my pants. Samara thought she could save me, and I loved her even more for it. It helped me make peace with the fact that I likely wouldn't survive the day. If the Moroi Queen got ahold of me, she would yank out every thought from my head before killing me or, worse, turning me into one of her mindless Strigoi hunters.

This might be my only chance to be with Samara, and I wouldn't fucking waste it. It was selfish of me, but I would take this moment, however short it was, and enjoy every second.

I would have preferred to have her all to myself, but if I told Vail to leave, he would have refused. The Marshal was still standing across the room, unmoving, focused entirely on Samara. I almost felt bad for him. Conflict was etched all over his face. Whatever had happened between the two of them was complicated, and he was clearly still hung up about it.

Not my problem. He could stay or he could go. Didn't matter to me.

My only concern was making Samara scream my name until she forgot about every single one of her worries. We would both get our moment of peace before reality crashed back in.

"Drav," she breathed out and pulled harder on the whip binding her arms above her head.

I nipped her neck, and she let out a hiss of pleasure. "Yes?" My hands trailed down her breasts to unlace her pants and tug them down her legs, but annoyance flickered through me when I couldn't get them over her boots. I wished we were already naked in that pool Kieran and I had used, that would have made this much easier.

"You're taking too long," Vail growled.

"You could help." I shot him an annoyed look.

"We shouldn't . . ." Samara's protest trailed off when Vail stalked over to us. For a second, I thought he was going to attempt to cut through my whips, and I readied myself to lash out at him. He would not ruin this for me. Not when he likely had his whole life ahead of him.

One with Samara, if he wanted it.

But instead, he knelt on her other side and yanked one of her boots off before glaring at me and dropping his eyes pointedly to her other booted foot still in my hands. "We have less than thirty minutes, which means this is going to be rough and fast. You're wasting time."

Samara inhaled sharply as I pulled off her remaining boot and helped Vail take off her pants and undergarments until she was standing in only her shirt that I'd pulled down to expose her full breasts. I took a step back to admire her. Some people might have shied away from being mostly naked and bound like this, but Samara just arched an eyebrow at me like she was still in control of this situation.

The fabric was bunched up beneath her breasts, and I wanted nothing more than to bury my face between them. Choices, choices.

"Thirty minutes," Vail reminded me. I glanced at him and saw his gaze was locked on her tits as well.

"Limited time." I glided around her, my eyes drinking in every inch of her glorious curves. Then I gripped her plump, luscious ass that I'd always wanted to bite. "And limited resources."

Vail moved to her front, and his hand disappeared between her thighs, causing her back to hit my chest as she let out a gasp. I laughed and reached around to cup her full, heavy breasts while Vail finger-fucked her. "Are you ready to scream now?"

"N-no." Samara shook her head stubbornly. "Kieran . . . and Alaric . . . did it better."

Then she moaned as I pinched her nipples and chuckled darkly. "Sadly, I don't have any oil with me, and we don't have time to prepare you. Otherwise, I would fuck this glorious ass of yours and watch it bounce while Vail buried himself between your thighs."

"Alaric has already claimed my ass," she panted and gave me a cheeky grin.

Samara yelped as my fingers wound around her long braid and sharply yanked her head back. "I don't want to hear his name on your lips again while my hands are on you."

"For once, I agree with the prince," Vail growled, then he did something with his fingers to make Samara let out a strangled moan, and I kissed her exposed neck when her head slammed against my shoulder. It wasn't fair that I only had this short amount of time with her. I wanted so much more.

I licked her neck before letting my fangs graze her skin. Life wasn't fair. I knew that better than anyone, so I would take what was offered.

"Is she wet enough for you to fuck, Vail?" I alternated between kissing and nipping Samara's neck, enjoying the little mewling sounds she was making from our attention.

Vail raised his hand from between her thighs, and his fingers glistened with slickness. "She's fucking dripping."

"Perfect." I looped my hands under her thighs and pulled them up until her feet were off the ground and her legs were spread wide. "Don't hold back."

"Oh fuck," Samara whimpered as she leaned further into me. Between my whips holding her arms and me bracing her body and holding her thighs, she was completely at our mercy.

"You okay, love?" I asked her quietly. Everything I picked up from her body said she was into this, but I needed to hear her say it.

"Yes," she breathed out before turning her head to give me a quick kiss. "I trust you, and him."

I wanted to tell her that I loved her. That I had for years and that she and Kieran mattered more to me than anything else, but it wouldn't be right because I couldn't give her a future. All I could give her was mind-numbing pleasure and a hope that Vail and the others would keep her safe when I couldn't.

As much as I wished I were sharing this moment with Kieran, I had to admit that Vail's intensity was turning me on. He gripped Samara's thighs right below my hands and tugged her closer to him, then she screamed as he impaled her with his cock and started fucking her hard. There was no hesitation and no easing into it to let her adjust to him.

Despite bracing myself for it, I still rocked back as she

slammed into me, and I laughed as I held her tightly, loving the way she felt between us. With Vail supporting some of her weight, I slipped my right hand between them and started toying with her clit.

"Oh fuck!" Sam cried out, followed by a torrent of words in the Fae languages and something else I didn't recognize. Then her head fell back against my shoulder, exposing her throat to me, and I didn't hesitate before biting down on the tempting flesh.

Vail growled, clearly not liking me tasting her blood, but I didn't give a shit. I'd wanted to know what she tasted like for too fucking long, and moonsdamn it all, she was divine.

Her rich, spicy blood splashed across my tongue, and I lost myself in the flavor of it, only vaguely aware of Vail pulling her legs away from me so she could wrap them around him. Samara leaned further into me, and my free hand drifted back to one of her breasts, squeezing it hard at the same moment I pushed down harder on her clit.

"Fuck," Vail cursed, and I had no doubt Samara's pussy had just clamped down on his cock. His thrusts gained a new, vicious edge, and based on the breathy way she was whimpering his name between moans, I knew she was enjoying every second of it. I didn't fully understand what it was between them, other than knowing it was different and more complicated than what she had with the other three, but whatever existed between Vail and Samara was clearly intense.

The scent of more blood filled the air as Vail roared, slamming into Samara one last time. She trembled against me, chest heaving as waves of pleasure rolled through her body.

"Not done yet, love." I chuckled and wrapped my arms around her waist before pulling her off Vail's dick, forcing him to release his claws from where they'd dug into her thick thighs. He stumbled back with a glazed-over expression, and I commanded my whip to unwind from Samara's wrists. Her

A Court of Bones and Sorrow

legs instantly gave out, but I was prepared and tugged her towards me, settling us both on the ground on top of the blanket she'd been resting on earlier.

My cock pushed into her pussy that was drenched with her and Vail's arousal, and we both groaned. "Ready to scream more, Heir?"

"I doubt," she panted and squeezed her legs on either side of me as she sank another couple of inches onto my cock, "that you can outdo—oh fuck." She gasped as I yanked her the rest of the way down.

"What was that?" I thrust up into her, and she leaned forward to grip my shoulders as her thighs trembled around me.

"I think," Vail said, appearing beside us, his dick already hard again as he gripped Samara's hair, tugging her back, "that she doesn't think you can make her scream more than I did."

"Hmm." I dug my fingers into her hips. "Is that so, Sam?"

She gave me a slightly dazed smile and nodded.

"Let's find out." I glanced at Vail. "If she gets too loud, I'm sure you can find some way to occupy her mouth."

"I'll think of something." He stroked his hard length, and Samara licked her lips, but with Vail's grip on her hair, she couldn't take him in her mouth until he wanted her to.

I hardened even more at the sight, and Samara gasped, grinding her hips down on me. That was all it took for me to lose the little control I had left. I thrust up, hard and fast, and kept the brutal pace. She let out a strangled scream as I pumped in and out of her, using my hands on her hips to shove her down on my cock so I could take her deeply with each stroke.

"Play with your clit," I ordered, and Sam's fingers immediately snapped down to fuck herself.

More words in all sorts of languages poured from her lips

as her eyes rolled back. "Look at me," Vail commanded, and Sam whimpered as she looked up at him. Then he pushed his thick cock against her lips and she obediently opened them. My balls tightened as I watched him slowly slide in and out of her mouth to let her adjust before tightening his hold on her hair and shoving himself all the way in. Sam gagged as he hit the back of her throat but leaned into him as she eagerly swallowed his cock again and again.

"Scream for us, Heir!" I yelled as my nails shifted to claws and bit into the flesh just above Vail's marks, heat exploding in her soaking wet cunt as I came hard. Vail yanked her off his dick so Samara could scream while he came all over her tits.

There was no force in this world that could have made me look away from her face as she unraveled between us. Vail sank to his knees next to us and pulled Sam to him, claiming her mouth with his. Then, to my surprise, he gently pushed her towards me.

Samara collapsed happily on my chest and kissed me deeply, and I ran my fingers down her back as aftershocks of pleasure made her tremble.

Worth it. Absolutely worth it.

Vail rose and grabbed three of the clean tunics stacked on a shelf against the wall. The Velesians tended to leave clothes scattered all over the place since they never knew when they'd have to shift. Vail pulled the canteen from his pack and poured a little water over the tunics before passing two to me, keeping one to clean himself off.

"I'm going to check outside." He got dressed and gave Samara a pointed look. "We'll have company soon. Be ready to leave."

Without me, because whatever they were doing, it was better if I wasn't a part of it. My plan to marry Samara and keep her safe that way was no longer viable. My mother was plotting something, and whatever it was, Samara needed to be kept

A Court of Bones and Sorrow

away from her. It killed me to admit it, but at this point, I was putting Samara in more danger with my presence, especially since I'd killed some wraiths.

I had no doubt Erendriel knew of my betrayal by now. If he came for me personally, I was fucked.

"Not one for pillow talk, is he?"

Sam laughed, and I automatically tightened my arms around her. Fuck, I loved that sound, even more than her screams of pleasure.

"This is only the second time Vail and I have done that," she admitted. "And the first time was last night, or I guess early this morning, and wasn't quite so . . . intense. So I can't really speak to his pillow talk habits yet."

"But you want to?" I asked. "Be able to talk to his pillow talk tendencies?"

She fell silent while she thought about it before raising her head to look at me. I loosened my arms so she could do so, immediately missing the feel of her against me.

"Yes." She tilted her head and kept her expression carefully neutral. "Would that bother you? Knowing I want him and the others? As well as you?"

I reached up and tucked a loose strand of hair behind her ear. Technically, the question was irrelevant since I wouldn't be part of this future Samara was already thinking about, but I answered her honestly anyway, allowing myself the delusion for just a moment longer. "No. There might be days when I want to steal you away from everyone else and keep you to myself, or maybe myself and Kieran." I grinned. "But as long as the others love you as I do, then I'm happy you have them in your life."

Her eyes widened. "Drav, I—"

"You don't have to say it back," I cut her off. "I just wanted you to know."

Truthfully, I didn't think Sam loved me yet. How could

she? I'd hidden so much from her, and while we'd always been friendly towards each other, up until recently, I hadn't allowed it to go any further. But if she did feel that way . . . and if she did say it . . .

I wouldn't be able to walk away, and that was too dangerous an option to pursue.

"I'll wait here while the two of you do whatever you came here to do." It was a lie. As soon as Samara left, I was going to run far away from her. A plan had already begun to form in my head. My mother would want me, but Erendriel would be pissed about the wraiths. There was a good chance he'd tell them to chase me rather than pursue Samara. Maybe I could lead them away and buy her a little more time.

The question was where to go. I was good at fighting wraiths one-on-one, but now that they knew I'd turned on them, they'd be more careful. I needed to run, go somewhere they'd have a harder time getting to me. The Furies were my best bet. Something about them made even Erendriel wary.

I hadn't gone to them originally because they probably would have laughed in my face and then thrown me out of their realm, but Cali loved Samara and would do whatever she had to in order to keep her friend safe. She'd protect me.

Or kill me if she determined that was the best way to keep Samara safe. I'd have to be very fast about my explanations.

Samara leaned into my touch as I trailed my fingers down her neck and chest until they rested over her heart, which beat strong and steady beneath my hand. I wished I'd had more time with her and Kieran, but this would have to be enough.

I breathed in her scent, which always reminded me of the spicy night blossoms of the plants that grew along the southern coastline. Reluctantly, she pulled away, and I let her go, watching silently as she cleaned herself up as best she could before getting dressed. There was nowhere for her to rinse off, and I reveled in the knowledge that she would smell like me all day.

And Vail, but I decided to not let that bother me.

Samara quickly rebraided her hair and tucked her throwing daggers into the thigh sheaths. By the time she was done, I'd already gotten dressed, my whip once again coiled at my hip.

"We'll be back soon." She cupped my cheek, and I closed my eyes to enjoy the feeling. "I think we might find something that can help you. Even if we don't, I will find a way to keep you safe. Promise you will wait here? Promise me, Drav?"

I opened my eyes and met hers. They were the perfect color of twilight, and I saw how much she believed her own words. The lie rolled off my lips, even as it felt like someone had stabbed my heart. "I promise."

CHAPTER TWENTY-SEVEN

Samara

I LOOKED at the cabin one last time before setting off to find Vail. It was a little surprising he had wandered so far away . . . and that Rynn wasn't here yet. Maybe it had just taken her longer than she'd anticipated to slip away without being noticed. I shook my head as I tried to focus my thoughts. They were still reeling from what had happened between me, Draven, and Vail in the cabin, but I needed to pay attention to the task at hand, and that meant bottling up my jumbled mess of emotions and tucking them away to be dealt with later. There were too many people counting on me to fail.

Draven didn't believe I could save him. That was fine. I'd just have to prove him wrong. This wouldn't take longer than a few hours, and then I'd be able to return to him. I'd told him to stay inside to avoid running into any Velesians, who may not be too happy about the Moroi Prince coming unannounced into their realm. Hopefully none of them tried to use the cabin today. He'd assured me they wouldn't be able to pick up his scent from outside, which had only led to questions on my end, but I hadn't bothered voicing them.

He was still hiding things from me, and whatever strange

magic he had was definitely one of them. Logically, I knew I shouldn't trust him, but my heart said otherwise.

Just as I started to step over a fallen log, my instincts screamed at me that I was no longer alone.

A broad hand covered my mouth and another clamped around my waist, pulling me against a hard body. Panic seized me, and I struggled for several seconds before recognizing Vail's scent.

"Quiet," he whispered faintly in my ear. "The Velesians are here."

Slowly, he dropped his hands and beckoned me forward, further into the forest and away from the cabin where Draven hid.

"Velesians." As in more than one. Rynn was supposed to have come alone.

Something had gone very wrong.

Vail and I quietly made our way through the woods. I was a little disoriented, but I was pretty sure we were headed back the way we'd come, which meant we were going away from Lake Malov. Not ideal, but what mattered more was staying undetected.

Maybe we could backtrack and then make our way around them to the lake? I also needed to find out what had happened to Rynn. Given her status with the Alpha Pack, I knew she wouldn't have been hurt, but maybe they had detained her somewhere.

Fuck, this was already turning into a political nightmare, and we didn't even know if it was worth it yet.

A low, rumbling growl caused us to stop dead in our tracks before a familiar, sleek, black form dropped from the branches above us, blocking our path ahead. The panther surveyed us with its cunning, green eyes.

Hello, Bastian.

Also. Fuck. Me.

All the Velesians were deadly in their own way. The ailuranthropes—usually just called ailurans or panthers—weren't the biggest. Both ursanthropes—bear shifters—and lycanthropes—wolf shifters—were larger than them, but the ailurans were the fastest, and their feline bodies allowed more flexibility in a fight.

I'd never actually seen Bastian fight, but I had no doubt he would be vicious. And he was no doubt very pissed off at us right now.

Vail shoved me behind him but didn't draw the sword strapped across his back. Instead, his hand hovered near the large dagger on his hip. He understood the situation just as well as I did. We were on Velesian land without permission. If we killed one of them . . . the fragile alliance between our people would shatter.

And it would be all our fault.

"I can explain." I stepped around Vail with my hands held out to my sides and dodged his hand when he tried to make a grab for me. The panther's ears flattened back against his head before releasing a high-pitched snarl, and Vail pulled his dagger free. "Let's just calm down," I said frantically. "This is all just a misunders—"

Bastian let out a startled cry as a large, white wolf plowed into his side. The ailuran went flying, his body slamming into a thick tree trunk with a resounding *crack*. Several green vines immediately shot forward, clearly thinking they had just found their next meal. They wrapped around the unconscious beast as the bark down the center of the trunk started to split apart, revealing a dark, cavernous mouth.

"Damn it, Rynn!" I hissed and lunged forward to cut the panther free. Vail joined me a second later, and between the two of us, we managed to free and drag Bastian a safe distance away from the apparently carnivorous tree. I eyed the other

A Court of Bones and Sorrow

trees suspiciously but couldn't tell if they shared the same food tastes.

Fucking Velesian forests.

Bastian wouldn't be unconscious for long. Velesians healed the slowest out of all the Moon Blessed, but they could still heal from just about anything, and unlike the Moroi, they didn't need spells or blood to do it. We needed to figure out a plan to fix this mess. Fast.

"Change back." I glared at the white wolf, whose back was higher than my waistline. Granted, I wasn't that tall, but Rynn's wolf form was massive. She exhaled sharply before turning away from me, a clear dismissal, and I fought the urge to strangle her.

I'd had everything under control before she'd decided to come barreling in. Mostly under control. Well, I'd possibly had things under control.

It wasn't like we could just leave. Bastian would wake up any minute now, and he would absolutely track us. It was hard enough to avoid the Velesians when they didn't know about our presence. We had zero chance of outrunning Bastian in these woods. Not to mention he would report this to Cade, and then we'd have the might of the Alpha Pack falling down on us.

Rynn's involvement only further complicated things.

"Fuck, I wish Kieran were here," I muttered and rubbed my face. Kier had a real talent for smoothing things over.

"It's good he's not," a deep voice drawled. Vail and I whirled around, Rynn somehow already between us and the enormous man who had managed to sneak up on us.

"We like Kieran," another voice rasped from behind us, forcing us to turn so we could keep both Velesians in our sights. "It'd be a shame to have to kill him along with you."

Rynn had been eying the first man warily, but she full-on growled at the second, aggression radiating off her. He cocked his head in a very wolflike gesture, a bright sheen rolling over his crystal blue eyes.

"Ryker," I said evenly to the man Rynn was snarling at in a way I'd never seen her do to anyone before. Then my gaze slid to the larger man. "Cade."

I didn't know Ryker all that well, but Cade I'd met fairly regularly, since he spoke for all the Velesians. He was quite possibly the only person I'd ever met who towered over Vail. He had to be at least six and a half feet tall, and it wouldn't have surprised me if he had to twist his ridiculously broad frame just to fit through doorways. Usually, his light brown eyes were calm, sometimes even welcoming if he was in a particularly good mood.

Today, they were cold and predatory.

"You shouldn't have come here, Samara," Cade said in a chillingly calm voice. "And you definitely shouldn't have attacked Bastian after that shit you pulled at the human settlement."

Guess that answered the question of whether Bastian had tattled on us to Cade. I never doubted he would, just hoped that maybe he hadn't had time to do it yet.

"We had our reasons." I glanced at the panther and then back at Cade. "You know me, and you know Vail. Trust that we wouldn't do anything to jeopardize our relationship with the Velesians, and definitely not with the Alpha Pack."

"If you wanted our trust, you shouldn't have kicked Bastian out of your lands." He shrugged. "And definitely shouldn't have snuck into ours. Your pretty face and words aren't going to get you out of this one."

"Think carefully about what you say next." Vail slid the long, curved dagger free from his hip.

Cade smiled. "Looks like we might get that fight we've been spoiling for all these years after all." He took a step forward, a blade similar to Vail's appearing in his right hand

A Court of Bones and Sorrow

before a raspy growl sounded from Ryker as tension bled through the air.

"STOP!" Rynn barked, her chest still heaving from shifting to her human form. "They're here at my invitation." She raised her chin high, exuding authority despite standing there naked while surrounded by males who towered over her. "As a member of the Alpha Pack, it is within my right to invite others into our territory. Bastian was interfering, and I was merely putting him in his place."

"Funny." Cade gave Rynn a flat look. "Only a couple of hours ago, you were telling me to take my pack and shove it up my ass."

"You must have misheard on account of your thick skull."

What in the actual fuck had gotten into my mild-tempered friend?

Ryker's growling gained an even more vicious edge, but Rynn paid him no mind, despite her back being to him. The insult was clear, and I raised my brows at the brazenness of my friend. She had definitely been leaving out a lot of information on how things were going with her and the Alpha Pack. We'd be having words about this later once we were alone.

Her mismatched eyes, one golden brown and the other a deep, vivid blue, slid to mine, and she pressed her lips into a hard line. Yeah, she knew I'd be grilling her about this later.

The growling abruptly cut off, and I looked away from Rynn to see Cade staring at Ryker, some unspoken communication passing between them. Ryker's lip curled in distaste before he tugged off his shirt and threw it at Rynn. She snarled, but he was already turning away and shucking off the rest of his clothing. Velesians rarely wore boots, as they preferred to stay in contact with the earth. A second after his clothes hit the ground, an enormous wolf with a grey coat flecked with white burst free from the cage of human skin.

Then he darted into the forest without another glance at

any of us as Rynn stared after him with a predatory focus before pulling his shirt on with jerky movements.

"*Rynn.*" Cade sank so much dominance into that one word that Rynn's head snapped towards him, almost of its own accord, and he smiled at the venom in her gaze. "Ryker's going to make sure we're not disturbed, and you are going to explain what the fuck is going on here."

"Is that an order?" she asked cooly, not looking away from the alpha stare she was on the receiving end of.

"Does it need to be?" Cade crossed his arms, making his biceps bulge.

Rynn's upper lip trembled in a snarl as she glared at Cade.

"Okaaay." I drew out the word and grabbed Rynn's arm, tugging her away. "We're gonna need a minute."

"I didn't say you could leave," Cade said in a low, threatening tone.

"And I don't give a shit," I snapped. "I need to speak with my friend. Once I've done that, we'll talk and get this all figured out." Bastian started to stir on the ground, and I glanced at Vail. "Why don't you help Cade check on the overeager pussycat."

"Both of you really try my patience," Cade grumbled and moved towards the ailuran, who had managed to shake his head and was blinking blearily at the world. Vail nodded at me. He'd keep them away from me and Rynn while we talked. Velesian hearing was very sharp, but if we kept our voices low, it'd be fine.

Neither of us said anything as I pulled Rynn through the woods. When I was confident we were a good enough distance away to not be overheard, I stopped. She immediately pulled her arm free and fixed her features into the stubborn look I knew so well. It was the one that said she knew what she was doing, she was absolutely in the right, and the rest of us were idiots for not realizing it.

So I did what I'd done every time she'd gotten into this mood while we'd been at Drudonia. I reached out and flicked her on the nose. Hard.

"Fuck off, Sam!" She rubbed her nose and glared at me.

"What in all the moonsdamned fuck is going on?" I mimicked Cade's stance from earlier and crossed my arms. Unfortunately, my biceps were nowhere near as intimidating as his. "Last I checked, you were worried the Alpha Pack didn't want you anymore because you hadn't been able to go to them right away." Rynn's mother had passed away last year. They'd had a strenuous relationship, but Rynn had still felt obligated to help her elderly mother in her final days. So she'd delayed leaving her pack to join the Alphas, but she'd *wanted* to go, and now she was looking at them like she wanted to rip their throats out.

Rynn's lips trembled, but it wasn't in a snarl this time. Tears welled in her eyes. "I'm being banished from the Order of Narchis."

"What?" My eyes widened.

She looked away as she tried to collect herself, tugging at Ryker's shirt. He was smaller than the rest of the Alphas, but it still drowned her lean frame, falling to mid-thigh. Tears rolled down her cheeks and dripped onto the shirt before she wiped the rest of them away.

"Remember last month when I went searching in Fervis territory?"

"You mean when I told you not to go there because if you got caught it would cause all kinds of problems?" Rynn raised her chin, still defiant despite the tears falling. "Let me guess." I sighed. "You got caught?"

She nodded miserably. "Aetanthrope scout spotted me. I should have known better, but there aren't many eagle shifters in the Order of Fervis."

I squeezed my eyes shut. Rynn *was* really good at sneaking around, but she got too cocky sometimes.

"What did they do?"

"Refused to release me back to the Narchis. They said I'd been promised to them before my pack changed its mind and made the deal with the Alphas. Claimed they were owed compensation. Cade sent Bastian and Ryker to *fetch* me." Her eyes sparked. "Bastian promised them I would be punished."

I was suddenly quite sure she hadn't slammed him into that tree hard enough. "The banishment is your punishment I take it?"

Rynn blinked away her tears as she fought to compose herself. It was strange seeing her cry. I wanted to hug her, but I knew she would have hated that. So instead, I pretended I couldn't see the wet streaks running down her cheeks or the way her eyes had reddened. Within a few minutes, she was back to her normal, cool and steady expression.

"They announced it this morning to everyone gathered." She looked back towards the trees we'd walked through, to where Cade and the others waited. "I'm to leave with them as soon as the meet is over. The agreement is that I'm forbidden from traveling through Narchis territory unless I'm in the company of one of them."

I took that to mean Cade, Bastian, or Ryker.

"And I can only go through Fervis territory if I get permission first—which they won't give." She looked back at me. "That leaves going through the neutral area of Drudonia my only option for getting to the Moroi realm, and Cade could easily tell the rangers who are posted in that area to not let me pass."

"He wouldn't do that," I said but couldn't hide the hesitation in my voice.

"I won't be able to see you, Sam." Panic flared in her eyes.

A Court of Bones and Sorrow

"I'll be trapped in the fucking Alpha House, cut off from everyone I care about."

A low whine punctuated her words. All her life, all Rynn wanted was to belong to a pack that respected and loved her. The one she'd been born into had cared for her, but only as a political pawn to be traded. The Valatieris were one of the strongest Velesian bloodlines, and her uncle ruled the largest of the Narchis packs. Rynn was basically a shifter princess.

"Hey." I ran a hand through her shoulder-length, chestnut brown hair. "Do you really think they could keep me away from you?" I snorted. "Better question, do you really think they could keep Cali away?"

She huffed out a laugh. "No, but I wouldn't let either of you get into trouble for me."

"Oh, my sweet, sweet wolf." I shook my head at her. "You don't *let* us do anything. If the Alphas are going to treat you this way, then they don't deserve you. We'll get you away from them and give you the chance to find a pack of your own choosing."

"Sam, you ca—"

I flicked her on the nose again, and she let out a low growl.

"Trust me. Now"—I rubbed my hands together—"any ideas on how we get out of this current predicament? We need to get to Lake Malov and search for the crown."

She sighed. "As pissed off as I am at Cade and the other Alphas, I think we should tell them. We kind of have to at this point anyway if we want to search that area, and we might need their help down the road. They are a lot of things, but I don't think there is any chance of them being involved in this. Ryker's family was killed by wraiths, and he was taken in afterwards by Cade and Bastian. They would never ally with someone who was working with the wraiths."

"Let's hope you're right." I smiled brightly at Rynn. "On the plus side, if you're wrong and they are working with Erendriel and Velika, then we can just kill them and solve your little problem."

Rynn shot me a wolfish grin. "Always looking on the bright side."

"This is exactly why everyone hates the Moroi," Bastian said after I'd explained our situation. Most of it anyway—I'd left out anything involving Draven. "The rest of us are just trying to survive in this fucked-up land, and you bastards somehow find the time to discover cursed Fae artifacts and use them to enslave others."

The ailuran had been his human form when Rynn and I had returned, wearing a pair of loose-fitting pants and nothing else. It was too bad the Alphas were such assholes and I had a high probability of killing them in the future, because every single one of them was hot. Even with the feline disgust stamped all over his face, Bastian was gorgeous.

Standing next to Cade, who was more of a ruggedly handsome type, Bastian looked almost pretty. I thought it might be his eyes. Even in this form, his bright, emerald green eyes had vertically slit pupils, and something about that with the chiseled cheekbones and full lips made him captivatingly stunning.

"No need to drool, Samara." He finally noticed me outright staring at him and gave me a sinful grin. "I don't usually fuck Moroi, but I'll slum it in your case."

Vail growled, but I just batted my eyelashes at Bastian. "Actually, I was just thinking Rynn should maybe have a go with you before I slit your throat and feed you to that tree that tried to eat you earlier."

His grin got a little sharper.

"Not helping, Sam." Rynn sighed.

"Sorry, I got bored listening to him prattle on about how

the Moroi are so awful and the Velesians are so perfect." I shrugged and then looked at Cade. He was the only one I needed to convince. "My mother believed the other half of the crown might be hidden near Lake Malov. We need to search that area."

"And if we find it?" Cade's fingers brushed the scar that ran from his ear down his jawline, the roughly healed, pale tissue standing out against his light brown skin. "If you think I'm letting you walk out of here with it, you're even more insane than I thought."

"Careful," Vail rumbled.

Cade glanced at Vail curiously, but it was Bastian who spoke. "For someone who got drunk with us on more than one occasion and talked about how you dreamed about killing the Harker Heir, it seems a little strange to find you defending her." His nostrils flared as he inhaled and tilted his head slightly. "Not to mention that we can still smell you all over each other. Pussy was that good, huh?"

Vail took a step forward, but I yanked him back, forcing Rynn to step to the side before I raised a brow at Bastian. "My pussy is, in fact, that good. Dream of me." Rynn laughed under her breath while I blew him a kiss before turning my attention to Cade. "It just so happens I agree about the crown. At this point, I don't know which Moroi are working with the Sovereign House. While I can vouch for myself and those close to me, we're also the ones most at risk of being captured."

"What do you propose?" Cade asked, his expression curious. He always was the most reasonable of the Alphas as long as we didn't push him too far.

"We destroy it," I said. "Something like that shouldn't exist to begin with."

Cade studied me for a long moment, and I fixed my features into a pleasant but neutral expression. Something told me he didn't buy it, but he glanced at Rynn, and something passed in his eyes that I couldn't quite read. Once again, I wished Kieran were here. He was better than me at picking up subtle cues like this.

"Fine," Cade agreed. "We destroy it. But I want to see it destroyed with my own eyes."

"Wonderful." I dipped my chin in agreement. "Can we head to the lake now?"

"Of course. Follow me." He turned and set off through the woods. I looked over my shoulder in time to catch Bastian reaching out for Rynn's arm but yanking his hand away when she snarled at him. Then he stalked off after Cade and we followed after him.

I kept glancing around the woods for Ryker but didn't see him anywhere. Despite that, I was pretty sure the wolf was following us based on how Rynn's gaze kept drifting deeper into the woods.

We walked in uneasy silence for almost an hour before the forest finally ended and revealed Lake Malov. Even before I saw it, I knew we were close because of how tense all the Velesians got. If they'd been in their animal forms, I had no doubt the hair along their backs would have been raised.

It was interesting to me that I didn't feel anything. Vail didn't seem to either, although I'd ask him later to confirm. Whatever was going on with the lake, only the Velesians could feel it, and Cali. She hadn't said if other Furies had the same problem she did though.

Even though I didn't feel whatever Cali and the Velesians felt, I still found the lake disturbing. I was used to the turquoise waves that crashed against our beaches or the crystal clear waters of the lakes and rivers scattered throughout Lunaria.

Lake Malov was black. Impenetrable, inky darkness. Not even a ripple ran across the surface. It was like looking at glass.

I bumped my shoulder against Rynn's. "No wonder you

A Court of Bones and Sorrow

always want to come to the Moroi Realm. Our lakes are way more enticing for swimming."

Cade looked over his shoulder. "You enjoy swimming?"

"Yes," Rynn said after a long moment.

"Hope you like swimming in frigid water," Bastian quipped. "Because the closest lake to our home is frozen for most of the year."

Rynn's brows furrowed, but before she could answer, Ryker appeared and rammed his shoulder into her as he walked past, wearing only a pair of loose-fitting pants. "Princess wouldn't lower herself to swimming in our lake."

Vail managed to grab Rynn just as she lunged for the lycanthrope. She twisted in his grasp and snarled in his face, but he just gave her a flat look in response. He'd spent plenty of time around Velesians and was used to their bullshit.

"Where should we start?" I asked, trying to break up the tension. "We could split up?"

"No." Cade shook his head. "We might run into some patrols, and it'll be easier to explain your presence if I'm with you. We'll start at the southern tip. Go up the west side and work our way around."

I nodded, and we continued on.

"Stop," I said softly after we'd been walking for less than five minutes. I could hardly believe it, but for once, luck was on our side. The feeling was so subtle, I'd almost walked right by it. "There's a lookaway spell here."

"What?" Rynn perked up, any resentment she felt towards the Alphas instantly forgotten as her academic mindset kicked in. "Where?"

Vail stepped up to my side as we both studied the edge of the lake. Several boulders rose up from the water, and there were several smaller ones on the shore, but none of them were the source. I walked forward a few feet and stopped, bending down to brush away the small greyish pebbles that made up the shoreline. A shiny, obsidian black stone greeted me, exactly like the ones we'd found at the human settlement. The kind that had been used centuries ago by the humans to turn us all into monsters.

"What does it say?" Rynn asked, crouching on the other side of Vail as we all studied the glyph that had been carved into the stone.

Based on how the ends of the symbol thinned out and twisted off sharply, it was an Unseelie glyph. My heart raced faster. My mother had been right. There was something here, and it had likely been hidden from everyone this whole time.

"Salvation." I swallowed. "It means salvation."

CHAPTER TWENTY-EIGHT

Samara

We all watched as I dripped some of my blood onto the glyph, the shallow cut on my arm instantly healing. The glyph carved into the black stone greedily drank in the offering until there was none left on the surface. The strange awareness I'd felt when we'd walked by grew stronger, like a humming in the back of my mind.

"I know this," I muttered. "Why do I know this?"

"Sam?" Rynn glanced up from the glyph to give me a puzzled look.

"It calls to me," I said softly. "I've never felt this way about any place in Lunaria."

"What does it feel like?" Cade asked.

"Belonging." I smiled as the feeling settled into my soul. This place was meant for me. I wondered if my mother would have felt the same way if she had found it. My smile slipped. Why did this place call to me . . . but drive everyone else away?

Before I could ponder that thought more, the dark, placid surface of the lake started to shiver, and we all took a step back as the water parted, revealing a set of stairs leading down.

"Holy shit," Rynn breathed out and took a step closer to

study the quietly churning water held back by magic. "I can't believe a spell as complex as this still works after all this time."

"It must have been really important to the Fae to keep it hidden and protected." I frowned. How did Erendriel not know of this place? Or maybe he did know . . . but couldn't reach it? Rynn had said even the wraiths didn't come here. Had the Fae crafted this spell to specifically keep the wraiths away too?

"It doesn't make sense," I said aloud as I tried to figure out this puzzle.

"What?" Vail asked, watching me instead of studying the newly revealed hideout.

"Let's consider the order of events. The Unseelie and Seelie existed here together, the Seelie did something to themselves that turned them into wraiths, and during that same time, the Unseelie disappeared." My brows furrowed as I glanced back at the glyph and then to the hidden stairs. "So who crafted this spell to keep this place hidden? It clearly targets the wraiths, so it's not like the Seelie did it."

"Maybe the Unseelie did it before they vanished?" Bastian suggested. "We know there was some animosity between the Unseelie and the Seelie. This could have been one last fuck you to the Seelie."

"If that's the case, then this might be one of the last places the Unseelie were before they vanished." I still felt like there was some big piece we were missing from all of this, but maybe we'd find answers inside.

Rynn glanced over her shoulder at me from where she was standing close to the water and shrugged. "Only one way to find out."

"Do not move, Rynn," Cade ordered, but she ignored him and darted down the stairs. Ryker growled and stalked after her.

"I told you this was going to be a problem," Bastian told

Cade, who was glowering at the dark passage where Rynn and Ryker had disappeared. I got the impression not many people disobeyed his orders.

"She'll fall in line," Cade said flatly.

I snorted. "You've had all this time to get to know her and yet you've failed spectacularly."

"Watch yourself, Moroi." For a second, Cade's tone gained a deeper edge, and I had to remind myself that, despite his usually calm demeanor, he could shift into a nearly two-thousand-pound bear at any moment. From a purely rational standpoint, that meant I should avoid pissing him off any further.

But he'd messed with my friend, so fuck that.

In a blink, I let my bloodlust rise and shifted my nails into claws. Cade didn't quite flinch when I suddenly appeared in front of him, but he did stiffen. The Velesians might be stronger than us and quite good at sneaking around, but the Moroi were still faster.

I tapped his chest with my index finger, right where his shirt parted to reveal warm, brown skin dusted with dark hair. Blood welled as my claw pierced his flesh with each tap. "Bite. Me."

Cade's nostrils flared, and Bastian laughed next to us. "Isn't that what Vail is for?" the ailuran drawled. "Or maybe whoever was hiding in that cabin?"

I killed the panic before it had a chance to show on my face and gave Bastian a bored look. "You need to get your senses checked, cat. It was just the two of us there. Or maybe you just don't know what a good fuckin' sounds like since you've never given anyone that kind of pleasure."

Bastian narrowed his eyes, but before he could open his mouth to likely say something smartassed, Cade pushed past us. "Come on. Let's go make sure those two haven't killed each other."

My money was on Rynn in that fight. I took a few steps towards the stairs and paused, biting my lower lip.

"Don't you want to see what's inside?" Vail asked, moving to stand beside me.

"Yes." I swallowed. "But this is what our parents died for. No matter what we find in there, it wasn't worth their lives, Vail."

"No." He slowly raised his arm and slipped it around my shoulders before pulling me against him. Somehow, this tentative hug felt more intimate than anything we'd done so far, including in the cabin. "But I think they'd be happy to know that we made it here. Together."

I sniffled and blinked back tears. "Don't tell me you're getting soft in your old age."

"I'm only three years older than you," he said dryly. When we pulled apart, he slipped his hand into mine. "Ready?"

"Yeah." I sucked in a breath. "Let's do this."

We walked hand in hand down the stairs, darkness quickly engulfing us. I had no problem seeing, but I was surprised they hadn't added Fae lanterns or something to light the way, especially considering how long we walked. A little claustrophobia started to set in when I thought about how far we were beneath the lake and all the water just lying above us . . . ready to crush in the walls.

"Samara?"

I realized my breath had started to quicken, and Vail was giving me a concerned look. "It's fine." I smiled faintly and took in a few steady breaths. "Just discovered yet another thing to be frightened of in Lunaria."

The corners of his mouth twitched before he swept his hand towards the open door in front of us. "We're here."

Light crept out into the hallway we were standing in from the brightly lit chamber.

Please let the crown be here, I thought as we swept into the room and paused. "Well, this feels familiar."

Rynn looked up from where she already had her nose buried in a large book. "It does?"

I nodded while looking at the walls lined with floor-to-ceiling shelves and the work tables in the center of the room. "We found a hidden room in that sea cave near House Harker." My eyes widened as I took in all the shelves *filled* with books. "But it was mostly empty. That's actually where we found the journals I told you about."

"Ah." Her eyes dropped down to the book in front of her. "I've barely scratched the surface of the knowledge in this room, but just from randomly selecting books off the shelves . . . these came from somewhere else. I think the Fae brought them from wherever they came from. Some of them are written in Unseelie and some in Seelie, but others are written in the common tongue."

"Really?" I moved to the table and started flipping through the book she was browsing. "You're right . . ." I turned more of the pages. On one side was a detailed illustration of a beast, and on the other were details about it. Size, location, behavior. It was a bestiary, but none of these creatures roamed Lunaria lands, and the language they were written in was like the one we spoke here but different. It was close enough that I could read it easily but not exactly the same. Maybe our language had descended from this one?

"Stop." Rynn's hand fell on mine when I went to turn the page.

A skeletal creature stared out at us from the page, its eyes far too large for its narrow face. The artist had drawn it with its mouth open, displaying fangs eerily similar to mine, but the rest of its teeth were sharp points as well. Its gangly arms ended in slender fingers, each tipped with a three-inch long claw.

Beneath the drawing was one word. *Vampyre*.

"'The vampyre have mostly been hunted to extinction, but there are still some populations left,'" I read aloud. "'In southern regions, they are often referred to as Moroi or Strigoi. Some locals in that area have managed to tame some of these creatures enough to be guardians of their towns, and they call them Moroi to distinguish them from their more vicious brethren, the Strigoi. Note: this practice has been largely abandoned due to instances of the Moroi turning on their masters.'"

"These are the creatures we're based on." My fingers traced the outline.

"I don't know how," Rynn said, "but I think the humans who crafted the spell to change themselves into the Moon Blessed read this book, or one like it."

Vail started searching the table next to us, and I knew I should be doing the same because we needed to find that damn crown, but I couldn't resist turning a few more pages. The library at Drudonia was quite large, but even they didn't have any books from outside Lunaria. Every bit of knowledge we'd managed to scrape together since the Fae had disappeared were from books and scrolls that had been written *here*.

This book, and potentially all the others in the room, could tell us so much about not only the history of the Fae but *our* history. I wanted more than anything to live in this room for the next year and not leave, but that wasn't an option. So I allowed myself a few more minutes.

"Huh." The section of the book I'd turned to had another page folded over the one containing the drawing. I carefully unfolded it and blinked when I had to unfold it again. "Wow."

Rynn and I stared at the enormous reptilian monster that took up three pages. Leathery wings were tucked against its scaly body, and a triangular head rested on a long neck, a crown of horns rising behind it.

We both tilted our heads as we tried to read the word beneath the sketch. It was one I wasn't familiar with, and I didn't know exactly how it should have been pronounced.

"Drakōn?" I guessed.

"It says here they're commonly referred to as *dragons*." Rynn frowned. "It's kind of weird that it doesn't have as much information about them as the other creatures. I wonder what they do," Rynn murmured.

"Hopefully we never find out. I don't ever want to fight anything that large." Reluctantly, I stepped away from the bestiary and started searching the room. Rynn did the same a few minutes later, choosing the part of the room that put her the furthest away from the Alphas.

For over an hour, we searched every inch of the room. We even carefully pulled the books from the shelves to check behind them. Nothing. No sign of the crown anywhere.

"It's not here," Ryker growled. "This was a waste of time."

"Seriously?" Rynn glowered at him and gestured towards the walls lined with books. "There is more knowledge in this one room than in all of Drudonia. Even if the crown isn't here, this knowledge is priceless."

The lycan scoffed. "It's knowledge of a place we've never been and will never go to. Nothing here is going to help you stay alive in Lunaria, Princess."

"I told you not to call me that," Rynn said in a low, threatening tone. "I'm sick of listening to your bullshit." A sheen rolled over her eyes as the wolf in her rose to the surface. Oh shit. I backed away from the two of them as Vail continued poking through some books and the other two Alphas seemed to be pointedly ignoring the fight that was about to break out.

Ryker stepped into Rynn's space, and I tensed, getting ready to intervene if I had to, since apparently the others weren't going to be of any help. "And what exactly are you going to do about it?" His gaze dropped to his shirt that she was still wearing, and he grinned wolfishly. "You look good in my clothes. *Princess.*"

A snarl ripped out of Rynn's throat before she shoved him. Hard. Clearly Ryker hadn't been expecting her to do that or to be so strong, because he stumbled back and hit the nearest bookcase. An answering growl rumbled from his throat as he pushed off the shelves, causing them to shake again, and then something rattled above us.

"Wait, what is that?" I stepped between the two Velesians who were sizing each other up and looked towards the ceiling. "There." I pointed at it. "There's a gap between the top of the bookcase and the ceiling."

We all peered up at the small crevice. As tall as Cade and Vail were, they still wouldn't be able to reach it. There must have been a step stool or something in here. I turned away to scour the room and then jumped when Rynn let out a high-pitched yip. I spun back around to find her glowering at Cade atop his shoulders, his head between her thighs.

"A little warning next time."

"Sure thing, Princess."

Rynn sighed but reached up and slipped her slender hand between the bookcase and the ceiling. I held my breath as she pursed her lips while searching the tight space. Suddenly, her eyes widened, and she slowly pulled her hand back, revealing a slender, gold crown.

"I'm so happy you shoved that asshole into the bookcase, Rynn." I stared at the glittering Fae artifact with a mixture of relief and awe.

Rynn let out an amused snort and glanced down at Ryker. "I guess violence really is the answer sometimes."

Bastian laughed and bumped his shoulder against Ryker's, who was still staring daggers at Rynn as Cade lowered her to the ground.

All of us gathered around and looked at the simple yet

elegantly crafted crown. Despite sitting up on that shelf for probably decades if not centuries, it still gleamed in the light with absolute perfection. Most of it was comprised of three gold bands woven together, and occasionally an ornate gold leaf would flow out from one of them, looking so dainty that I was worried Rynn would accidentally snap it off, but when her fingers carefully swept over one of them, it seemed clear it wasn't so easy to break.

"I can feel the magic," she murmured, flipping the crown around as she studied the inside. "But I don't see any glyphs anywhere, so I have no idea how it works."

"Doesn't matter," I said. "We need to destroy it."

Rynn pursed her lips. "I know but . . ."

I shook my head. Rynn didn't like mysteries. While I could appreciate that from an academic standpoint, even if this half of the crown was the lesser of two evils, it still couldn't be allowed to exist, especially considering the Moroi Queen had the other half, and nothing good would come from them being reunited.

"Sorry, Rynn." I waved at the rest of the room. "You'll just have to settle for the greatest find in probably all of Lunarian history."

She grinned sheepishly. "Fair enough."

"The question is, how do we destroy it?" Vail looked at Cade. "Melt it down?"

"We could try." The large Velesian grimaced. "Something tells me it won't be that easy."

"Even if we are able to melt it . . ." Rynn pondered the crown, running her fingers along the inside. "We don't know exactly how the magic works. Usually there is a glyph, but in this case, I think the entire crown is spelled. I don't know if melting it down would destroy the spell or just change the shape of the crown."

Vail held his hand out, and Rynn passed the crown to him,

then we all watched as he tried to snap it. Muscles bulged along his forearms, but the crown didn't so much as crack. He passed it to Cade, who also had no luck.

"I think melting it will be the only chance we have of breaking it apart," Vail said. "We could melt it and separate it into a few different pieces while it's in liquid form, then scatter those chunks afterwards."

"Dump some into the ocean and bury others," Cade suggested.

"If the spell persists in the gold even after it's melted though, will splitting it apart weaken or destroy it?" I grimaced. "Or will each piece retain the full functionality of the spell?"

"We might have to use the crown to test it." Rynn sighed. "And then again after we split it up."

Everyone tensed at the suggestion. Sure, we used the remnants of Fae magic regularly. Our wards were reactivated Fae spells and the glyphs that we used around our fortresses were all repurposed Fae magic, but something about this crown felt different. Everything else we used was for defense or making our lives easier.

The soul crown was made to see into the souls of others and control them. It was made to do *harm*.

"Maybe we can find an answer in here?" I looked around at the wealth of knowledge surrounding us. "In the meantime, we need to keep the crown hidden and safe."

"We could leave it here?" Bastian suggested. "Nobody else knows about this place, and the spell keeps it secure. Thousands of Velesians have walked past it, and none of them detected the spell the way you did."

"How did you do that, by the way?" Ryker asked, eying me suspiciously.

"I don't know." I thought back to how it had felt when the spell had skittered across my skin. "Something about the glyph, the salvation one, called to me. I didn't feel anything else while going through the passage or in here."

Rynn hummed, and my lips twitched in amusement, knowing I'd just given her another mystery to solve.

"I think you should take it, Rynn," I said seriously. She jerked slightly as my declaration and looked at me wide-eyed. I held the crown out to her. "This place has remained hidden for a long time, but there is a chance that someone followed us here or will detect our scents above. Velika likely has spies everywhere, and we don't know if the wraiths avoid this area because they don't like it or because they can't come here. Until we know for sure, I'd be more comfortable with you keeping the crown on you at all times."

"Alright." She looked at the crown and then down at the shirt she was wearing before walking over to one of the shelves on the wall and grabbing a leather satchel. She carefully emptied the contents and then strode back over to Cade with her hand held out. He passed her the crown and Rynn dropped it into the bag.

Vail averted his eyes as she raised the shirt, flashing her goods at all of us, and wrapped the bands attached to the satchel around her waist. I'd seen Rynn naked more times than I could count, so it didn't bother me in the slightest.

An annoyed sound slipped from Rynn as she tried to hold the shirt up while also tying the bands together.

"Would it kill you to ask for help?" Cade grunted and grabbed the bands, shoving away Rynn's hand as he tied them and stepped away. Rynn stared at him with an unreadable expression as she dropped the shirt and looked down to inspect how it looked.

I glanced at Bastian and Ryker and was surprised to find that, like Vail, they had averted their eyes for this whole thing.

Wow. Rynn and the Alpha Pack were even messier than I'd thought. I couldn't wait to tell Cali all about it.

"Good enough," Rynn said as she finished fussing with the shirt. She was right, it was baggy enough that the satchel beneath it was barely noticeable. "When I get back home, I'll find a better solution—something that will work in both my forms—but I'll keep it on me at all times."

"You can do that while you pack up your things to move to your new home," Bastian said smoothly, his gaze once again on Rynn.

"Fuck you, Bastian," Rynn snarled.

"You would be so lucky."

"I'm not joining your stupid pack!" she screamed. "I'll figure out a way out of this."

"The fact that you're wearing his shirt"—Bastian pointed at Ryker—"says otherwise."

She took a step towards him, a snarl bubbling from her throat, when Ryker slid between them, causing Rynn to bump into his chest and stumble back. The lycan's hands darted out, gripping her around the waist, and his head leaned down closer to her shirt—his shirt, technically.

Ryker's nostrils flared, and his gaze dropped to Rynn's chest before he practically growled in her face. "Why were you crying earlier?"

"Seriously?" she snarled and shoved him away.

I bit my lip, not really knowing what to say to make this situation better. Rynn snatched a few books from the table and stalked towards the door, only to be thwarted when an invisible force seemed to wrap around the books and prevent them from passing the threshold. Rynn's body jerked as she was yanked back, and my brows rose as she tried to pass through again, but it was pretty clear the books were not leaving this space.

The Fae had clearly been determined to not only keep this place hidden but to protect the books inside as well. I was dying to know why, but it would have to wait.

After one more pissed-off snarl, Rynn slammed the books

down onto the nearest table, causing me to wince at the harsh treatment of books that were likely centuries old, before storming out.

Apparently the crown could leave but the books couldn't. Interesting. Maybe the books were part of the original spell that kept this place safe, and the crown had come here afterwards?

"I'll go check on her," Vail said.

I watched him go, a little surprised that he cared, but I knew he respected Rynn and had dealt with the Alphas a lot in the past, so maybe he could offer her some words of wisdom.

"Explain the clothing," I said quietly.

Bastian looked like he'd bitten into something sour, and Ryker clamped his mouth shut, suddenly looking very young and unsure.

"When a Velesian joins a new pack, it's customary for them to wear the clothing of the other members . . . once they've accepted it," Cade explained in a somewhat strained tone. "It shows to others that they're happy with their new life . . . and family."

"You're not keeping her." I met Cade's stare and held it even as his dominance slammed into me and the other two Velesians let out warning growls. "We're in agreement for the crown, and that takes priority, but if Rynn wants to leave your pack, know that I will do everything in my power to help her, and if you hurt her"—I pushed my bloodlust until I was sure my eyes were jet-black—"I will cut out your heart and eat it in front of you."

The dominance exuding from him pushed against me one more time before vanishing like it'd never been there.

"Understood. I have no interest in harming Rynn." Cade nodded calmly before striding towards the door and tossing over his shoulder, "But I have no interest in giving her back either."

CHAPTER TWENTY-NINE

Samara

"Where'd they go?" I frowned when we reached the surface again. There was no sign of Vail or Rynn anywhere. Rynn had been really pissed, so she probably just needed some distance between her and the Alphas to calm down. Vail would keep her safe.

Apparently not everyone shared my opinion, because Cade let out a frustrated growl and Ryker looked like he was on the verge of shifting again just as Vail appeared from the trees.

"She's fine," he said. "Just pissed off. I tried to calm her down, but I think she just needs time to cool off. She's on her way home now."

Not her home anymore. I closed my eyes. It was always expected that Rynn would go and live with the Alphas up north, but being exiled from her own fucking Order was an entirely different situation. I still couldn't believe Cade had gone along with that plan.

"Princess needs to learn she doesn't get everything she wants in life," Bastian snarled and took off after her. Ryker shucked off his pants and shifted, and the enormous white wolf followed.

A Court of Bones and Sorrow

"You'll never find her," Vail called. "These are her woods."

Cade snorted. "We'll always find her. I'll get the others to give her a little space. Just for the trip back. She'll need to be with us tonight as part of the celebration."

The muscles along Vail's jaw flexed, but he didn't argue. I didn't like leaving Rynn here. Unfortunately, I didn't see any other options.

"Come on," I said to Vail. "We better get going."

Draven was probably losing his mind in that cabin, and I wanted to return to him so we could figure out our next move. We had the crown, which meant Velika wasn't getting it. For the first time in a while, I was starting to feel a little optimistic.

We parted ways with Cade and headed south. I allowed myself to get lost in my thoughts, and I put my trust in Vail to keep us undetected by Velesian patrols and safe from any monsters that roamed during the daylight hours.

We would need help to get the other half of the crown away from Velika. After my conversations with Aniela and Ary, I thought they made sense as our first potential allies to approach, but I wanted to wait until we'd destroyed the crown in our possession. I might have trusted them not to side with the wraiths or anyone working with the wraiths, but that trust didn't extend towards Fae artifacts. They might argue that we should keep the crown or use it in the fight. Every part of my soul told me it needed to be destroyed, and until that was done, I wouldn't be able to trust anyone enough to tell them about it.

Ary and Aniela would probably be pissed, but they wouldn't be able to do anything about it.

We were halfway back to the cabin when several cloaked forms melted out of the trees like they were wraiths themselves. They weren't, but they were something almost as bad. Sovereign House rangers. At least twenty of them, which was far more than Vail and I could fight on our own.

"Greetings, Samara Harker," a tall, dark-haired ranger

said, then he nodded at Vail. "Marshal, both of your presences are requested by Queen Velika."

My heart hammered inside my chest. At least Rynn had the crown. Unless they had captured her too? No. She had three of the deadliest Velesians in existence with her, and they would have fought hard enough so she could have escaped. Rynn wasn't a coward by any means, but she knew what was at stake. She wouldn't let the crown fall into enemy hands, and no Moroi would stand a chance at catching her in the forest.

"Any particular reason?" I asked, struggling to keep my voice even. "This all seems a bit much." I gestured towards the rangers surrounding us. All of them had their swords drawn, angled towards the ground, but the threat was clear. I was a little surprised Vail hadn't sensed them closing in on us, but these were likely the best of Velika's rangers.

"It is not my place to question the queen, nor is it yours." His gaze hardened. "Your aunt is currently a guest of the Sovereign House. If you care about her health, you will come with us and not impede the journey in any way. Understood?"

"Yes," I ground out. We should have rescued Carmilla first instead of leaving her as a hostage. I'd been so concerned about getting the crown before Velika that I'd left the last of my family at her mercy.

"Marshal," the ranger addressed Vail, "we will leave you and the Heir with your weapons for now, as we will continue traveling through the night to make it back as quickly as possible. Do not make me regret doing so."

Vail jerked his head in a nod. I could feel the fury rolling off him but didn't think he was capable of speaking at the moment. He wouldn't do anything to risk Carmilla, and neither would I.

I'd trust Vail to keep me safe on the way to the Sovereign House, and I'd be plotting how to keep both of us alive once we got there.

A Court of Bones and Sorrow

TWO DAYS LATER, we arrived at the Sovereign House. Usually, the trip would have taken twice as long, but there had been fresh horses waiting for us at each outpost, and we'd had extra protection at night . . . wraiths.

I hadn't seen them clearly, but as we'd raced along the roads, I'd seen shadows keeping pace with us in the woods, keeping the worst of the monsters away. The only attack we'd suffered had been from some howlers during the day. They'd picked off the ranger at the end of the line and carried his screaming body off into the woods before anyone could intervene.

The other rangers hadn't seemed all that upset. They'd just carried on like nothing had happened. I was pretty sure Velika had used the magic of the crown she possessed to bind them. During the journey, they'd rarely spoken to each other or displayed any sort of emotion. The man in charge had been the only one who had displayed the slightest amount of individuality.

They'd also kept Vail and me apart as much as possible, so we'd barely been able to speak the entire time.

I didn't know what Draven had done when I'd failed to return to the cabin. He'd surely looked for me, but where? Had he tracked down Rynn only to learn that I'd parted ways with her already? Had he returned to House Harker to let Kieran and the others know that something had gone very wrong?

Dread coiled in my gut. Or had he returned to the Sovereign House despite the pain and misery that awaited him there, because he knew that was where I'd likely been taken? I'd promised him I would keep him safe, and I'd failed.

I shoved back the grief and despair that had been building the last couple of days. They would do me no good, and I still had friends and family to protect. The situation wasn't ideal, but the other half of the crown was out of Velika's reach for now. If she suspected I knew where it was, she wouldn't kill me, which meant I had something to barter with. I'd never give up its location, but she didn't know that, so I could string her along while Vail and I figured something out.

Curious stares fell on us as the rangers marched us through the halls of the Sovereign House. This Fae fortress was similar to the other Houses but considerably larger. The main tower alone was the size of all of House Harker. Whispers echoed off the walls as the courtiers and advisors took in our state. Vail and I were both covered with a fine layer of dirt and probably looked a little worse for wear given how hard we'd been traveling the last week.

I hoped the queen choked on my stench.

Two guards stood in front of large double doors that I recognized immediately. They were gilded in silver and had an enormous tree engraved on them. We'd been brought to the throne room.

"Queen Velika wishes to speak to Samara first," one of the guards said at our approach. "The Marshal will wait out here."

"Not a chance," Vail growled. The rangers escorting us tensed, and the guards at the door reached for the swords at their hips.

"It's alright." I slid between Vail and the guards, placing my hands on his chest. He tore his gaze away from the guards to look at me, his eyes dark grey storm clouds with silver dancing amongst them. I stood up on my tiptoes and brushed my lips against his. "I'll be okay."

We may not have had a choice in coming here, but we hadn't been dragged here in chains either. That could mean any number of things. Velika could still be feeling us out to find out exactly how much we knew. In that case, she might pretend like nothing was wrong at all and come up with some cover story for why she'd wanted us brought here so urgently. Or maybe she'd just wanted to rattle me, having me brought to the Sovereign House like this, and now wanted to separate me from Vail while she questioned me about the crown.

As much as I wanted Vail by my side so I could draw strength from his presence, he was absolutely terrible at hiding what he was feeling. She'd see every emotion written on his face, not to mention, he might let something slip in anger if he spoke. Between the two of us, I had a better chance of playing this game with the Moroi Queen.

Assuming she didn't just kill me as soon as I walked in. That would be unfortunate.

Vail's expression softened, and he cupped my face with his left hand. "I'll be right here. Just yell if you need anything. These guards won't stop me from getting to you."

The guards in question shuffled nervously before opening the door for me.

I kissed Vail one more time and then took a deep breath before turning and striding into the throne room with my chin held high. The door clanged shut behind me, and I let my gaze skim over the dozens of courtiers and advisors standing around, talking softly.

The throne room was not particularly large, but it made up for that in opulence. The walls and ceiling were made of white marble with silver running through it all, creating elegant patterns. A deep blue stone made up the floor—so shiny, you could almost see your reflection in it.

What truly made it extraordinary was that everything appeared to be one piece. There were no visible seams anywhere. No imperfections. We struggled to keep the wards operational while the Fae had probably created this gorgeous room in an afternoon with barely a thought. I wondered what they would think of this beautiful space they'd created being used by the descendants of humans. Maybe I could ask Erendriel someday.

The exhaustion and stress must have finally gotten to me because I laughed at the thought.

"Something funny?" a light, breathy voice asked.

A tall, slender, fair-haired Moroi female strode into the room, her light blonde hair falling down her back in a wave of curls and her blue gown flowing around her with each step. She took a seat on the throne made of the same blue stone as the floor that rested on top of a dais. The Moroi Queen always did love to make an entrance.

My breath caught in my throat when I spotted the silver crown that rested on her head.

She can't use it on you, I reminded myself. Without the other half, anyone who belonged to one of the House bloodlines couldn't be controlled by its magic. We could be driven insane until we became Strigoi, but that took time. So that was a tomorrow problem. Right now, I just needed to survive this encounter.

"It's nothing, my queen," I said lightly. "Just silly musings about the Fae. I find myself rather exhausted from the ride here, as you can probably tell from my appearance."

She smiled at me, but it didn't reach her golden brown eyes. I saw very little of Draven echoed in her.

"You *are* looking rather ragged," Lucian said in a bored tone.

I glanced at the consort standing at the bottom of the dais. Despite being with Velika for almost three decades, she had never married him or allowed him to stand by her side. I'd never liked Lucian. He represented the worst side of the courtiers. Someone who thought their elevated status made them better than everyone beneath them . . . and enjoyed reminding them of that.

There were whispers of cruelty that had befallen the staff and lower-ranking courtiers, but I'd never been able to confirm anything for sure. Despite keeping Lucian in his place, Velika clearly favored him, and no one wanted to go against the queen.

Instead of responding to Lucian's comment, I ignored him, and his mouth tightened at the dismissal. Velika's lips twitched in amusement, and tension roiled in my gut. Considering how little I knew about this situation, I had no idea how to play this other than to continue pretending everything was normal. Or as normal as it could be when one was summoned to the Sovereign House by twenty armed guards.

"Why were you in the Velesian realm?" Velika asked. "Seems odd for you to leave your House unattended since Carmilla is here with me."

The reminder that she had my aunt sent a chill down my spine. I'd been subtly looking around the room but hadn't seen Carmilla's face amongst those gathered.

"I'm working on arranging a larger trade of malachite with them, my queen," I answered smoothly. "Several of our outposts have been dealing with increased attacks, and we may need to expand the wards that protect them."

"Interesting." She hummed. "That's not what I heard."

I sunk every ounce of will I had into forcing my heartbeat to remain steady as she raised her hand and flicked her fingers forward. Then my resolve broke when the guards dragged a bloody and beaten Draven into the room.

"No!" I cried and stepped forward, only for strong arms to yank me back against a hard chest.

"Don't make a spectacle of yourself, Samara," Demetri purred into my ear, and I went absolutely still. "Good girl."

Then I twisted free and slashed my claws across his face before he could react.

"Fuck!" he screamed as blood streamed between the fingers he'd pressed against his cheek. Damn it. I'd been hoping to scratch his eyes out. I lunged towards Draven, but two guards rushed in and restrained me. No matter how much I struggled in their grasp, I couldn't break free.

Demetri straightened, his hand falling away from his face to reveal three deep gouges. The bleeding had already slowed when he stalked towards me, eyes burning with fury. My head snapped to the side as he backhanded me hard, and I saw stars for a few seconds.

Then a growl rumbled throughout the room.

"Restrain him!" Velika ordered.

I raised my head despite the blinding pain shooting down the left side of my face to see the guards clamping thick, iron chains onto Draven's wrists and attaching them to the nearby pillars. The chains forced him to stand, and the way his arms were pulling against them, I suspected they were all that was keeping him upright. One of his beautiful eyes was completely swollen shut, his face a mishmash of bruises and cuts, and the dark tunic he wore was nothing but blood-soaked rags at this point.

Nobody in the room moved to help him. They just looked at him with amusement or disgust. Sometimes both.

"What did they do to you?" I whispered in horror before turning my wrathful gaze to Velika. "He's your fucking son!"

She shrugged one dainty shoulder. "Technically, this is your fault."

"Bullshit." I seethed. "You're just a sick, twisted fuck with too much power."

A fist slammed into my jaw, and I heard something crack. The guard who had punched me yanked me back when I leaned over and spat out a mouthful of blood. "Do not speak that way to our queen," he warned.

"No." Lucian grinned at me. "By all means, keep going. This is fun."

"Just don't damage her too much," Demetri said mildly as a servant handed him a wet cloth so he could wipe the drying blood off his face. To my annoyance, the gouges I'd inflicted on him had already healed. "She is to be my wife again after all."

"You're fucking delusional." I stared at him in disbelief.

"The two of you can fight about that later." Velika rose from her throne and stepped down the dais to stand in front of me, Lucian moving to stand behind her like the obedient consort he was. "This"—she gestured at Draven, who looked like he was on the verge of passing out—"is your fault because you allowed him to drink from you. He has too much Harker blood in him right now for me to compel him to answer me."

I deliberately kept my gaze on her face, refusing to look at the crown on her head.

"You can stop pretending." She laughed. "I know you're aware of what this crown is, and more importantly, what it does. Just like I know that you're searching for the other half." She reached forward and twirled a loose strand of my hair around her finger. "And I suspect you've found it."

My face hurt from where I'd been hit, twice, but that didn't stop me from raising my chin and spitting in her face. Her hand froze where it had been playing with my hair before moving it to slowly wipe away the blood-tinged saliva.

She pondered it, looking more curious than angry before glancing at Draven and then back at me. "Figures my son would fall in love with the only other Moroi in existence foolish enough to spit in my face." Then her lips curved into a cruel smile. "Demetri was with the guards who captured him leaving the Velesian realm. He confirmed that my worthless son smelled of you. That he never broke while we ripped his body apart is only a testament to how much he loves you."

Tears streamed down my face before I could stop them as I looked at Draven. His wounds weren't healing—blood still leaked from all of his cuts, and the bruising looked even puffier than it had when he'd been dragged in here. I didn't know if it was because his magic was taxed out or if something else was at work.

Where the fuck was Vail? There was no way he hadn't heard the commotion in here. Had they done something to him? No. There was no way they could have hurt him quietly, and I hadn't heard a fight. Maybe he was just biding his time?

I didn't know what one person could do against all this, but I was desperate for anything at this point.

"Here's what's going to happen, my pet." Velika wiped her hand on my clothing, drawing my attention back to her. "I'm going to bring some of your friends here, starting with that pretty blond courtier, or maybe the advisor with the pretty eyes. By the time they get here, your blood will be out of my son's system." She clapped her hands together excitedly. "And then I'm going to command him to inflict every bit of pain on them that we've done to him over the last two days. Now, for all his shortcomings, the prince is quite hardy, so they probably won't make it the full two days."

"Doubtful they'll make it more than a day," Demetri said, and Lucian laughed with him.

A bloody and broken version of Kieran flashed before my eyes, followed a second later by Alaric. I'd have liked to pretend that I would remain strong, that I wouldn't give over the knowledge of where the crown was, and that I wouldn't put Rynn and the rest of Lunaria in danger, but I would break. Even knowing that we were all damned regardless, I would break eventually.

"Ah." Velika gripped my chin, and I stared hatefully into her beautiful face. "Now you get it. There is no one who can save you from this, so you best cooperate with me, and I'll spare you some pain." Her nails shifted to claws, and I felt them bite into my skin. "But trust me, there will be pain."

Devastation and hopelessness threatened to break the strong front I was trying to present. I had no chance of fighting my way out of this. I was good at plotting, but Velika was better. She'd outmaneuvered me, and there was fuck all I could do about it now. The chains rattled again as Draven stirred enough to pull against them.

"I'm sorry." I looked at him through tear-filled eyes. "I'm so sorry."

Lucian opened his mouth, likely to taunt me again, when the doors to the room slammed open and Carmilla stormed in with Vail following her.

Hope rallied inside me, followed immediately by confusion. I'd assumed Carmilla was being held prisoner and Vail restrained . . . but the rangers who had been guarding the door made no move to stop them. Instead, they followed after Carmilla and Vail at a respectable distance. What the fuck was going on?

"Carmilla." Velika released my chin and shot my aunt an annoyed look when she stopped a short distance away from us, Vail standing just behind her, his eyes on the queen. "I thought we agreed I would handle this? You're too sentimental."

What?

Velika glanced back at me, and I realized I must have said that out loud. She frowned and returned her attention to Carmilla, her eyes drifting to Vail behind her and then to Demetri, who had casually strolled over to stand beside them. "What is the meaning of this?"

"I'm sorry, my friend." Carmilla shook her head ruefully. "I've always stood by you, but I can't any longer. You never should have bargained with the wraiths. I cannot abide by that."

Realization dawned on Velika's face, and she stalked towards Carmilla. I tugged against the grip of the guards, but they held me firmly in place so all I could do was watch this unfold.

"You treacherous bitch!" Velika's eyes sparked with rage as

she stopped a foot away from my aunt. "All these fucking years of me helping you, and this is how you repay me?" She scoffed. "It doesn't matter. All of the Sovereign House is bloodsworn to me. You have no power here, *friend*." She bit out the last word.

I tried to catch Vail's eyes, but he wouldn't look at me. Instead, his gaze was fixed straight ahead . . . on Lucian.

"No." Carmilla shook her head slowly. "Everyone in the Sovereign House is loyal to the crown . . . and the head upon which it rests."

A gurgling sound came from in front of me, and I tore my gaze away from Carmilla to find Velika clutching at the sword protruding through her chest. Blood dribbled out of her lips as she gasped, and Lucian wrapped an arm around her like a lover before twisting the sword more as he yanked her back onto it.

The Moroi Queen's legs gave out, and she collapsed to the floor as blood pooled around her. I stared in stunned silence as Demetri strolled forward and took the sword from Lucian before swinging it down. The sound of metal slamming against the hard marble floor echoed across the room as Velika's head rolled away.

Then Lucian knelt down, picked up the crown, and then walked over to Carmilla before kneeling in front of her and offering it up. "Your crown, my love."

CHAPTER THIRTY

Samara

"Thank you, Lucian." Carmilla took the crown from him and settled it onto her head, then her dark eyes fell on the guards still holding me. "Release my niece."

"Yes, my queen," they both replied and immediately stepped back. I staggered and almost fell without the support. Demetri stepped forward to steady me but halted at the look I gave him.

"Carmilla," I croaked. "What the fuck is going on?"

"I'm so sorry, Samara. It was too risky to tell you what I had planned considering the company you've been keeping lately." She glanced pointedly at where Draven was chained up before striding towards the dais. Lucian rose and guided her around Velika's still warm body before standing beside the throne as she took a seat.

Everyone in the room knelt before their new queen, except me and Draven, but he was barely conscious at this point and couldn't have kneeled anyway with the chains holding him up.

"The crown . . ." I started and then stopped, drawing in a deep breath. She must not know what it was truly capable of, because she never would have placed it on her head otherwise. "You have no idea what it can do. We have to dest—"

"It's half of the soul crown." She smiled at me. "This part binds souls, the other half sees them. Without that second half, it's quite time-consuming to instill your will on others. A blood exchange is required, and if their will is strong, they can still fight it, but the two halves together will solve that issue."

Dread filled me. "What are you saying?"

"Don't give me that look, Samara," Carmilla chided. "You understand the threat Erendriel and the wraiths pose. We cannot allow infighting amongst the Moon Blessed to weaken us at a time like this."

"I understand that, but enslaving people against their wills cannot be the answer." I shook my head. This couldn't be right. The Moroi leader I'd looked up to for the last decade . . . the person who had raised me after my parents had died . . . she couldn't possibly be doing this. "Please, Carmilla," I rasped. "Take the crown off."

"I was worried you'd react this way." She sighed and traded glances with Demetri, who stepped closer, causing me to tense. The guards who had released me a minute ago moved to my other side, boxing me in. "I'm sure you'll come around eventually. You always were a smart and ambitious girl."

She didn't have the other half of the crown. I wouldn't tell her, and despite everything, surely Carmilla wouldn't resort to torturing Kieran and Alaric to get it out of me? Uncertainty flickered through me. Exactly how much had I gotten wrong about who Carmilla really was?

Draven's labored breathing drew my attention. His skin was pale and clammy, and an alarming amount of blood soaked his clothes. I needed to get him help and figure out why he wasn't healing, then I'd try to talk some sense into Carmilla.

This was still fixable. I could fix this. I could—

"Vail?" Carmilla called as she held her hand out.

"No," I whispered. Demetri's hand clamped down on my arm, and I was rooted in place as Vail strode towards the throne, not looking at me once, and withdrew the gold half of the soul crown from beneath his cloak.

The same crown Rynn had been in possession of.

"I'll go check on her."

He'd gone after Rynn as soon as she'd been alone and taken the crown from her. She never would have given it to him willingly.

"What did you do, Vail!" I screamed, and he finally looked at me.

"I did as my queen ordered," he said calmly, even as I saw the regret in his eyes.

"Rynn . . . Is she—" My voice broke as tears streamed down my face, and I couldn't bring myself to finish the question.

"She's fine," he assured me. "I just knocked her out and then placed a keep-away spell around her so Cade and the others wouldn't find her right away."

"'Just knocked her out?'" I stared at him. "She was your friend. She trusted you. *I* trusted you."

"What did you expect?" Demetri drawled. "He had to choose between one of you. His queen or his latest fuck. Who did you think he would pick?"

"Demetri," Carmilla snapped. "Watch how you speak about my niece or I'll change my mind about our arrangement."

I couldn't even bring myself to care about what that meant. All I could do was stare at the gleaming gold crown in Vail's hand. "Don't," I begged him.

Vail swallowed . . . and then passed the crown to Carmilla.

Something inside me shattered into a thousand pieces, and I couldn't stop the pained sound from slipping from my lips. Demetri's grip on me tightened, and I yelped.

"Don't fucking touch her," Vail growled, and Demetri had enough sense to look a little worried before loosening his hold, but he didn't completely let me go.

"Oh, that's rich." Lucian laughed. "You can stop pretending now, Vail. I mean, honestly, I didn't think you had it in you, but good on you for mixing work and pleasure."

"Fuck you, Lucian," Vail snapped before sending me a pleading look. "It wasn't like that, I swear. What happened in the cave, in the cabin, all of it. It wasn't . . . I wasn't . . ." He struggled to explain, but I just turned away, not able to look at him anymore.

I was such a fucking fool. This whole time, I'd been worried about Draven stabbing me in the back when I should have been looking at the male who'd already betrayed me numerous times and had told me to my face more than once that he hated me.

"Sam, I—" Vail tried again, but I cut him off.

My head snapped back to glare at him, hoping he saw every wrathful promise about how much I would make him pay. "You don't get to call me that." Vail's face fell, but he could go fuck himself.

Then I looked at Demetri's fingers still wrapped around my wrist and raised my gaze to meet my ex-husband's light brown eyes. He stroked his thumb across my skin, and I wanted to hurl. "I told you when you left House Laurent that we could come to an understanding about our marriage, but you didn't listen."

"And I told you," I purred and leaned into him, and Demetri's eyes darkened before his gaze snagged on my lips, "that the only understanding I was capable of coming to was one that involved your cock flopping around on the floor and you bleeding out at my feet."

His eyes widened, and he screamed as I dug my claws into his crotch. I was pretty sure I'd missed and mostly gotten thigh, unfortunately. Then I was slammed into the floor as he flung me away from him. Vail was there in an instant to help me up, but I snarled in his face before rising on my own.

"You fucking whore!" Demetri screamed as he cradled his wounded dick. Apparently I had gotten him after all.

Vail growled, and Carmilla let out a long-suffering sigh like we were children fighting over sweets. A pained laugh rang through the air, and I whirled to Draven. He was conscious again and standing but still looked like shit.

"I hope she tore it off." His laugh turned into a cough, and the chains clinked together as he struggled to breathe.

"We need to get those chains off him." I stepped forward, but Vail wrapped his arms around me, pinning mine to my sides. Unlike Demetri, Vail knew I was perfectly capable of violence and made sure I was completely immobilized. "He had no choice in obeying her!" I struggled in Vail's hold even though I knew it was pointless. "Draven is not our enemy!"

Carmilla rose from the throne, taking Lucian's hand as he guided her down the dais. I still couldn't wrap my head around the fact that Carmilla was involved with Lucian. Based on how he was looking at my aunt like she was one of the ancient gods reborn, this was more than just a political arrangement. He was in love with her. Had he always been? Or was this something new?

Exactly how much had Carmilla been hiding from me? Another stabbing pain shot through my chest. Her betrayal hurt just as much as Vail's. I loved her. She was my only family left. I didn't know if she had suggested Vail get close to me or if it had been his idea, but either way, two people I cared for deeply had conspired against me.

Some dark part of me wondered if Alaric was in on it too. I would bet every piece of the shattered remains of my heart that Kieran and Roth had no idea this was going on. Kieran would never have lied to me, and Roth would have told them to go fuck themselves.

"There is so much you don't understand," Carmilla said sadly as she stopped in front of me. Then she raised her hand to tuck my hair behind my ear like she'd done my entire life, but I jerked my head away from her as much as I could, which wasn't much thanks to Vail's iron grip. Though it was enough to make her lower her hand and take a step back.

"Vail informed me of what you all saw in the temple."

"Of course he did," I ground out, and Vail stiffened behind me. "But Draven had no choice! He had to serve Velika because of that fucking crown!" My eyes flicked up to the united gold and silver crown that now rested atop Carmilla's dark hair. "The one that you're planning on using to enslave our people."

"You're being a bit dramatic, dear." She gave me a small, placating smile. "This crown was made for the Fae and it responds to our magic . . . oddly. I'm not going to just walk around Lunaria and make everyone kneel to me. Logistically, that doesn't make sense, and I have no desire to do so anyway. I will only use it in situations where I have no choice."

"Forgive me for not believing you, Aunt," I said evenly. "It seems I've chosen poorly about who to trust these days."

"Draven is Erendriel's son," she said without any preamble. "He is half Fae."

For a brief moment, shock cut through the rage I was feeling. Draven was half Fae. Erendriel's son . . .

Fuck it. I didn't care. Draven was *mine*.

"If you think . . . I'm loyal"—Draven coughed harder and sucked in a breath. I could hear his lungs rattling from here—"to my piece of shit father, you're even crazier than my mother." He rushed out the last words before doubling over and vomiting blood.

I frantically pulled against Vail. "Let me help him, damn you!"

"It's the iron," Carmilla explained. "The Fae can't stand it. Velika used to cut him up with it, and I'm pretty sure there are still some pieces buried in his chest. She really did hate him," my aunt mused. "I never did understand why."

"Please," I begged. "Just let me help him before it's too late."

"He's not dying," Lucian said dismissively. "Trust me—he's looked way worse than this. Haven't you, boy?"

Speaking seemed to be beyond Draven now, because all he could do was glare at Lucian.

"I understand you care for him," Carmilla said softly, "but we don't know how much control his father has over him. He cannot be trusted, and it's a risk to let him live."

"Please," I pleaded. I couldn't lose Draven. Not only because I'd promised to keep him safe, but because I was pretty sure I was falling in love with him. Something in his soul called to mine, and I couldn't let that go. Plus, he loved Kieran, and my sweet Kier loved him in return. "I'll work with you. Help you. Just please don't kill him."

"Seriously?" Demetri sneered at me. "Fuck this." He stalked towards Draven, who pulled against the chains but had nowhere to go.

"Stop!" I screamed, and for a second, I thought Vail would let me go, but then he tightened his grip again.

"Demetri!" Carmilla barked.

But the House Laurent Heir didn't hesitate as he grabbed a sword from one of the nearby guards and shoved it through Draven's gut.

"He's alive," Carmilla said from where she stood on the other side of the bars. After Demetri had stabbed Draven, I'd absolutely lost it.

I was still a little murky about what had happened. The ground had trembled, I remembered that much. Maybe Draven had tried to rally his Fae magic? At some point, Vail had either let me go or I'd slipped free from his grasp to dash towards Draven.

I brushed my fingers together and looked down at the cold and sticky blood on them. Draven's blood. I had reached him. Freed him. I remembered a spark of magic and then the chains disintegrating like they'd never been there.

But that couldn't have been right . . . I must have somehow unlatched them.

Everything had been so chaotic. Draven had sagged against me, the building had shaken, and then . . . darkness.

I'd woken up in a cell, presumably in the dungeon of the Sovereign House.

"It's admirable that you think I'd take your word about anything at this point," I rasped and moved to a sitting position against the wall. My throat felt like it was on fire.

She tossed a leather waterskin through the bars, and I snatched it up. I sniffed it but didn't detect anything obvious in it. Carmilla let out an annoyed sound when I hesitated for another second before guzzling the water down. It's not like I could refuse to eat and drink forever.

Besides, she had a crown capable of binding souls. Poisoned or spelled water was the least of my worries.

I wondered if my bloodline would protect me against the crown. It hadn't protected Draven, at least not entirely. Would Carmilla use it against me?

Had she used it against Vail? Or was I just desperate to believe he hadn't had a choice in betraying me?

Carmilla laughed under her breath. "I can practically feel

you thinking from here, trying to puzzle out what has happened and planning for possible contingencies." Her dark purple eyes, which were identical to my own, danced with amusement in the dim lighting. "You make me proud."

"Funny." I wiped the back of my hand against my mouth. "Your decisions lately have made me sick."

The corners of her mouth tightened. "You're young. It's easy to be idealistic when you haven't been dealing with everyone's bullshit and ridiculous demands for almost a century."

I stared at the roughed-up stone floor of my cell. Moroi politics were frustrating because every House was out for themselves. We were desperately fighting for survival, but instead of cooperating, everyone was plotting how to spin the deal in their favor. It hadn't always been like this. I had no actual proof of that, but I had to believe it because there was no way we would have survived as long as we had if we hadn't worked together before.

The Moroi hadn't always looked down on the Velesians or feared the Furies, the Velesians hadn't always been so distrustful, and the Furies hadn't always been so isolated. The Moon Blessed were falling apart.

I refused to believe that using magic to control them against their wills was the answer though, because what was the fucking point of that? There were monsters . . . and then there were *fucking monsters*. I had to make my aunt see that.

"Perhaps, you're right," I said, making sure to add a clear reluctance to my tone. "But surely you see things from my point of view? I mean, you had the Marshal of our House spy on me, betray me, and you commanded him to use our relationship to—" I inhaled sharply. The pain I felt with each breath wasn't an act.

"I didn't tell him to do that," Carmilla said quickly. "In fact, I specifically warned him off that path. Given your future with Demetri, that didn't seem wise."

"What future?" I asked, ignoring the fear igniting in my gut. "Our marriage is over. You fucking agreed to it!" I slapped my palms against the cell floor.

As the leader of House Harker, her signature had been required on the dissolution paperwork, and she'd signed it without hesitation.

"This isn't an agreement with House Laurent," Carmilla said carefully. "Marvina is . . . a problem, but the Laurent bloodline is important, and Demetri and I have come to an understanding."

"What did you promise him?" I asked sharply.

"Not what you're thinking," Carmilla hissed. "If you truly don't want him, then we'll figure something out, but you have to at least give him a chance—"

"I was married to him for three fucking years!" I shot to my feet and slammed my hands against the bars. Carmilla jerked back. "I only did that because I wanted to make you fucking proud of me!"

"Samara." She gave me a chiding look. "Be reasonab—"

"Fuck you!" I screamed. "I've done everything you've ever asked of me, including marrying that asshole! You don't get to tell me who to love anymore!"

"You're a Harker." Carmilla drew herself up and gave me a steady look. "Love is irrelevant. You had to have known your future didn't involve marrying courtiers or advisors."

I was acutely aware of every beat my heart took, and I felt my bloodlust rising in a protective wave around me as my eyes bled black and my nails hardened into claws.

"My future is my own." I bared my fangs at her, and I could have sworn I felt the cell bars trembling beneath my grip. "And I fucking dare you to try to take that from me."

Carmilla touched the crown on her head. "We'll see."

CHAPTER THIRTY-ONE

Vail

HOURS BEFORE THE SUN ROSE, I found myself walking silently down to the prison buried beneath the Sovereign House. For a moment during my trek down the winding stairwell, I stopped at a solid wood door and rested my hand against it.

On the other side was a room that contained three large cells. They were nicer ones than the levels below, but a gilded cage was still a cage.

I could feel the lone prisoner stewing in rage over the betrayal she hadn't seen coming.

It had never been my intention for things to play out this way. I'd thought I could obey Carmilla while protecting Samara from herself. She needed to understand just how much of a danger Draven was to her despite the sweet lies he whispered in the dark.

Yet you were fine with fucking her while he watched, a dark voice whispered in my mind. *And watching him slide his cock into the pussy that was still dripping with your seed.*

I'd fucked up. Badly. I let my fingers glide across the rough wood, wondering how much of her rage was directed at

Carmilla and how much at me. Just like I wondered if she could feel this pull between us. I'd noticed it a couple of days ago. It had been so faint, I'd thought I'd been imagining it.

Now it felt like a burning chain around my soul.

My fingers curled against the door, and for a second, I almost opened it, but based on how much anger I could feel through this strange magic that bound us, I suspected she'd only spit in my face if I went to her now.

I forced myself to take a step back and then continued on my way to the lowest part of the prison. A few screams and pleas sounded from the other levels I passed. We'd rounded up anyone who had served Velika and contained them for now. Carmilla promised most of them would be released once we figured out who could be trusted.

It bothered me a little. The rangers, I understood. Many of them had chosen to follow the now dead queen even before she had found the crown and bound them with its magic, but most of those contained in the cells were advisors and courtiers . . . and their families. Surely they weren't such an active threat that they needed to be locked up?

I'd speak to Carmilla about it tomorrow. She had a lot to handle in this tumultuous period of taking over the rule of the Sovereign House. Maybe I could offer to do an initial screening of those imprisoned and promise to assign rangers to keep an eye on those who were released?

An iron door awaited me when I finally reached the bottom. The walls contained large amounts of iron too, enough to make even my skin crawl a little bit. Something about our Moroi blood didn't like iron, but not nearly to the same effect as the Fae.

I pushed the door open, and it swung silently inward. There was only one prisoner on this level. Brushing my fingers against a glyph on the inside wall, I activated the Fae lanterns, and the flames flickered to life, bathing the small room and the cells that lined the walls in a warm glow.

"Come to finish me off?" Draven drawled from where he was stretched out on the ground of the cell at the end of the room. He leapt to his feet with a grace I hadn't thought he was capable of in his current state and stood with his hands clasped behind his back. "You're welcome to open these doors and try it." Solid red eyes that promised death locked onto me. "I dare you."

I kept the surprise off my face as I slowly walked over to his cell. Draven was a predator, and it was never wise to let a predator know they unnerved you.

"You're looking better. Last time I saw you, I was pretty sure we'd be digging your grave within the hour, or you know, chucking your Fae corpse off a cliff."

Casually, I let my eyes drift over him. He hadn't been given a change of clothing, so he was still coated in dried blood, but I could see patches of smooth skin beneath the tattered fabric. Even if he had used healing glyphs on himself, he should have been exhausted from the effort without someone to drink from.

Had someone snuck down here and fed him? No. There were guards loyal to Carmilla posted at the entry door to the stairwell, and that was the only way in here.

"Half Fae," Draven corrected. "But it does come with its benefits."

I tapped the iron bars of his cell. "I bet."

Despite his healthier-looking appearance, he was standing in the center of the cell, as far away from the walls and doors as he could get. Clearly the iron bothered him, but it hadn't blocked his ability to heal. Maybe because he was half Moroi, he wasn't as sensitive to it as most Fae? I'd have to tell Carmilla. We might want to have guards posted in this room as well.

"So"—he cocked his head—"if you're not here to attempt to kill me, why did you bother coming down here? Too scared to chat with the dark-haired beauty who you so thoroughly betrayed?"

I winced before I could kill the movement, and Draven laughed.

"Samara will understand," I snapped. "She just needs to calm down for a few days, and then I'll tell her everything. Carmilla has the best interests of the Moroi at heart."

Draven shook his head. "Oh? Is that why she imprisoned children? I can hear their cries even down here."

"It's temporary," I ground out.

"Ah. So cruelty is fine so long as it's only for a short amount of time. Such a wonderful leader to follow."

"She's a vast improvement over your mother." My fingers curled into fists at my sides. "We dumped her body outside, by the way. Figured the monsters could use a snack."

If my words caused him any pain, Draven hid it well. He raised one of his hands in front of him and studied his nails as he let them shift to claws. "Trust me when I say that nobody was happier than me to see my mother's headless body on the floor." He frowned. "Actually, I wish I had been more with it so I could have truly appreciated the moment."

"And your father?" I closely watched Draven's face, looking for any reaction. "How will you feel when it's his corpse in a pool of blood?"

Draven let out a chilling laugh and sank back to the ground in a cross-legged position. Then he let his hands sink into the floor on either side of him, and I noticed some of the stones had been broken up enough that it was more dirt than anything at this point. His posture relaxed, and some of the red receded in his eyes.

"If I were you, I'd walk back up those stairs to where Samara is locked up and plead for mercy. She loves you and,

A Court of Bones and Sorrow

despite everything, would at least grant you a swift death." My heart clenched at the admission that he knew Samara loved me.

"She'll forgive me." Even I could hear the uncertainty in my words though.

Draven just smiled. "She won't. If you had only betrayed her, perhaps over time she would have, because again, my fierce love is kindhearted, but your actions have put Kieran, Alaric, and Roth in danger. Carmilla isn't a fool. She knows the way to controlling her niece is through those she loves. And that"—he leaned forward slightly—"is not something Samara will forgive."

I looked away from the fallen prince, because he was right. Samara would never forgive me if something happened to those she loved because of all this. It had never occurred to me that Carmilla would use Kieran or Alaric like that. Maybe Roth because Carmilla wasn't as close to them as the other two, but even then, Roth was clearly an asset.

I also hadn't thought Carmilla would imprison children, so maybe my judgment of character wasn't as good as I'd previously believed.

"None of it really matters though," Draven continued, drawing me out of my dark contemplations. "Because Erendriel will come, and then all of you will wish you'd had the foresight to just slit your own throats rather than deal with his wrath."

"I thought you said your father didn't care about you?" I sneered. Of course he'd been fucking lying.

"Oh, he doesn't." Draven shrugged. "I mean, he probably wants to carve me apart himself, given that I killed several of his best soldiers, but Velika was important to his plans, and her death will set him back. He has a bit of a temper when it comes to that kind of thing."

"We can handle him." I crossed my arms. If anything, it

might be easier if he came to us. We could get this over and done with once and for all. "I've fought wraiths before, and Erendriel is just one Fae."

Draven chuckled darkly, and the hairs rose on the back of my neck. "He's not though. Erendriel is the Seelie King.

Want to see some NSFW art and read more spicy scenes?

Signup for the Alex Frost newsletter at <u>alexfrostauthor.com</u> to read some of the emotional and spicy scenes from an alternative character's point of view and get all the NSFW artwork delivered to your inbox!

Guide to the Characters and Places of Lunaria

THE MOROI

Broken up into six Houses, each controlled by the bloodline the House is named after. All six Houses are ruled by the Sovereign House.

Sovereign House

Queen Velika Nacht - Ruler of Sovereign House and all of the Moroi realm.
Consort Lucian - Velika's plaything for the last few decades. Must be very talented with certain body parts.
Prince Draven Nacht - Son of Velika. Suspected father is Lucian but never been confirmed. Sure that won't be relevant later.

House Harker

HEAD OF HOUSE | Carmilla Harker - Samara's aunt.

Raised Samara after the death of her parents; Samara's mom was Carmilla's sister.

HEIR OF HOUSE | Samara Harker - Raised in House Harker before moving to House Laurent for an arranged marriage with Demetri Laurent. Only lasted three years on account of him being a tool. Beloved niece of Carmilla.

Kieran Blake - Courtier of House Harker. Childhood friends with Alaric and Samara. Still besties with Alaric. In love with Samara. Has a complicated ex-lover. Originally from House Corvinus.

Alaric Lockwood - Grew up with Kieran and Samara. Besties with Kieran. Rivals with Samara. Also totes in love with her but won't even admit that to himself. Following in his parents footsteps of being an advisor to House Harker.

Roth Devereux - Librarian. Hot nonbinary librarian. Oh you need more? Hot nonbinary librarian who has magical ropes. Met Samara while studying at Drudonia. Their aunt runs House Devereux.

Vail Ferenc - Marshal of House Harker. Very devoted to Carmilla who raised him after his parents were killed. Has a complicated history with Samara. Might have tried to kill her once. It's complicated.

Nyx Corvinus - Ranger for House Harker and a part of Vail's unit. They met Samara at Drudonia but left their studies to become a ranger. Their parents run House Corvinus and their sister is Heir. Have a complicated history with their original House on account of their parents being assholes.

Adrienne - Ranger for House Harker and a part of Vail's unit. Very protective of Nyx and view them as a younger sibling.

Emil - Ranger for House Harker and a part of Vail's unit. The oldest of the group but still manages to kick everyone's ass and look hot while doing it. Major "Yes, chef!" vibes.

Guide to the Characters and Places of Lunaria

House Laurent

HEAD OF HOUSE | Marvina Laurent - Massive snob with no plans on handing the House over to her son anytime soon. Rumored that she killed her husband, Demetri's father, shortly after her son was born.
HEIR OF HOUSE | Demetri Laurent - Marvina's son. Was in an arranged marriage with Samara until he fucked it all up and she realized she could do better.

House Corvinus

HEAD OF HOUSE | Mora & Darius Corvinus - Both wicked shady and obsessed with gaining more political power.
HEIR OF HOUSE | Tamsen Corvinus - Nyx's older sister. On the surface she seems crafty and shady like her parents, but she's also done everything she could to protect Nyx, including encouraging them to get the fuck out and join House Harker.

House Devereux

HEAD OF HOUSE | Thessalia Devereux - Warrior and a scholar. Incredibly paranoid, especially against the Sovereign House for currently unknown reasons. Has no marital partner or children which is why she named her nephew as the Heir.
HEIR OF HOUSE | Taivan Devereux - The most quiet and mysterious of all the Heirs. Not much is known about him at this time. Obviously he's wicked hot though.
Severen & Celestina Devereux - Severe is Thessalia's brother. He has three children with his wife, Celestina: Taivan, Desmond, and Roth.
Desmond Devereux - Middle sibling between Taivan and Roth. Perpetually involved in relationship drama.

Guide to the Characters and Places of Lunaria

House Tepes

HEAD OF HOUSE | Raoul and Sylar Tepes - more concerned with hunting monsters than in their words, "bullshit Moroi politics". Raoul is Ary's biological father but both men raised him.
HEIR OF HOUSE | Ary Tepes - Takes after his fathers in that he'd rather be out in the wilds killing shit than dealing with politics. However, he is more adept at it than they are. Him and Anniela and have hated fucked.

House Salvatore

HEAD OF HOUSE | Dominque Salvatore - Head of House Salvatore; youngest of all the House rulers on account of her parents and older sister getting killed.
HEAD OF HOUSE | Anniela Salvatore - Dominque's cousin and Heir of House Salvatore. Her and Ary have hate fucked.

THE VELESIANS

Lycanthropes - shift into wolves. In human form their eyes are typically blue, but it's also common for them to have mismatched eye color.
Ailuranthrope - shift into panthers. In human form, their eyes are always green with vertical pupils.
Ursanthrope - shift into bears. In human form their eyes are always brown.
Aetanthrope - shift into eagles. In human form their eyes are alway some variation of yellow.

Broken up into three Orders—Narchis, Avala, and Fervis—each one consists of multiple Packs. Hierarchy and dominance

is a big deal with Velesians. Currently the Alpha Pack of the Avala order oversees everyone.
Not everyone is happy about that and they're constantly battling to maintain their position of authority.

Rynn Valatieri - Best friends with Samara and Cali. Born into the Order of Narchis. Her aunt and uncle run the Valatieri Pack which is at the top of the Narchis hierarchy. Because of her high-ranking status, Rynn was promised to the Alpha Pack to cement the alliance between them and Narchis. Rynn is less than pleased by this.

Alpha Pack

Cade - Leader of the Alpha Pack. Calm and steady. Until he isn't. Ursanthrope.
Bastian - Second in command of the Alpha Pack. Charming face with a ruthless personality. Ailuranthrope.
Ryker - Youngest member of the Alpha Pack, close to Rynn's age, hot-tempered and usually serves as a scout. Lycanthrope.

THE FURIES

The Furies mostly keep to themselves and will appear more in the later books. Most of the badlands are in their realm.

Calypso Rayne- most powerful Furie of the current generation, possibly ever. Best friends with Samara and Rynn. Capable of wielding shadow magic with far more skill than anyone else. Her friends think she is keeping a secret from them… she absolutely is.

If you enjoy fantasy romance with morally grey characters and slow burn angst you may like this series...

Lost Legacies

A Shift in Darkness*

A Shift in Shadows

A Shift in Fate

A Shift in Fortune

A Shift in Ashes

A Shift in Wings

A Shift in Death

*A Shift in Darkness is available for free download at maddoxgreyauthor.com.

About the Author

Alex Frost is… actually Maddox Grey. Dun dun duuuuun!

Okay probably not that dramatic of a reveal since it isn't exactly a closely guarded secret. The pen name Alex Frost was created to publish the spicier fantasy series that fall under the "Why Choose" genre.

Why Alex Frost? Because Maddox is a freaking nerd. After being trained by local baristas to respond to the name "Alex" instead of Maddox, it seemed like the perfect pen name. Half of it anyway.

Since Maddox already shares their last name with Jean Grey of the X-Men, it seemed fitting to borrow Emma Frost's last name for their other persona. If you know, you know. (insert smirking face)

To get regular email updates about new releases and other announcements, be sure to sign up for the newsletter on alexfrostauthor.com

facebook.com/alexfrost.author
instagram.com/alexfrost.author
tiktok.com/@greymalkinpress

Made in the USA
Middletown, DE
21 October 2024